"Charming and fun, *The S[...]* [...] opportunity, to believe in y[...] to fill your life with wonderful experiences that will become cherished memories . . . A book to read today, not someday, and Morgan is clearly a writer to watch."

—Stacey Ballis, author of *Recipe for Disaster*

Sometimes when your life flashes before your eyes . . . you realize—you need a better life.

Mid-slurp, the coiled lemon rind shoots down my throat as if sprung from a slingshot and lodges in my esophagus.

I drop my martini and glass shatters. I thump my chest. *Oh, God.* I'm choking. Choking! My throat burns and my lungs cramp as if a boa constrictor has wrapped around my ribs.

Jesus. This is it. This is my end. These are the last moments of my life.

With horror, my mind flashes to an image of my body lying on a cold, stainless-steel bed at the morgue. Oh, crap. I think there's a hole in my underwear.

From the corner of my bulging eye, I see the man jump from his seat. He slides his arms around my waist and lifts me off the ground. His fingers brush under my breasts as he squeezes me against him—I was right about the stone-hard abs—and thrusts his entwined fists into me.

Nothing happens. I'm still choking. My fingers and lips tingle numb.

Oh, God. Oh, God. Oh, God.

Moments of my adult life flicker through my mind. *Sorting stacks of documents. Oil changes. Scrubbing clean the condo's baseboards. Sunscreen.* Diligence. Order. Routine.

Then, thank everything holy, with one more heave, the man launches the lemon free. It flies from my mouth and the slimy fruit smacks the bartender on his forehead . . .

the Someday Jar

Allison Morgan

BERKLEY BOOKS, NEW YORK

BERKLEY

An imprint of Penguin Random House LLC
375 Hudson Street, New York, New York 10014

Library of Congress Cataloging-in-Publication Data

Morgan, Allison.
The someday jar / Allison Morgan.
pages cm
ISBN 978-0-425-27939-7 (paperback)
1. Single women—Fiction. 2. Man-woman relationships—Fiction. 1. Title.
PS3613.O725S66 2015
813'.6—dc23
2015003050

PUBLISHING HISTORY
Berkley trade paperback edition / July 2015

PRINTED IN THE UNITED STATES OF AMERICA

10 9 8 7 6 5 4 3 2 1

Cover photos: *Stardust Jar* © _ta'_/Getty Images.
Wedding Rings with Stars © Alexandre Marques/Getty Images.
Cover design by Sarah Oberrender.
Interior text design by Tiffany Estreicher.

Penguin
Random
House

To my family and friends

one

Don't panic, Lanie.

Don't freak out.

Don't shove your hand into the paper shredder. It won't fit.

Sifting through the contracts piled high on my desk—I swear twelve trees are chopped down each time a house is sold—checking the trash can and digging through my purse, I find nothing. Nothing!

How is this possible? I'm twenty-seven years old with dental floss, multivitamins, and spare staples in my desk drawer. I have no past due library books or expired tags on my car. I never litter. Never chew with my mouth open. I lift heavy things with my legs, not back. A responsible adult by any account. Yet, someway, somehow, I've carelessly gone and lost the single most important thing I *shouldn't* lose. My engagement ring.

"Lanie?" Evan, my fiancé, calls from his office.

Crap.

"Just a minute." I push my chair aside and search underneath the desk, finding no more than a few paper clips and a fuzz ball. Apparently, the maid has gotten a bit lax with the vacuuming. Oh right, that's me.

"Where are you?" he calls, sounding closer this time.

Quick to stand, I bonk my shoulder on the desk and hear the silver picture frame of the two of us from last year's Realtor Awards ceremony fall over.

"Oh, there you are." Evan strides toward me in his crisp Armani button-down shirt and creased pants, with a smooth gait that only good breeding spawns—his mom's a tenured English professor at Stanford and his dad's a venture capitalist. Evan is smiling, the same smile that garnered him a number six spot on last month's most-attractive-businessmen poll in the *Arizona Republic*. More than his Ken-doll good looks and crackerjack genes, Evan's a proven asset in the real estate community. He's respected and admired.

And he's mine.

But great. Just great. I've gone and lost his token of love.

Obviously, I could ask him to help me search, but what would I say? *Hey, funny thing, I've misplaced my ring. You know the one—diamond-encrusted platinum band, passed from generation to generation. Wasn't it your great-grandmother's?*

As a perfectly timed distraction, the office door swings open and in walks my dear old friend, Hollis Murphy.

He's decked in his usual navy blue, one-piece jumper. The matching belt droops around his waist. He smooths his thin white hair with a finger comb, and his cheeks and nose, laced with a few broken capillaries, flush pink.

My whole world just got brighter.

"Hollis, what a nice surprise." I slide around the desk and open my arms for a hug.

His skin is cool and clammy, he smells of too much cologne, and staleness heavies his breath, but I don't care. I love this old man.

We met several years ago, when I crashed my shopping cart into the side of Hollis's truck. In my defense, *People* had just released the Sexiest Man Alive issue and a shirtless Ryan Reynolds, along with each one of his gloriously defined abs, was pictured on page thirty-seven. Who wouldn't be distracted? Besides, it was only a scrape. Okay, dent. But Hollis was forgiving and we've been friends ever since.

He grasps my hand and says, "Zookeeper chokes to death eating an animal cracker."

Nearly every time we talk, Hollis rattles off a peculiar obituary. It's a sick ritual and I'll likely rot in hell for making light of someone else's misfortune. Still, I can't help but chuckle. "That's awful."

"Good one, don't you think? My Bevy clipped it out."

"How is Mrs. Murphy?"

"A slice of heaven. Today is our fifty-fourth wedding anniversary."

"Congratulations!" I say, making a mental note: *Send Murphys wine*. "Any special plans?"

"She's making meatballs tonight. My favorite."

"Sounds perfect. When will you bring Bevy by? In all this time, I still can't believe we've never met. I'd sure love to meet her."

"She says the same about you, but I swear that woman never has any free time. She's busier than the tooth fairy at a crackhead's house."

Evan approaches, extending his hand. "Mr. Murphy, it's nice to see you."

"Likewise."

"To what do we owe this honor?" Evan asks.

Hollis fishes in his pocket and pulls out a candy cane, his favorite treat that he carries year-round. He offers it to me. "Just came by to give Lanie-Lou something sweet." He eyes me, waiting for my answer.

"Because every woman deserves a candy cane."

"That's right." He squeezes my arm and says, "Everything good?"

"Everything's great, thank you." *Except for the fact that I can't find my ring.* I quickly scan the carpet.

"All right," Hollis says. "I'm off."

"Good to see you," Evan says.

"Give Mrs. Murphy my best," I say, walking Hollis outside.

"I already gave her my best this morning," he chuckles, and then he drives away.

Evan waits for me beside my desk. He holds out his open palm. "Look what I have."

Damn. He found it first.

I step toward him, conjuring up a witty explanation like, *Silly little bastard, that ring must have legs,* but words escape me as I stare into his hand.

He doesn't hold my ring. He doesn't hold the symbol of my future. He holds a piece of my past. My Someday Jar.

"My God." I try to hide the tremor in my fingers as I reach for the glass crock. Nostalgia surges through me like a desert flash flood and all at once I smell my dad's cologne masking his one-a-day cigarette habit and hear his voice, usually light and high-spirited, pivot adamant and stern when he said a dozen years earlier, "This jar is for your goals and aspirations, Lanie. None too big. None too small."

"Where did you find this?" My voice is no steadier than my hands.

"In a box at the bottom of my office closet. Found your ASU graduation cap, too. Maybe you can wear that to bed later?" He teases, but he must see the focus in my eyes because he strokes my arm. "What is it?"

I lean against my desk, my body heavy with sentiment. "This is my Someday Jar. A gift from my dad. God, I haven't seen it in years." The last time I held this, I wore bubble-gum-flavored lip gloss and braces dotted my teeth. With the jar close to my ear, I give it a little shake and listen to the slips of paper tumble inside.

"What's in there?"

"Fortunes."

"Fortunes?"

"Yeah. Every year for my birthday Dad took me to the Golden Lantern, a Chinese restaurant in Mesa." I half smile, remembering the dome-shaped chandeliers covered with crushed red velvet and dangling tassels decorating the dining room. "They had this wall with dozens of fortunes pinned to it. Dad plucked a handful of slips, flipped them to the blank side, and said, 'Write your own fortunes, Lanie. Create your own path.'"

I remember scribbling *Learn something new* on the first slip, thrilled with his nod of acceptance as I tucked the goal into the jar.

Now, as I rub my thumb along the nicks in the glass, a lump forms in my throat. "Dad made me promise that I'd empty the jar. He made me promise I'd claim my own stake in the world, fulfill my desires and dreams. He made me promise I'd do this . . . before I got married." I'd forgotten that last part until just now.

Evan tucks a strand of hair behind my ear. "Your dad was never afraid to throw caution to the wind, was he?"

"No, he definitely wasn't," I whisper, staring at the jar.

"You okay?"

I shake my head to clear it and force a little laugh. "I'm fine. It's just an old piece of glass that brings back a lot of memories, I guess."

Evan pulls me close and holds me for a minute.

Though it serves no purpose but longing and regret, I let my mind wander to my childhood days with Dad. The days where pancakes were dinner, chocolate cake was breakfast, and jokes and laughter filled our bellies in between. I hate to admit it, but I wonder what Dad would think of me now, so different from the carefree teenager he knew. Would he be proud of the woman I've become or disappointed by my structured life? Worse yet, indifferent?

Evan steps back and says, "Listen, I don't mean to rush this moment for you, but I'm in a tight spot and sure could use a favor."

I blink away tears foolhardily forming in my eyes. "Yes, of course. What is it?"

"Can you pick up Weston Campbell from Sky Harbor Airport, executive terminal? He's flying in from Los Angeles."

"A new client?"

"No, a business associate of my parents turned family friend. You've never met him?"

"The name doesn't sound familiar."

"Well, anyway, he's going to lend me a hand with an upcoming project."

"How will I spot him? I have no idea what he looks like." For some reason, the name Weston Campbell evokes an image of a wirehaired and well-fed Irish farmer stabbing bales of hay with whiskey breath spewing from his toothless grin. I should work on being less judgmental, but honestly, where's the fun in that?

"No problem recognizing him." Evan aims his phone's camera in my direction. "Smile."

"Wait." I set the jar on my desk and comb through my shoulder-length brown hair, fluffing the bangs that hover over my Irish green eyes, thankful I wore my favorite sleeveless dress cinched above the waist with a ridiculously cute Michael Kors belt. "Okay, go."

He snaps a photo of me.

Dang. I think my eyes were closed.

"This is Lanie Howard." He punches at the keys. "There, I forwarded your picture to him. All you have to do is stand outside the security gates and he'll find you. The executive terminal isn't very big." Evan slides into his jacket and steps toward the leather-framed mirror hanging on the wall to study his reflection. He swivels his head side to side and checks for any budding "parasites," as he called the two gray hairs discovered earlier this year on his thirtieth birthday. "I'd go myself, but Weston changed his flight and I've got that 1031 Exchange lecture tonight."

"What time is Weston arriving?"

"Six." Evan spins around and catches me peeking at the clock. "I know, the Cardinals game. Maybe you'll miss the first half, but you'll be home in time to catch the rest. I'll make it up to you tomorrow." He winks. "You'll take care of Weston for me?"

Waiting in a stuffy airport is the last thing I feel like doing, especially if it means missing a Monday Night Football game.

But Evan's in a pinch and business outweighs pleasure, so I hide my discontent with a smile and reply, "Sure."

"Great. Weston's staying at the Biltmore. Just drop him there." Evan slips his hands around my waist and pulls me toward him again, my Someday Jar wedged between us. His lips brush my neck and he whispers, "I'm such a lucky man."

After his quick kiss, I watch his Mercedes drive away, then slump into my chair. With the tip of my forefinger, I trace the jar, top to bottom, following a crack. "Promise me you'll explore life," Dad had said with narrowed eyes and hands clasped around mine. "Promise me you'll color outside the lines."

Now, here I am, a grown woman, many years later, wondering if I should twist off the cork. Reach beyond my comfort zone and tackle my ambitions, challenge myself like I vowed. *Should I color outside the lines?*

My inbox chimes with an e-mail, jarring my thoughts to the present. Glancing toward the computer and spotting the lotion bottle, I'm reminded why I took my ring off—for age-defying, triple-moisture smooth hands—and see the jewel behind the knocked-over frame.

Thank God. With relief, I slip the ring on my finger and decide that my future is what deserves my attention, not the painful reminder of days behind. I tap the jar's brittle cork and drop the keepsake into my purse. *Those days are gone.*

An hour later, I lock the office and head toward my car, juggling an armful of files and a ringing cell phone.

"Hey," says Kit, my best friend of countless years. She's chewing on something, odds are a papaya granola bar as she lives off those things, admitting they taste like cardboard, but loves the fact that they can double as a kickstand for her son's bike, should the need arise. "Want to catch the game and share a plate of greasy potato skins?"

"God, I'd love to, but I'm on my way to pick up a colleague of Evan's, then hurrying home to catch what I can of the second half with a mound of paperwork piled on my lap. Dammit," I say as much to myself as her, "I need to swing by Nordstrom's. Evan's out of shaving cream."

The judgment in her silence is deafening.

"What?" I ask.

"I'm just wondering what happened to my nutty BFF who used to hustle pool tables and dance on the bar after a couple drinks. Has she been eaten alive by the responsibility monster?"

"I don't know what you're talking about."

She chews another bite, then says with confidence, "The Vine, Labor Day weekend, senior year. You danced on the bar in that denim miniskirt. The bartender's arm was sticky from your sloshing lemon-drop martini. He was pissed."

I can't help but laugh. "Next time we'll grab drinks."

Kit sighs. "Okay. Just promise me that cheeky girl I've known since grade school is still in there."

"She's there." *Somewhere.* "I've been busy." *For three years.* "Did I tell you? We have nineteen listings in escrow right now. Evan Carter Realty is poised to rank number two in residential sales this quarter, in all of Phoenix. Evan's worked really hard."

"*You've* worked really hard. Come out and play sometime."

"I will."

"Swear?"

"Swear."

"Okay, I'll talk to you later."

"Sounds good. And Kit, for the record, it wasn't the Vine. It was Club 99. I rocked the hell out of that miniskirt."

༄

Interstate 10 is the direct route to Phoenix Sky Harbor, but since traffic is light and I've a few extra minutes, I find myself steering through the side streets of downtown. I turn onto Washington Avenue and pull up curbside at the almost completed City Core construction site. Chain link surrounds the seven-acre urban complex, which combines condos and commercial space built within two sharply angled towers. I don't know much about the project, other than I'm impressed by the architect's vision, for he or she must've known that at this time of early evening, the towers' glass captures the sun setting over Camelback Mountain and reflects on the city, dual sixty-story murals of the desert's incredible landscape.

I step from my car and wrap my arms around myself, grabbing hold of the fence, uncertain if I'm chilled from the hint of fall in the breeze or the memories from where I stand. The City Core is very different from the building that once stood here, the one my dad worked in when I was a kid. The one with the corner deli where he let me order my own coffee. Side by side, we spent mornings sorting through photographs of him rafting, hang gliding, rappelling, choosing the best shots for his next freelance magazine article.

"Are these dreams from *your* Someday Jar?" I'd ask, holding a glossy photograph of some snow-covered mountain range, praying I didn't sound too eager. Too much like a child.

"Nah, I don't need a jar." Dad nudged my elbow with his own. "You're my greatest adventure."

My heart flickered. Actually tickled inside my chest when Dad said those words. *You're my greatest adventure.* I'd never felt more loved. Or more protected. The most important person in his world.

He moved out six weeks later.

I release my grasp on the fence as if it's buzzing me with voltage and chastise myself for letting a silly childhood token rattle my thoughts. Honestly, what has gotten into me?

As I drive toward the airport, my engagement ring catches the sun's light and I think about my life. In three months I'll be married to a beautiful man full of integrity and principle. A man who is kind to my mom, finishes my crossword puzzle, and still half stands when I join him for dinner or return from the restroom. Thanks to this man, I have a solid job with clients I adore. A stable future.

I nudge the jar deeper into the depths of my purse. I'd be a fool to uncork the pain and splintered promises of my past. Yes, my dad is the first man I ever loved. But he's also the first man who broke my heart.

two

FLIGHT #819—LAS to PHX
DELAYED

Delayed? Until when? The game started ten minutes ago. Another set of stacked monitors stands fifty feet away. Unfortunately, the same word flashes on the screen. DELAYED.

I reach for my cell phone and call Evan.

No answer.

When his voice mail cues, I say, "It's me. Weston's plane is delayed. Guess I'll wait. Just thought I'd let you know. Bye."

Beside the security gates, I claim an available seat in a row fixed against the wall. Next to me, a snoring older woman's *People* slips from her relaxed fingers. I lean over her, angling my neck like an ostrich, toward the cheers and claps from the sports bar down and across the hall. Every square inch of the wall space is plastered with neon beer signs and TV screens. The game is tuned in on like one, two . . . three screens.

"Go! Move your million-dollar legs." Some fan in the bar shouts.

"Cut right. Cut right," yells another fan.

Sounds like a good game.

I glance at the Jetway. No plane.

Okay . . . just a couple plays.

I spring from my seat and hurry toward the bar like a toddler running toward her mommy. "Excuse me." I weave through the crowd formed at the entrance, stopping beside a man whose suitcase blocks the narrow walkway between tables. He's fixated on the screen.

A super-fast Cardinals running back plows through the Giants defense for thirteen solid yards before getting tackled.

"First down," the man cheers.

We high-five like old friends.

There's one open seat at the bar. I step over the suitcase and wiggle myself comfy on a bar stool.

"What can I get you?" The bartender slides a napkin in front of me.

"Oh, nothing, thanks. I just want to catch the game for a minute."

"Gotta order something then." He points at a sign behind him. PURCHASE REQUIRED FOR BAR SEATING.

I scan the room; everyone has a drink. Those who don't jam the bar's entrance squinting through the glass walls like middle schoolers trying to see what the cool kids are doing.

"Well?" he asks again.

At that moment, the air conditioner kicks on and a cool breeze blows in my face. I once read that the recycled air in airports can be incredibly drying. Since I'm a firm believer in hydration, and really, I have no other choice if I want to watch the game, I say, "Lemon-drop martini, please."

Kit would be proud.

Truth is, it's been ages since I've done anything mindless and rash like Kit mentioned. Not that I want to relive my college days or dance on a bar again, but a little fun now and then wouldn't hurt. Maybe spend a date night with Evan over a game of pool, a pitcher of Blue Moon, and saucy hot wings, teasing while I sink the eight ball into the corner pocket for a winning shot?

The bartender places the pale yellow drink in front of me. I nibble sugar off the rim and swallow a healthy sip of the bittersweet cocktail. *God, I've missed you.*

I lift my drink in appreciation.

The bartender nods as he wipes a wineglass.

Yes, of course, drinking a martini isn't *exactly* what I should be doing. I should wait by the gate and review the real estate market's daily hot sheet or calculate the company's third-quarter tax payment. But, *c'mon* . . . the game's on. Kit's right. When is the last time I've relaxed? Besides, it's only one drink. And I won't miss Weston's flight because hanging on the wall at the bar's far end are blue-screened monitors. I can make out the word *delayed*.

Love that word.

⌒

I'm such an idiot. *How long have I been rambling?* "I didn't mean to go on and on like that." My words snag on my tongue and sound a bit slurred, even to myself. "I wish you would've stopped me."

"I tried," says the man seated on the bar stool beside me.

"Oh, you did? Sorry." I hiccup, then quickly cover my mouth.

Never again should I drink multiple lemon-drop martinis on an empty stomach in an airport bar. Number one, they are a total rip-off at eighteen dollars apiece. Number two, I wind up blabbing like a lunatic. And number three . . . *whatever.* I sip.

"No problem." He swallows a swig of beer.

He's not gorgeous. No chiseled model-type face and flawless micro-dermabrasion skin like Evan. There's a crescent scar above this man's lip and the hint of evening stubble pokes along his chinny-chin-chin. Even so, there's a rugged attractiveness to him with his dark eyes and hair. He's like a headstrong, one-screw-up-away-from-being-fired kind of cop I'd see in movies.

The crowd roars. I glance at the screen and catch the play in action. The Cardinals are deep within their own territory, but I watch with delight as the quarterback lobs a long spiral down field. It's a little high, but #11, Larry Fitzgerald—the best wide receiver ever—skyrockets like eighty feet in the air and catches the pass, one-handed. "Go. Go. Go."

The announcer calls, "Fitz's at the thirty, the twenty, the ten, touchdown. Wow, folks, what a miraculous catch. The Fitz does it again. He goes all the way for the score."

Okay, so maybe my enthusiasm for the game gets carried away at times. Blame it on my football fever, blame it on the martinis, blame it on the wind for all I care, but I can't stop myself. I jump up and down, high-five the bartender, fist-pump a busboy, and hug every cheering stranger within a fifteen-foot radius. Everyone except the man I've been talking with.

With a smile as wide as the flat screens on the wall, I plop into my seat, keeping an eye on the game. Fitzgerald runs the football over to the referee. "Did you see that?" I tug on the man's sleeve. "See what he did?"

"The touchdown? Yeah, I—"

"No, not that." I wave my hand. "Fitzgerald handed the ball to the referee. He always does. After every play. Instead of chucking it on the ground, forcing the ref to chase after it like other players do, Fitz gives it to him. Every time. I hate arrogant football players, don't you?" I don't give the man a chance to answer. "Did you know Fitzgerald used to be a ball boy for the Minnesota Vikings? He's really nice."

"You know him?"

"Well, no . . ." My voice trails off.

"Football fan?"

"Little bit." I sip my martini, then shake my head. "That's a lie. I'm a *huge* fan. Borderline obsessive."

"I can see that."

I giggle and focus on the curled lemon rind at the bottom of my glass.

The man points at my business card peeking from my purse pocket and reads, "Evan Carter Realty. You work there?"

"Yes." I sit taller and smooth my dress, which has risen to my thighs. I meet his eyes and offer a professional smile. Perhaps he's in the market. There's a cozy two-bedroom loft-style in Gilbert that'd be perfect for him.

"Real estate agent?" he asks.

"Broker, technically."

"So why isn't your name on the card, too?"

I open my mouth to reply, then close it again. *That's a damn good question.* I reach for a napkin.

My phone, lying on the bar, chimes with a message, likely from Evan. The screen shines on my face as I check the text. It's not Evan. It's Stacee, our wedding planner. *Evan wants to meet Tuesday, late afternoon. Please confirm.*

Setting the phone down a little harder than I intended, I say,

"Did I mention we're engaged? See. Getting married in three months." I wiggle my three-carat, square-cut diamond solitaire ring in the man's face. Except I lean too far and the stool wobbles underneath me, throwing me off balance. I wind up scraping his nose with the edge of my diamond before I catch myself. "Oops. Sorry."

"It's all right." He wrinkles his nose, which now has a tiny, red scratch.

"Evan's so excited about the wedding." I tear off a long strip of the napkin and curl it around my finger. "He talks with our wedding planner more than I do. They've made everything so easy for me, selecting the date, the venue, the food." I tear off another corner of my napkin. "Everything is meticulously arranged. All I have to do is pick out a dress."

"It's dead."

"What's dead?"

"The napkin." He eyes the shredded mound beneath my hands. "It's officially deceased."

I push the pile away and fold my hands in my lap. *Why haven't I been named broker?*

"Well, I'm sure the wedding will be flawless."

"Yes, it will. Thank you." Glancing at the arrivals monitor, I still read: *delayed*.

We sit in silence for a few moments, watching an ad for Kay Jewelers. After the closing jingle, *Every kiss begins with Kay*, I say, "You know, I disagree with that."

"Yeah?" He pushes the peanut bowl between us.

"Yeah. I bet more kisses begin with an empty bottle of cheap Zinfandel."

He laughs, nearly choking on his beer. After wiping his mouth with the back of his hand, he says, "Tell me more."

The alcohol relaxes me, so I don't hesitate. "Well, I detest poor grammar. Irregardless is *not* a word. I'd rather be stabbed in the neck than watch a movie with zombies, clowns, or Cameron Diaz. Or eat anything with mustard. I had my tonsils removed when I was eight. Broke my tailbone when I was ten because apparently jumping off the top of the slide into the pool isn't the best idea. I've never solved a Rubik's cube. And you"—I point at the man—"are looking at Roosevelt High School's senior prom queen."

He eyes me quizzically, like I asked his tampon preference. I stare back.

What did he say his name was? Okay, so yes, maybe he's good-looking. Early thirties, I guess. Though his sideburns are a few days away from needing a trim, his slightly disheveled hair and five-o'clock shadow are mildly appealing. Some women might even quiver when his lips curve into a half smile.

I mean, I'm not dead. I can find other men attractive. It's not against the law or anything. If I weren't in love with Evan, I might even notice that under this man's charcoal-colored shirt, his abs look harder than this steel bar stool I'm sitting on, which, by the way, has completely numbed my ass.

"No shit?" He flicks a peanut shell off the bar and signals the bartender for another beer.

"No shit, what?"

"Prom queen?"

"Is that so hard to believe?"

He shrugs.

I snatch the peanut bowl from his grasp and cradle it with my hands.

He laughs, reaches over my arm, and pops another peanut into his mouth.

Murmurs from the bar crowd shift my gaze toward the game. "Watch the blitz." I scream. "The *blitz*!" Seconds later, and exactly as I feared, a Giants linebacker barges through the Cardinals offensive line and flattens the quarterback. "I told you." I wave my fist at the screen, then turn toward the man. "I told them."

"You did." He reaches for his ringing phone. "Will you excuse me?"

"Of course."

He swivels his bar stool around. "Hey. How are you?" His voice sounds sweet. Interested. Sincere.

Afraid he'll think I'm eavesdropping, I call the bartender for another drink. Quickly, of course, so I can eavesdrop.

"Trevor, he's good?" the man says. "How's the project? Excellent. Tell him I'll call him tomorrow. Okay, love you, too." He slides his phone into his pocket and spins toward the bar.

"Your family?"

"Yeah. Trevor, he's seven and has been working on a science project for a couple of weeks, trying to determine if plants grow differently with microwaved water versus straight from the tap. He made a chart and everything. He's clever, that kid."

"Sounds adorable."

"Yeah, he's cool."

"Your turn," I say, cracking a peanut shell in half. "Tell me something."

"Okay, well . . . *irregardless* of what you say, I love mustard. And, I, too, was crowned prom queen."

"Whatever."

"All right. Let me think." He picks at his beer label. "I make a killer apple pie, never remember birthdays, and know a guy who has this weird quirk. He sniffs whenever he's bugged by something."

"Sniffs?"

"Yeah, he's great to play poker with. I always know when he has bad cards."

I laugh and reach for the ChapStick in my purse. As my fingers brush against the Someday Jar, an image of my dad's face floats through my mind. "You know, my dad was kinda quirky, too, prattling off random Irish sayings all the time."

"Yeah, like what?"

"*B'fhearr liom thú ná céad bó milch.*"

The guy scrunches his face in confusion.

"I prefer you to a hundred milk cows."

"A hundred milk cows?"

"Yeah, it's a compliment."

"Milk cows is a compliment?"

"Yes." I playfully smack his forearm.

"Are you sure?"

"Yes."

"Totally sure?"

"Yes." I'm smiling. Smiling a lot. Then it hits me.

My hand still rests on his arm.

I jerk my hand away. *Jesus, Lanie. Get a grip. You're flirting with this man. Flirting.*

The bartender slides over the other martini I forgot I ordered. I take a massive gulp, swallowing half.

"You like to drink?"

"No, not normally. Actually, I'm supposed to pick up Evan's associate, some guy I've never met, and his plane is delayed. Speaking of which, what time is it anyway?"

He checks his watch. "Nine thirty."

"Nine thirty?" I practically scream. "Are you sure?" My eyes dart toward the TV. Two SportsCenter commentators discuss the game's highlights with an empty field behind them. The football game is over. The bartender arranges liquor bottles and only a couple of patrons remain, their beers nearly gone.

I confirm with my phone. Nine thirty. *How did three hours pass without my realizing it?* A pang of clarity socks me in the gut as I glance at the monitor and though I struggle to focus, all the flights display *arrived*.

Shit.

"Listen, I've gotta go." I slide off my bar stool, tip my glass, and slurp the last sip of my expensive-yet-delicious concoction. A little more juice pools underneath the lemon garnish at the bottom. I tilt my glass high and tap at the base.

That's when I almost die.

Midslurp, the coiled lemon rind shoots down my throat as if sprung from a slingshot and lodges in my esophagus.

I drop my martini and glass shatters as I thump my chest. *Oh, God.* I'm choking. Choking! My throat burns and my lungs cramp as if a boa constrictor has wrapped around my ribs.

Jesus. This is it. This is my end. These are the last moments of my life.

With horror, my mind flashes to an image of my body lying on a cold, stainless-steel bed at the morgue. Oh, fuck. I think there's a hole in my underwear.

From the corner of my bulging eye, I see the man jump from his seat. He slides his arms around my waist and lifts me off the ground. His fingers brush under my breasts as he squeezes me against him—I was right about the stone-hard abs—and thrusts his entwined fists into me.

Nothing happens. I'm still choking. My fingers and lips tingle numb.

Oh, God. Oh, God. Oh, God.

Moments of my adult life flicker through my mind. *Sorting stacks of documents. Oil changes. Scrubbing clean the condo's baseboards. Sunscreen.* Diligence. Order. Routine.

Then, thank everything holy, with one more heave, the man launches the lemon rind free. It flies from my mouth, the slimy fruit smacking the bartender on his forehead.

"Thank you." I wheeze and cough, drying the tears that drip from the corners of my eyes. I collapse onto the stool. "I don't know what happened. One minute I was fine and the next minute, I couldn't breathe."

The man returns to his seat. Beads of sweat have formed above his lip, and he wipes them away with the back of his hand.

Awareness swarms through my body as the color presumably returns to my cheeks. I stare at the man with a serious face. "What if I choked on that lemon peel and died? What if that was my last breath?"

"Maybe a glass of water?" he asks the bartender, who dabs at his forehead with a napkin.

"I could've died. My obituary will read, *Lanie Howard dead*. That's it. Nothing else. No lifetime accomplishments. No list of accolades. Just white space."

"I'm sure it isn't that bad."

"Yes, it is. My bobblehead collection is the most exciting thing I've done in just about forever."

"Bobbleheads?"

"Exactly."

"Who do you have?"

"Yoda, Statue of Liberty, Martin Luther King, Robin—"

"Robin? As in Batman and Robin?"

"Yes."

"Why not Batman?"

"Because Robin does all the legwork and gets none of the credit. Sidekicks are underrated." I shift my feet. "Look, it doesn't matter. You're missing the point."

"What exactly is your point?"

What is my point? All at once I get it. All at once I understand what my dad meant, what he wanted for my life. *Color outside the lines.* I pound my fist on the bar. "My Someday Jar."

"Your what?"

"My jar of aspirations."

"Like a bucket list?"

"Yeah, exactly. I'm gonna uncork it."

"You should."

"You're right, because you know what else my dad said?"

"I'm afraid to ask."

"'Follow your dreams, unless it's the one where you're running naked through church.' So that's what I'm going to do."

"Run naked through church?" He arcs his left eyebrow.

"No." I press my lips together to quell my smile. "But I will not stand and watch life pass me by a moment longer. I can balance a bit of adventure with responsibility."

"Sure you can."

"Sure I can. I will open the jar. I will accomplish my goals. For me. Before I become Mrs. Evan Carter. Just like I promised Dad." *Even if he isn't around to see it.*

"Good for you." He thanks the bartender for the water and, before sliding it toward me, plucks out the lemon wedge. "Just in case."

"Ha-ha." I chug the water, the cool liquid soothing my aching throat.

The bartender comes around and sweeps up the broken glass.

I offer an apologetic smile, then return to the man beside me. "Look, it's nice meeting you, but I have to go."

"You sure you're all right?"

"Totally fine, thanks."

"What about the guy you were supposed to pick up?"

"Oh, damn." I text Evan, but he still doesn't answer. Maybe that's a good thing because I'm pretty sure I misspelled every word. There are two *e*'s in *airport*, right? "I don't know. It's so late, I'm sure whoever he is, he found his own way to the hotel by now." I dig into my wallet, which apparently is made of the slickest leather in the Western Hemisphere. A couple twenty-dollar bills, three quarters, ChapStick, a worn credit card, and my driver's license scatter under the bar stool.

"I got it." He stops me, putting his hand on mine.

His hands are scarred and weathered from hard work in the sun. Determined. Dependable. Capable hands.

Not that it matters, of course.

He gathers my things and stares at my driver's license for a moment longer than I think he should. What's he doing? At least the picture's not half bad, but I don't want him criticizing me for not being an organ donor. I snatch the license and hold my purse open for him to dump in everything else.

"Well, thank you again for saving my life."

I ask the bartender for my bill and slide off the stool, but my legs buckle and I'm forced to hold on to the counter for support.

"Listen." The guy tosses a hundred-dollar bill on the bar and thanks the bartender. "I'm leaving, too. I'll walk you to a cab."

"I can pay for my drinks."

"So can I. Let's go."

My disappointed mother shouting "stranger danger"

screams through my mind. "No, really, I'm fine." I take a couple of wobbly steps toward the exit, but the doors are all squiggly. What do they put in those lemon-drop martinis anyway? Jet fuel? Maybe I do need a little help. And really, he's not a total stranger. We've talked for hours. Plus, he has nice teeth. White and strong. That has to count for something, right? Serial killers don't have good teeth, do they?

He moves beside me.

"Um, okay. I guess walking me to a cab might be a good idea." I lick my lips, which seem to have thickened into two gelatinous blobs.

We walk in silence and I'm painfully humiliated. I got drunk at an airport bar, choked on a lemon rind, and now need an escort to a cab. Tomorrow, I'll be some hilarious story this guy tells all his buddies. I'd hate him for that if I didn't need his forearm to lean on.

He motions toward the open door of a taxi.

"Listen, thanks again," I say, climbing inside, guilty that I can't remember his name.

"No problem." With slightly parted lips, he folds a stick of gum onto his tongue. His jaw flexes with each chew.

My God, his eyes are piercing.

"Um, right." I clear my throat. "Anyway, I really appreciate your help."

"My pleasure." He steps inside and slams the door behind him.

three

"Lanie, now!" My dad calls from the driveway below the balcony where I stand. His elbow is wrapped with gauze from a recent snowboarding accident—or was it ice sailing this time?—and his perpetually tan face broadens with laughter.

From the bucket near my feet, I grab a red water balloon. It wobbles like Jell-O in my cupped hand.

"Do it." He laughs. "Do it now."

Hard as I can, I chuck the balloon. *Splat*. The latex bursts the instant it smacks against his well-used golf cart. Water shoots out in all directions and splatters the concrete.

"A direct hit." He cheers. "Again, again."

I reach for another balloon, a blue one, and whip it at the tire. *Spoosh*.

Dad dances as water splashes his shins, and I break into a belly laugh. My face hurts from smiling. My fingers are ice cold from the water, and any minute now, Mom will order us to stop, but I don't care. This is how we wash the golf cart.

"Hurry, Lanie," he yells. "Throw another one. Get the backseat."

Before I do, someone taps on my arm. *Tap-tap-tap.*

I brush it off and grab another balloon.

"Lanie," says a man's voice, sounding far away. At the same time, the balloon shrinks into nothing and Dad disappears from my view, fading into black.

"Wait," I cry out.

"Lanie," the man calls again, closer now.

After a deep breath, I realize I was dreaming. My head pounds and the hint of lemon sours my mouth. I'm too exhausted to open my eyes. It can't be morning yet. *Please, don't let it be morning yet. I'm too tired for morning.*

Tap-tap-tap.

Go away.

Tap-tap-tap.

Ugh. How annoying is this? Why can't I sleep? I just need a few more minutes, a little more time with Dad and . . . *tap-tap-tap.*

"Lanie. Get up."

Reluctantly, I lift my head and check the alarm clock.

"It's only forty-nine fifty," I snap. "See, it's early. Let me sleep." My head settles back against the most comfy pillow ever. But there's a buzz in my brain. A nagging bouncing around in my head like a fly trapped in a windowsill and at last I realize. *What kind of time is that?* I lift my head again and rub my eyes.

Within seconds, I gain my bearings and discover we've stopped in front of Evan's condo. The guy from the airport is beside me. Apparently I fell asleep. In his lap. *Is that drool?*

Wiping my mouth, I quickly grab my purse and reach for

the door handle. With a swift move, I hop out, slam the cab door, and run toward Evan's condo like a track star. Never in my life have I made such a fool of myself. Accidentally farting near the microphone during my fourth-grade choir concert was nothing compared to this humiliation. Nothing!

As I cross the street, the crisp nighttime air sobers me. *Oh, Lord, this is bad. Very, very bad.* This man knows where I live.

I unlock the door and quickly close it behind me. Through the frosted window of our front door, I watch the cab's taillights disappear down the street. *Thank God.*

"Hi, love."

I spin around and find Evan standing beside the kitchen sink, an empty water glass in his hand. He sets the drink down, loosens his tie, and unfastens the top two buttons on his shirt. "I just got home myself and noticed you called earlier. Everything okay? Did you find Weston?"

"Funny thing." I sway slightly and grab the dining room table for balance.

Evan frowns and steps close. "Have you been drinking?" He picks at my bangs and scrunches his eyebrows together. He's due for a wax, but there are better times to mention that. "Is that sugar in your hair?"

"Probably."

"You and Weston got drunk?"

"No. Just me." Which sounds even more pitiful out loud.

"Want to tell me what's going on?"

No, not really, thank you very much. I can think of a thousand other things I'd rather do. A colonoscopy, for one.

"Where's Weston?"

"I'm not quite sure. His flight was delayed and well, the game was on and—"

"Lanie, this was important to me." He pulls out his phone and dials. "Weston, it's Evan. Sorry for the mix-up at the airport. Give me a call; let me know you made it to the hotel." Evan drops his phone into his pocket, slips his tie from his neck, and lines up the ends. He folds the silk tie precisely in half, then half again. Without looking at me he says, "It's late." Before I can utter a word, he pounds up the stairs.

I'm such an idiot. What was I thinking? *Sure, I'll have another martini. Sure, I'll blab to a stranger. Sure, I'll drool in his lap. Jesus, Lanie.*

After gulping two glasses of water and eating several slices of bread—I once read that wheat soaks up alcohol, and for half a second I contemplate swallowing spoonfuls of flour—I trace the walls and crawl up the carpeted stairs toward the bedroom. Quietly, I tiptoe inside the bathroom, close the door, and turn on the light.

Though I'll regret it tomorrow, washing my face or brushing my teeth now seems more challenging than climbing Mt. Everest with a broken leg. Screw it. I'll scrub extra in the morning.

I strip out of my clothes, drop my purse beside Evan's row of neatly aligned shoes, and turn off the light. My face smacks into the closet door, because apparently it has to be *open* to walk through it. With a whimper from my pain and behavior, I slide into bed, thankful that Evan's asleep, snoring. I don't have the energy to explain this evening. All I want now is sleep. And the room to stop spinning.

four

Evan's text screams at me the following morning. It takes longer than I like before my head clears and I am able to focus on the words. *Call me. By the way, it's airport, not aeeport.*

It wasn't a bad dream.

After a long shower and countless vows to the water spray that I'll never, never, never drink again, I gag down a dose of Green Power—Evan's favorite vegetable drink that looks and smells like baby poop (especially when hungover). Thankfully, my symptoms subside. All that's left is a sledgehammer pounding my head every three seconds. Given how I let Evan and Weston down, I deserve the pain.

It isn't until I reach inside my purse and keys jingle in my hand that I remember my car is parked at the airport.

Awesome.

I call Kit. "Hey, it's me." I burp a pungent combination of lemon, vodka, broccoli, and kale into her voice mail. "Call me when you get this." Before I finish the message, my phone chimes with an incoming call.

"You're a lifesaver." Kit's voice smiles through the receiver. "I've searched for my phone all morning. It just rang inside the Cheerios box."

Naturally calm and maternal, Kit juggles her four-year-old son, Dylan, like a pro. She's happily married to Rob, an insurance adjuster, and they live a few minutes away in a house that is snuggly-warm and slightly disheveled like a page straight from *Restoration Hardware*. Her kitchen smells of cinnamon and there's always whipped cream in the fridge.

"I'm sorry to ask, but can you drive me to the airport? I left my car there last night."

Kit pulls the phone away from her mouth. "Honey, the dog doesn't want Play-Doh in his ears." To me she says, "Why is your car at the airport? You and Evan elope? I'll be furious, you know."

"No, we didn't elope. Long story. I'll explain on the way."

"I love long stories. It means it's gonna be good. Okay, listen, Rob's home this morning so he can watch Dylan." Her voice turns sinister. "Let me bust out the finger paints."

"You're awful."

"Me? It's good for Rob. The other day he claimed to have eaten a bad plum and was in bed all afternoon. A bad plum? Give me a break. He spent the day watching *Breaking Bad* reruns."

I giggle, then wince, for every fiber in my head stabs with pain. "I'll see you soon?"

"Yep, be there in a couple minutes."

We hang up and I fix myself a piece of peanut butter toast. I munch and delicately swallow, for my throat is still tender, and grow irritated with myself, recalling my behavior last night. *Blabbing for hours. Flirting with that guy?* Yes, okay, in my own defense, I was drunk. Not thinking straight. Nobody should be taken seriously after several martinis.

And honestly, what was with me spouting off all that crap about my Someday Jar? Sure, it was a big part of my life at one time, but I've pushed that keepsake out of my mind for so many years, no sense in thinking of it now. No sense in uprooting the pain I've worked for years to bury.

Kit honks and I step outside into the blinding light.

"Hey," she says as I slide into the passenger seat of her silver Audi. Dressed in worn jeans and a black T-shirt, she wears no makeup, doesn't need it. Just a bit of gloss shines her lips. It's times like this, staring at her glowing, wrinkle-free skin, I wonder if she's right about a diet of grass-fed humanely killed meats and nonprocessed foods.

She flips her long black ponytail behind her shoulder and, with a frown, grabs my chin. "Honey, you're pale. You know vampires aren't popular anymore, right? We're supposed to have a little color again."

"I miss that look. It's easy to look tired and malnourished."

"Me, too." She releases my chin. "By the look of your swollen eyes, this is going to be a really good story." Kit steers away from the curb and heads us toward the airport. "So?"

"I almost died."

"Swear?"

"Swear. I choked on a lemon peel. The guy beside me saved my life. Did the Heimlich thingy."

"That works?"

"Apparently, because here I am."

"Thank God you're all right." She pats my knee. "Tell me what happened."

I tell Kit everything. The delayed flight, the game, the

martinis, right down to my flirting and passing out in the guy's lap. "Who does that?"

"So, you had a few drinks and some guy saved you. Big deal. It's about time you had a little fun."

I rub my pounding head.

"Wait a second. Where did you say this guy was flying from?"

"Los Angeles. The screen said the LAS flight was delayed. Why?"

"Honey, LAX is the code for Los Angeles. LAS is Las Vegas."

"What?" I spring my head up and look at her. "Are you sure?"

"Do you forget I folded brochures at that travel agency for like nine months my senior year? I'm sure."

"That means Weston was there. Waiting for me and I missed him."

"Sounds like it."

I bury my head in my hands.

"What did Evan say when you got home?"

"He wasn't happy." My voice garbles beneath my palms. "He stormed upstairs and went to bed. I'm such a twit."

"You're not a twit." Bless her heart; Kit bites her lip and suppresses a laugh.

We can't help it. We've known each other since grade school and when she holds back her laugh, it's only moments before she . . . there it is . . . lets out a snort and we break into a belly laugh, marveling at what a complete jackass I am.

Ten minutes later, Kit pulls into the airport and stops curbside underneath the DEPARTURES sign, near the parking structure.

"Thanks, I appreciate it."

"Think nothing of it. I always enjoy a hearty laugh; it's good for my core." She pats her abs.

Stepping out of the car and leaning through the window, I

thank her for the ride and beg her not to tell anybody what happened.

"You mean besides Rob, Rob's colleagues at work, your mom, my mom, Rob's mom, all of our friends, Dylan, Dylan's friends, Dylan's teacher—"

"Fine, fine. You made your point. I feel bad I let Evan down. Plus, I left Weston hanging and made an ass of myself. Ugh. I'm just so embarrassed."

"Don't be." She waves her hand. "I'm glad you didn't choke to death and I'm really glad you had a little fun. You deserve it. Stop taking yourself so seriously."

"Okay, you're right," I say with relief. "Besides, it's not like I'll ever see that guy again."

five

The moment I walk in, Evan's voice echoes through our spacious office, well appointed with a black iron coffee table and Nantucket beige walls, which his mother and I agree make the room warm and inviting, "Lanie, we need to talk."

My stomach twinges with apprehension. Not because Evan intimidates me or I feel inferior in an argument—I'd already passed the LSAT and earned an honorable mention from my undergraduate debate team when Evan and I met—but because we've had so few arguments in our relationship . . . two? . . . maybe three? One was a slightly heated discussion over toothpaste, so it hardly counts (I was right, anyway). All the same, I pride myself on our amicable connection. Our ability *not* to push one another's buttons. Dad and Mom fought so vehemently, especially during the last couple years of their marriage. Tension stifled our house, making it hard to pass their bedroom without a clenched jaw. So now, in my adult life, I cherish, even crave, an even-keeled relationship.

Evan was mad last night. Very mad.

When the phone rings, I'm grateful for the temporary interruption.

"Good morning, Evan Carter Realty."

"Morning, sweetie."

"Hi, Mom. I just got in to work, can I call you—"

"I'm at the hospital."

"What?" I grasp the phone tighter and press it hard against my ear. "Are you all right?"

"Fine. In fact, good news. I left the lab and my white blood cell count is five point two. Right on target."

"Oh, that's good." I plop into my chair, flooded with relief. "I didn't know you were sick."

"Oh, no." She laughs. "I'm not. You remember? It's my monthly checkup. Gotta know ahead of time if I'm coming down with something. You should think of doing the same."

"Right." My screen prompts and I type in my password. *OREO*. Milk's favorite cookie. Mine, too.

"Anyway, today in the cafeteria they're serving chicken alfredo. Want to join me for lunch?"

"Mom, I don't get it. You're afraid of getting sick. You won't come over to the condo if anyone within a three-block radius so much as sniffles. Why do you eat at the hospital?"

"Considering the reviews I've read, the hospital is the cleanest place around town. All the doctors eat here."

"Doctors who have had their hands drenched in sick people."

"Oh, Lanie. Don't be such a snob. Lunch is a bargain at four twenty-five and that includes a drink. How about Evan? Would he like to join me?"

"I don't think so."

"Well, we must get together soon. Time is ticking away for your wedding. There are a few others I'd like to include on the guest list and my friend Liz doesn't hear well in her left ear. Where will you seat her? Place me near the present table."

"No one will steal our presents, Mom."

"Well, lots to discuss. Just think, soon you'll be Mrs. Evan Carter. It has such an illustrious ring to it. Don't you think? I don't know how you did it, Lanie, nailing down Evan."

"Gee, thanks."

"I didn't mean it like that. Good-looking, caring, and successful." Her voice peaks with the last word. "He's a wonderful man. Nothing like the featherbrained boys you dated over the years, and what is more important, nothing like your father." She sighs. "Oh, Lanie, I can't tell you how happy it makes me, knowing my daughter has found a solid man and won't have to worry about the things I did. So flighty, your father. If that man hadn't walked out and—"

"I know, Mom. We've discussed it many times. Neither of us was reason enough for Dad to stay."

Half listening to Mom ramble about devoting her good years to a man who tossed aside his wedding vows like a used condom, I reach for the Someday Jar and hold it in my palm, allowing my mind to drift to the days before their arguments, before the strain, before the exhaustion.

"Are you there?"

"What? Oh, yes, sorry." I pick free a piece of lint stuck in the cork. "Mom, do you remember my Someday Jar?"

"Not that silly trinket your father gave you. Toss it in the trash, Lanie. Right now. Don't you see? This is exactly what I mean. There is no reason you should hold on to such a childish token when you have a glorious life waiting for you with Evan. Be smart. Don't you recall how your father hurt us?"

She's right.

I squeeze the jar within my palm, tempted to shatter the delicate glass into pieces. Why should I care about this dumb jar? Why should I waste a fraction of my thoughts on broken promises? Why should I hold on to anything from my dad?

Because it's all I have.

I release my grip and set the crock on the desk.

"Sorry, Mom, I better go."

In the background, a doctor is paged over an intercom and she waits for it to finish before saying, "All right, dear. I'll call tomorrow after I get results from my liver panel. Bye."

Evan buzzes me on the intercom the moment I hang up. "Lanie?"

"On my way." I head toward Evan's office with confident steps. I'll simply explain that we all make mistakes and I didn't purposely mean to confuse LAX with LAS, forget Weston, get drunk, or drool in a stranger's lap. Maybe I won't mention any of that.

Evan stands behind his oversized mahogany desk, with his back to me. The wood shutters are open and he stares out the large picture window that lines the far wall, allowing the magnificent view of Camelback Mountain.

I'm reminded, as I wait for Evan to say something, that he's always so formal. Unhurried. Exact. His posture screams respect and patience. Whether it's Monday morning or Saturday afternoon, his belt matches his waxed shoes. His shirt and slacks are pressed smooth. Come to think of it, in our three years together, I've never seen him in grimy clothes or dirt under his nails. Does he even *own* a sweatshirt with grass-stained elbows?

That goes back to Evan's upbringing, I suppose. Not quite a silver spoon in his mouth but close enough. Taught in highly accredited private schools, Evan grew up the shining star in his parents' lives. As a single child, he never had to divide his

Legos or fight for the front seat of the family Jaguar. He's never had to fight for anything.

Quite different from my modest childhood; with my mom always on the hunt for a bargain, the closest I got to a silver spoon was if families like Evan's donated one to the thrift store.

Evan says nothing.

I wish he'd say something.

Maybe I should go first? Where do I start? The delayed flight? The one-too-many martinis? The handsome guy? *What?*

"I just got word that Hollis Murphy might list his fourteen-thousand-square-foot mansion in Fountain Hills. I've been waiting a very long time for this day. A very long time. More than anything, I want this listing. Murphy is such a prominent figure in the Valley; it'd be huge for this company. Huge. The commission alone is half a million."

"I'm sorry. I shouldn't—" Wait. Did he say Murphy mansion? He said work stuff, right? No *what the hell happened?* No chastising wag of the finger? I shift my train of thought into work mode. "I know Hollis well. I'll give him a call and offer a market analysis."

Evan eyes me curiously.

"Well, think about it. The market is hot right now, especially for high-end properties. With the currency exchange rate, the Canadian demographic alone is scooping up luxury homes for their winter residences. Not to mention, the latest job-growth predictions show a strong upswing. The market looks the most promising in years. If I draw up an evaluation and give the Murphys an idea of what their home is worth, maybe they'll consider selling. I'm sure they're poised for a sizable profit and there's talk the capital gains tax rate may increase in the coming years. Now might be the best time to sell."

"Lanie, that's genius. Absolute genius. That's what I love about you, always quick with an idea." He steps close and kisses my cheek; toothpaste lingers on his breath. "I must admit, your clumsiness a few years ago might prove the best thing that ever happened to this firm."

"It was an accident."

"Knock his socks off with your market analysis. Show him I have a professional, solid firm. No reason to think of listing at any other time or with any other firm." He smiles.

That's it? No mention whatsoever of last night? With this weight lifted off my shoulders, it's all I can do not to swirl around the room like a helium balloon with a pinhole leak. I head toward the door.

"Hold up," he says. "I want to talk to you about last night."

My head starts to pound again.

"I'm disappointed with your behavior, but I spoke with Weston this morning and he made it to the hotel with no problem, so all in all, I guess no harm was done."

"Thank you, that's good."

"I trust that sort of carelessness won't happen again?"

"Never." I reach for the handle.

Evan lifts a hand. "There's something else."

The guy? Did he see the guy in the cab?

"Yes?"

He steps toward me and says, "What time do we meet with Stacee today?"

"Four o'clock."

Evan slips his finger behind the waist of my skirt and tugs me close. "After that, I'm taking you to dinner. I have a surprise for you."

"A surprise?"

"Yes, and it's big." He steps back and outstretches his arms like a preacher welcoming a Sunday congregation. "Life-changing big. Something I think you've always wanted."

"Can you give me a hint?"

"Nope."

"Even a tiny one?"

He shakes his head.

"At least tell me where we're going for dinner."

"The Hill."

"Wow. This is a big deal."

"I thought you'd be pleased. Now off to work because tonight you're mine." With a pat on my ass, he playfully shoos me away.

I hurry out of his office while my mind inventories my closet. What am I going to wear? Not the red strapless (too slutty) or the black floor-length (too witchy). Maybe my cream V-neck dress with the puckered hem? Perfect. I need to borrow Kit's snakeskin heels that make my legs look slender and sexy.

"Evan's taking me to The Hill for dinner," I say to Kit when she answers on the first ring.

"Swear?"

"Swear."

"What's the occasion?"

"He has a surprise for me."

"Really? What do you think it is?"

"No clue. He already proposed and—" Like a firecracker, the airport guy's voice pops into my mind. *Why isn't your name on the card, too?* "Oh my, God, Kit. Do you think he'll promote me to broker? I mean, we've talked about it briefly—albeit very briefly—and I do have my license."

"You think?"

"What else could it be?"

"Oh, Lanie, that's awesome. You've worked so hard. Clearly you deserve this. Okay, what are you wearing tonight? Not that powder blue pant suit."

"You don't like that outfit?"

"I would if you were my grandmother. Burn it."

"Whatever. I'm thinking my cream V-neck dress. The one I got at Nordstrom's Rack."

"You'll need my snakeskin heels."

It's like we have one mind.

After we hang up, and though my head's still a bit woozy, I focus on work. There's a lot to do today. First things first. I call Hollis. His voice mail cues after three rings so I leave a message asking him to call.

The rest of the day, I sell an East Valley split-bedroom to a young couple, list a lot in Mesa, swallow a couple more aspirin, complete and pass two of Evan's and my broker renewal classes, send a birthday card to Evan's godmother in San Francisco, haggle with the electrician over an outrageously high bill—four hundred dollars for a defective circuit breaker. Seriously?—and cram a day-old bagel in my mouth moments before Hollis Murphy walks in the front door.

"Recovering alcoholic struck in crosswalk by Budweiser truck."

"Awful," I say, trying not to laugh and sliding close for a hug.

"Mr. Murphy," Evan steps from his office. "It's good to see you again."

"Yes, well, Lanie left me a message and since I was in the neighborhood, I thought I'd stop in."

"I'm glad you did. Yesterday I forgot to thank you," Evan says.

"Thank me? Whatever for?"

"I read your article a few months back where you said the secret to your financial success is a rich marriage with a good woman."

"That's right. Hard to trust a man whose feet aren't planted firmly in the ground."

"Agreed." Evan wraps his arm around me. "That's why I took your advice and popped the question."

"She's a good woman." Hollis winks at me.

"I proposed during a sunset gondola ride at Gainey Ranch, spared no expense." He glances at me. "You probably already told him this."

I shake my head and offer an apologetic smile.

"Well, I don't know why not." Evan chuckles. "Have you seen her engagement ring? Lanie, show Mr. Murphy your diamond."

I place my hand in Evan's open palm—grateful I found my ring yesterday—and give him a little squeeze. How lucky am I, cushioned between my two favorite men? Evan, youthful, disciplined, and intelligent, stands across from Hollis, looking at the older man with admiration. What does Hollis see in Evan? Talent? Drive? Focus? A younger version of himself?

"The stone is over three carats," Evan continues. "VVS1 rated and nearly flawless. My jeweler said F color, but I lean more toward E. I had the new diamond set in my great-grandmother's wedding band."

"Lovely ring," Hollis says. "Well, Lanie-Lou, what did you call about?"

Evan nudges my shoulder.

My cue.

"Hollis, a little birdie said you might consider selling your home."

"What dumb-ass bird said that?"

Crap. The last thing I ever want to do is irritate this sweet, sweet man.

My heart flip-flops with compassion as I glance at Evan. He stands so rigid that I fear he'll snap in two if I so much as blow in his direction. He really wants this listing.

"Bevy and I have lived there for as long as I can remember. Why would we want to sell it?"

"I apologize. We just thought—" I pause. "Actually, Hollis, would you mind if I compiled a market analysis and gave you an idea of the value? Just for fun. You might be impressed with the numbers."

"Fun is slathering Vaseline on the handle of my neighbor's mailbox. I don't know that a market analysis is *fun*, but you've piqued my interest. Put something together and I'll show it to Bevy. She's the brains in the duo."

Out of the corner of my eye, I see Evan's face break into a satisfied smile.

Yes. "Will do, thanks."

"Okay, I'm off." Hollis waves good-bye with a slight tremor in his hand, and then the dear man shuffles out the door.

"Nicely done," Evan says. "Get a jump start on the analysis, okay?"

"Absolutely. I'll call the title company and order a property profile right away. That'll get me started."

"You can't imagine how badly I want this listing." Evan straightens his tie in the mirror, then turns toward me. "No one else better get it."

six

At four p.m., Evan and I step inside Stacee's Boutique. Bells, wrapped around the handle, jingle as he closes the door behind us. The room smells of love and lavender. Yards of flowers drape along the windowsills and soft cream-painted walls rise behind comfy-looking couches with bridal books spread across the coffee table.

Evan places his hand on the small of my back and guides me inside.

Stacee, sweet and plump, looking sleek with ruby red lipstick, stands beside her desk in a loose blouse and one-size-too-tight black pants, nodding into the phone.

A moment later she hangs up. "So sorry about that. I have the cutest bride you ever did see, but she can't stick with a decision to save her life." Stacee laughs, reaching for a long lacy veil. She waves it in the air. "We've gone from long veil, to short veil, to no veil, back to long veil again, at least a dozen times."

She's teasing. I don't know her all that well, but well enough to hear the lightheartedness in her voice.

I'm not like most girls. Sure, I've dreamed of getting married since my Barbie made out with Ken on the hood of her pink Corvette, but I've never been one to obsess about the tiny details. Not unnecessarily concerned whether we have three or four tiers on the wedding cake, custom labels on the wine bottles, orchids instead of roses for the centerpieces. As long as the man I love is waiting for me at the end of the aisle, the rest seems inconsequential. Evan enjoys the particulars. It's cute, really. Watching him resolve the details like he's negotiating a fair deal on a house. Evan is inviting many clients and investors to attend our big day. He wants things just right.

"Enough of that. Now, Miss Lanie, don't you look beautiful." She air-kisses both my cheeks.

"Thank you. Evan has special dinner plans for us."

"How sweet is he? I must say, Lanie, you've got yourself a keeper." She playfully squeezes Evan's biceps, looks at me, and wiggles her eyebrows. "A definite keeper."

Evan's cheeks redden.

Stacee tosses the veil on her desk, then tiptoes—she once said a lady never makes noise with her shoes—into the back room, calling out, "I promise not to keep you long." She returns with two flutes of champagne. "Cheers to love."

We take our drinks and clink glasses.

"Three months until the big day. Let's see how we're doing." Stacee sits on the desk's edge and, referring to notes in front of her, she rattles off details quickly. "Okay, invitations will go out next week. I've ordered the china and charger plates, glasses, flatware, and we finally decided on a writing style for the hand-scripted place cards. Evan, wasn't that a chore?"

She leans toward me. "Who knew the letter *a* could be written so many different ways?"

Evan shrugs.

"I've made Lanie's hair, makeup, and nail appointments. The photographer and wedding album designer have been coordinated," she says to herself as she marks off the items on her list. With a little huff, Stacee sets her notes down and frowns at me. "Lanie, when will you pick out your dress? We're running out of time."

"I know. I'm sorry. Kit and I plan to come very soon."

"You're lucky you're so adorable and anything will look gorgeous on you, but all the same, you'll likely need alterations. We're cutting it close."

"Agreed," Evan says. "Now, love, I hope you don't mind, but Stacee and I decided on white chocolate hand-dipped cranberries as table snacks rather than almonds because my aunt Diane has a nut allergy."

"Okay, that's fine."

"The cellist confirmed."

"Excellent," Evan says. "I was worried he'd already be committed elsewhere."

"I pulled a few strings," Stacee jokes. "Oh, I almost forgot." She grabs two linen samples from a nearby table. "Ecru or eggshell?"

Evan weighs a napkin in each hand, baffled, as if choosing which of his dying twin children gets his pancreas.

"Which one, Lanie?" he asks. Honestly, they look exactly the same. Without reason I point at the eggshell napkin.

"Are you certain? Because I fear the hint of beige overpowers the cream." He throws his arms in surrender and with a smile tosses the napkins onto Stacee's desk. "Lanie says eggshell, so eggshell it is."

"Okay, then. That should do it for now."

Evan stands and I join him. He wraps his arms around me.

Stacee's right. He has amazing biceps. Almost as amazing as the man from the bar. *Whoa! What the . . . ?* Instinctively, I peek at Evan with hopes he can't read my thoughts. Although, really, what's the big deal? If Evan saw the guy's biceps, he'd be impressed too. But still, why does that guy from the bar keep prickling my thoughts like a rash?

"We'll talk soon," he says to Stacee.

"Sounds good." She wags her adorable pudgy finger at me and scolds, "Pick out your dress."

"She will." He plants a quick kiss on the top of my head. "Won't you?"

"Of course. Actually, I like that veil. Will you order me one?"

"I'd love to. Oh, Lanie, it will look stunning on you. Just stunning."

Outside, Evan presses his car remote and starts his Mercedes. The alarm responds with a *beep-beep* and the engine roars.

Before pulling away from the boutique, I watch Stacee replace the veil on a mannequin, smoothing the lace. She and Evan have worked hard on the wedding, ensuring an impressive ceremony. *Mr. & Mrs. Evan Carter.* I'm very lucky. Very lucky indeed.

So why am I feeling unsettled? What's with this underlying current that my Someday Jar has sparked? Then it hits me. My wedding day. I'm surprised I hadn't thought of this earlier. Coupled with the fact that I promised Dad I'd finish the jar before I married, his absence seems heightened as the biggest day of my life approaches. The emergence of the jar reminds me that my dad won't be dressed in a tux, fidgeting with his stiff bow tie and blinking away tears he'll pretend aren't forming in his eyes, as he grabs my hand and says, "Ready, kiddo?" He won't pat Evan on the back or shake his hand with a firm take-good-care-of-my-daughter grip. He won't be there to fold his hand over mine and walk me down the aisle, hold me for the father/daughter dance, or offer last-minute advice to me, his little girl. Seeing the jar again reminds me how far away I am from my youth. How far away I am from him.

"Now about that surprise." Evan pats my thigh, jarring me to the present.

I inhale a deep breath, erasing all other thoughts except what's ahead. "Yes." I clasp my hand around his. "About that surprise."

seven

Under the oxidized-steel-and-wood porte cochere of The Hill, the valet opens my door and I step onto the stamped concrete. A 1950s converted mansion, Scottsdale's most exclusive restaurant sits above the city at the end of a curvy torch-lit drive. Most of the waiters are Italian and speak with the most charming accents, saying things like *"buona sera"* and *"il piacere è tutto mio,"* which could mean *your hair looks like shit* or *there's risotto stuck in your teeth*, but I don't care. I love the sounds. People wait three weeks for a reservation. Evan sure has connections. We sold a house to the executive chef and his wife last summer.

Evan and I head toward the double-door glass entrance, passing under cascading sheets of water that drape off either side of the porte cochere's roof and splash into ponds filled with large koi and bordered with smooth boulders.

We walk inside, greeted by the chatter of diners, clinking wineglasses, and smells of garlic, tomatoes, and pasta. Is there anything better? What a perfect place to unveil a surprise, especially a surprise for me.

Lanie Howard, *Broker*. I never compared myself professionally with Evan before, but as I stand here thinking of my efforts at the office, I don't know why not. Haven't I researched, previewed, and shown property after property, spent countless hours in negotiations, perused pages of contracts and escrow documents, salvaged broken deals, and managed all the small yet immeasurably important details? Haven't I done as much work as Evan—arguably more—over the years? Come to think of it, why haven't I become a broker already?

He must've known this all along. Silently, he's recognized my contributions to the business, appreciated my results, and tallied them in his mental vault, realizing that I deserve to stand side by side with him. That I'm worthy of his love *and* a promotion.

We are a great couple. Totally in sync. He thinks of things before I realize I want them. This is right. This is real. Though I'll never admit it, I worried there was a fraction of truth to my rambling and flirting last night. Worried that my life might be the slightest bit insipid with Evan. And okay, part of me was excited about uncorking the jar and the notion of learning something new. Several times today I caught myself bouncing ideas around in my mind, like scuba lessons or parasailing. But just as dust has settled in the cracks of my Someday Jar, awareness has settled in me. I've grown up. My childhood is no more reclaimable than melted snow. Though there's beauty in my youthful dreams, Evan is the next chapter of my life.

"Lanie, lips."

"Oh, yes. Thank you." At the bottom of my purse, I find

the Dior lipstick he bought me and spread Bright Amber #24 on my lips.

Within moments we're escorted toward our table, and after I sit our waiter drapes a linen napkin in my lap. Unfortunately, it's not a secluded table for two and our waiter leaves behind the third place setting, but I don't complain. I smile broadly as he hands me a heavy leather-bound menu.

"Good evening. My name is Santo and I have the honor of serving you."

"Good evening," Evan and I say in unison.

The two men compare a 2005 Pahlmeyer Merlot and a 2008 Spottswoode Cabernet, while I envision my name etched alongside Evan's on the office door.

When will he tell me? After Santo pours our glasses of wine? During a comfortable and relaxed discussion over entrées? Will he tease and hold back until dessert? God, I hope he doesn't wait that long.

Evan decides on the Merlot, and Santo disappears with the wine order. Reaching for my hand, he says, "You look pretty tonight. I like your hair that way."

"Thank you." I fiddle with the end of my low-slung ponytail.

"Lanie." His eyes glow in the candlelight, and I hope mine do the same. I'm glad I painted my lips and bought that twenty-seven-dollar tube of mascara, because Evan's entire focus is on me. Just me. Other diners and hurrying waiters have grown misty in my view. The smells and the chatter have dissolved. All I see is Evan.

This is it.

He pauses.

I slip my other hand, supportively, over his. "Go on."

"You know as well as I do that the success of our relationship is because we blend well and work hard."

"Yes." My stomach tickles with anticipation.

"Because of that, I—"

"Excuse me." Santo presents his wine.

"Wonderful, thank you." Evan leans back, allowing Santo to uncork the bottle and pour a taste in a glass. Evan swirls the wine and watches the liquid flow down the sides. Particular about his grapes, he once returned a $250 bottle of vintage Mosel Riesling after a couple of sips because it didn't pair well with his trout fillet.

While I wait, my eyes dart around the room, taking in the sights and smells. Waiters rush from table to table; diners laugh and spoon into their desserts. A tall man in a navy blue button-down shirt walks toward us, a mother links arms with her—wait, I'm drawn back toward the man. My eyes squint for clarity. Is that?

He sure looks like—no, it can't be.

He comes closer and without any doubt, I know exactly who it is. The same quiet confidence. The same dark eyes. The same scratch on the tip of his nose. It's him. It's definitely him.

The man from the bar. He's getting closer.

Oh, God.

What's he doing here?

"Lanie?" Evan asks. "Do you like your wine?"

There's a full glass in front of me.

"Um . . ." What if the guy recognizes me? What if he stops and says, "Hey, aren't you the drunk I brought home in a cab?" I snake a menu from underneath Evan's hand and duck behind it, nose to nose with the seafood specials.

Sweat seeps under my arms. Why did I wear that god-awful aluminum-free, organic deodorant Kit raves about? Sure, doctors say aluminum gives you cancer, but the deodorants without aluminum are crap. Total crap.

Evan barks at me, something about embarrassing him, but I disregard his words. It'll be a lot more embarrassing having to explain how I know this man.

A quick peek over my menu.

The guy smiles.

Shit. Shit. Shit.

Okay, no problem. It'll be fine. Totally fine. Just don't come over here. *Please Jesus, Buddha, Gandhi, witch doctor, Tom Cruise, anyone, please, please, please, don't let him come over here. Please don't—*

"Evan," a familiar voice says, "it's good to see you. How long has it been?"

Huh?

Evan stands and shakes hands with *him*.

They know each other?

"Too long. Glad you made it, Weston."

I stare at him in disbelief. So much for my fat Irish farmer theory.

"Thanks," Weston says. He glances at me and his eyes flicker with recollection.

Oh, this will be awful. Just awful. Weston will spill everything.

"Lanie?" Evan tugs the menu from my death grasp. "What are you doing? Say hello to Weston." Evan turns toward him, nodding in my direction. "Again, our apologies for the mix-up last night."

"No problem." Weston extends his hand toward me. "It's

nice to meet you, Lanie. Call me Wes. I dropped the '-ton' years ago, right after my boy band fell apart."

He's joking.

"Hello," I say, filled with amazement. He's not ratting me out. He's not letting on one tiny bit that we met last night.

"Excuse me, I'm going to grab our waiter's attention." Evan disappears around the corner.

"The girl with the Someday Jar. How's your throat?"

"A little sore." I stare at him, puzzled.

"I bet." He releases my hand.

"Hold on a second. You mean that whole time at the bar, you knew who I was and you didn't say anything?"

"You were snockered on martinis. Lemon drops, I believe."

I shudder at the thought. "Still, you could've said something."

"Yeah, I could've."

"All right, then." Evan rejoins us. "Santo will be right over. Wes, have a seat. Lanie, your cheeks are flushed. You okay?"

"Yes, I'm fine." I wring the napkin over and over in my lap. My brow creases with wariness. *Who is this guy?* Sure, he didn't divulge that we met or broadcast to Evan my moronic display at the bar, but he played me for a fool. Okay, yes, I helped in the "fool" department. But still. Why not tell me who he was? After a long sip of wine, I say, "Tell me again, Evan. How do you know Wes?"

"Well, he's worked with my parents on various projects, so we've met many times over the years, spent that one New Year's in Park City with my folks." He turns toward Wes. "Remember that double black diamond, east side?"

"That wasn't a ski run, that was a suicide attempt."

Evan laughs. "Those moguls were insane. All the same, my parents can't speak highly enough about you."

"Thank you, I enjoy them as well," Wes says.

Oh, no. A thought paralyzes me with fear. He's an associate of Evan's parents. A likely confidant. Does he plan to expose me to them? Make known my behavior and save their son from marrying a loose-lipped drunk, garnering himself an even closer alliance with them and their rich real estate developer friends? Oh, God, they'll hate me. They'll think I'm an awful match for Evan.

I can imagine it now. At the wedding, his parents will shake their heads in disapproval and whisper to friends and flown-in family members that I'm the daughter-in-law who flirts with random strangers. "Likes to get drunk at airport sports bars," they'll say with a certain tone. Except they won't refer to me by name. I'll simply be known as *her.*

Evan continues, "You know, the last time I saw you, Julie was with you. How is she?"

"Fine, thank you."

Instinctively I glance at Wes's ring finger. No ring. Ha! This explains a hell of a lot about his character. Typical Southern California guy slips off his wedding band when he's out of his wife's sight. Such a schmuck.

I'm about to call him on this, point out that his relationship isn't perfect and who is he to make assumptions about mine? And, now that I see clearer, his sideburns *definitely* need a trim.

Evan asks, "And the boy?"

Wes's face lights up like it did at the bar. "Trevor's seven already, can you believe it?"

"Already?" Evan shakes his head.

"He's a good boy; still struggles a bit. Julie's really great with him."

"I'm sure," Evan says.

"Um, speaking of surprises." Even though we weren't. I mean, enough about Wes. I'll worry about him and his motivation later. Tonight is about me.

"Right, right. That's what tonight is about."

See?

Evan reaches into his jacket pocket.

Paperwork for me to sign? A little formal at dinner, but that's okay, let's sign, seal, and deliver this partnership. We can borrow a pen from Santo.

Evan doesn't pull out an envelope full of tiny-worded documents with my name in capital bold letters underneath a *Sign Here* line. He doesn't pull out a business card with *Lanie Howard, Broker* scribed in fancy font. Nor does he pull out an etched nameplate for my desk. He pulls out a baggie of . . . *dirt*.

"Surprise." He sets the clump of rocks and sand before me.

What the hell does a bag of dirt have to do with my promotion? "What is this?"

"I bought it."

"A pile of dirt?"

Merlot laces his breath as he laughs. "I bought the house that accompanies the dirt. Twenty-eight ten Orchid Lane."

Orchid Lane? I rack my brain for an answer. Nothing comes to me. This is payback for drinking myself silly when I should have reviewed the market inventory. Damn karma. "What house on Orchid Lane?"

"You're going to love it. It's located in a prime area of Paradise Valley. I bought it before the listing went public, closed escrow this afternoon." He leans back in his chair. "Consider it an early wedding present."

My brain is abuzz. A house? By *house* does he mean *broker promotion?*

Evan glances at Wes. "Look at her. She's completely surprised."

As if on cue, Santo arrives with another bottle of wine and three clean glasses. "Celebration?" he asks.

"Indeed. I bought my bride a house."

"Congratulations, miss." Santo uncorks the bottle and after Evan's protocol, fills each glass, starting with mine.

I smile at Santo, then ask Evan, "What about the condo?"

"You'll list the condo tomorrow. I want it to hit the MLS first thing in the morning."

"You said escrow closed today?"

"Yes, I've got the keys in my pocket. Did a good job of keeping this a secret, didn't I?"

"I had no idea." Trying to act nonchalant, I swirl my wine, but confusion weighs heavily inside me. *He* bought a house for *us*. Isn't that an oxymoron or something? I had nothing to do with it. Not a thing. "Evan, I didn't sign anything. How can it be *ours?*"

He puts his drink down. "Lanie, aren't you happy about this?"

"Yes, I suppose I am. I'm just shocked." I speak more softly, as if lowering my voice a decibel won't allow Wes, sitting twelve inches away, to hear. "We discussed buying a home together and splitting the down payment. Remember? You know how important that is to me. If your name is on the deed, then technically it's yours, not ours."

"Lanie, can't we discuss legalities another time?" He leans close. "I was quite excited to surprise you with this. I never expected this type of reaction." He stares at me for a response.

Now I feel like an ass.

Okay. Stop. Think this through. I swallow another sip of Merlot and mull over the situation. Yes, I feel sidelined that Evan didn't include me in this significant purchase. Yes, I'm disappointed that I'm not walking out of here a new broker, but as wine seeps through my body, invades my belly, and numbs my reserve, I decide that just because I'm caught off guard—totally off guard—doesn't mean I should sabotage his special reveal. He did say we'll discuss details later. Isn't his word enough for now?

As far as the promotion goes, maybe Evan doesn't appreciate how important becoming a broker is to me. Sure, once we're married I'll likely have claim to the business, but I don't want it that way. I want to earn it. On merit. On my own. *Have I ever told him that?* I shouldn't throw him under the bus for not promoting me when he didn't know I wanted it in the first place. Come to think of it, the office is a better venue to discuss work anyway. I will ask about the promotion. At the office. Tomorrow.

I glance at Wes. *She didn't even appreciate the house he bought her*, he'll likely tell Evan's parents. *Did nothing but complain. Look here, she drooled on my leg.*

For another moment I consider Evan's perspective. He's pleased with himself. Is it fair of me to sour his enthusiasm? Ruin the evening with my criticism and nitpicking? To a person looking in from the outside, a new home is hardly something to sneeze at. My mom will be thrilled.

What is more important, I won't give Wes the pleasure of watching me quibble another moment.

"You're right." I raise my glass to him. "Thank you. The house sounds wonderful."

"Quite the wedding present, wouldn't you say? Wait until you see the place." He smiles, then motions toward the menus. "Shall we order?"

A question plagues me as I scan the entrées. "So, Wes, I'm not quite sure why you're here." *In other words, when are you leaving?*

Before Wes answers, Evan folds his menu on the table and says, "I'm glad you brought that up. You know, Lanie, you're the reason I called him."

"Me?" I laugh a bit too loudly. "I don't see how that's possible."

"You're familiar with the City Core, yes?" Evan asks.

"Of course. It's an incredible property. The seamless combination of steel and glass with acute angles is breathtaking."

"Thanks," Wes replies.

Wait . . . what?

Evan aims a thumb toward Wes. "He's the architect."

I don't mention that my dad would've loved the City Core development with the tower's penthouse balcony serving as an ideal zip-line post to the pool. Instead I manage, "I . . . I don't understand. What does that have to do with us?"

"Orchid Lane needs an update, cosmetic as well as a few structural changes. Nothing major. I want to eliminate several walls, possibly open up the kitchen, restructure the dining room, add a Jacuzzi tub in the master bathroom. All of which requires an architect. Wes happens to be one of the best."

Wes dips his head in gratitude.

"Meet the architect for Orchid Lane. You're surprised again, yes?"

"Stunned." I stare at Wes. He mentioned none of this last night. Not a single word.

"Wes bounces back and forth between here and Los Angeles frequently, so I contacted him and after a bit of pleading on my part, he agreed to the project."

"I'm happy to do it."

"Evan, I—"

He grabs my hand and says, "Wait, there's more."

Dear God. More?

"I haven't run this by Wes yet"—he turns toward him—"but when I mentioned to my mother you were visiting, she dished me out a serious tongue-lashing for putting you up in a hotel. She says you're practically family and family doesn't stay at a hotel."

"The Biltmore is fine, thanks."

"Please, I insist. Help me get my mother off my back," Evan says with a laugh. "Besides, we'd love to have you. Wouldn't we, Lanie?"

"Um, well, if Wes is more comfortable at a hotel then he should . . ." Heat spiders up my neck as I glance at Wes.

He holds my gaze and offers that damn half smile. "You know, on second thought, I'd love to."

"Great," Evan says.

Santo walks by and I snag his perfectly crisp shirtsleeve and hand him my wineglass. "I'll have a lemon-drop martini."

eight

The next morning, a prickly sensation courses through my body. I scratch at my nightshirt's itchy tag above my hip, but it's not the problem. Could it be the tiny blister formed on my pinkie toe from Kit's heels? There's no way I'm still tired. I came straight to bed after dinner. Nor am I hungover. I drank less than half of the martini.

Evan has opened the blinds as he normally does once dressed and ready for work. Maybe it's the morning light? I pull the blankets over my head. I've never grown used to daybreak in Evan's bedroom as the sun casts rays on the north wall rather than the south like it did in my old apartment. Is that what makes me restless?

At once, Evan's surprise, my lack of a promotion, and Wes's face flash through my mind. I discover what this irritating sensation is: annoyance. Before I can stop myself, I slide toward the middle of the bed and kick my legs and flail my arms, wildly and erratically like a bouncy ball ricocheting inside a shoebox, until I've exhausted myself. *Phew. That felt great.* I remake the bed, shower and dress, then head downstairs.

At the table, Evan's focused on the *Arizona Republic* with a steaming mug of coffee beside him.

Light peeks out from underneath the guest bathroom door. By the sound of running water, Wes is showering.

I'm tempted to flip off the water heater breaker.

"Good morning," Evan says. "Sleep well?"

"Yes, thanks." I pour myself a glass of juice and join him at the table.

"Take a look at this." He taps the lower right-hand corner of the Lifestyle section.

Pictured with varying photos of a dozen or so other men is my fiancé, taken from a recent "Save the Libraries" fundraiser we attended. He stands in a tux, one elbow on the bar, smiling at the camera while lifting a glass of champagne.

Sorry, Ladies . . . They're Taken, the headline reads, and a short article follows listing each man's attributes and accomplishments along with the one thing Phoenix's most-desired bachelors are afraid of. Evan's answer was mediocrity.

"You've got good taste." He takes the paper and regards the write-up for a moment longer. "Evan Carter, a young, attractive, and accomplished broker . . ." He continues to read aloud, but my mind lingers on one word. *Broker.*

"Evan, there is something I'd like to discuss with you at the office today."

"Anything." He tucks the paper under his arm. "First, let's swing by Orchid Lane. I don't have Kit's number, but I already called your mom and gave her the address. I figured you'd want to share this with her. She'll meet us there in a half hour. Ready to see the house?"

I'm eager to get to the office and discuss the broker situation, but equally anxious to see the house. There's a wide grin plastered across Evan's face. He's excited. "Yes, let's go."

"Great." He kisses my cheek. "I'm gonna make a quick call to Stacee because I changed my mind about the garnish for the entrée, and then I'll be ready."

Evan heads into the den and I can't help but sneak a peek inside Wes's room. Thankfully, my bobblehead collection rests undisturbed on the dresser, but Wes's suitcase is flung open on the unmade bed, a half-filled water glass rests on the nightstand—without a coaster—and there's a sock on the floor. A sock.

Evan and Wes really are different. To think, he'll be living here for weeks.

"Need something?"

Wes's voice startles me. I spin around and see him step from the bathroom, dressed in dark gray jeans and a pale blue button-down shirt. Wes's hair is slicked neat, his face clean-shaven, and damn him, he smells a bit like heaven.

"Uh, yes." I glance at the den, then whisper, "Thank you for not letting on that we met at the airport. And for everything else . . ." My voice trails off in embarrassment.

"Don't mention it."

"Look, I want you to know, I don't normally drink like that. And whatever I said, well, it was the martinis talking." With a short laugh, I add, "Whoever said alcohol is a truth serum is an idiot."

"Really?" He stuffs his hands in his pocket and leans against the door's threshold. "You're not an obsessed Arizona Cardinals fan?"

"I meant that part."

"You've never been compared to a hundred milk cows?"

"I'm *preferred* to a hundred milk cows, thank you very much, but that's not—"

"So Evan's not afraid of hummingbirds, frozen yogurt, and polyester?"

Did I say that?

"Don't tell me there's no Someday Jar."

"Of course there is." I shift my feet and slide my hands onto my hips.

Wait a minute.

There's a smile on Wes's face. He's enjoying this.

"Are you finished mocking me?"

"Not quite."

"I'll have you know—"

"What are you two hushed about?" Evan asks.

"Um . . . I . . ." I step back. "I . . . I was checking to see if Wes needed anything. You know, like towels, more pillows, a conscience . . ." I mutter the last word under my breath, then turn and hurry toward Evan.

Wes coughs in his hand, but I know it's just to cover a smug laugh.

Fine, you little smart-ass. If that's the way you want to play, then fine. Just fine.

"Lanie, is something wrong? You're gritting your teeth."

"Am I?" I relax my clenched jaw, slide into Evan's arms, and say loud enough for Wes to hear, "Good thing your love always makes me feel better."

"Let's get going, shall we?"

We decide it's best if Wes rides with Evan and I follow behind in my white Ford Flex, so afterward I can head straight to the office. After the fifteen-minute drive through the curved, mountain-lined roads of Paradise Valley, we turn into a cul-de-sac. Evan types in a code on the keypad and waits for the gate to swing open onto a semicircular driveway, lined with fist-sized copper-colored gravel and evenly spaced barrel cactus.

On my left is the house. I blink several times, trying to make sense of what I see. Heavy and ornate dark-iron outdoor lights with smoked glass decorate the stuccoed walls of the sprawling southwestern-style house, which is landscaped with tall palm trees and oversized boulders. A four-car garage sits at the far end. We park beside it.

Wes steps ahead and unlocks the double front doors.

"What do you think?" Evan asks as I step from my car.

I think this house is incredibly indulgent and how in the world will I afford my share? Especially with my current non-broker salary.

We turn at the *toot-toot* of a horn and there's Mom, parking her car behind mine. She climbs out, wearing her favorite light brown pants and tweed jacket she bought at the senior center for two dollars. "They're Jones New York. Quality slacks," she says every time she wears them. Her shoes clop-clop over the cobblestone walkway and she embraces Evan with a warm smile. "How's my darling soon-to-be son-in-law?"

"Excellent, Jane."

"Nice write-up in today's paper."

"Want me to autograph it?" he jokes. Sort of.

Mom beams at him and grasps each of his hands after a quick scan of the house. "Heavens me. My daughter is so lucky to have you. So lucky indeed. Lanie will have everything I didn't. This is very different from the one-bedroom apartment I raised her in." Tears pool in her eyes as she looks apologetically at Evan. "It was all I could afford raising a teenager as a single mother." She returns to me and wags her finger. "Don't screw this up, Lanie Howard."

Hi, Mom. Yes, it's good to see you, too. Fine, fine. I'm fine. You?

Mom notices Wes, who now stands beside Evan. "Who is this handsome young man?"

"Wes Campbell." He extends his hand.

"Wes is an architect and offered his expertise with the remodel," Evan says.

"What is there to remodel?"

I wondered the same.

"A few things," Evan assures.

"Well, Evan, you know best. It's a pleasure to meet you, Wes."

"You as well."

Mom steps toward me. "Evan bought you a palace. Can you believe it?"

Did he mention he bought it without me?

"Shall we?" Evan motions toward the house.

Mom eyes me for a moment, then reaches for my arm. "You boys go on ahead. We'll join you in a minute."

"All right. Don't keep her long."

She grabs my hands. The safety chain on Grandma's white-gold watch swings underneath Mom's wrist, and I smell White Shoulders perfume. She twists my ring straight and wipes the diamond clean with the cuff of her jacket. "Honestly, Lanie, you're not doing justice to this ring. When's the last time you had a decent manicure?"

I jerk my hands from her grasp and say with a biting tone, "What did you want to talk about?"

"Do you remember when you were nine years old and asked me for the truth about Santa Claus? After I told you, you cried for two hours."

"Yes, because I didn't know *that* was the truth."

"Well, on that day you had the same look on your face as you do now. What's wrong?"

"Nothing."

She raises an eyebrow in disbelief.

I chew on my lip and stare beyond her at a palm frond waving in the breeze. Yes, I decided not to make a fuss about Orchid Lane, but that was *before* I saw it. Now, standing beside this expansive house reminds me that I contributed nothing. No capital. No viewpoint. Not a single thing. I can't help but feel a bit left out, second-class. Controlled.

"Honey?"

"It's just . . . I know this house is really something, most girls would kill to live here."

"I'll say. It's the grandest house on the street."

I nod. "I didn't know anything about it. I didn't help pick it out, didn't assist with the down payment, didn't sign escrow docs. Nothing. Evan knows I wanted to buy our first property equally. If his name is solely on the deed, how can it really be ours?"

She grabs me by the shoulders. "You stop right now. There's a man inside that house, a loving man, who adores you. He adores you so much that he bought this house to share your lives together. Financially, you'll never have to worry, so stop your brooding."

"I'm not brooding. There's more to a relationship than a man's tax returns. I want to be equal, in all ways. Kept out of the loop makes me feel like my opinions don't matter, like they aren't important, like *I'm* not important. Besides, given how you've always said Dad left you with nothing, I'd think you'd want me on the deed, protected."

"Evan is nothing like your father. That man couldn't keep his feet on the ground. Dashing off here and there, always chasing the next adventure. He was unfocused and I will not let you make the same mistakes I did."

"Mom, I'm not—"

"Don't tell me this is about that ridiculous Someday Jar. Has it gotten you discombobulated already? Damn that man." She pats underneath my chin. "Listen to me, Lanie. Evan is a solid man. He's good to you. He wants to take care of you. Let him. Stop asking for more; you'll wind up alone. Trust me, I know."

My eyes drift toward the house. Evan stands behind the front window. He waves me inside. *Maybe Mom's right. Maybe the stress of the wedding, Wes, work, and stirred memories from the Someday Jar have gotten me flustered. Maybe I am making too big a deal out of this. I mean, honestly, Evan isn't peddling heroin to Girl Scouts. It's just real estate. Lumber and tile.*

"How many men buy their fiancées houses as wedding gifts, Lanie? How many? I bet most buy a necklace or a bracelet, if anything at all. Your father bought me a spoon."

"Are you coming?" Evan slides the window open and pokes his head outside. "I want you to see inside."

Yes, I wish he had included me in the house decision, in *any* decision that affects us, but he will in the future. I'm certain of it. Evan's heart is in the right place. He did this for us. That's what matters.

I nod at my fiancé, then clasp Mom's hand. "C'mon, let's go."

We enter the double-high foyer with a massive crystal chandelier hanging overhead and I'm speechless. There are no words to describe this delicious house. Bright and spacious with high ceilings and creamy beige marble floors, it's a showplace.

"Oh, Lanie." It's all Mom can say.

Beyond the formal dining room, we cross a long hallway extending in each direction, lined with doors, presumably for bedrooms and bathrooms.

Ahead, we step two stairs down into the living room with super soft carpet and muffin-colored walls. Banked along the far, curved wall stand floor-to-ceiling glass windows. Not a fingerprint or smudge blurs the view of the grassy lawn and kidney-shaped swimming pool outside.

I walk closer for a better look and notice a stunning rock formation. Almost as tall as the house, it spans the length of the pool's opposite side. The rock looks volcanic, black, rough, and pitted. In the center, a waterfall trickles from its highest peak. On the right, a carved slide winds and twists before dropping into the pool's deep end.

"What do you think, Jane?" Evan asks, wrapping his arms around me. "Will this suffice for your daughter?"

She claps her hands. "I'll say. Glorious, Evan. Simply glorious."

"Is that a cave?" I point at a secluded section of the rock, overhanging the water.

"Sort of. There's a Jacuzzi hidden inside. Watch this." He steps toward a nearby wall and punches a few buttons on a built-in computer panel, the size of an iPad, then motions toward the pool. After a couple of puffs, billows of fog escape from the cave.

Mom and I gasp in unison.

"Spectacular, wouldn't you say?"

"Yes, Evan, it is. It really is." Mom's right. Only a fool

would screw this up. Plus, I'm sure once we move in, our furniture will soften the echo, and with a few personal touches, the house will feel like a home.

"I'll poke around the rest of the house if you don't mind," Mom says.

"Sure thing, Jane. Check out the media room at the end of the hall. The chairs vibrate."

"Ooh," she says, and disappears in that direction.

Wes comes around the corner, clutching a measuring tape, notepad, and pen.

"Wes, let's show Lanie the other side of the house and explain what we're thinking with the remodel."

"I don't see a single thing wrong with this house. Let's leave it as it is." I extend my hand toward Wes. "Thanks for coming, but we won't be needing your services."

"Don't be silly, Lanie." Evan pats my lower back, then steps away, disappearing into the kitchen.

"Yes, Lanie," Wes smirks, "don't be silly."

Ugh.

We turn the corner into the kitchen and I'm stunned. It's the largest kitchen I've ever seen, larger than my old apartment. My entire apartment. The Wolf refrigerator hides behind two paneled doors, and the stainless-steel stove is some fancy European style with more dials than a cockpit. There's a built-in espresso maker and two dishwashers, one on either side of the fifteen-foot, yes, fifteen-foot-diameter round granite island.

Wes knocks on a couple of walls. "This is a bearing wall, so it'll need to stay put." Pointing at another, he says, "You can rip this one down."

"Good." Evan taps on the wall himself. "See, Lanie. It'll really open the space."

Nodding, I walk toward a breakfast nook, shaking away negative thoughts and picturing Evan and me on weekend mornings with the *Republic* divided between the two of us. He'll comment on the Middle East chaos and I'll mention the week's stock exchange rally or predictions for the Cardinals' upcoming game while stirring Bailey's into our Sunday morning coffee with a shared spoon. Well, Evan will want his own spoon. But still.

The pool with the dark rock, blue water, and green grass surrounding catches my eye. Stepping toward the window, a smile spreads across my lips as I imagine how fun it'll be to barbecue with friends and family in this backyard, Evan standing by the grill with a spatula in one hand, Rob and Dylan splashing in the pool. Kit and I will sip mango margaritas and munch on chips dipped in her homemade salsa. I'm excited now. This will be a great house. I peek at Evan and smile. Regardless of how we got here, this will be *our* house.

Evan's preoccupied watching Wes measure a wall, so after a moment I disappear from the kitchen and investigate the rest of the house. I meander through the six guest bedrooms, family room, office, and I forget how many bathrooms, comparing this home to the tiny apartment with the windowless bathroom and narrow kitchen Mom and I shared after Dad left. Orchid Lane reminds me nothing of my childhood and yet, I find myself thinking of Dad. *Again.* Not because he'd marvel at the hand-carved balusters, his-and-hers closets, or the laundry room large enough to park a Chevy truck, but for this long hallway I stand in. I can picture him now, slipping off his shoes and saying with the slightest flick of his chin toward the hallway's end, "You got what it takes?" Then, with a troublesome grin across his face, I imagine him sliding in socks along the smooth marble, his laughter echoing off the walls.

Why not?

I'm about to step out of my shoes when a woman's voice, other than Mom's, calls from the front door. "Evan? Hello? Anyone here?"

I find an expertly dressed, tall and thin woman standing in the foyer, a clipboard in her hand. "Hi," I say. "May I help you?"

"Oh, good, you're here," she says. "Did you see the stain in the corner of the dining room? I think it's red wine or something. Make sure you get it out."

"Excuse me?"

"I didn't stutter." She forces a smile and scans me from head to toe.

Even though I copied my outfit from a Pinterest post—dark jeans, white scoop-neck blouse, light blue checked scarf, silver drop earrings—I feel like an unwanted stepchild in hand-me-down clothes compared to her.

"You're with the cleaning crew, right?" she asks.

Cleaning crew? "No, I'm Lanie Howard, Evan's fiancée."

"Oh goodness, of course. I'm sorry." She pats my forearm. "It's just, with the hair, I thought . . ."

My hair? I reach to touch it but stop and fiddle with my earring. I can't help but notice *her* shiny blond cropped hair. A style I've never had the courage to try. Her eyebrows are angled and plucked, her earrings dangle but don't sag, and though her eyes are set slightly far apart, her face has an exotic appearance instead of that of a dazed circus animal, like I'd have preferred.

"I'm Paige. Congratulations on catching the big fish."

"Sorry?"

"Evan. But don't worry. I'm not here to steal him away. At least not on purpose." She winks.

Before I punch her in the mouth, Evan and Wes stroll in from the kitchen.

"Paige, I appreciate you coming," Evan says.

"I'm so glad you called." She walks all glossy and confident toward him.

"Lanie, Wes, this is Paige. She's an incredible interior designer and she's agreed to help us with the house."

Help? Why do we need all this help? First an architect and now an interior decorator? We don't need Paige. I can do it. I've got skills. My Yoda and Lady Liberty bobbleheads, lined up along the fireplace mantel, pop into mind. Okay, maybe I don't.

I slide my arm into Evan's and comb my fingers through my hair—which I planned on doing anyway—and accidentally-on-purpose catch the sun's ray hoping to blind Paige with my diamond. Then, with a sugary-sweet tone, because after all, he's engaged to me and there's no point in making a big deal out of this, I say, "Sounds great."

"Shall we start in the kitchen?"

Walking toward us, Mom peeks at her watch. "Gotta run. My adrenal cortex evaluation is in twenty minutes. Remarkable home, Evan." She nods at Paige and Wes, then pats my cheek. "Remember what I said, okay?"

"Okay."

"Good. I'll call you later, honey."

We all say good-bye and Mom shuts the door behind her. Evan pulls away from me and leads Paige toward the kitchen. "Let's show Paige what we're thinking." Quite honestly, I really don't mind that she's here, even if she is extraordinarily beautiful, has an ass rounder than a Victoria's Secret model, and probably wears sexy underwear, the itchy kind. She'll simply prove to Wes that Evan only has eyes for me and that we are a great, solid couple.

"Your thoughts?" Evan asks.

Shit. I wasn't listening. "I—"

"Well, I agree with . . ." Paige starts.

My stomach wobbles with embarrassment. Evan asked Paige. Not me.

Oh, well, no matter, I convince myself. Of course Evan asks Paige questions. She's here for her opinion and I'm here because Evan loves me.

After they finish their discussion, we step outside.

Evan says, "We'll be in touch?"

"Yes, I'll get back to you with some ideas."

"Excellent."

Paige backs out of the drive in her Range Rover SUV with her DECOR8 license plate and speeds off.

Wes dips his head good-bye to me and slides into Evan's car.

"You like the house?" Evan asks.

"It's amazing."

"I thought you would. Listen, Wes and I are stopping for breakfast and then we have an appointment with the planning and zoning department for permits and such. I'd love for you to come, but I'd rather you got started on the Murphys' evaluation." He squeezes my shoulder. "I'm counting on you, babe." He steps toward his Mercedes and says before pulling away, "The house looks beautiful with you in it."

For a moment I stand there, staring at a stray piece of gravel on the driveway. With a swift kick I sail the rock high and watch it spin and twist in the air, hovering for a fraction of a second against the cloudless sky before it plummets onto my windshield and, with a loud smack, chips the glass.

nine

"Are you Phoenix's newest broker?" Kit asks, wearing a cleavage-revealing peach sundress that Rob says is his favorite for two very obvious reasons, which jiggle as she chops an onion. She's making tacos. Rob grills fish outside while Dylan and a friend play hide-and-seek. Evan had a dinner meeting, so after I finished Hollis's evaluation, I came by myself. Truth be told, I'm thankful for the time alone with Kit.

"Not yet." I pick at my beer label.

"Evan didn't offer you a promotion?"

"Nope. I planned to bring it up today, but he was out of the office all day."

"What was the surprise about?"

"He bought a house."

"A house?"

"A fancy place on Orchid Lane."

"Wow. That is a surprise." She grabs her beer and clinks mine. "Congratulations!"

"Yep."

She looks at me, unconvinced. "We're not excited?"

Before I answer, Rob walks inside unwrapping the plastic cover off a new barbecue spatula. He tosses the cellophane in the trash, steps close to Kit, then sips her beer.

"Hey." She elbows him and halfheartedly protests.

He takes another swig and with the wood end of his spatula pats her right boob.

"Get your own beer."

Goose bumps trail along her arm as he plants a kiss on her shoulder. "Fish will be ready in ten minutes," he says, flipping the spatula end over end and heading toward the door.

Kit's starry gaze follows her husband until he disappears outside.

I slump in my chair and fight for a breath not weighted with envy. Over the years, I've spent countless hours with Kit and Rob. We've shared Thanksgiving dinners, football Sundays, handfuls of Vegas weekends with each other. I know how they act together. This display is nothing new. But now, all at once, I'm jealous. I'm jealous of the simplicity between them. I'm jealous of their spirit and the sexiness spewing from their pores. I'm jealous of the spark that ignites as their bodies brush one another.

"Yoo-hoo. Are you there?" Kit asks, waving a knife in the air, directing my attention.

"Yeah, sorry." I straighten in my seat.

"So tell me why we aren't excited about the house." She dumps the onions into a rust-colored bowl and starts on a tomato.

Not wanting to rehash my poor-me speech, I wave my hand and say, "No, I like it. I mean, it's a beautiful place, huge with many bedrooms. The pool has a rock mountain–type thing with a hidden Jacuzzi. Evan and I just need to work out a few legalities."

"I can't wait to see it. Are you moving in right away?"

"Not right away. Evan wants to remodel a few things." Wes's face pops into my head. "Remember the guy I told you about from the bar?"

"Hmm . . . let me think"—rapping her fingernails on the counter—"was he the guy you got drunk with and choked in front of and then repaid the favor of saving your life by slobbering on his pants?"

"You're cute. Do you know that? Anyway, he came to dinner. He's Wes, not Weston, the guy I was supposed to pick up at the airport."

"Swear?"

"Swear."

"No way."

"I know. He played me all along. Wes knew who I was and didn't say one tiny word about it. Can you believe it?"

"Crafty. I like him."

"That makes one of us."

Kit pops a tomato chunk into her mouth. "Why was he at dinner?"

"He's an architect. The lead on the City Core project."

"Some architect. That place is sharp."

"Well, anyway, he's drawing the plans for the house remodel and, get this, he's staying in our guest room for a couple weeks. The rat now sleeps under the same roof as me."

Kit snorts, holding back a laugh.

"Kit!"

"C'mon. You have to admit, it's pretty damn funny."

"Whatever."

"Oh, c'mon. Stop sneering at me and cut the rat some slack. He did save your life. Is he cute?"

"What? How should I know?" I wipe a chip crumb off my thigh. "I mean . . . I don't know . . . I suppose he's not ugly or anything."

"Oh, really?"

"Give me a break. He doesn't hold a candle to Evan."

Kit finishes the tomato and heads toward the sink.

"Oh, and I met Paige."

"We don't like Paige either?"

"Sure, if we like flawless ivory skin and an ass that G-strings were made for."

"We hate her." Kit rinses the knife, then her hands. "Invite her over. We'll pick on her until she develops an eating disorder."

I laugh and nearly spit out my beer.

"Who is she?"

"Our interior designer and she's hot for Evan."

"Slow down," Kit yells at the boys, who chase one another through the living room. Once they're gone she slides onto the bar stool beside me. "Okay, so how long are we going to dance around the issue?"

"What?"

"When are you going to tell me what's really wrong?"

"That obvious?"

"My blind grandfather could see the worry in your eyes. What is it?"

I peel away the label in one square piece, grateful Kit's in my life. She's one of those people I can truly confide in. Ever since fourth grade, when one of the popular girls called me a whore for wearing a skirt on the swing set—*how was I to know the boys were peeking?*—and Kit pulled me aside, telling me to wear shorts underneath, I have trusted her. When we talk, it's genuine. Whatever I say goes nowhere, stays in her vault.

So, I'm not surprised to hear myself reveal feelings that I've pretended for the past couple of days didn't exist. "Do you ever worry that life is passing you by while day in and day out you're focused on what you're supposed to be doing, rather than what you want to be doing? Then, before you know it, you're old and curled up on your deathbed, weigh ninety pounds, nothing but elbows and knees, consumed with remorseful thoughts that obligations and function controlled your life while you sat idly by and watched it happen. Feeble and unable to eat anything but chicken broth or ice chips, you think, *Golden years my ass, I'll never get the chance to shout my name from the rooftop and why didn't I take advantage of my youth?*"

"Holy shit, Lanie."

"I know, I know." I shrug. "Ever since I choked last night, my mind keeps bouncing in a million directions. I keep thinking about my life. I keep thinking about Dad."

"Oh, sweetie. I know you miss him."

I lick my lips while nodding. "I think I know a way to settle my nerves."

"Really, how?"

"Well, it might sound ridiculous, childish actually, but do you remember my Someday Jar?"

"Of course." She grabs two more beers from the fridge.

"What if I uncork it? What if I uphold the promise to my dad and tackle my goals?"

Kit raises the beers in the air. "Yes, absolutely."

I smile at her enthusiasm. "Okay, but here's the thing, Evan won't be too keen on the idea. We have a big listing on the bubble, the biggest of our careers. He'll prefer I focus on the wedding and work, not make waves."

"Give him a blow job. He'll forget all about it."

"Kit!"

"Don't be such a prude. How do you think I got that Pottery Barn armoire?"

"I knew you didn't snag it at a garage sale."

She shrugs and sets the bottles on the counter. Returning to her stool, she swivels toward me so our knees touch. "Listen, all jokes aside, I love my husband, and waking up to him and Dylan every day is honest to God my greatest joy on earth."

"You're an amazing mom."

"Thing is, I jumped into marriage and a family. Now I don't regret it, but there is a part of me that wishes I'd taken a little time to explore life first. Found out who *I* am, you know? This is your chance, Lanie. Grab it. Do something for yourself."

"My goals aren't all that ambitious."

"Who cares?"

"What if I screw up?"

"Then we'll get drunk and laugh about it."

Breaking a chip into pieces, I think about her words. I have wanted to fill the jar and accomplish my goals. I have wanted to broaden my boundaries, explore new challenges, and push myself toward adventure like Dad wanted me to do. But to this day, I haven't. I haven't done anything. Afraid to fail, I've made a decade of excuses and kept the jar corked, putting off my *someday*, and been disappointed with myself for doing so.

My insecurity isn't the only reason I've kept the keepsake at bay. Twelve years ago Dad left. Walked out. Erased me from his life. Since then, the jar has been a painful reminder of my past. I've kept it tucked away, out of sight, out of mind, safe-guarding my heart.

What does that say about me? That I'm a quitter? That I can't handle adversity in life? That I cast aside my ambitions just because Dad found something greater? Bullshit. Don't I matter? Don't I deserve my *someday*?

And what about Evan? How can I move forward with him and uphold a promise to my future when I haven't upheld a promise from my past? Maybe it's crazy but tackling this jar, without Dad's presence, is therapeutic, solidifying my inde-pendence. Solidifying that I've grown strong and healed. That I *can* color outside the lines.

Kit squeezes my knee. "Tackle those ambitions, honey. Close that chapter in your life; then you can start the next one."

"The jar is with me now."

Her eyes widen.

"As a kid, I only filled out a couple slips. Dad left and . . . well, I figured anything more was pointless."

"Fill the rest out. Right here. Right now."

"Swear?"

"Swear."

I pull out the jar and set it on the counter between us.

Kit claps. "This is so exciting."

My heartbeat pounds as I twist off the cork and dump the folded slips into my hand. The papers spot my palm like a flock of small white birds. I catch a glimpse of sweet-and-sour sauce on one paper's edge and the youthful nature of my hand-writing: *Learn something new.*

None too big. None too small. Create your own adven-tures. My dad's words swirl through my mind.

Kit retrieves a pencil and shoves it into my hand. "Do it."

I unfold a fortune, flip it to the blank side, and write. *Broker.* I drop the goal into the jar.

"Absolutely. What else?"

I don't read the manufactured fortunes; I'm focused on shaping my own. My ambitions come to mind with ease. "Break a record."

"You can cram a thousand hot dogs in your mouth," Kit teases. "Or build the world's largest igloo out of sugar cubes."

I tap the pencil on my chin.

"Bungee jumping." Kit squeals.

"Make your own list," I joke. "I will scuba dive."

"Close enough." She adds the slip to the jar. "Okay, more."

"Touch an official Cardinals game ball," I jot. "Silly, huh?"

"None of these are silly." She grabs and reads my next slip. "Make a sacrifice. My, my, Lanie. How very profound of you."

"Yes, well, I'm a beautiful spirit."

Kit chokes on her beer.

I slug her.

"What else?"

"Volunteer."

"For what?"

"As a Big Sister or something."

"Excellent idea." She folds the slip and hands me another. "This is so much fun. Why haven't I done this years ago?"

"See? One more."

I say as I write, "Laugh until tears run down my face."

"Good one."

She reads silently, the other slip I wrote as a kid. A soft, wholehearted smile spreads across her face. She waves the slip in the air. "This one is my favorite."

I reach for it, but she quickly drops it into the jar.

"I want to read it."

"Not now. You'll know when the time is right." She folds the remaining slips and before adding them to the jar, she slides me the *Learn something new* goal.

"Start with this one."

"Wait. How many are there total?"

"Nine."

"There are only three months until the wedding."

"You better get crackin', then." She seals the cork tight and shakes the jar before handing it to me. "Okay, they're all mixed up. The rest is up to you. Promise you'll do this, Lanie."

"I promise. I will empty my Someday Jar."

ten

"Got it."

"Got what?" Kit answers on the first ring.

"Kickboxing."

"Kickboxing?"

"For my *Learn something new* slip." I twirl it between my fingers. "Why not? I'm bored with running, and spin classes make my butt numb. On my way to work today, I spotted a boxing gym on Ray Road. They have women's classes daily at four p.m."

"I adore you, but let's be honest, kickboxing requires coordination and you can barely walk across the street without stubbing your toe. Not to mention, you fell asleep during *Rocky V*."

"Everyone did," I protest. "It's exhausting trying to understand more than three consecutive words from Sylvester Stallone."

She laughs.

"So, you'll go with me? Tomorrow after work?"

"What? Hell, no. These are your adventures."

"C'mon, please." I feed a purchase contract through our scanner. "Don't you have a Maui vacation coming up soon? A little exercise might do you good." This will touch a nerve.

"Bitch," she moans. "Fine. Sign us up."

"You're the best. Now wish me luck. I'm on my way to talk to Evan about the broker promotion."

"Go get him."

"Thanks."

After we hang up, I retrieve the contract and jot myself a note regarding the grading permit. Then, with confident steps, I head toward Evan's office feeling good about myself for pulling a slip from the jar. Granted, I haven't accomplished anything yet, but I like the fact that I'm moving forward. Kickboxing. *Why, Lanie Howard, you're a bit of a bad-ass, aren't you?*

"Hey, there."

"Hi." I slide into one of the barrel chairs opposite his desk.

"Is that the blouse my mother sent last month for your birthday?"

I glance down at the ivory lace cap sleeve with pearl buttons. "Yes, it is."

"She'll be pleased you like it. Tell me: How's the Murphy proposal coming along?"

"Done."

"Already? You're incredible." He leans on the desk's edge. "What'd you come up with?"

Mentally I review the proposal, optimistic with the thorough package I put together. Resting on ten acres, the Murphys' home spreads over fourteen thousand marble and Calamander-wood-floored square feet. With twelve bathrooms (a lot of toilets to clean), two theater rooms (one in each wing), and a garage larger than Home Depot, the hilltop property boasts a killer view overlooking the East Valley.

I spent yesterday analyzing recent sales, pending escrows, price-per-square-foot comparisons, median days on the market pre-sale, and replacement construction costs. I explored every shred of pertinent information available, leaving no fragment of data untapped, no statistic unaccounted for, and, hopefully, no question unanswered.

"Considering my calculations, my instincts were spot on. The market is strong for their price point and the Murphys are poised for a sizable profit. All they need to do is agree to sell."

"And agree to sell with us," Evan says.

"Absolutely." From the corner of my eye, I see the tip of Evan's latest commission check peeking out of the top pocket of his jacket. I secured the buyer for that sale, showed her several properties. Three weeks later she closed on a triplex in Tempe. Cash. No contingencies. A nice sale. Evan gets the credit. And the bigger paycheck.

"Did you get the condo listed?"

"Yes. I also finished the listing packages for the two lots in Chandler."

Evan tosses his hands in the air as he returns to his chair. "What would I do without you?"

"Curl up in the fetal position and cry."

"Without a doubt."

I glance at the check again. This is a perfect opportunity. As Dad used to say, "You can't learn how to swim on the kitchen floor."

"Evan, remember I mentioned wanting to discuss something with you?"

"Yes. What is it?"

I clear my throat. "Well, I've worked very hard for our clients for some time now. Although I haven't minded managing the paperwork, cleaning the office—okay, I've minded that a little—and helping you establish the firm, you promised that was a temporary situation. It's been over three years. I have my broker's license. I have the knowledge and fortitude. I deserve to be named co-broker. I've earned it. It's time."

Phew. That feels good to get off my chest. Now Evan knows, without a doubt, how I feel.

"You're right."

Wow, that was easy. In an attempt to maintain composure, I force away my enormous smile and say with a professional voice, "Great. Let me get the paperwork." Once through his door, I hurry toward my desk and retrieve the change forms while my mind floods with ideas. First, I'll call my friend Chett at the real estate department and have him implement the change. Second, business cards and letterhead will be ordered. Third, the logo will need a rework, and so will all of our advertising, including the website, brochures, and signs. They all need to read *Lanie Howard, Broker*. Holy hell, this is fantastic. I can hardly stand it.

Never have I been more excited about my future. Never.

Guilt pours through me. Except my future with Evan, of course.

A moment later, I hurry into his office, place the documents on his desk, and spatter my words like a loaded semiautomatic rifle. "Okay, it's only a matter of initialing these few forms where I've marked and signing this check for eighty-five dollars, which Evan Carter Realty graciously agrees to pay for filing and licensing fees. I'll call Kinko's and order letterhead and business cards. I'll—"

"Whoa!" Evan raises his hands in surrender and says with a short laugh, "Slow down. Let's talk about this for a minute."

"Okay." I slide into the leather chair and ignore the tiny voice in my head whispering that Evan will attempt to bow out of the promotion.

"Lanie, there is no question how invaluable you are to this firm. No question at all."

Besides, expecting him to make excuses is an awful assumption about the man I plan to marry.

"I'd be a mess without you here."

He probably wants to iron out a few minor details. Like health insurance or a 401(k) plan.

"You're extremely integral to the success of this firm."

Or vacation days.

"I can't imagine a more qualified person to shoulder my responsibility with."

There's a *but* in there somewhere.

"But."

There it is.

"This is a tough, fierce game we play. They don't call us real-a-sharks for nothing."

"Snakes," I correct him.

"Pardon?"

"Snakes. They don't call us real-a-snakes for nothing."

Evan evens his laptop with his desk's edge. "Lanie, I'm ready. I'll sign the paperwork today."

"Great." I perk up, ashamed with myself for misjudging him. "I've highlighted where you sign. It'll only take a minute."

"I don't think *you're* ready."

My breath catches before I respond. "What? Why not?"

"You're so kindhearted and slightly naïve," he says with a wink. "I don't want my sweet future wife corrupted by the dog-eat-dog mentality of this business. I don't want it to change you."

"Change me? Why would it change me? It hasn't yet." I can't help but recollect that I, more than he, negotiate with the so-called dogs on a daily basis. Or are they snakes? Or sharks? It's a friggin' wild kingdom. *Okay, deep breath, Lanie. Don't lose focus. Center.* Nothing is gained from a temper tantrum. "You agree my name belongs on the logo?"

"I do."

"Then I don't understand."

"You're upset."

"Damn right I am. I deserve this. You know I do." I rise and prop my hand on the edge of his desk, surprised by my own resolve. I'm so ticked I may not even wipe off my fingerprints. "This makes no sense. I don't need to be sheltered from life. I'm fully capable of tough negotiations." *Go, Lanie, go.* "Frankly, I've done more of the tough negotiating over the years than you have."

Evan frowns, and irritation laces his words. "I'm shocked. You more than anyone knows this company isn't about whose name is on the door. It's about assisting people with the largest investment of their lives. We smooth a pathway for their dreams."

That's *my* line. I used it on the web page.

"It's bigger than us, Lanie. I must admit, I'm a little taken back with your adamancy. Have you lost focus on who matters? Forgotten about our clients?" He shakes his head. "Life isn't always about you."

There's a familiar pang in my chest. Aren't those the exact words Dad spat at Mom before he slammed the moving-truck door and drove away? *Life isn't always about you*. Perhaps I've pushed too far. Perhaps I've demanded too much from Evan. From my dad. Perhaps my worries and concerns have always been self-absorbed, one-sided. All in vain. My dad left. What am I doing? Trying to chase Evan away, too?

His voice softens as he invades my thoughts. "I didn't want to bring this up again, but the other night you completely dropped the ball at the airport. We're fortunate Wes was so understanding, but had it been someone else, a new client, you could've blown a deal."

"I told you, that won't happen again."

"I trust you want to keep our personal relationship out of this broker arrangement?"

"That's right. I want to earn it on my own."

From behind me, a loud pop jolts us both. Evan squints, and following his gaze, I turn around and look through the front window of our office. Hollis's truck swings into a parking spot. It backfires again before the engine sputters and shuts off.

Mr. Murphy doesn't travel in a black tinted limousine or obnoxiously pretentious helicopter, which he surely can afford. Rather, the driver's-side door wrenches open and the old man totters from a lime green 1980s Chevy pickup truck with a cracked windshield, torn upholstery sagging from the ceiling, and a dent near the rear fender—made by some adorable and charming distracted shopping cart driver—toward our office.

"Tell you what." Evan regains my attention. "I'll make you a deal."

"A deal?"

"You have a way with Hollis. He likes you. He trusts you. Get me the Murphy listing and I'll make you partnering broker."

"He doesn't even want to sell."

"He wants to sell. He just doesn't realize it yet. Otherwise, he wouldn't have been curious about the value. Acquiring Phoenix's most coveted property will, without a doubt, escalate my firm into the number-one slot in Phoenix. Evan Carter Realty will be the most sought-after company in town. I want that listing. Nail Murphy down and get me the deal."

"Evan, I—"

"I know you care for the old man."

"Of course I do."

"If he lists elsewhere, Lord only knows what type of attention he'll get. Can you live with yourself if he's misrepresented by another firm when you had a chance to prevent it?"

"I know what you're doing, Evan, pulling at my heart-strings, but Hollis is a strong man, perfectly capable of handling himself."

"Is he?" Evan peers over my shoulder.

I turn and see Hollis struggle with the weight of our office door. He appears frail and weak—more so than the other day—trying to hold the door open and balance his steps at the same time. I spring from my chair and rush to help.

He manages to get through the door before I reach him. "Lanie," he says, slightly winded.

"Hollis, what a lovely surprise."

He embraces me, then steps back and says, "Man walks in on naked mother-in-law."

"Oh, no." I press my lips together.

"The sight scared him into cardiac arrest. True story." He laughs, which turns into a cough.

"You okay?"

"Yeah, I'm fine. My youngest boy insists I get a flu shot. Damn thing makes me sick every year. Mind if I sit?" He motions toward the couch.

"Please do." I hurry and fluff the pillows for him. "Can I get you some water?"

"No. I don't need anything."

I slide in beside him and pat his knee. "Maybe you should lighten up on the morning swims."

"You sound like Bevy."

"Thank you." I smile.

"You know why I exercise early in the morning?"

"Why?"

"So my brain doesn't have time to figure out what the hell I'm doing."

"Good plan."

"Have you treated yourself today? Had anything sweet?"

"Not yet."

Hollis fishes out a candy cane and hands it to me.

I reach for it and at the same time he jerks it away. Laughing, I reach again only to be outfoxed by the old man. Finally, on the third try, I snatch it from his fingers. "Ha!" I wiggle the peppermint in the air. "Got it."

"I let you—" He pauses to catch his breath.

My heart sags. "How about that water?"

He nods.

"Stay put."

Evan's got me thinking as I fix Hollis's drink. If he lists with another company, one of the impersonal real estate firms with their stuffy faux-painted reception areas and artificial flowers, will they pay mind to him like he deserves? Will they know he likes rooibos tea with a splash of whole milk, not cream? Will they laugh at his jokes? Warm his liver-spotted hands with their own? I gasp. Will he bring *them* candy canes?

I would be devastated if he decided to list but did so elsewhere. Not for the ridiculously huge commission—and my God, it's huge—but because I truly love the old man currently swallowed up in the pillows of our couch.

And dammit, I don't want to share my candy canes.

Hollis thanks me for the drink. After a long sip, he says, "I came by for the analysis. You called and said it was ready."

"I told your housekeeper I could drop it off."

"I know, but it's a beautiful day for a car ride. Besides, I enjoy seeing that smile of yours."

"Same to you. Hold on a second, I'll get it."

I grab the shiny folder with the Evan Carter Realty logo sprawled across the cover. Inside, I've compiled a neatly arranged and thoroughly detailed portfolio, complete with color-coded pie charts, graphed sales predictions, current market conditions, and various other calculations. I squeeze my eyes shut and exhale. I hope they're impressed.

"Here you are, young man," I say, returning a moment later.

"I've grown rather curious to see what you've come up with. Who knows? Maybe we will sell."

"Only if it feels right."

He places a trembling hand beneath my chin, holds his eyes on mine, and says, "You're a good girl, Lanie."

"Thank you."

"Well, I need a nap."

"Of course." I help the old man to a stand, saddened he's not feeling well.

"I'll call you after Bevy's had a chance to look at this and she gives me *my* opinion. After fifty-four years, I've learned we share the same opinion. Hers."

"Smart man."

Hollis and I walk arm in arm toward his truck. Once inside the cab, he leans through the window and blows me a kiss.

I catch it in my palm and press it against my heart. Though I never told Hollis, he's the closest thing to a grandfather I've ever had. Both sets of mine died young, three of them before I was born and the last, nine days after my second birthday. And while it's true Bevy and I have never met, listening to Hollis boast about his bride has made me fall in love with her, too. Never did I have a Nana who wore my colored-noodle necklace to lunch dates or hung my clothespin-reindeer ornament on the Christmas tree year after year. Never did I have a Gramps teach me how to ride a horse, squeeze my cheeks too tight, or slip me a ten-dollar bill for a good report card. Whether it's right or it's wrong, endearing or presumptuous, I consider Hollis more than a tender old man with bad jokes and candy canes. I consider Hollis family.

The truck billows black smoke as it drives away.

As the fumes dissipate, my determination grows clear. No way in hell will I let some other agent take Hollis from me.

Back inside, I march into Evan's office, fueled by the challenge. "The Murphys list with us and you'll make me partner?"

"You get me that listing, Lanie, I'll make you anything you want."

eleven

The following afternoon, dressed in sweats and old T-shirts, Kit and I nervously walk into Rudy's Martial Arts Academy for a kickboxing class. Other than the distinct smell of body odor, it's not your typical gym with heavy dumbbells or weight machines requiring an engineering degree to adjust the seat.

Quite the opposite, it's a warehouse-style, echoey metal building with a mirror-paneled wall, a chain-link cage on the far end, and a big blue squishy mat covering the entire floor. Several punching bags with *Everlast* emblazoned down the sides hang by meaty chains from the ceiling, and five or six other bags with black plastic bases—presumably filled with water for stability—are scattered about the mat.

As I scan the room, I decide it looks friendly and unthreatening. This won't be so hard.

"Hello," says a Hawaiian-looking thirty-something man from behind the office counter. "I'm Rudy. First time?"

"Yes, I called earlier today."

Several women trail in behind us and wave hello to Rudy

as he hands us the necessary waivers. With their idle chitchat and playful banter, they seem so comfortable. My mood perks up even more. I whisper to Kit, "This will be fun."

Kit frowns as she reads the form. "'Possibility of injury that could lead to paralysis or death.'"

I snatch the paper from her hand and initial it. "They have to say that. For insurance reasons. Heck, walking to the mailbox could result in paralysis or death."

"No, it couldn't."

"You could trip on a stone and fling yourself into oncoming traffic. I saw it happen once in a Lifetime movie."

"Are you serious?"

No. "Yes." I hand Rudy our waivers.

"Grab a ball." He points at a rack built above the mirrors, lined with large exercise balls. "Then find a seat anywhere on the mat. All I ask is that you leave your cell phone, gum, shoes, and worries off the mat. And you might want to take off your rings."

We tuck them safely in our purses.

The room isn't crowded, maybe a dozen or so women, varying in age, size, and shape. Like copycats, Kit and I each grab a ball and plop down on the mat, which feels cool on my feet. A girl about my age sits beside me. She wraps a long yellow strap around her wrists, weaving it between her fingers just like I've seen UFC fighters do on TV. She throws her neck from side to side and I hear a couple of pops.

In front of me, another girl with long dark legs and hair to match pumps out twenty push-ups like she's weightless. I dare look behind me at a third woman, who raps punches at a hanging bag with the rhythm and speed of an expert Morse coder.

Good Lord. Maybe this won't be so easy. "Now I'm nervous," I whisper to Kit. "You?"

She looks at me with concrete fear in her eyes. "I already peed my pants."

Rudy bows with hands at his side before stepping onto the mat. His voice echoes throughout the room as he says, "How are we all doing?"

Several of the women reply.

Rudy says to Kit and me, "Welcome."

"Thanks," we answer in unison with uncertain voices.

"Your names again?"

"I'm Lanie Howard and this is Kit Reese."

"Welcome, Howie."

"Excuse me?"

"Everyone in here gets a nickname. Yours will be Howie." He points at the woman with the long legs. "That's T-Bird. Next to her is Peanut. She's Avatar, and never mind. You'll figure the rest out. Let's get started."

"Wait. What's her nickname?" I point at Kit.

"Kit, right?"

"Yes."

"How about Kitty-litter?" he says with a harmless chuckle.

Her face drops.

"Perfect." I laugh.

She rolls her eyes at me and mouths, *I'll kill you.*

Rudy steps away and fiddles with his iPod. "Pour Some Sugar on Me" by Def Leppard blares through the speakers. "It's eighties day."

"Hold on to your panties, everyone. I'm coming," a woman yells over the music.

We turn toward the entrance and see an older lady rush

inside. She's dressed in a cream velour sweat suit with hair swept up in a tightly pinned bun and a set of blue pearls bouncing around her neck.

"Jesus Christ, the old people in this city need to learn how to drive." She tosses her oversized Louis Vuitton bag onto the bench and with a quick unzip sloughs off her jacket, revealing her jeweled *I kick like a girl* black T-shirt. She slips out of her leopard-print ballet-style flats and steps on the mat.

"I'm behind some geezer for fifteen goddamn minutes. I swear he drove twelve miles an hour." She looks at me. "Twelve."

I giggle. This feisty old woman with more wrinkles than a shar-pei puppy can't be more than five feet, four inches tall and one hundred pounds soaking wet. Given her appearance, she seems more suited to volunteer at the library or knit blankets for the homeless, but her attitude registers spot on for a kickboxing class. She's a whirlwind.

"I'm Blue," she says to me with a broad smile. A teeny smudge of red lipstick dots her bottom tooth.

"It's good to meet you, Blue. I'm Howie and this is Kitty-litter."

She looks at Kit and nods toward Rudy. "He's a bastard, isn't he?" She grabs her ball, smacks Rudy on the ass, and says before plopping onto the mat, "All right, Rudy, whip me into shape."

I laugh out loud. I don't know who this woman is, but I like her. A lot.

Rudy orders, "On your backs."

We spend thirty painful minutes on sit-ups, push-ups, and squats, using muscles I never knew I had.

Rudy finally says, "Okay, ladies, put the balls away."

"Oh, thank God," I gasp at Kit, lying beside me on the mat with her arms and legs spread wide like a starfish. Her hair is a mess: sweat-soaked, stringy, and wild. She reminds me of our junior year in college during spring break, the morning after she fell in love with pomegranate margaritas and some guy named Tyler.

Rudy bellows, "Warm-up is over. Get your gloves on."

"That was warm-up?" Kit wipes sweat from her brow. "He's kidding, right?"

"Howie. Kitty-litter"—God, that'll make me laugh every time—"you'll find gloves in the bucket over there." Rudy points across the room at a red plastic container.

I contemplate curling up in the corner of the room, lying in a pile of my tears and sweat. But no. I'm determined to tackle this, and every future slip, with everything I've got.

Kit and I each grab a pair of midknuckle gloves. We help each other pull the Velcro strap tight around our wrists and pretend not to notice that the leather smells musty, like someone else's sweat.

Kit grabs my index finger. "At least your nails look great."

"I know. I told you that BioSil vitamin is awesome." I wiggle my fingers but stop and pull at the glove. "Ouch. The stitching on the inside of my glove is scratching my knuckles."

"Want to switch?"

"No, thanks. I'm just not used to wearing gloves." There's no time to fuss anyway because Rudy has arranged various stations around the mat using heavy bags, ropes, and weighted medicine balls. He calls us over. All the women head toward a different spot. Kit and I stand in confusion.

"Kit, Blue will show you what to do. Howie, you'll start with me." Rudy slips on a pair of black oval-shaped boxing mitts. He smacks them together, and the sound, louder than a gunshot, echoes through the metal building.

Oh, God. "Really, it's okay, I don't need to go first." I scan the room, hoping to find a volunteer, but all the other women are in place.

"Don't worry, everyone gets a chance." He waves me close.

My BFF of eighteen-plus years pushes my back, nudging me toward likely paralysis and or death. "Go, Howie."

I'm terrified and I feel sick. Rudy has mitts. Hard-looking mitts. All I have is a pair of ill-fitted and scratchy gloves. Shouldn't I wear headgear or a chest protector or, at the very least, a mouth guard?

I let out a long breath and tell myself to suck it up. Not only is this for my Someday Jar, but I'm expanding my comfort zone, trying something different, stepping out of my box. Isn't this what I wanted? Truth is, I already feel stronger. Besides, if Evan doesn't promote me, I can use my newfound strength to beat him up. *Ha-ha-ha.*

"Okay, Howie." He grabs my shoulders and faces me toward him. "Spread your legs, shoulder width apart, and put your left foot slightly forward."

I do.

"Good. This is your horse stance." He raises my gloves to ear level. "Keep your hands up. Always protect your face."

You can count on that.

Rudy holds his mitts opposite mine, mirroring my position. "Let's start with a jab-punch. Your left hand is your jab. Right hand is your punch. Hit my mitt." He wiggles it. "Hit your right into my right and your left into my left. Keep your elbows up and cross your body with your strikes. Make sense?"

Absolutely not.

"Aim for the center of my mitt. Jab, then follow with a punch. Go."

My whole body jumbles with nerves. I stare at the center of the mitt. *Which one is the jab?* Crap, I've forgotten already.

"This one first." Rudy wiggles his left mitt. "Ready?"

I nod and squeeze my hands into tight fists, filling my head with confidence-building thoughts. *Someday Jar. Stronger. Solid wife to Evan. Doing this for me.* I jab my left hand into Rudy's steady mitt and, without a flicker of hesitation, follow quickly with my punch into the other.

Holy hell, I did it. Just like he told me. Just like the fighters I've seen on TV. Just like a bad-ass.

Kit grabs my attention with her claps. Blue, at the station beside us, shakes her fists encouragingly in the air.

My shoulders give way to laughter. I did it. I actually did it. And it felt great. I'm incredibly awakened. Fresh. Feisty. Fierce. I clap my gloves together, totally alive, ready to climb mountains or walk through fire. Hell, I can do anything.

"Did you hit me?" Rudy asks.

I stare back at him, deflated.

"My niece hits harder than that and she wears Dora the Explorer Pull-Ups."

I'm speechless.

"C'mon, Howie. You can do better. Soften your entire body and relax. Breathe. Use your kiai," he says, which sounds like *key-i.*

"What's a kiai?" *Does it help with the friction? My knuckles are killing me.*

"In karate, a kiai is your shout. To shout one must breathe."

Rudy's coffee breath spreads across my cheeks as he yells, "Hi-yah!"

I almost giggle. Seriously? He wants me to yell *Hi-yah*?

My smile disappears as he pokes my stomach and says with a serious voice, "A sharp exhalation contracts the muscles, particularly the abdominals. Tight abdominal muscles are essential for any solid technique. Hi-yah!" He shouts again. "Understand?"

"I think so."

"Find it inside and before you know it, you'll be able to knock over that bag with one punch." He nods toward the freestanding bag near the mat's edge.

"I don't know—"

"No excuses." He smacks his gloves again.

I inhale a long breath and close my eyes for a moment, calling out to my inner strength. Whatever the hell that means. Apparently my inner strength has something to do with Ralph Macchio from the old *Karate Kid* movies because I picture him standing one-legged atop a wooden post with ocean waves slapping below him as he prepares for a crane kick. But there is no way I'm going to shout like an idiot.

As I exhale, somehow my breath, or Ralph's quick wink before he disappears from my mind, renews me and I promise to give this my best shot. I can do this.

Rudy says, "Let's try again. Think of something that infuriates you. Something that really gets your goat. Pull that from inside and direct that frustration toward my mitt. You're here for a reason. Release it."

Like a ticker tape, my frustrations parade through my mind: the promotion I don't have, the house I didn't buy, the decorator I don't want, my dad that I do, Wes smirking, and surprisingly, the face of that little pig-nosed girl who called me a whore. It all builds inside me, churning with intensity like a desert dust devil.

I flex my whole body, tense with strength and determination, tighten my abs, and pull back my left arm. *Fine, Rudy. You want some of this?* Energy surges from my shoulder. Resolve floods through my bicep. Grit shoots from my hand like a bullet blasting out of a shotgun. I belt out an ear-shattering "Hi-yah!" and, hard as I can, jab my fist into Rudy's mitt.

My knuckles burn with pain, but I don't stop. I cock my right hand and with the same conviction and power deep from within, I punch my glove right into Rudy's . . . eye.

Oh, shit.

I watch in horror as he staggers backward, drops his mitts on the floor, and shakes his head clear. "I'm so sorry. Are you okay? Is there anything I can do?"

"No." His eye is scrunched shut, already starting to swell. This is awful. Awful.

Blue steps close. "Should I get him some ice? Do you have ice here?"

T-Bird rushes to Rudy's office. She returns with an ice pack and presses it against his eye.

"I can't believe I punched him in the face," I whisper.

Blue pats my back and says, "Don't worry. I kicked him in the nuts my first time."

"I'm so sorry. I didn't mean to hit you. I missed the mitt and—"

He lifts a hand and says, "Class is over."

Grunts from the women echo throughout the room. God, I ruined their workout. Their hour of calorie burning is shot.

Kaput. I can't make eye contact with any of the women. I'm afraid they'll kick me in the head.

"Sorry, Rudy," I apologize for the forty-seventh time before Kit and I walk out the door.

"Nice shot," she says as we climb in the car.

"Are they coming?" I turn and look through the rear window.

"Who?"

"All the women." I lock the car door.

Kit rubs my shoulder. "Don't be ridiculous. No one is coming after you."

"I'm such a twit and good Lord, my hands are throbbing."

Twenty minutes later, after I drop off Kit and step inside the condo, I notice I still have Rudy's gloves with me.

That means I have to go back.

At least my panic has worn off. After all, the women don't know where I live. My shame over punching Rudy subsides enough to allow my knuckles to scream even louder with pain. The burning sensation tells me my skin must be scraped raw. If not for the padding inside the leather, I'm certain I'd see blood.

Slowly, I slide off the gloves and cringe at the sight of my hands. Pea-sized circles of raw skin decorate each knuckle except one, my right pinkie. A trail of dried blood snakes along my index finger, and my thumb has a flap of skin still connected on one side.

Yuck.

I wince beneath clenched teeth and wash the blood away in the bathroom sink. After letting my hands air-dry, because even my 820-gram Pottery Barn luxury towel will feel cruel, I place a dab of oop-a-goop—Dad's name for Neosporin—on each knuckle and lie down. I'm exhausted. My Someday Jar hasn't started out that great. But I can't feel sorry for myself. Imagine what Rudy's eye feels like.

⁓

"Where's your ring?" Evan wakes me, the room dimly lit from the setting sun.

"In my purse." I yawn.

He flips on the nightstand light and lifts my hand. "What happened? It looks like you got in a fight. And lost."

"Kit and I went to a kickboxing class."

"Kickboxing?" he says with a tone as if I cursed in church. "Why?"

"It's a slip from my Someday Jar."

He eyes me curiously. "Wouldn't you rather focus on *our* future, not the past?"

"This jar is important to me. These are my goals."

"Brutalizing yourself is a goal?"

I peek at my shiny, medicated knuckles. "No. *Learn something new* is."

"Kickboxing sounds barbaric. What will the clients think sitting opposite a bloodied and bruised young woman?"

"Today was my first time. My hands are just tender, that's all."

His eyebrows knit together and the vein on his temple puffs out. He doesn't like it.

"I don't like it."

See?

He glances at his watch and shakes his head. "We have the Davenport signing in an hour."

"Oh, right. I forgot about that." I swing my legs off the bed.

"Hold up. You can't be seen like this."

"I don't have leprosy. It's just a few scrapes."

"I'll take care of it." He runs his fingers through his hair. "You know, it's been nearly two days since Hollis picked up your proposal. Did you cover all the bases? Are you certain your data was comprehensive enough?"

"Relax, Evan. It's a lot of information to process." I rub in a glob of oop-a-goop. "I'll give them this weekend to discuss it, then call on Monday."

"All right. They're close. I can taste it and I sure as hell don't want to lose it." He drapes a blanket over my legs. "Just so we're clear, my fiancée likes to punch things."

"Kinda, yeah."

"Should I be worried?"

"No. Trust me; I'm not very good." Rudy's swollen eye comes to mind. "Rather a bad aim, actually."

"I'm glad you got it out of your system." He steps through the door, threatening to disappear.

"Wait!" I stop him. "What do you mean?"

"Kickboxing. Now you know what it's like, I'm sure you won't do it again."

"I might," I blurt before realizing how I feel. I was awful, but if Rudy and the women will let me in the door, I'd like to give class another try. Who knows? Maybe someday I will be strong enough to knock over the freestanding bag with one punch.

"You can't be serious?"

"Yes, I am. It's great exercise. Besides, it's important for me to do this."

"Kickboxing is *important*?"

"Not just kickboxing. It's more than that. I made a promise to my dad. And myself. I want to honor that. I plan to fish out all the slips and give them a shot."

"Look, the jar is a sweet memory, but Hollis's mansion is the deal of a lifetime, plus the wedding, and Orchid Lane. I need you sharp these next few weeks. On task. The jar is a likely distraction."

"The jar won't interfere with any of it."

"Don't tell me your hands will look like this at the wedding. We can't have that. My clients and the food and the pictures—"

"No, they won't. I promise."

He looks unconvinced. "Are all the slips so violent?"

"No."

Evan folds his arms across his chest. "For the record, I'm not happy about this jar. You beating things up doesn't sound very ladylike. Lord knows what other hazards the jar holds."

"Don't worry, there's nothing too outlandish."

"All right." He sighs. "Get some rest, Rocky."

twelve

As if sinking into a too-hot Jacuzzi, I inch lower into my chair Monday morning. Not because I want to. Because I have to. Ever since Rudy's class, every part of my body, except my eyelashes, screams with pain whenever I move a fraction of an inch. Never have I realized how much it could hurt to move my legs. Or arms. Or breathe.

One hour and several ibuprofen later, a package arrives from FedEx. I sign for the parcel and notice the driver's puzzled look at my knuckles. Afraid he'll think I'm a weekend diesel mechanic, or do in fact have leprosy, I explain, "Kickboxing."

"Ah." He nods. "Take it easy on those hands."

"I will, thanks."

The phone rings.

Before picking up the receiver, I tap it and whisper, "Let's hope you're Hollis, calling to say you want to list your mansion with a brilliant agent named Lanie." I press line one. "Evan Carter Realty."

"Hey, Lanie, it's Larson."

"Larson. How are you?"

"Great. You?"

"Just fine, thanks." I set my purse on my desk, noticing Wes and Evan inside his office.

Larson and I met a few months ago when he toured one of my open houses. Even though he stands at six foot nine, his ego hasn't stuck his head in the clouds. I pretend to like basketball because Larson is so nice, but let's be honest, unless Larry Fitzgerald takes to the court, my heart forever lies with football.

A couple of weeks ago, we showed Larson and his girlfriend a split-bedroom in Gilbert. I remember her well because her cleavage was pushed up high enough to brush the ceiling fans and she leaned close to Evan, touching his arm whenever she asked a question. She asked twenty-three questions.

"Is this the pantry?" Touch. "Is that a guest house?" Touch. "Are these hickory cabinets?" Touch. Touch. Touch.

Larson wrote an offer and I did some master negotiating, but the deal fell through a few days later. Little-Miss-Painted-On-Jeans decided the six-thousand-square-foot house was too confined and, dear God, she might see her housekeeper fold towels or scrub the toilets from time to time. Imagine the horror.

"How's the season so far?" I ask.

"We're in first place, but the Lakers are threatening."

"Well, Larson, try to remember the bouncy ball goes in the basket with the dangling white strings."

He laughs. "Thanks for the tip."

"No problem. Did you get the properties I e-mailed you?"

"I did. Thanks for that. I want to look at a few of them, but I'm on the road the next couple of weeks. So, when I get back?"

"Okay. I'll keep my eye out for any new listings you might like."

"Sounds good. Though I'm not calling about a house."

"Well, I can't reveal my chicken tortilla soup recipe. It's a family secret."

He laughs. "Listen, you've done so much for me the past few months and I wanted to express my gratitude. I know you're a huge Cardinals fan and I've got four tickets to the next game, fifty-yard line, front row. They play the Forty-Niners. Know anyone who might want them?"

"Are you serious? Front row? Larson, I'll be inches from the players. I'll hear the ice rattle in the cooler, smell the sweat of Fitzgerald." Okay, that last part sounded creepy. "My God, this is amazing. The Forty-Niners are Evan's favorite team. I don't know what to say."

"Say yes."

"Yes! Thank you so much."

"Here's the catch."

"A catch?"

"Yeah, I only scored one locker room pass. You and Evan will have to fight over it."

"Locker room pass? Like to the Cardinals locker room?" My knees wobble. I should sit. Oh, I'm already sitting.

"I thought you'd be happy, even though I'm completely offended you never want to come to my games."

"Oh, I do. I totally do. I'm your biggest fan."

"Liar." He jokes. "I better run. I'll messenger the tickets over soon."

"Thanks again, Larson."

"My pleasure. Talk to you when I get back."

We hang up and it takes all my decorum not to tumble back

handsprings around the room. That, along with the fact that I don't know how to tumble back handsprings.

"Evan." I rush into his office. "Guess what?"

He lifts his gaze from an outstretched set of house plans spread across his desk and eyes me with a curious face.

Okay, I'll admit, I sound like a crazy person, but I'm just so damn excited. Never have I sat in the front row. Never have I been inside the locker room. I'll hear the slam of metal lockers, the tap of cleats on the concrete floor, and the pregame smack talk. I love smack talk.

Wes stands a few feet away and talks on his phone. Though I try my best to ignore him, by his gentle tone, I infer he must be talking with that Julie girl again. Well, good for him. Very good indeed.

"What are you so excited about?" Evan asks me.

"Larson called and offered four tickets to the Cardinals-Forty-Niners game. On the fifty-yard line. And a locker room pass. Can you believe it? This is a chance of a lifetime. In all the years of watching football with Dad, we used to fantasize what it'd be like meeting face-to-face with the NFL's greatest."

And the icing on the cake? I'll complete another Someday Jar slip. There's bound to be a game ball in the locker room.

"That's very generous of him," Evan says, straightening his burgundy tie. "I know you'll enjoy that. My Forty-Niners are tough this year. Your Cardinals have their work cut out for them."

"We'll see about that."

"Did Larson express interest in the homes you sent him?"

"Yes, we're going to view some in a couple weeks."

"Good. Keep after him about the house."

"Yep."

"Any word from Hollis?"

"Not yet."

Evan taps his pen on the desk. "Keep on him as well."

"Will do."

Wes hangs up and walks toward Evan's desk. "Hi, Lanie."

I nod, still puzzled about him and even more puzzled why I regret not swiping a brush through my hair.

"Listen, while you're here." Evan points at the blueprints. "The previous owners of Orchid Lane let me forward a set of plans to Wes a couple of weeks ago. He's completed a preliminary revised set. Come take a look."

I step close.

Wes points on the page, the scratch on his nose all but healed. "If you knock out this wall, you'll have to reroute the drain lines for the kitchen. They run along here."

"What about relocating the vent?" Evan asks.

"You've got ceiling joists and I'm sure a strong-back tied on here. This is likely a knee wall, which poses more of a challenge."

I wish I understood half the shit they're saying. *Note to self: Study architecture terms.*

"Of course, you could eliminate the second dishwasher and move the vent here." Wes draws a box on the page.

"Yes, that's agreeable."

Wes taps at another section of the prints and alternates glances at each of us. "Lanie might like the dining room area opened up here, as it will bring in more light."

"Yes, the more light the better."

Wes starts to X the wall, but before he does, Evan lifts his hand. "Let's not make a hasty decision. We'll give it some thought."

"What's there to think about?" I ask.

He pats my shoulder patronizingly like one would a bemused grandmother. "I've got a million things on my mind. We'll talk about this later?"

"Why later? I'd like more light."

There's an uncomfortable silence between Evan and me. A nun in full habit with one leg on the bar chucking down shots of whiskey would be less awkward than the heaviness in the air.

I peek at Wes.

Crap.

What sort of impression have I given him? Other than the minor squabble with Evan at the restaurant when he surprised me with the house, the day at Orchid Lane with too-perfect Paige, and now the discussion over plans, Wes and I have hardly seen one another. Those less-than-ideal encounters, mixed with my behavior at the bar, don't give Wes the best perception of me.

Yes, fine. I realize he hasn't given me any reason not to trust him.

My dad didn't either until he was gone.

I wish Wes had seen Evan and me under better light. Not that I *want* him underfoot. Obviously. It's just that the past few days have been sprinkled with tiny spats and I don't want Wes to think that's all there is to Evan and me.

"I promise, I'll add this to my list of things to consider." Evan squeezes me close.

"We don't have to decide this second." Wes marks a *?* in the box.

"Um, okay." I calm myself, ignoring the voice in my head that screams, *What the hell? Why can't I make a decision? Isn't this my house, too?*

The phone rings.

I excuse myself to answer it. "Evan Carter Realty."

"Hey," Kit says. "Are we still on for four o'clock? This time I insist on grabbing a drink afterward."

Four o'clock? What is she talking about? Does Dylan have a school play? A soccer game? I scramble for my phone and check the calendar. Nothing is listed. Not even a hint of what I've forgotten trickles through my mind. Good Lord, I'm a terrible godmother. I probably agreed to something really important and I can't ever remember what. Bake sale? Car wash? Field trip?

Then it comes to me.

Wedding dress.

Kit and I are supposed to try on wedding dresses today. *Jesus, Lanie. How could you forget that?*

"Yes, of course. I can hardly wait."

"Right." Kit's voice sounds unconvinced.

Okay, so maybe I laid my enthusiasm on a little thick.

"Stacee's shop. Four o'clock?"

"Sounds good." I scribble a note and paste it firmly on my monitor's frame.

᷍

"This is a train wreck." I stand on a platform in a wedding dress and examine my reflection in a three-way mirror. Even the boutique's flatteringly pale lights, well placed to highlight a bride's features, can't hide the fact that a hideous A-line floor-length gown with a drop waist stares back at me.

"It's not *that* bad," Kit says. She steps onto the platform and fluffs the large bow tied at my hip, which doesn't quite puff in the right place. It droops toward the floor. "Okay, you're right; it's awful."

"What about the empire style with pink sash? That was pretty on you."

"No, it made me look pregnant. I don't want guests whispering, 'Is Lanie knocked up? How far along is she? Three . . . four months?'"

"Pregnant my ass." She pats my flat stomach. "What I wouldn't give for your body. You know, if I didn't love you so much, I'd strangle you with a veil."

"Then you'd have those pesky murder charges to deal with."

She waves her hand. "A minor technicality."

"How are we doing, girls?" Stacee strides toward us with a napkin draped over her cupped hand and a clipboard tucked under her arm.

"Hi, Stacee. You remember Kit? We came here right after Evan proposed and thumbed through bridal catalogs."

"Of course. Who could forget that beautiful skin?" Stacee smiles at Kit. "It's nice to see you."

"You, too."

Stacee extends her hand toward me, revealing a small paper cup. "The white chocolate cranberries arrived today. I thought you might like a sample."

"Sure, thanks."

I step off the platform and with each step, tulle swish-swishes beneath my skirt. I pop a cranberry in my mouth and nearly choke with disgust. *Blech.* They taste like chalk. *Evan likes these? They're revolting.*

Stacee lifts her eyebrows, waiting for my approval.

"Yum," I say, trying not to gag.

"Kit?" she offers.

Kit grabs a couple and, by the squint in her left eye, I can tell she feels the same. She thanks Stacee, then heads back toward the rack of dresses and along the way, spits the cranberries into a nearby potted ficus.

Stacee doesn't notice. "In case you want more." She sets the remaining berries on the table, then refers to her clipboard and runs a pen along her list. "Tell Evan his tux will still be a few weeks. Armani hand-cuts each tuxedo, so they take a while, but trust me, it'll be worth it."

"Sure."

"We've decided on lilies and pussy willows for the centerpieces?" She glances from her sheet.

"Yes, that's fine." That's what I wanted, anyway. Evan probably knew that.

"Oh, and please tell him that yes, the restroom attendants' ties will be a full Windsor knot and the *exact* hue of the table napkins. He was worried about that."

"Um . . . okay."

"The cake, still as we discussed?"

"Yes, three tiers, cascading flowers on one side, vanilla cake and icing," I say, triumphantly. At least I know something about this wedding.

"So, no raspberry filling?"

"God, no."

"That's odd. For some reason I have a side note penciled in that Evan added it on the eighteenth." She frowns and nibbles on the end of her pen.

"Oh, that's right," I lie, trying to hide my growing frustration behind a forced smile. "Raspberry filling. I forgot. So much to remember, you know."

"Don't I know it." She tucks her clipboard under her arm. "I'm going over invitations with another couple, but holler if you need me. And, Lanie, if I may, that style is not right for you. You're much too pretty for that dress."

I thumb through the rack of remaining dresses. The metal hangers, drawn heavy under the weight of silk, scrape against the pole and I wonder, *Why is this so hard?* I'm blessed with normal proportions, no longer arm or shorter leg to contend with. I need no specially designed sleeves, high neckline, or fully covered back to hide a tramp stamp or regrettable barbed-wire tattoo on the day I'm wearing virginal white. But of the countless dresses I've tried, each is either too sheeny, too poofy, or too something-just-not-right. I reach the end of the rack, finding nothing else that I want to try on. "I give up, Kit. I'm calling it a day."

"You can't. There isn't much time left." She pushes the row of dresses to the beginning and starts to look through again.

I plunk into a nearby chair and gulp three quarters of my complimentary champagne. Then, with my free hand, I smack the tulle like a flyswatter, smashing it flat.

"Don't give up, sweetie. We'll find one." Kit discovers a strapless, straight-lined dress and folds it over her arm. "I want to try this one on myself."

Ignoring her, I steady the glass between my knees, dip my middle finger in the drink, and circle it along the rim, round and round, until a dull ring fills the room. A trick Dad taught me one night at the Golden Lantern. He'd planted a hefty tip in our waiter's hand and asked for a pitcher of water and eight more glasses. Dad filled each with varying amounts of water, opting for a variety of pitches. Our dinner plates long cleared, we stayed for hours, long after any other diners, long after the busboy had wiped the tables and vacuumed the dining room. We stayed until I mastered "Twinkle, Twinkle, Little Star."

Kit hangs her dress on the rack and kneels beside me. She cringes at the sound of my music, grabs the glass, and sets it on the nearby table.

"This isn't about dresses, is it?"

"Do you and Rob make decisions together? Do you feel, I don't know, like you guys are equals?"

"Rob and I aren't equals. I only let him think that every once in a while." Kit's smile fades when she notices me picking at a loose bead on the dress. She squeezes my hand, mindful of my sore knuckles. "What's going on?"

"Shouldn't Evan at least discuss things with me? We're a couple, one unit."

"Are you talking about the house?"

"That, too."

"Honey, he wants *you* to live there. No one else."

"That's what Mom says. But don't you think he could've said, 'Hey, can you pass the salt, and by the way, I'm thinking of investing our future in a house, hiring a hot decorator, having an architect live with us for weeks, making you land a nearly impossible listing before becoming broker, and by the way, adding raspberry filling to our wedding cake?'"

"Think of it this way: Evan's in the real estate business. He looks at a property with a different perspective than most. He sees investment potential and doesn't stop to consider anything else." Kit strokes my hand. "Who cares about the filling? You'll be too busy shaking hands and air-kissing Evan's stuffy friends and family. You won't have time to eat cake."

I shimmy out of the dress and toss it on the pile of a dozen or so discarded gowns draped over a barely visible upholstered chair. Even without the dress, standing in nothing but my bra and panties, I feel heavy under the weight of my concern. With a long sigh, and before I realize what I'm saying, I ask, "Am I making the right decision, Kit?"

"I'll take a bullet for you. You know that. Should you die suddenly, I'll clear all the porn off your computer history. That's what I'm here for."

I chuckle. Leave it to Kit to lighten the mood.

"Seriously, Lanie, it doesn't matter what I think. It matters what your heart and brain think. Evan's a great guy. He's gorgeous. He's successful. He's charming. On paper, he's everything a woman wants. Is he what *you* want?" She hands me my jeans and shirt. "You've got a lot on your plate right now. It's okay to be freaked out about forever."

Wait a minute. My eyes meet hers with revelation. I know what's going on here. "It's just cold feet, isn't it? That's all this is. It's perfectly normal to be worried about forever, right?"

"It is."

"It is," I nearly shout, securing the button on my jeans, fully dressed and fully relieved. "God, I've been a swirl of emotions, but now it makes total sense. Thank you, I feel so much better having talked this out. Brides have jitters all the time." I click my shoes together three times, and laugh. "See, my shoes are on. Feet no longer cold. Ha-ha-ha."

"You're a bit of a whack job."

"Jitters." I shrug. "Blame it on the jitters."

She glances at her watch. "Well, I know exactly how to fix them. Come with me."

thirteen

Not too far from Stacee's Boutique is a trendy bar attached to the lobby of an even trendier hotel. They have swanky appetizers served on square white plates, square tables, and square, uncomfortable chairs. Lots of businesspeople meet here. When we step inside the entrance doors, the lobby is filled with people waiting outside a closed meeting room door.

"I wonder what's going on?" I yell.

"You'll see." She grabs me by the wrist and pulls me through the crowd.

Once on the other side, Kit and I sit at a high table near the bar. We order two Chardonnays and the spinach-artichoke appetizer.

Kit tells me what Dylan and his friend did last night, something about one folding the other inside the hide-a-bed and leaving him there. Rob didn't notice until he sat on the couch and was kneed, repeatedly, in the butt.

I'm half listening because this whole cold-feet thing has me frazzled. Much as I don't want to admit it, as the wedding day draws closer, I have become thick with doubt. Is this normal? Is this what brides typically feel? A natural drawing back as the pending promise of forever approaches?

Or maybe since Evan and I have bickered more than normal the last few days, our disputes have surfaced harbored memories from my parents' failed marriage. *Am I afraid to make the same mistake?* After all, weren't they in love once? Convinced there was no one else they'd rather spend their lives with? Now look at them. Is my tension built around the fear that Evan and I will fall into the same misfortune?

It'd be easier if I could pinpoint my displacement. If I knew for certain that the stress of daily life, work, the house, the wedding, Wes, my jar, is the reason for my agitation. Because what if it's not? What if it's something more? What if this hovering cloud is one that won't pass, a storm that I shouldn't ignore? It's this, the unknown, that scares me the most.

"Lanie? Are you there?" She waves a pita chip in front of my face. I hadn't noticed our order had arrived.

"Sorry."

We take sips from our wine and munch the appetizer, but several times I catch Kit sneaking peeks behind me and checking her watch.

"What's going on?" I turn and can't make out what the banner over the meeting room says, but given Kit's smile, there must be a sale inside. Probably knockoff purses.

"They're starting."

"Huh?" I watch the group funnel like cattle through the opened doors.

After the mass disappears, two women remain in the lobby, and from what I can tell at this distance, they each have the same style name tag. The woman closest to us, middle-aged with wiry gray hair, a plum tent dress, and Velcro-strapped sandals she should reconsider wearing in public, smiles at her handheld counter. "Ninety-eight," her proud voice echoes in the tile lobby to the other woman. "Ninety-eight," she says again. "We're so close."

I turn back toward Kit. She dials her phone.

"Who are you calling?"

She holds up her index finger. "Hey, baby. I'm at Sofitel with Lanie. Lucinda Wilkinson is here. Yep, same dress. Can you come? Darn. Oh, oh, they're closing the door. I better go. I'll be home in a bit. Love you."

I poke around again and see this Lucinda person close the door behind her. What the hell is Kit talking about?

"Hurry. Finish your wine. We gotta go."

I swallow it in one chug while Kit throws some cash on the table and pulls a laminated card from her wallet.

"Where are we going? Who's Lucinda Wilkinson?"

"She'll help you with your jitters. If anyone will make you feel better about getting married, it's her. I guarantee it." Kit drags me through the lobby toward the closed door. She stops right outside. "Give me your ring." She's already taking hers off.

"My ring? What for?"

"You can't go inside with your ring. Here, I'll keep it with mine." She opens a zipper pocket in her purse. "C'mon."

I slide it off and drop it beside hers. Now I wonder why I trust her as much as I do.

It's then I notice the banner hanging above us.

LUCINDA'S BLIND SPEED DATING—5:30 P.M.

"Speed dating? Isn't that a room full of desperate people?"

"Exactly."

"You're kidding, right? You're married to Rob. Have you forgotten?"

"Of course not. Rob and I did this before. That's why I called him. Trust me, Lanie, it's totally hilarious. It'll ease your jitters. I promise."

"Rob did this?"

"Yeah. We went home even more thankful to be married to each other and had the best sex of our marriage." She wiggles her eyebrows.

"Why does it say *blind dating*?"

"That's the best part. You don't *see* any of these people. It's pitch-black inside. They have a few ushers who walk around with flashlights so you don't trip and stuff, but otherwise it's dark. Lucinda says that way we experience the spirit and inner beauty of each individual, not clouded by external motivations.

"Lucinda sounds like a freak."

"C'mon, we're missing it."

Against my better judgment, I allow her to open the door and we walk inside. As promised, it's totally dark. On my left, a young woman holds a flashlight under her chin and welcomes us. A mole dots below one eye.

Kit flashes her card and the woman smiles. "Welcome back."

"Thank you." Kit pats my shoulder. "It's her first time."

"Very nice to have you. Very nice indeed," the lady says to me, quite enthusiastically. "Hurry to tables twenty-six and twenty-seven. We're about to start."

My eyes gradually adjust to the dark. Across the room, glow sticks are shaped into numbers fixed onto the backs of chairs.

We walk past other tables toward ours. It's creepy. I sense bodies around me but can't see them, only vague shadows. I'm not a fan. Not in the least. Fortunately, another late arrival opens the door behind us, lighting a path, and we settle into our chairs.

I lean in what I think is Kit's direction. "I'm going to kill you."

"Me?" a male voice whispers back.

I think he sits across from me.

"No, sorry," I reply.

"All right, everyone." Another woman's voice sputters in the microphone and echoes within the room. She, too, holds a flashlight below her face. It's the same woman with the wiry hair from the lobby. "Welcome to Lucinda's Blind Speed Dating. I'm Lucinda."

Claps resonate through the room.

"Thank you," she gushes. "We're so glad you're all here today. A fantastic turnout. I know you're eager to get started."

"Hell, yeah," screams a man from the other side of the room.

A few others laugh.

This is weird.

"Okay," Lucinda continues, her breath heavy in the microphone. "Real quick, let me go over the rules for our newbies. You'll each have two minutes per table. When you hear this sound"—she rings a bell—"gentlemen, that's your cue to move on to the table to your right." She emphasizes the last word. "Ladies, you stay put. Please remember and wait for the bell and move when you hear it. It's dark in here, folks, and it's easier if we all work together. Now another important point, blind speed dating is all about trust." Feedback squeals through the microphone and Lucinda steps forward, quieting the noise, before continuing. "Okay, men in the room, remember to place your forearms and palms upward on the table. Ladies, your hands and forearms will rest on top of theirs. That is the only part touching, nothing above the elbow. Everyone understand?"

Not only do I have to talk to these strangers for two minutes, but I have to touch them as well? That's it. I will knock Kit senseless with a glow stick.

"Remember, it helps to close your eyes when talking with your seatmate. Breathe in their voice and embrace the spirit of the individual. Enjoy the beauty of blindness. Well, that covers the rules. Let's get started."

A few seconds later, the bell rings and the man seated across from me says, "My palms are up. I'm ready."

My stomach tightens. Sweet Jesus. I feel molested and we haven't even touched yet.

He clears his throat. "Um, we only have like two minutes."

"Right." Forcing myself to move, I hover my hands on top of his forearms.

"Hi." He clasps his hands around my elbow. "I'm Seth."

He sounds young and harmless, like a surfer from Southern California. "Hi, Seth. I'm Lanie." *Ah, crud. Why did I give him my real name?* Kit just introduced herself as Alexandria.

"Lanie, that's a cool name."

"Thanks."

"Ever play Black Ops?"

"Sorry?"

"Black Ops. It's a war game on Xbox where you kill your friends and stuff. It's bitchin'."

"No, I've never played."

"Dude, you're totally missing out. It's killer, especially wasted." His hands squeeze tighter around my elbows and I tense. "You should totally get an Xbox. That way we can chat and shit. I have mine set up in the basement of my mom's house. She's cool. I can play it whenever I want."

You have no girlfriend, Seth? Shocking.

"You seem pretty dope. I'll take it easy on you. I won't kill you that much." He laughs.

"Awesome, thanks."

The bell rings and I eagerly say good-bye to Seth.

The next man sits across from me. "Look," he says with a thick East Coast accent, massaging my forearms like he's kneading pizza dough. "I'm lookin' to get laid. You interested?"

Bile creeps up my throat. "I'm a lesbian."

"Even better. Bring your friend."

"I have genital herpes."

He releases his hands as if I'm toxic. His chair grinds across the floor as he scoots back. "Jesus."

Kit giggles beside me. "Lanie, be nice."

I whisper through gritted teeth, "You. Are. So. Dead."

The bell rings, not soon enough, I might add, and I hear one more man sit across from me. My body fills with dread. Kit's right. Evan is nirvana compared to these freaks. I was a fool to think anything else and I will rush into his arms when I get home.

This is the last nutcase I will subject myself to. I sense the third man's arms on the table and with hopes of getting this crazy ordeal over with, I quickly lay mine on his.

Warm hands. Strong forearms. He smells good, too. Maybe this guy will be tolerable. Maybe I'll have two enjoyable minutes with a stranger. Maybe I'll—"

"Hi, Lanie."

Fuck.

I try to yank my hands away the instant Wes speaks, but he clamps down like a boa constrictor.

"Relax."

"What are you doing here?"

"Me? I was having drinks with a client. I saw you and wondered why an engaged woman would walk into a singles meeting. What are *you* doing here?"

"So, you're spying on me? Am I some sort of game to you? First deceiving me at the airport, now following me. What's your agenda? Report to Evan's parents what an awful daughter-in-law I'll be?"

A few people shush us from across the room.

I ignore them. "Just because I flirted with you a teeny tiny bit, and said a few less-than-positive things about Evan the other night, doesn't mean you have the right to hold it over my head. Soon, Evan and I'll be happily married with lily centerpieces, new granite in the kitchen, and a cave that bellows fog. So leave me be."

"You're engaged? What the hell are you doing here?" shouts a man a few tables away.

"Yeah, this is for singles," calls another.

"She's got herpes," says my second "date."

"Why exactly *are* you here?" Wes asks.

"Kit thought it'd be fun." There's no way in hell I'll mention my jitters to him.

"Isn't Evan fun?"

I snake my hands away out from under his. "Kit, let's go."

"I'm right here." We find each other's hands and march toward the exit.

"Can you believe him? He has some nerve walking in here, following me around. Of all the arrogant men in the world, he tops the list."

"Calm down. You'll give yourself a heart attack."

"Lanie."

I instinctively turn around at the sound of my name, and though I can't see anyone, Seth's familiar voice shouts, "Call me."

By the light of the EXIT sign, I stop and snatch Kit's purse from her hand.

I tear through her pocket, digging for my ring. "I can't believe I ever second-guessed marrying Evan. He can never find out about this. Never." *Please, Lord. Don't let Wes tell him.*

"Ladies and gentlemen," Lucinda stammers into the microphone as she tries to regain control of the murmurs that gurgle in the room, "let's all settle down. We'll continue in a moment."

I slide on my ring. "This is not coming off again." I press open the door.

"Wait!" Lucinda calls after us. "Girls, please wait."

With an exasperated growl, I spin around and face Lucinda's flashlight-lit face across the room.

"Yes, thank you. Folks, I forgot to mention, that young lady on the right, who is leaving, albeit with a rather harsh disruption." She points at me. "Anyway, she's new today and folks, let me be the first to announce she is our one-hundredth guest. She took us over our highest attendance to date. I'm sorry, I don't know your name."

"Lanie," Seth shouts.

Thanks, Seth.

"Congratulations, Lanie. You broke our attendance record."

Kit pats me on the back and giggles. "You broke a record."

The slip from my Someday Jar comes to mind.

I storm out the door.

"You were right. I'm convinced more than ever that I want to marry Evan. All doubt has washed away. You know what else? Raspberry filling will be delicious." Before she can say a word, I hurry toward my Ford and drive off like a carjacker. It's not until my fingers ache that I discover I am gripping the steering wheel as if trying to choke the life out of the steel.

The City Core, a 2,000,000-square foot mixed-use, urban complex built on seven acres, is touted as one of the Southwest's greatest architectural feats. The highly regarded conceptual master plan for the project was designed by Wes Campbell & Associates, who laid out the project with approximately 250 condominiums and 800 commercial office spaces all distributed within two high-rise towers around an ultra-high-end retail and entertainment district.

"It's designed to have all the commodities of daily life, while encompassing the changing future," Campbell says. "We incorporate extensive use of green technology along with xeriscaping, thus reducing our draw on the desert's crucial water supply. We're quite pleased with the project."

The estimated cost of the project is $110 million. The complex is expected to open with a ribbon-cutting ceremony early next month.

"Impressive write-up, don't you think?" Evan asks as he cuts into the pizza I picked up on my way home.

I say nothing, fold up the *Arizona Republic*, and peel olives off my slice. "Where is Wes, anyway?" I try not to let on that his name pricks me like a cactus.

"The Patriots are playing tonight. He's watching the game with some of the City Core engineers."

"A game?" I perk up. "We should do that." At a different bar, of course. An entirely different bar. One far, far away from Wes. "C'mon, let's go have some fun."

"Not tonight. There's a pile of RSVPs we need to sort through on the kitchen counter, and then I'm hoping for a good night's sleep."

"Right." I pause, then say, "You know, I was thinking, Rudy has coed classes. Maybe you'd want to come sometime?"

He blots the corners of his mouth with his napkin and looks at me. "I don't like you doing it. Why would I want to?"

"How about skydiving or horseback riding, or maybe we can rent Jet-Skis on Tempe Town Lake?" I sound desperate. *C'mon, Evan. Something. Something fun together.*

"What's with you? Are these ideas from that jar?"

"No. I just thought we could step out of our box, try something new."

He eyes the Scrabble board, pushed aside to make room for the pizza box. "How about we finish our game?"

"No, that's all right." I stack olives on top of one another. They wobble and fall over. One rolls off my plate toward the newspaper article. "Evan, how well do you *really* know Wes? He seems rather arrogant, don't you think?"

"Arrogant? That's not how I'd describe him at all. He's probably the most modest man I know. He's incredibly respected in the architectural arena, yet doesn't brag about it."

"I'm surprised you invited him to stay with us." I add a sixth olive to my rebuilt stack.

"It's the least we could do."

"This girl, Julie, are they close?"

"Well, I'd hope so. She's a lovely young woman. I think she's an elementary school teacher."

She's sweet *and* admirable. Ugh.

I flick my olives.

Damn that Wes for getting me all worked up. Who does he think he is, sneaking up on me, questioning my whereabouts and motivations? I'm crazy about Evan. Yes, we've disagreed a couple times lately. Big deal. Doesn't every couple?

I glance at my fiancé and recall Wes's words: "Isn't Evan fun?" Yes, he is. I'll prove it. What would Wes think of this?

I grab Evan's fork and toss it on the table. I push his plate aside.

"Lanie?"

With my eyes seductively fixed on his, I straddle myself across his lap and kiss him hard on the mouth.

He murmurs, wraps his arms around me, and returns my kiss.

This is good. Yes, very good. This is exactly what we need. No question. This is fun. This will squelch the minor squabbles we've had.

My gorgeous fiancé kisses my neck. His lips trace along my skin, teasing with his touch, and it feels, well, it feels . . . fine. I mean, it doesn't feel *bad*. I'm just not in the mood, I guess. I'm sure I will be. Any minute. I'm sure to get all gloppy and turned on by his wandering hands.

I shove aside the pizza box, knocking Scrabble letters off

the racks, and climb onto the table's edge. With a tug on his belt loop, I pull him close.

"Lanie, what's gotten into you?" He leans toward me and his lips playfully tug on my earlobe.

Any minute now.

I fold my legs around his hips, arch my back, and push myself into him.

Nothing.

Focus, Lanie. Focus. You started this. Isn't this what you want? I wrap my arms around his neck and concentrate. His body presses against mine and his warm breath breezes across my cheek. His hands caress the shape of me.

Patriots fan, huh? Typical. It's easy to be a fan of a consistently winning team. Try being a Cardinals fan. That takes grit, endurance, and years of disappointment. Where does Wes get off following me into Lucinda's, squeezing my forearms, and smelling so—knock it off, Lanie. Pay attention to Evan. Who cares what Wes thinks?

Determined to jump-start the fireworks, I unbutton my shirt and slink it off my arms, letting it fall onto the table. Slowly, and with approval in Evan's eyes, I slide each bra strap off my shoulder, then reach behind and unclasp the hook. My lace bra drops from my fingers. Cool air tickles my nipples as I post my arms behind me and lean back, fully exposed to Evan. Let the games begin.

The front door swings open.

Wes walks in.

"Aagh!" I clutch my chest and hop off the table, scrambling for my clothes. *Oh, God. Oh, God. Oh, God.* My dumb-ass bra strap is caught on the chair and I yank it, hard. After a painfully embarrassing few seconds—which feels like days—it snaps free. I bang into the table, and the pizza box falls on the floor.

"Shit. I'm sorry," Wes says, shielding his face with his hand. He turns around, bumping into a picture hanging on the wall. "Fuck, sorry. I should've knocked. I'll come back later."

I don't hear Evan's reply because my half-naked and fully humiliated body races up the stairs. It hits me then and there. I do care what Wes thinks. That makes me run even faster.

fourteen

I dashed out of the house before Wes woke with hopes that when he did, he'd suffer from a severe case of dementia and forget he saw me half naked. Honestly, how am I supposed to look him in the eye ever again?

With a stack of listing documents in my arms, I walk toward the office door and notice Maria, the soft, round, sweet Mexican woman with broken English and zebra-print press-on nails who stops by every couple of weeks selling the best home-made tamales in all of Phoenix, standing on the curb in front of her car.

"Everything okay, Maria?"

"*Hola*, Miss Lanie." She points at her car. "I deliver my tamales, then find tire flat like pancake. This lovely man pull up and offer to help."

"What lovely man?"

Wes stands.

Oh, God.

My breath catches and I take half a step back. My knees

threaten to buckle from the crushing weight of my embarrassment.

"Hi, Lanie." He brushes off his hands. He wears a crisp white shirt that floats over his stomach and contrasts with his tan skin but matches his teeth as he offers his familiar half smile. "Got a jack? Maria doesn't. Nor does my rental." He thumbs toward the Dodge Charger behind him.

"Are you sure you no mind?" Maria asks Wes.

"Not at all. It'll only take a minute." Wes rolls up his sleeves and nods toward my car. "Jack?"

I stare back at Wes, full of conflicting emotions. I was mad at him for fooling me at the airport. Furious for following me into Lucinda's last night. Mortified at home. And now, he's so nice to Maria. I don't know what to feel. *Naked. He saw me naked.* Mortified. That's how I feel. "In the trunk," I manage.

He finds the jack and lug wrench, then crouches down beside Maria's tire.

She steps close to me and whispers, "He's very cute, Miss Lanie."

With swift moves and flexing forearms, Wes hoists the jack and effortlessly removes each nut, lining them up in a row on the pavement.

"How you learn this so well?" Maria asks.

I'm curious myself. Evan would call a tow truck. Or buy a new car.

"My grandpa had a tire shop in Savannah." Wes spins the tire freely until it plops into his hands. "My brother and I spent a few summers there as kids. Worked at Grandpa's shop during the day and chased the farm girls at night."

He winks at Maria.

She blushes.

I clutch my papers closer.

"When we'd get a full set, Wade, my brother, and I, would race. We'd each pull two tires and see who could swap them the fastest." He pauses to laugh. "I've never had more bloody knuckles in my life."

Instinctively, I glance at my sore hands.

"He older than you?" Maria asks.

"No, a year and a half younger." Wes rests the bad tire against the curb and reaches for the spare. "This one time, we got so caught up in trying to beat each other, one of us forgot to tighten the lug nuts on the rear tire of a Chevy pickup. Neither could remember who did it."

"Uh-oh," Maria says.

"The poor guy got a quarter mile down the road before his tire fell off and rolled into a ditch half filled with cow shit." Wes quickly corrects, glancing at Maria. "Pardon my language. Manure."

"Shit," Maria says. "Go on."

Wes laughs. "Well, Grandpa was livid, to say the least. He made Wade and me get the tire and roll it all the way to the shop. Then he made us stay at the garage all night long, loosening and tightening lug nuts on his tow truck, over and over. No food. No shower."

"No girls either, eh?" Maria teases.

"Not a one. That shit stench stuck for so long, no girl came near us for weeks."

Maria lets out a long laugh.

I can't help but giggle.

"You're all set." Wes lowers the jack and again brushes off

his soiled hands with a towel Maria provided. "You should get a new tire on here soon. Want me to follow you to a station?"

"Honey, I gave birth to five kids. If that didn't kill me, then neither will the drive to a tire shop. Now, how can I thank you?"

He eyes the basket of tamales on her front seat. "How about one of those?"

"Yes, of course." Maria hurries toward the passenger seat and stuffs three tamales into Wes's hands. She plants a juicy kiss on his cheek, leaving a red lipstick imprint. "Thank you, Mr. Wes."

"My pleasure."

"You sure you're okay?" I ask.

"I'm fine," Maria assures me, and waves good-bye.

Wes returns my jack, then moves beside me.

I swallow hard, more self-conscious than a sixteen-year-old on a first date. I can't look him in the eye. *Naked.* "Evan's probably wondering where I am. I better get inside."

"Right." Wes holds the door open and I walk past him. He heads into the restroom only to step toward my desk a minute later.

Not even a bra.

"Listen, Lanie. I think we got started on the wrong foot. Maybe it was insensitive of me not to reveal who I was at the bar, and though I don't understand why you were at a singles hot spot yesterday, I wasn't following you. I'm not a spy for Evan's parents. There's no familial covert operation."

"Well, that's good to know. For the record, I wasn't there to meet guys. Evan and I have a great relationship."

"From what I saw last night, I gathered."

My cheeks flush hot. "Let's not talk about that. Ever. I hope you finally believe me. I didn't mean what I said about Evan at the bar."

"I do believe you. I always have."

Not knowing what else to do, I open my desk drawer and reach for a nail file.

"You know, you could thank me," he says.

"Thank you? What for?"

"I kept you from dying, remember?"

"Oh, that." I wave the file nonchalantly.

He slides his hands in his pockets. "You're lucky my ninjalike reflexes kicked into gear and saved your ass."

I press my lips together, hiding my smile. "Ninja?"

"You heard me."

"Fine. I'm grateful for all you did, but still, you could've told me who you were. Why didn't you?"

He shrugs. "You threw me for a loop."

"Me?"

"I wasn't expecting someone like you. I've met one or two of Evan's girlfriends over the years and well, they were different."

"How?"

"I don't know. I never paid much attention, but you know, the done-up nails, fake tans, smiles pasted on. That sort of thing."

"Like Paige?"

"Exactly."

"I'm nothing like that sort of girl."

His eyes meet mine. "That's the point."

"What's going on?" Evan asks as he walks from his office. "What are you two so deep in discussion about?"

I back away from Wes and blurt, "We, uh, we're discussing

whether the Cardinals should start with two or three wide receivers."

Evan laughs. "Good luck debating Lanie. She's something."

"Indeed she is." Wes's phone rings and he steps away.

"Paige and I are going over the house plans in my office. Join us?"

"Oh, I didn't even know she was here."

"Yes, for a while now. You coming?" He thumbs toward his office.

"Certainly. Give me a minute to forward the septic certification to the title company." I pat a nearby file. "They're waiting on it to close escrow."

"Excellent. What about the Murphys? Have they called to schedule an appointment?"

"Not yet."

He rubs his temples. "I'm losing sleep over this, Lanie. Do you appreciate what's at stake here?"

Yes, my promotion.

"They'll call soon."

"Keep on them. I think I've made it clear how much I want this listing."

"And I want to be named broker."

"We're equally motivated." Evan smiles at me. He catches Wes's eye across the room and motions toward his office.

A minute later, Wes joins me by the copy machine. We stand inches apart. "How about we call a truce? If you and I are going to live together for the next couple of weeks, we need to get along. For Evan's sake."

I press random buttons on the machine to buy some time. For the past few days, I've envisioned Wes devoured by tiger sharks or spontaneously combusting into flames—well, not really—but now, something about his smile and considerate nature softens my reserve. Wes seems genuine. Truth be told, *I* was the drunk idiot at the airport and *I* was the one caught at a singles' meeting. How could he not be skeptical? Not that I'll admit this, of course.

"Fine. I will no longer poke pins into my Wes voodoo doll."

"So that's why my neck hurts." He offers his hand. "Friends?"

"Friends."

We shake hands and his shirt, with a small grease smudge on the upper sleeve, stretches tight across his shoulders. Only for a moment do I wonder how he looks without it on.

Paige laughs, grabbing our attention.

"They're discussing the house. We should probably get in there."

"After you." Wes moves out of my way and I walk around him, aware of my every step.

Evan and Paige aren't discussing the house. They stand beside his bookcase. A deep purple satin scarf peeks from behind the lapels of her well-fitted jacket. She looks brilliant in white tailored pants that reveal neither panty lines nor unsightly ass-dimples.

Kit's right. We hate her.

"Hi, Lanie."

Evan holds a picture frame in his hands. I know the picture. I've dusted it countless times. Evan poses knee deep in a river with waist-high yellow waders and a salmon in his hand during a recent fishing trip to Alaska. He hated the trip. Not much of an outdoorsman, he complained of mosquito bites and lack of quality bedding at the lodge. Who gets adequate rest on mere three-hundred-fifty thread count sheets? A client with a medical complex in escrow invited Evan and, with a pending commission, he couldn't say no.

"Anyway." He returns to Paige. "I panicked."

"What did you do?" Her tone implies they're discussing a bloody grizzly attack and not a defenseless salmon the length of a Subway sandwich.

"Well, while this fish floundered inside my waders—" Evan points toward his pants. "It's powerful—"

Paige tilts her head. "I can imagine."

Oh, please.

"I try to scramble out of my waders, but this fish thrashes so much it throws me off balance, I lose my footing on a slippery river rock, and I fall face-first into the river."

"You didn't." Paige covers her gaping mouth.

"But I will not let this fish get away."

"No?"

"No. The salmon swims up and out of my pants. I bear-hug it. It flails and twists, but I hold it steady, squeezing tight while I call for help. Finally, after what felt like hours, the boat captain rushes over with a net and I drop the fish into it. That"—he sets the frame on the shelf—"is my fish story.

Paige rests her hands on Evan's forearm and throws her head back in laughter. "Evan, that's hilarious."

He notices me in the doorway. "There you are. Come join us."

"Oh, if I may." Paige glances apologetically at Evan, then returns to me. "Lanie, be a doll and get me something to drink." She taps her throat. "I'm parched."

"Uh, sure. Tea? Coffee? Lots and lots of cream?" I say the last word louder as if the mere sound alone will instantly glop cellulite onto her ridiculously toned thighs.

"Never," she says, stunned. "Water, please."

When I return a moment later with Paige's drink, she stands across the desk from Evan and beside Wes, each bent over the unrolled set of plans. I step beside Evan, the plans upside down from our view, and hand Paige her water.

"You're an angel." After taking a sip, she sets the glass on a coaster Evan provides, digs into her purse, and pulls out several five-by-five-inch stained samples of wood. She holds a couple in her hand and scatters the others on the plans. "We really should decide on the cabinets before selecting the granite or paint. This step is crucial as it sets everything in motion, not to mention the atmosphere of the entire home."

"I've narrowed between the cherry and the walnut." Evan reaches for the two wood squares.

"Cherry will look fantastic with that sandalwood granite we saw the other day," she says to Evan.

"What other day?" I ask.

"You were showing that commercial lot on Thomas when Paige called. Good thing I didn't bother you to come, as they wrote a solid offer. Remember?" Evan winks at me, then continues his discussion with Paige. "I do especially like the movement in that slab. It has an appealing seductive flow."

"I totally agree." Paige smiles at Evan. "There's a smooth sexiness to it."

They're still talking about countertops, right? Neither one looks at me. Even Wes scribbles notes on the plan's edge. It's like I'm not even here. Isn't this my house, too? Why isn't anyone asking me about granite or cabinets? I have thoughts and suggestions.

Here I am, sitting on the sidelines. As usual. Letting others control my life. This is raspberry filling again. No more. It's a new me. I uncorked my Someday Jar, dammit!

I grab a light, clean-looking wood sample propped against her purse. "I like this one. It's very smart and contemporary with the straight lines and simple markings."

"Oh, Lanie, you're precious," Paige says.

Evan grasps the sample and taps it a couple times with his index finger. "This is the backside." He flips over the square and reveals the espresso-stained side. He drops it back into my hands.

"I knew that." Damn. Why didn't I know that?

"Anyway—" Paige waves her hand. "Moving on."

Before I strangle myself with Paige's scarf, Hollis walks in the front door, saving me. Never have I been more excited to see the man, especially since there is color to his cheeks.

"Lifeguard drowns at *own* pool party," he says, and we embrace.

I shake my head, trying not to laugh. "So awful."

He hands me a candy cane and says, "I need to discuss that market analysis you gave us, but can I trouble you for a tissue?"

"No trouble at all. I'll just be a second." My body flutters with excitement. Hollis may be one step closer to listing his house.

I poke my head into Evan's office. "Mr. Murphy is here."

"Now? I didn't know we had anything scheduled."

"We didn't."

"Hollis Murphy? *The* Hollis Murphy?" Paige squeals.

Evan nods and straightens his tie.

When I return with a box of Kleenex, I find Evan and Paige hovering around Hollis like a vulture circling a dead rabbit on the roadside. Strange how people act around those with money. He's a human being, not a bag of cash. Wes stands a few feet off to the side with hands clasped behind his back.

Evan announces, "This is my architect, Wes Campbell, and Paige Davis, my interior decorator."

Paige snakes around Evan and sits on the arm of the chair, closest to Hollis. "It's such an honor. I've read all your articles and seen your home in *Phoenix Home and Garden*. I've always admired your eclectic style of decorating. Such a lovely balance of old world charm with modern enhancements, and the array of colors really brings life and warmth to the structure. I also—"

Mr. Murphy lifts his hand. "Thank you. My wife is the decorator. I'll pass along your compliments." Hollis takes a tissue and thanks me with a smile.

"Mr. Murphy, if I may." She rummages in her purse.

Hollis blows his nose.

"Where are they?" She flashes a nervous smile, then digs like a ferocious raccoon trying to bore a hole into a trash bag. "Found them." She nearly shoves her business card into the old man's hand. "If I may ever be of decorating service, please call."

"Lanie, I'm busy the next few days. How's your schedule early next week?"

"Wide open," I say without checking. "Would you like to make an appointment?"

He nods. "Turns out we're ready to make a change in our life. You're the gal to help us."

Yes! I can feel satisfaction spewing from Evan's pores. "How's ten o'clock on Monday?"

"Perfect. I'll tell Bevy." With a shaky hand on the couch arm, he flounders to stand.

Wes rushes over to help.

"Thank you, son." Hollis waves good-bye as he and I walk toward the door.

I swing it open.

"Bye, Mr. Murphy," Paige calls. "Hope to hear from you someday. I'm always available. Anytime. Anytime at all."

He dips his head toward her in acknowledgment, then leans close to me and whispers, "Is there something wrong with her?"

"Be nice." I wag my finger, then say, "And yes, I think there is."

We laugh and step outside.

"See you later." I wave and watch him drive away.

Back inside Evan practically prances toward me with a smile so wide that I notice a silver filling on a back molar I never realized he had. "I knew it. I knew we could nail this listing." He plants a hard kiss on my lips. "Damn good."

"Congratulations, Lanie," Wes says.

"Yes," Paige adds.

I nod at them all and try not to rocket my hopes too far in the sky. "Let's not jump the gun. They still have to sign."

"This gets me thinking," Evan says. "The past few days we've all worked so hard and I'm quite grateful for all the effort put forth. So, I say, let's take a day and relax." Evan squeezes me close. "Wes, Paige, we'd like to invite you both to a Cardinals game."

In shock, I stare at Evan. *What?*

"That sounds like fun. Doesn't that sound like fun?" Paige asks Wes.

"Yeah, a blast. Thanks."

"It's settled then. Paige, come by the condo, next Sunday, around ten. We'll go for lunch before the game."

"Perfect." She gathers her bag. "I better run. Make a decision on the cabinets. It'll give us a starting point."

"Sure thing. Thanks for your input today."

"My pleasure. Good-bye, everyone." She tosses us air kisses, winks at Evan, then blows out the door.

"Why did you invite her?"

"Why not?"

"Seriously? You don't see it? She's crazy about you."

"Don't be ridiculous. You never struck me as the jealous type."

Wes's phone rings. "Excuse me."

I return to Evan. "I'm not jealous. These are my tickets." At first I thought about inviting Kit and Rob or the Murphys, but since I've felt distanced from Evan and can't shake these jitters that infect me like bacteria, I'd hoped we'd spend the day together, reconnect.

I grasp his hands. "I hoped to spend the day with you. Just you. We're not going to be able to focus on one another with Wes and Paige around."

"Babe, I just bought a house. I'm designing and remodeling it to perfection. I'm planning a wedding most girls dream of. Surely, you're getting enough attention? And surely, you aren't upset about sharing a couple of football tickets with those making our house a home?"

When he says it like that . . .

"Fine. Next time ask me first. Whether you're buying a house, adding raspberry filling to our wedding cake, or inviting semistrangers to an all-day event with us, ask me first."

"Yes, ma'am." He pats me on the butt. "There's that feisty attitude I like so much."

"I'm serious."

"So am I."

fifteen

I've been sitting in the parking lot of Rudy's gym for ten minutes, painfully aware that the courage I felt on the drive here is gone. Vanished. Kit's not coming. She texted me a few minutes ago that Dylan has a fever, and without her, I fear that once I'm inside, Rudy will seek revenge and have the women use me as their punching bag. I sucked last time and ruined class. Ruined it for everyone.

But I should go inside. I *want* to go inside. I want to get better. I want to knock over the bag with one punch. The slip says *Learn something new*, not *Half-ass a challenge*. Regardless, I need to return his gloves.

"Welcome, Howie," Rudy says when I swing open the door. There's a black, purple, and gold semicircle underlining his eye.

"God, I'm so sorry."

"A job hazard." He laughs, patting his swollen skin. "I'm glad you're back."

My anxiety subsides with his gentle smile. "Check out my knuckles." I fan them with a sense of pride.

"Nice."

"How's Kitty-litter feeling?"

"Cursing your name every time she squats to pee. As am I."

He laughs. "Everyone starts off that way. Take it easy on those hands today."

"Will do."

"Howie, come join me." Blue smacks a spot on the mat beside her.

I grab my ball and sit close. "Hi. How are you today?"

"Fine as frog hair. You?"

"A little nervous to be here. I was afraid everyone would be mad at me."

"Think nothing of it." She nudges my elbow. "Gonna do that again today? Shoot for the rib cage this time?"

"God, I hope not."

"Hi, Blue," says a muscled fighter with railroad tracks tattooed across his chest. He and a group of guys walked in a few minutes after me, some already inside the fenced practice cage at the far end of the room.

She taps her cheek.

He places his gloved hand on her shoulder, leans over, and kisses Blue on the cheek.

"Sweet boy." She smiles. "Now go kick some ass."

"Yes, ma'am." He catches up with the other guys.

"You sure have a way with people."

"I don't know about that, Howie. Be good to them and they'll be good to you. That's my motto. Truly, there's only one man that matters to me."

"Your husband?"

"My husband," she confirms with a sparkle in her eye.

"What about you? A darling young woman like you must have someone special in your life."

"Yes, thank you. I'm engaged."

"Lovely. Tell me how you met. I always love hearing the story."

"Well, at a Starbucks of all places. I was having coffee with a friend." My heart dances at the thought of three years ago when Hollis and I met to discuss the damage to his truck. He insisted the dent gave his old Chevy character and refused to let me repair it or pay for any more than a cup of coffee. "Anyway, my friend left, and when I went to the counter for another shot of whipped cream, this handsome man approached me."

"Ooh, I like this story already."

"I had an instant crush. Who wouldn't, seeing a good-looking man expertly dressed in a dark suit and tie? Those broad shoulders . . ."

"You didn't stand a chance," she says.

"I know, right?" I laugh, reminded that Evan really is a catch. "We shared a slice of lemon cake and talked for hours. He took me out for dinner the following night and a couple weeks into dating, persuaded me to come work with him. We've been together since."

"So, you're sleeping with your boss?" She winks.

I laugh. "Yes, technically. But after I secure a certain business deal, he promises to make me a partner." I don't want to say any more; Evan wouldn't approve of me sharing our business with a relative stranger.

"Let's get started," Rudy calls.

At the end of class, I sit on the bench and guzzle my water. I'm tired. Exhausted, actually. Rudy said my jab-jab sequence still sucks, and I'm nowhere near knocking over the bag, but he did compliment me on not punching his face and the women were nice, so all in all, a good day.

"You go and get yourself that business deal," Blue says on her way out the door.

"Thanks, I will."

ᥴ⁓

Later, when I walk through the front door of Evan's condo, I find Wes on the couch, reading official-looking documents with fine print and scribbled notes in the margin, a pencil in his hand. He wears jeans and a faded black T-shirt, revealing a thick snakelike scar that starts at his elbow and disappears underneath the hem of his sleeve. A beer rests on the coffee table.

"Hi," I say, and head toward the fridge, setting my purse on the counter.

"Hi." He flicks his pencil on the stack of papers. "Evan's upstairs."

"Okay, thanks." I pour myself a glass of orange juice.

"What's with the sweaty look?"

My soaked shirt clings against my chest, my soiled towel is thrown over my shoulder, and I can only imagine what my face looks like. Oddly enough, I don't care. "Kickboxing class."

"I wondered how you got the scraped knuckles. That's bad-ass."

"Thanks. I had no idea kickboxing could be so intoxicating. I love smacking the hell out of a bag."

"Pent-up aggression? Anger management issues? Violent tendencies?"

"Ha. Ha. Ha."

"Was this a Someday Jar slip?"

"It was." I sip the juice, hiding my pleased reaction that he remembers the jar.

"Cool. I can tell you're excited."

"It's only my second time and I did much better today. The first time, well, I gave my trainer a black eye."

"Seriously?"

I chuckle and step toward the couch, surprised with my ease around him. "I felt really bad, but luckily he's cool about it. And, I've made a new friend named Blue. She's this saucy older woman wrapped up in pearls who'd embarrass a truck driver with her potty mouth."

"Good for you, Lanie Howard."

A tiny tickle wiggles up my spine.

"Um . . . anyway." I set the glass in the sink and grab my purse. "I'm gonna take a shower."

"Yeah, okay." With his hand clasped around the papers, he steps from the couch and heads toward his room, stopping at the threshold. He turns, meets my eyes, and says, "Lanie?"

"Yeah?"

"You should be proud of yourself."

"Thanks. I am."

We say no more, but neither of us moves.

I silently count to five before looking away.

"Hi, there." Evan sits on the edge of our bed in a white polo shirt and navy twill pants, clasping his watch. A couple of water droplets dampen his shoulder. "Just got cleaned up from my run."

Guilt floods through me for the moment I felt with Wes—what was that about anyway? I drop my purse on the ground and practically lunge toward Evan. I kiss him with a passion as if he's just returned home from war.

"Whoa," he says, almost immediately, pulling away. "What is this all about?"

"Just trying to finish what we started last night."

We kiss again, this time, soft and slow. Comfortable. Rhythmic. Familiar. In our time as a couple, we've developed a pattern. Lips slightly open, then closed. Open. Closed. Open. Closed. It reminds me of a goldfish's gaping mouth.

For shame. *Stop it! What the hell is wrong with you?* Be thankful for Evan. Just like his kisses, he's steady and predictable. Safe. Besides, it was just a look with Wes. A look. Nothing more. Not worth remembering.

"Lanie?"

It's only then I notice we've stopped kissing.

"Sorry." I pull him closer. "Where were we?"

He steps back, eyeing my sweaty clothes. "Where have you been, anyway?"

"Kickboxing."

"Really? I hoped you'd gotten over that by now."

"No. I love it. Next week I'm learning kicks."

"I still don't think fighting is an appropriate activity for a young woman. How about tennis?"

"I don't want to play tennis."

"Golf?"

"No."

"What about your knuckles?"

"They're getting better."

"You keep me on my toes. I grant you that." He glances at his watch. "Okay, I'm off."

"Where are you going?"

"Dinner and then catch the Suns game with Wes. Don't wait up." He kisses my cheek.

Deflated, I sit on the top step of the stairs, listening to the voices of Wes and Evan until the garage closes and only silence remains.

I meander toward the dresser and trace my finger along the top drawer groove, one side to the other, then back again. Something sparked between Wes and me. I can't deny it. Nor can I deny it's something I don't feel with Evan. So what was it? A connection? Yearning? Desire?

No. No. No. This is absurd. Totally absurd. Damn cold feet. It doesn't matter that I feel confident and sexy whenever Wes stands close. It doesn't matter that I fall boneless when he says my name. It doesn't matter that my mind wanders to him, occasionally. All the time.

I am *not* with the wrong man.

With a long sigh, I gather my purse and on my way to the closet, think of my Someday Jar. The exact distraction I need. Focus on something else. I reach for the crock, pop off the cork, and dump out a slip.

My heart sinks further as I read the words. *Oh, God*. This is the slip Kit talked about. Her favorite. The one I wrote as a kid. I twirl the fortune in my fingers and shake my head in disbelief. Could there be two more difficult words in the English language? A more unobtainable goal? No, I can't. I can't do it. There is no possible way. None.

I tuck the slip back into the jar and pull out another.

Scuba dive.

Yeah, I can do that.

sixteen

This is very exciting. Terrifying, but very exciting. I sit at a front table in Dave's Diving School. The brick walls surrounding me are decorated with framed pictures of diving trips, colorful reefs, and an underwater shot of a rather large shark that I'm going to pretend is fake.

A few people trickle into the room. An elderly couple sit behind me and two men—father and son, perhaps?—situate themselves at the table on my left. I glance at the worksheets I was given when I arrived as my foot raps against the floor, eager to get started. Evan is meeting me here at one p.m. for a late lunch at the Mexican restaurant across the street, and then we have an appointment with Stacee to finalize the cake. Since he wasn't thrilled with scuba diving, as it "seems far more dangerous than kickboxing," I don't want to keep him waiting.

Luckily, I was able to take the instructional portion of the class online last night. I learned all sorts of stuff like oxygen/nitrogen ratios, diving do's and don'ts, and how pressure affects the body—a lot. If I pass the quiz today, and after the required in-class lecture, I can attempt my first pool dive, which I hope is soon, because my bathing suit is creeping up my ass.

A few minutes later, a man with curly hair on his head and upper arms walks into the room. "Welcome to dive school." He reaches for a marker and spells *DAVE* on the whiteboard. "I'm your instructor and I gotta tell you, I'm thrilled to be back." He snaps the lid on the marker and pauses. "You guys are my first group since the accident. But I'm sure it won't happen again, right? I mean what are the chances of two groups drowning?"

I stare at him in shock. *Oh, God. What have I gotten myself into?*

He tosses the marker in the air, catches it, and says with a laugh, "Kidding."

Ha-ha-ha.

After ninety minutes of discussion about equipment and safety and thirteen more lame jokes, Dave wraps up the lecture with coral reef preservation and responsibility.

"Any final questions? Comments? Complaints?" He passes out the one-page quiz, stopping in front of my desk. "When you walk out of here today, remember at least one thing. One thing. I cannot stress it enough." His words are sharp. His stance solid. His eyes focused on me.

"Yes?" I'm rapt with attention.

"Never go diving alone."

"Okay."

"Reason one, if you have equipment problems, your partner can help you."

"Got it."

"Reason two, if you run out of air, your partner can share."

I nod. Share air. Good.

"Reason three, if you come upon a shark, odds are fifty-fifty your partner will become lunch instead of one hundred percent you."

He laughs. "Kidding."

After I pass the test—a perfect score, thank you very much—Dave fits me with a dive regulator and a scuba buoyancy compensator and adds weight to my belt. With fins and mask in hand, I follow Dave and the others toward the pool. One of his assistants, Tracy—a broad-shouldered and tan twenty-something—rolls scuba tanks toward the pool's edge.

I slip the mask to my forehead, snagging it briefly in my hair, then adjust the weight belt that digs into my side.

"Sure you want this?" Dave pats the scuba tank. "I think oxygen is for wussies." He laughs. "Careful now, it'll be heavy."

I brace my legs. "Ready."

He hoists the steel tank and straps it to my BC.

I nearly topple over. *Good Lord.* For once, he wasn't kidding. Tracy helps the others.

Dave waits for me to lower my mask and affix my regulator.

Okay, now I'm a bit freaked out. With this mask snug around my face, I find it hard to breathe. This growing tightness in my chest reminds me of the time Dad taught me how to suck air underwater in a Jacuzzi. He'd guided my fingertips to an airstream flowing from the seat bottom and said, "Purse your lips real tight around the air, like you're gonna kiss it."

I dove underneath the bubbles, did as he said, and took a breath. All was fine until the cycle shut off and midbreath I swallowed a lungful of water.

Mom was pissed.

Dave must see the apprehension in my eyes. "You'll be fine. Trust me." He wraps his hands around his neck and pretends to gasp for breath.

Funny.

He double-checks the air connections and tightens the strap of my weight belt. "Once you're in the water, you won't feel the weight of the tank or the rigidness of the equipment. Remember, keep an eye on the air level."

I nod.

"You're all set." He moves me so my butt faces the pool. He inches me backward until my heels dangle off the edge.

Oh, God.

"When you're ready, hold your mask and jump backward into the pool." He moves on to the teenage boy beside me. He's adjusted and fitted in no time and before I can blink, he effortlessly plunges into the pool.

Show-off.

I'm convinced none of the others will have his same level of fearlessness, especially the older couple, but within seconds, I'm the only one on the surface.

"You're still here?" Dave jokes.

Lanie, don't be a wuss. People do this all the time.

With a gentle nudge from Dave on my shoulder, I fall into the pool. The water swallows me slowly, cooling my skin.

Dave splashes into the water and offers an *okay* sign. I return it. He motions me toward the opposite end of the Olympic-sized pool. In the distance, I see my fellow classmates and the obstacles Dave mentioned beforehand. There's a hula hoop to give us a feel for the size and span of our equipment, a large plastic turtle and several fish tethered on the pool bottom to practice swimming near animals without endangering them, a net where we'll learn how to untangle if our tank gets snagged, and my favorite, a makeshift coral arch to swim through.

All the same, I'm nervous as I flick my fins and follow Dave toward the deep end. But, hey, look at me. I'm breathing in and out, underwater. I'm scuba diving. This is easy. This is fun. I swim with the others along the pool bottom, play catch with a rubber torpedo, tossing it back and forth with Dave, and twirl around the faux fish.

Ten minutes later, Dave swims through the arch and motions me to follow.

Cool. I'm ready.

Midway, my hand accidentally snags my breathing hose—okay, maybe I do flail my arms a bit—and the regulator pops out of my mouth.

Oops. It's okay. Don't get flustered, Lanie. Just because Dave and the others swam to the shallow end, leaving you here alone, is no reason to panic. Dave explained what to do in this situation. All I need to do is calmly grasp the regulator, gently insert it into my mouth, purge it, and, remaining relaxed and in complete control, take a breath. Simple. There is a backup regulator should this protocol not work.

The hose seems to have drifted out the other side of the arch. *Silly little bastard.* No problem. *Keep calm.* My lips are pressed tight and, though my lungs have developed the slightest ache, I'm in ten feet of water. If need be, I can shoot right up.

I tug on my breathing hose but it's caught. Caught on the stupid coral arch. I yank again, hard, but it won't come loose. My lungs burn and bright-colored specks dot my vision.

My backup regulator. Of course. I pat around my body, trying to find the damn thing. *Where is it? Where? Oh, God.* I'm going to drown. Right here and now. I've read that most people drown in shallow water, but I didn't think that was true. I didn't think anyone could be stupid enough to suffocate in water with air a few feet away. But I'm proof that *I'm* stupid enough. Won't this make a good obituary for Hollis to read? *Dumb-ass drowns with a full oxygen tank strapped to her back.*

Fuck the regulator, I need air. Now! I need to blast up and suck in a lungful of sweet mother-loving oxygen.

I crouch low and with a mighty push, spring toward the surface. After a foot or so, I'm yanked back to the floor as if fixed to a bungee cord pulled taut.

What the . . . ?

I tug and tug but nothing happens. My secondary regulator is nowhere.

I need air.

I try to bolt for the surface one more time.

It's too late.

Blackness.

$\sim$

"Lanie, wake up." Evan's voice registers in my brain. Kneeling beside me, he pats my cheek. "Lanie?"

I open my eyes, inhale, and then cough, sputtering water out of my mouth.

"You okay?" he asks.

I moan as my head swirls. There's a ringing in my ears. The bodies behind Evan are fuzzy. I blink to clear my vision, but it doesn't help. I do *not* feel well.

Dave rushes over with an ice pack and places it on my head, though I'm not clear why.

Bile creeps up my throat. "I'm think I'm going to be sick."

"Let's sit her up." The ice bag slides to the ground.

"First kickboxing and now this?" Evan shakes his head.

I'm much dizzier sitting up. Facing Evan, I press a hand to my lips.

"Really, Lanie. Enough. These so-called goals of yours are insane."

"I *really* don't feel well."

"I told you this jar wasn't a good idea."

"Evan, I—"

Before I can stop myself, I throw up in his lap.

"Jesus!" He jumps up and stares at his pants in shock. "These are Armani." With a clenched jaw, Evan marches toward the restroom.

I'm on my knees now—feeling much better, thank you—and realize what I've done. *Oops.*

Dave crouches beside me and hands me a towel. "You all right?"

"I think so." I wipe my face. "Just a bit weak."

"You gave us quite a scare."

"Yeah, the arch snagged my regulator hose and I couldn't find my backup. What exactly are your safety measures because I don't think—"

"You hit your head."

"What?" There's a sudden pain on the top of my noggin.

"You were flinging your arms through the arch, doing . . . well, I'm not really sure what you were doing."

Swimming. Obviously.

"You hit your head on the arch. Sank like an anchor."

"I did not. Your equipment is faulty and your arch . . . ouch, my head hurts. I did?"

"You did."

"I remember tugging on my hose and needing air."

"Lanie, you were in the water for only a few seconds before we pulled you up. You've been lying here for a couple minutes and yes, while unconscious, you kept reaching for your regulator. You smacked Tracy in the face with it."

A baggie of ice is pressed to her cheek.

"You knocked out four of her teeth and dislocated her jaw, too. She'll likely need surgery."

"What? Oh my God. I'm so sorry." I dart apologetic glances between Tracy and Dave. He wiggles his eyebrows.

At once I realize.

Together we say, "Kidding."

"You should've seen yourself." He mimics my swimming and chuckles. "You were all over the place."

We laugh for several moments until I notice Evan and the large wet stain in the crotch of his pants.

A disgusted look is plastered on his face.

Oh, please. It was mostly water.

We decide I shouldn't eat or drive, so Evan takes me home after canceling our lunch reservation and appointment with Stacee. "Lanie's priorities are a bit jostled at the moment," I heard him tell Stacee. "She's very sorry to disrupt your schedule."

Regardless of the ruined afternoon plans, Evan's snippy attitude, or the fact that a bag of ice rests on the knot on my forehead, my excitement can't be bruised, for in my lap is my freshly printed Certificate of Completion signed in Sharpie by Dave. I passed all the requirements before smacking my noggin. So, hooray for me. I'm a certified scuba diver. Technically, I'm only *Discover Scuba* certified, but still.

And I've completed another Someday Jar slip.

We merge into the carpool lane and I settle against the headrest, thinking about the morning. Truly, the whole incident is hilarious.

I hit my head on a makeshift arch.

Knocked myself out.

And threw up on Evan.

But I shouldn't laugh about that.

seventeen

The following evening, I slip into my little black dress and slide my feet into matching heels that I bought at Macy's last fall, marked down from $169 to $79, which makes them all the cuter. A half a size too small and they pinch at the heel, but hey, no one said being adorable was easy. My hair is wrapped into a loose-yet-stylish knot at the nape of my neck, and the sterling silver drop earrings I wore when Evan proposed shimmer in the light. Evan is taking Wes, my mom, and me to dinner at Ivy House, a newly opened Italian restaurant in Mesa.

"Ready, Lanie?" Evan calls from the foot of the stairs.

He's much cheerier since Hollis confirmed our appointment for Monday and the dry cleaner promised his slacks weren't permanently stained.

I'm *still* cheery considering all that I've accomplished to date. I broke a record—attendance, yes, but a record's a record—am learning kickboxing, became a certified Discover

Scuba diver, and most importantly, am a day away from securing a co-broker position. *Whoo!* Life is good.

So, when I woke this morning and gazed at Evan's sleeping
face—well, the parts outside his eye mask—I promised myself
to be a better fiancée. To regard him with more love and
attention. To appreciate all that he is and accept what he isn't.
Try not to make any more waves.

I grab my purse and meet Evan downstairs.

"You look lovely," he says.

"Thank you." I receive his kiss.

"Mom is meeting us at the restaurant."

"Great. Wes is already outside."

Evan backs out of the driveway. He and Wes start discussing various aspects of Orchid Lane, the drywall texture, the
trim height. They lose me at offset toilet flange.

I pull down the visor and check my lip gloss.

In the mirror, Wes catches my eye.

My stomach flutters. The exact sort of thing I've promised
myself to ignore from here on out. Enough is enough. It's a
silly pre-wedding crush, anyway. Meaningless. He'll be gone
and out of our lives in a couple of weeks. All the same, I stare
a moment longer, wondering what he's thinking. His eyes give
nothing away. I flip the visor closed.

Several minutes later, we arrive at the restaurant and find
Mom seated at the table in a navy knit dress. A Chianti bottle
candleholder with wax dripping along the sides illuminates
her smile as she sees us.

"Jane, is that a new dress?"

See? This is exactly what I'm talking about. Evan's adoringly
sweet to my mom. How many sons-in-law treat their future

mother-in-law with such kindness? She even lists him as her emergency contact, after me, on her medical questionnaires.

She stands and hugs Evan. "Why, yes, thank you for noticing." Mom blushes. "Don't you look handsome as ever."

"It's the look of love." He winks at me.

"Charmer." She laughs.

"Hi, Mom." I hand her the napkin I retrieved off the floor.

"Thank you, sweetie. I knew this dress was a steal. You know, I got this and a toaster oven for six dollars at St. Vincent's yesterday," she whispers while smoothing out my bangs. "Have you thought about doing something different with your hair? It's much too long and drapey for someone engaged to Evan."

"Hello, Jane." Wes extends his hand. "We met at the Orchid Lane house, remember?"

"Yes, of course. The architect."

"Looks like you're my date for tonight." He slides into the chair beside her.

"I should warn you. I'm a cheap date. One drink and I babble on and on like a schoolgirl."

"Must run in the family," he mutters so only I can hear.

After we're settled, the waiter offers Evan a wine list and he selects a bottle.

"I took the liberty of preordering dinner for us," Evan says a few moments later as the waiter pours us each a glass.

"How thoughtful." Mom beams.

We all raise our glasses for Evan's toast. "To friends and family. A gift greater than life itself."

"He's such a sentimental man." She pats my hand, then sets her glass down, nearly sloshing the wine above the rim, and grabs my forearm. "Good Lord!" She examines the scabs on my knuckles and Tootsie-roll-sized bruise on the side of my hand. "What happened?"

"That?" I shrug. "It's nothing."

"Jane, your daughter is fighting. Didn't she tell you?"

Mom gasps. "What? Fighting? Who are you fighting?"

"I'm not really *fighting*, Mom." My eyes briefly flicker toward Evan. "I took a couple of kickboxing lessons and . . . *ouch*!" She presses her index finger deep into my black-and-yellow bruise. She frowns. "What is kickboxing? It sounds violent."

"Because it *is* violent, Jane," Evan adds.

"It's not violent," I protest, bugged by their alliance. "Kickboxing is fabulous exercise. We do all sorts of core strengthening, push-ups, squats, lunges, and yes, throw punches and kicks into the trainer's mitts. I'm not hurting people." *Except Rudy.* "I smacked the bag wrong the other day. That's how I got the bruise. And the scabs, I have tender knuckles, that's all.

They aren't impressed.

"I don't understand why you'd do this to yourself." Mom leans toward me and says with a frown, "Kickboxing doesn't sound very ladylike."

"My words exactly." Evan lifts his glass and air-toasts her. She responds with a confident nod.

"Who cares if it's ladylike?" I snap. "I'm learning something new and it feels good. Damn good. I like feeling strong. It's empowering and motivating. What's wrong with that?"

"I've seen these so-called women fighters. They're thick in the middle and boxy in the shoulders. It's quite unflattering. Think about how you'll look in your wedding gown."

This is infuriating. "Mom, I—"

"If I may?" Wes jumps in.

"Please," Mom says, reaching for her wineglass. "Talk some sense into her."

"For what it's worth, the idea of Lanie taking a kickboxing class is rather smart."

"I don't see how that's possible," Mom says.

"Neither do I." Evan folds his arms across his chest.

I stare at Wes, curious myself.

"Think of it this way." He focuses on Mom. "Your daughter is learning how to punch and kick, and yes, potentially hurt someone."

"Sounds like fighting to me."

"Fair enough." Wes nods. "Consider this. She's gaining strength and confidence along with learning basic self-defense skills. Let's face it, Phoenix isn't small-town Mayberry. There are a lot of creeps out there. Lanie's a beautiful woman. She needs to know how to protect herself. What's the harm in developing a few skills that one day may save her life?"

I never thought of it that way. Not only am I getting great exercise, but I'm learning how to defend myself, kick the crap out of someone. A mugger or something. Or Paige. I hide my giggle with my napkin, rejuvenated by Wes's argument that kickboxing is beneficial for me. A life skill. A valuable tool that will prove . . . wait, did he say . . . *beautiful*?

He dips his head and offers a little smile. He thinks I'm beautiful.

I feel myself flush.

"Lanie?" Evan regains my attention.

I jump as if caught with my hand in the cookie jar. *Jesus, Lanie.* "Yes?"

"Tell your mom about the scuba diving accident and how you nearly drowned."

"For heaven's sake. What has gotten into you?"

"Nothing has *gotten into me*, Mom. I—"

"Here we are." Our waiter arrives with our dinner and places a plate of chicken Marsala before each of us. He pours us more wine.

"This looks delicious." Mom flattens her napkin on her lap.

"Enjoy," says our waiter.

"Lanie, seriously, why all of this now? What's made you want to entertain"—she glances at Wes—"practical or not, these activities when you're a couple of months away from the most important day of your life?"

"Remember, I found the Someday Jar? I decided to accomplish the tasks, before the wedding, finish what I started and prove to myself—"

"Prove nothing. That jar and your father are ancient history. Get rid of it. You have other matters to focus on. Like your dress. Shouldn't you have one by now?"

"Yes, Lanie. Stacee said you came in the other day but left without one. Said you and Kit hurried out of the shop. Where'd you rush off to?"

A quick glance at Wes reassures me he isn't going to say anything about the speed dating. "Kit had an appointment. Don't worry. I'll find a dress soon." I force a smile, telling myself to enjoy the dinner and not press on about them bulldozing my ambitions. Stuff my mouth with Marsala and let the conversation go. But I feel a pang of irritation and not just from the bruise. Listening to them ambush my goals, I grow defensive.

I set my fork down. "I'm sorry you two don't support my Someday Jar, but it's important to me. That should be enough for you." I glance at Evan and then Mom. "Yes, I've hurt my hands and made a few mistakes, but who cares? Like it or not, Dad gave me this jar and though he checked out of our lives"— I exhale a long breath—"I think he'd be proud of me."

"Damn that man," Mom says. "He filled your mind with unnecessary fantasies, gallivanting across the world. No responsibility. No maturity. No dependability. All these years later, he seems to be doing it again through that silly jar." She shakes her head. "He lived carelessly, Lanie, and you grasped onto his words as if they were your breath of life, listening to his stories of adventure and recklessness."

"So?"

"So, do you know he never had health insurance?"

"There are worse things."

"Your Someday Jar is full of his irresponsibility."

Evan offers us more wine, but I lift my hand and refuse. Mom accepts.

There's a strange realization coursing through my veins as I watch the Chardonnay gurgle into her glass. An awareness. A truth, perhaps? Dad divorced her, wrote her out of his life, but what about me? Why did he divorce me, too? It's never made sense. We were so close and then nothing.

"Mom, what happened with Dad? Do you know why he cut me out of his life?" It occurs to me that I've never asked her this before.

She pokes her tongue under her cheek. Her signature move when she's nervous. "Evan this Marsala is lovely." She takes a bite.

"Mom?"

"Sweetie, what does it matter? You have Evan now and your life is falling into place. All the things I didn't have." Mindful of my scabs, she squeezes my fingers. "I didn't want you throwing your future away, chasing after daydreams like I did with your father."

"What exactly are you saying?"

"You were young and impressionable. You idolized your father so very much."

Tension builds in my shoulders and my tone turns rigid. "Wait a minute. You do know why he stopped calling me, don't you?"

Wes stands. "Evan, how about I buy you a drink at the bar?"

Evan disregards him. "Lanie, let's discuss this another time."

"Why, Mom?"

"It all worked out, anyway."

A stab of sorrow works its way to my heart. My chest is heavy, weighted by loss. I can barely utter the words. "You told him to stop?"

The look in her eyes confirms my question.

Oh my God. "How could you?"

"It wasn't easy for me either," Mom says. "Thanks to me, you didn't get muffled up in his irresponsibility. You went to college, got your degree, and now you've got yourself a wonderful man. Your future is set. Who knows what would've happened if you'd followed your father's reckless path."

I can't believe this. I can't wrap my head around what she did. She took Dad away. Took him out of my life. How could she? How could she alter the course of my life? How could *he*? And why did Dad give up on me so easily? Why did he cast me aside like a cracked oar from one of his rafting trips? Didn't he miss me? Even a little?

As if she can read my mind, Mom says, "He did call. Many times. For years, actually. The man wouldn't give up." Mom glances at Evan. "I threatened to file a restraining order. It was too much." She returns to me and clasps my wrist, but I yank it free. "Honey, please, it's a little jar full of fanciful notions, all in the past. Really, there's no point—"

"No point?" I jab at my chest with trembling hands. "*I'm* the point."

"Calm down, Lanie. You're causing a scene." Evan's voice is pained with embarrassment.

"This broke my heart, Mom. You watched me pace back and forth by the phone and cry myself to sleep when he didn't call. I hated birthdays, hated Christmas. Cried every Father's Day. Everything hurt too much without my dad. You never thought about that, did you? You never thought about Dad or me. You thought about yourself, just yourself. How could you be so goddamn self-serving?"

Tears cloud her eyes. "I'm sorry you feel hurt, but you must understand, it was for your own good."

"No. It was for *your* own good. You were angry with Dad for walking out. Hell, you still are. You figured keeping me from him was the closest you'd get to revenge."

"How dare you!"

"How dare *you*. You used me as leverage." I yell back, throwing my napkin on the table and rising from my chair.

"Lanie, sit down." Evan says.

I remain focused on Mom. "All these years I assumed Dad thought I was a waste of time. That he didn't care about me. I was wrong. Truth is, *you* didn't care about me." I march out the door before anyone can stop me.

"Lanie," she calls after me. "Wait!"

My mind swirls with rage and disbelief as I distance myself from the entrance, weaving among the cars in the parking lot. I march farther and farther away from the restaurant's lights, farther and farther away from that moment of truth, farther and farther away from *her*.

My nails dig into my palms as I pace with clenched fists. I bite my tongue so as not to scream. How could she? And what did Dad think? Did he wonder why I never took his calls? Did he check the mailbox as often as I did? Did he hurt as much as I did?

And yet, as angry as I am with Mom, there's a voice whispering in my mind, questioning if she's right. Is the jar pointless? Is it a silly token from my childhood and nothing more? Should I forget about it?

Dad has.

I reach the far end of the asphalt and sit on the curb, slipping my aching feet out of my too-small shoes.

He did call. Many times.

What does that mean to me *now*? For years I've stuffed the pain from feeling abandoned and forgotten in the depths of my heart. Spent nearly as many years without Dad in my life as I have with him. Am I all of a sudden supposed to erase the heartbreak? Forget the missed birthdays, skipped track meets, and empty seat at my graduations? Wipe the slate clean and reach out to him? Call him and say, "Hey, remember me? It's been a while."

Truth is, it isn't *all* Mom's fault. Dad didn't need to agree to Mom's restrictions. He could've fought. He could've surmounted any obstacle she threw at him. He tackled challenges in all other aspects of his life, the highest mountain, the wildest river, why not claw and climb to get to me? Wasn't I his greatest adventure?

Damn you, Dad. Why didn't you try harder?

Regardless of the obstacles Mom put up when I was a minor,

he hasn't contacted me as an adult. What Mom did or didn't do doesn't matter. I close my eyes and accept the fact that if Dad wanted to be in my life, he would be. It's that simple.

And yet, playing over and over in my head like a scratched record album, I hear Mom say, *He did call. Many times.*

I gaze at the cloudless sky with hopes a shooting star will sail across the night. "Wish for tomorrow," my dad used to say fireside during our Labor Day camping trips. But because of the city smog and overhead streetlights, the stars are obscured. With a heavy heart, I let my eyes drift toward the strip mall across the street.

It's then I see it.

I step toward the street's edge, vying for a better view. My pulse pounds in sync with the flickering letter *G* on the weather-beaten sign. I hadn't realized we were so close. I hadn't realized I'm a stone's throw away from my childhood. A stone's throw away from some of the best moments of my life. I don't know whether to laugh or cry. I stand across the street from the Golden Lantern restaurant.

I slip into my shoes and hurry across the road toward the building, swinging open the heavy glass door and inhaling wafts of warm air laced with fried rice, sweet spices, and stir-fried veggies. I breathe in the memories.

Beyond the hostess stand, where a teenage girl sets her math book aside and gathers a few menus from a tray behind her, are several tables bordering along the windows. I spot the worn booth Dad and I shared.

"How many?" the hostess asks, and then we both glance at her cell phone, which lights up with a message beside her book.

"No, I'm not here to eat. I just wanted to take a minute and look around. Is that okay?"

"Whatever." She reaches for her phone.

A man, presumably her father, for they share the same crook in their nose, joins her at the lectern and chastises her in Chinese with excessive enthusiasm; the teenager drops her phone into her purse, then returns to her studies.

He smiles at me before heading to the dimly lit dining room. I recognize him. He's the owner. His hair has thinned and his belly grown, but I recall him pulling up a chair beside our booth and talking with my dad every time we came. I glance at the girl. Her mother was the hostess and this girl was just a baby at the time. She bounced in a play saucer with a giraffe-colored rattle. She's all grown up. Funny, how time flies.

I step toward the wall on my left. The wall I came to see. Painted a lighter hue of pink than previously, as the uneven ceiling edge reveals a darker shade, the wall is coated with fortune slips, pinned with tiny tacks. Just like I remember. Just like so many years ago. All the tacks are snug against the wall, except for one, which threatens to fall onto the ground. I push the pin and the fortune catches my eye. *Happiness is truth.*

I glance at the girl, surreptitiously texting on her cell phone. I snag the fortune and, with a clear head, make my way toward the Ivy.

In the parking lot, I find Evan waiting for me. "There you are. I've been looking all over for you."

I point across the street. "That's where Dad and I went for my birthdays."

"Really?"

I can tell he's not impressed.

"Yes." I hide the fortune in my palm and wrap my arms around myself. "Where's Mom?"

"She left in a cab. She's truly upset."

"That makes two of us."

"Listen." Evan faces me. "I've been preoccupied with Orchid Lane, the wedding, and work. I've failed to appreciate the importance of this jar and the longing you obviously feel for your father. All the same, I think you'll agree that I've been patient and more than understanding with your behavior lately. Chasing adventure before the wedding, I get that. I honestly do. Hell, the other day I passed the Porsche dealership and nearly pulled in for a test drive. But, in light of everything that's happened, especially seeing how upset your mom is, don't you think it's time to put the jar away?"

"Did you not hear what she said? She chased my dad away."

"I heard her say she was protecting you. Just like I'm trying to do now. Let this go before it inflicts more pain on you or anyone else."

I step back. "You're kidding, right?"

"No."

"I don't get it. You haven't approved of this jar since day one."

"Can you blame me? Look at the havoc it's caused."

"Jesus, Evan. It's not a tsunami. It's a jar of wishes."

"I'm aware of what it is."

Wes clears his throat, standing underneath a nearby streetlamp. "Sorry to bother you, but the valet's pulled the car around. It's blocking other cars. We should probably . . ."

"Thanks, we're on our way." Evan rests his hand on the small of my back and says, "C'mon, babe. Enough of this. Let's go home."

We reach Evan's car and before separating toward our respective seats, he squeezes my hand as if to say, *So glad we worked this out.*

I glance at the Golden Lantern one last time and feel the fortune paper crisp in my palm, then climb inside his Mercedes. "I won't do it."

"Won't do what?"

"Give up on the jar. If anything, I'm determined more than ever to see it through." I click my seat belt. "Just thought you should know."

"Lanie, it's best—"

"I'm going to finish it, Evan. Not you, Mom, or any other naysayer can talk me out of it. Now, let's go home." I flick down the visor and wipe the mascara from under my eyes.

It's then I see Wes sitting in the backseat, staring at me. This time his eyes give everything away. Approval.

eighteen

It's several hours later, long after midnight, and I lie in bed, listening to Evan snore. I blink away tears into the darkness, my skin crawling with all sorts of emotions. Anger. Resentment. Hope.

He did call. Many times.

Twenty minutes later, I tiptoe downstairs with hopes that a cup of hot tea will ease my nerves.

Moonlight slips through the shutter slats, lighting my way into the kitchen. Already I feel better with the cool tile against my feet, preferring the calm, constant hum of the refrigerator to Evan's snoring.

A shadow sneaks toward me.

Oh, God. Oh, God. A chill snakes up my spine. There's an intruder in the house. An intruder!

It's getting closer.

In a knee-jerk reaction, I dart toward the silhouette and thrust my punch into the darkness, smacking my fist hard into the flesh with a loud thump. *Ouch! That felt like concrete.*

He groans.

I raise my fists again, wishing our largest kitchen knife wasn't buried in the dishwasher.

The man grabs my wrists.

I start to scream.

"Shhh, Lanie. It's me," Wes says.

"Wes? You scared me."

He releases me.

I bend over and catch my breath while he flips on the stove's night light.

The dim glow does nothing to conceal the fact that he's shirtless, wearing only a pair of jeans.

"You've got a hell of a punch." He rubs his chin.

"I'm sorry." I squeeze and release my hand, growing stiff with pain, convinced that should my broker career not pan out, becoming a fighter is not a viable second choice. Cool air blasts my face as I open the freezer and fill a Ziploc bag full of ice cubes. "Here." I offer him the bag.

"Thanks." He nods toward my clenched fist. "Why don't you put it on your hand?"

"It hurts like hell."

"I bet." He rests the bag on my knuckles. Ice slides around my fingers and the coolness is instant relief.

"Do you always punch your houseguests?"

"Only those who prowl around at night."

He laughs. "Sorry, I couldn't sleep."

"Me neither. Want a cup of tea?"

"Sure, but I'll get it. Keep that ice on and go sit."

"Thanks." On my way to the couch, I peek toward the stairs, wondering if Evan woke from the commotion, but I neither see nor hear any sign of him.

A couple minutes later, Wes silences the kettle at the hint of its whistle. "Here you go." He hands me a mug.

Shirtless. Did I say that already?

"Thanks."

"You okay?" I sense he doesn't mean my hand.

"Yeah." I set the ice on the table and blow on my tea. After a few moments, I say, "Not really."

"You know, your whole face lights up like a Christmas tree when you talk about the jar. I can tell it's really important to you."

"It is," I say, grateful for his objectiveness.

"Tell me the story."

"What story?"

"There's always a story. Tell me more about the jar."

"Well, it's the typical poor-me scenario of my dad leaving when I was fifteen, causing all sorts of abandonment and self-worth issues. Blah. Blah. Blah. Before he left, Dad bought the jar while visiting Cabo San Lucas, said it reminded him of me when he saw it."

"Long skinny neck, fat bottom?"

"Funny."

"Fine. No more jokes." There's a playful tone in his words.

I tuck my legs under myself and rub warmth onto my calves.

"Hold this." He hands me his tea. Wes retrieves the blanket from the love seat across the room and drapes it over my legs.

"Thank you," I whisper. "So . . . um, my dad had a wanderlust, spent his time traveling the world, hiking, parasailing, river rafting, you name it. Anything fun, he did it."

"A wealthy man," Wes says.

"He was a freelance journalist. I suppose he made enough money to chase his dreams and—"

"No, I meant wealthy with life."

"Oh, good. I was afraid you might ask to see his tax returns."

"W-2s are fine."

I giggle, but talking about my dad heavies my mood. I stare at my tea.

"I gather you don't see him much?"

I shake my head. Tears form in my eyes. "At first, I didn't want to. I was hurt. Hurt that he could leave Mom and me. Then weeks turned into months, months into years. After so long not hearing from him, I was too stubborn and proud to call. Figured if he didn't care, then neither did I. Until tonight, I didn't even know he tried to contact me."

So at ease with Wes, I allow the pain and thoughts of Dad that I buried for so long to flood my mind. "The night he left, I wrote a couple of wishes and tucked them in my Someday Jar. My plan was to fill it with all sorts of adventures. Goals that would impress him. Certain that once he saw how much fun I could be, he'd come home. Guess I was young and naïve."

Wes says nothing.

"All these years I thought he didn't care, but now I wonder if he did. If he still does. Maybe he . . ." My voice trails off.

"What are you going to do?"

"I don't know." I fiddle with the blanket string. "One thing I don't get is why do Mom and Evan make such a big deal out of me having a little fun? I know scuba and kickboxing lessons sound silly, but that isn't the point. The jar is my connection to my dad. It's all I have. It's for me. Just me. Does that make sense?"

"It does. Forgive me if I'm overstepping, but I think your mom's afraid you'll risk all that you have going for you and wind up alone. She doesn't want to see you struggle. That's a powerful sentiment. And for Evan, maybe he doesn't like your independence. I've noticed a building confidence in you the past couple of weeks."

"Really?" I sit taller. "Accomplishing these tasks, foolish or not, makes me feel great." I glance out the window into the darkness. "I don't need their approval, but I would love their support."

"I get that."

I blink to clear my damp eyes. "Anyway, what about you? What would your Someday Jar slips say?"

"Start a bobblehead collection."

"Oh. You think it's silly, too."

"No, I don't. I really don't. Look, I'm sorry. I'm sorry your dad—" He pauses as if thinking what to say. "Finish the jar, Lanie."

I nod, then reach for the bag of ice. "Enough of my pity party. What's your sad story?"

"Me?"

"Sure. You said there's always a story. What's yours?"

Wes stares at the window. "You don't want to hear it."

"Spill it."

"All right." He shrugs. "After graduation, I landed a job at an architecture firm. I was stoked. Not only because I worked in this huge, glass-walled building that overlooked downtown Los Angeles, but because at the desk next to mine was this sharp-tongued brunette. She had a smile that made me stutter like a twelve-year-old boy." His shoulders give way to a slight laugh. "We compared ARE scores."

"How much higher was hers?"

"Whatever." He sips his tea. "She may have scored higher, but she was a compulsive thief, always stealing my highlighter."

"A highlighter? Big deal."

"It was a big deal. I loved that highlighter. It had a resounding click when you put the cap back on, nice angle to the felt tip, too."

"Right."

"Well, after a dozen times of finding it carelessly left on her desk, hidden in her drawer, or nestled between her lips, which made it impossible to concentrate, I told her she could keep the damn thing if she went out with me."

"Nice technique."

"We married the following October at the same place her parents did, a Spanish-style chapel not far from here. A year later she was pregnant."

"That's no sad story. It sounds perfect."

His focus fixes on the window.

In the shadows I see his jaw clench.

Oh.

He says with a crisp voice, "At first she thought her achy back and nausea was morning sickness. I told her to get it checked out, but she brushed it off, saying they were common symptoms and didn't mind the discomfort, she was happy to be pregnant. It'd pass soon enough."

My stomach tightens, fearing what he's about to say.

"A couple days later, we sat at her doctor's office and she choked back tears, doubled over in pain. We feared a miscarriage, but the heartbeat was steady in the ultrasound. They ordered a CT scan and found a kidney stone. She was relieved. Stubborn as she was, she refused any pain medication because of the baby, said she was feeling better. They sent her home, telling her she'd pass the stone soon." He swallows, nodding. "Like an idiot, I went to work. When I came home, I found her shivering underneath a mound of blankets, a bucket of vomit by the bed, and a purple bruiselike rash covering her lower back. She was unconscious."

"Oh, God."

"There were more scans, drain tubes, I lost track of how many times they pricked her veins with needles." He is trying to hold back tears. "Twelve hours later she was gone. Septic shock, they called it." He gazes out the window again. "It happened so fast. We never found out if she carried a boy or a girl."

"Wes, I . . ." I don't know what to say. I long to reach out to him, pull him close, take away his pain. I can't imagine the hurt and guilt he feels. The loss. Finally, I manage, "I bet she would've been a wonderful mother."

He clears his throat and sits taller. "Since that day I've poured myself into work, focusing on commercial or industrial projects. Still can't bear to draw a residential home for a young family, nurseries, that sort of thing." He nods. "Work's been good to me. I opened my own firm eighteen months ago and I've been full-throttle ever since. I'm proud of what I've accomplished. Proud of the City Core."

"You should be. It seems you've come a long way."

It's then I think of Julie and how his voice softens when she calls. Stripped from love before, it sounds like he's found it now. I can't help but wonder what their life is like, especially in the quietness of night once Trevor's in bed and the two of them are alone. Do they share a glass of wine while cuddled on the couch and talk with soft, relaxed voices about their day? Does she massage his back and shoulders, tight from a long afternoon drawing plans? Does she aimlessly trace her fingertip along his chest, or nuzzle skin on skin, in the crook of Wes's arm while they sleep? Does she appreciate him? Appreciate his tenderness, his honesty, and his quiet resilience?

Most of all, I wonder if she trembles when he's close. If his touch prickles then steeps deep inside her skin and weaves through every bit of her body long, slow, and reckless, winding toward each nerve like a drawn-out vine.

Or is that just me?

Dammit. Why do I keep thinking of him this way? Why can't I shake these thoughts? Is it truly wedding jitters? Is it something more? Something real.

"By the way, the microwaved-water plant is dead."

"Seriously? I'm never going to use a microwave again. Tell Trevor I learned something from him today."

"I will, thanks."

We sit in the quiet before I muster enough courage to ask, "And Julie? What's she like?"

"She's the best. I swear that woman gets more centered every day of her life. She—"

"Babe?"

I jump as Evan calls me from the top of the stairs.

"You coming to bed? We have a big day tomorrow."

"Yeah, coming." Guilt clutters my conscience. I shouldn't be this casual with Wes. I shouldn't be sitting in the dark, inches from his skin, whispering sad stories of our past. I shouldn't have these thoughts. "Yes, I'm coming."

"Bring me a glass of water, will you?"

"Of course."

Evan's footsteps reverberate toward our bathroom.

"Time for bed." Wes pats my knee.

I start to get up and the blanket slips toward the floor. We both reach for it. Our forearms brush one another and warmth threads through my skin like a flame burning away its wick. I tell myself it's from the tea, but I know that isn't true.

Wes grabs our mugs and sets them in the kitchen sink.

I follow behind.

He turns toward me, clutching his jaw. "Thanks for slugging me in the face."

"Anytime."

He doesn't move.

Nor do I.

We stand close, close enough that his breath tickles my neck. Close enough that I could place my palm against his bare chest, feel the beat of his heart. We hold our gaze for several moments and I find myself more comfortable than I've felt in a long time. More comfortable than I've ever felt in Evan's condo. Or with any man. Looking at Wes, I find myself home.

I force my gaze toward the floor, afraid of what I'll see in his stare. Afraid of what I won't. And mostly, afraid of what I want.

nineteen

Hollis and Bevy will be here shortly.

It's business as usual between Evan and me. Neither of us has mentioned last night's dinner, which I'm grateful for. I don't want to explain or justify my feelings to him or anyone else. I will finish the jar. For me.

Evan spent the morning pacing his office, reviewing my market analysis and proposal, while I arranged the bouquet of daisies and assortment of muffins I picked up this morning.

If all goes well and the Murphys sign a listing agreement, I will be Evan Carter's new business partner. Though my heart is thick with emotions about Dad, Mom, and Wes, I push them aside and focus on the task at hand.

I wipe a scuff off my desk and clean a smudge on the nearby mirror with my rag. After a final scan of the office and myself—I free a piece of fuzz from my cocoa-colored cardigan and comb my low-slung ponytail—I'm ready.

A few minutes later, Hollis walks in with the help of a cane. "Hello, Miss Lanie."

"Good morning."

"Carjacker dies rear-ending a patrol car."

"Where do you find this stuff?" I laugh, then point at the cane. "What's with this?"

"Bevy. She says I'm a bit shaky. What the hell? I'm nearly eighty years old. I've been shaky the last ten years."

"She's right. Better safe than sorry."

"You women always stick together," he says in defeat. "It's like a cult."

A quick glimpse out the door assures me Bevy isn't with him. My heart sinks. *Damn.* "Um, Hollis, I'm starting to take this personally. Where's Mrs. Murphy?"

"My fault. She told me *not* to make our appointment before noon. I thought the opposite. She already had a facial scheduled. Apparently it takes weeks to get into this place and she couldn't cancel." He jabs the carpet with his cane. "I don't know what you gals do at those spas. All I know is she comes back with a shiny face and it costs me a couple hundred bucks."

"Ah, but I bet there's a relaxed smile on her shiny face."

"See, I told you, a cult." He laughs. "Bevy was impressed with your taste in Chardonnay as well as your evaluation."

"Good." *I wish she were here today.*

"Mr. Murphy." Evan walks from his office with an extended arm. "How are you?"

"Still kicking." He shifts his weight. "My wife told me you bought the house on Orchid Lane."

Evan looks surprised. "I did indeed. You know it?"

Hollis nods. "Sharp place. Bevy wanted to pick it up and flip it. Is that your plan?"

"No. After a small remodel, Lanie and I will move into it."

Hollis glances at me, then questions Evan. "Before you're married?"

Evan stammers, stroking his tie, "Well, we—"

"Actually, Hollis"—I scrunch my nose apologetically—"we already live together. In Evan's condo."

"Never mind. It's none of my business. Silly notion I had when I was your age. I insisted on getting married before we moved into *our* first house. It was important that we cross the new threshold united." He waves his hand. "Pay no mind to me. Times have changed."

"It's sweet." I squeeze his hand.

"Anyway, let's get started," Hollis says. "I've got a bocce ball game in an hour and if I'm late, I'll get stuck with that cheatin' son of a bitch from Glendale."

"We don't want that." I gesture toward Evan's office.

Hollis and I sit down beside one another in the barrel chairs.

Evan flips open my report and clasps his hands together. "What we've gathered here is exploratory. Our purpose today is to give you an idea of the marketability of your home, discuss promotional opportunities, and provide you with specifics why my firm is your best choice for optimum price point potential. And, of course, the listing documents—"

Evan's voice is drowned out when Hollis fishes in his top pocket for a candy cane. Fiddling with the crinkly plastic wrap, his hands tremble as he concentrates on the stubborn wrapper between his fingers. Finally, he rips it open and a chunk of peppermint falls on the floor. He glances at me like a toddler wanting direction from his mother.

I shrug.

With a mischievous smile, he plops the remaining candy cane in his mouth.

My shoulders give way to a tiny laugh.

"Yes, as I was saying," Evan continues. "Based on a thorough examination of recent sales in the area, factored with influx projections from the Arizona Real Estate Department and demographic studies for the Valley . . ."

I chew on the inside of my lip. I know what Evan says is important, a necessary discussion, but I wish he'd make this presentation a little less *boring*. I collected the data and it's interesting, but the way Evan speaks, all monotone and with the enthusiasm of a tollbooth operator, I find myself distracted and counting the circles on Evan's tie.

Hollis leans over and whispers in my ear. "How many times must I nod and smile, pretending like I'm interested?"

"Pay attention." I scold under my breath, and then a giggle leaks out.

Evan glares at me. "Given the data—"

Hollis stands. "Let me stop you there. I appreciate your approach and you clearly are on top of the market, but hell, son, I can read. Do you know how many years Bevy and I have lived in this house?"

"No. I—"

"Since the year after our first daughter was born. We've raised all six of our children here, three foster kids, and Lord knows how many hamsters, fish, and dogs. Bevy's made forty thousand peanut butter sandwiches and kicked countless boys out of our teenage daughters' rooms. I don't want to talk about sales numbers or projections." He points to the analysis. "I want to talk about why I should list."

Evan squirms in his chair.

"This house isn't just a number to us. It is *us*."

"Well, we . . . um . . . yes, let me just . . ." Evan flips through the analysis.

Hollis stands. "Thanks for your effort, but I think I'll just give Lanie her candy cane and call it a day."

Evan's pissed. His knuckles are white from his grip on the report. He releases the paper and scratches his head before saying, "Candy cane. Of course."

Hollis hands me one. "Sorry to waste your time, kiddo." He winks at me, then shuffles out of Evan's office, leaving my fiancé speechless.

That didn't go well.

Without looking at Evan, I jump to my feet and catch up with Hollis.

He moans under his breath as he climbs inside his truck.

I muscle shut the door and wait for him to roll down the window.

"Hollis, I'm curious why you have such a sprawling mansion. It doesn't seem like you."

Hollis smacks the door frame. "I've had this baby since it was brand new. Drove it off the lot with Bevy by my side. It hasn't let me down once. Nor has Bevy. You're right. I don't care about fancy stuff." Hollis leans closer. "It's not always about me."

I cover my hand over his, rubbing my thumb across his thin skin, sprinkled with age spots and thick veins.

"My Bevy." His tender eyes soften as he says her name. "She wanted a home with bells and whistles, and every woman deserves a candy cane."

Tears build in my eyes as I think about how much Hollis

loves his wife. Truly loves her. Down to the center of his being. She is his life. His greatest adventure.

I can't help but wonder if Evan feels the same about me. Or, more importantly, I about him. The mere question alone hints at my answer.

Blotting my teary eyes, I watch Hollis's truck grumble to a start and bellow black clouds of smoke as he drives away.

I'm melancholy as I step inside the office, partially from the meeting, but mostly because I'm tired of trying to ignore the constant fog loitering around me that I can't seem to shake. Is it allergies? The beginning of a cold? Mom? Dad? Or should I finally be honest with myself and admit it could be Evan? Will Evan share his candy canes with me? Do I want him to?

His voice jars my thoughts. He tosses my report on my desk, scattering the pages, and paces back and forth. "Dammit, Lanie. We need this listing. That fancy house we're about to live in, your wedding, this office, our life as we know it, takes money. A lot of money."

All the more reason to have consulted me before buying Orchid Lane.

I've never seen him this upset. Not even after a valet mistook his Mercedes for a Kia.

"That man has lost his senses. He doesn't know what the hell he wants." Evan throws his hands in the air. "That meeting was a complete waste of time."

"It wasn't a waste of time, not in the least. It revealed everything. Don't you get it? Hollis wants a handshake."

"A what?"

"Hollis is old school. He holds on to things made well, appreciates the value. He can't be wooed by projections or data. His kids' growth charts marking up the doorjambs are the only numbers he's concerned with."

Evan folds his arms across his chest.

"He doesn't want a sterile, formal relationship for something so close to his heart. He's a pat-on-the-back, I-take-care-of-you-and-you-take-care-of-me kind of man. A handshake mentality. Hollis cares about the *type* of person he works with more than anything else. And, remember, Hollis wasn't certain he wanted to sell. Sure, I gave him promising projections, but it might take some time for them to decide. It's a big deal. Maybe they want to consult with their family. Maybe they—"

"What did you say?"

"Well, first off, I don't appreciate the attitude. And, what I said was, maybe they want to consult with their family."

He pinches the bridge of his nose. "Shit. How did I not see this coming?"

"See what coming?"

"Timothy Bane."

"Who's that?"

He shakes his head in frustration. "And you want to be broker?"

"Excuse me?"

"Bane's a real estate developer in the Valley. He typically handles industrial developments, but for the size of the Murphy commission, I fear he'll take on their mansion. Dammit. We blew our chance today."

"If he wanted to list with Bane, wouldn't he have done so already?"

Evan says nothing, just marches back and forth, and I fear he'll wear a hole into the carpet.

"Why would Hollis care about Timothy Bane?"

"Bane is Hollis's niece's husband."

We are screwed. "That does suck. If Timothy is family, then I'm sure Hollis would rather—"

"Bullshit." He glares at me. "You need to find dirt on Bane. Suspicious deals, kickbacks, favors for investors, anything. I want to know if he's so much as jaywalked in the last ten years. Given the types of developments he represents, I'm sure he's stepped on a few toes and crossed a few legal lines over the years. If we're lucky, we'll find he's been slapped with a fine or two." Evan's face lights up. "Maybe jail time. Or better yet, caught with a hooker. Embellish if you have to."

"What? No way."

"This is what I'm talking about. This is how the game works. You don't become a top broker by playing nice."

"Well, you don't have to be an asshole, either."

He inhales a deep breath and combs his fingers through his hair.

"Forget it, Evan. I'm not going to dig around for ammunition against some guy I don't know, then tattle to Hollis. I won't stoop to that level."

His face relaxes and his voice turns sweet. "All I'm suggesting, babe, is prepare yourself. If he even hints at calling Bane, have some artillery to make Hollis reconsider. Won't you agree that our job is to represent the Murphys the best way possible?"

"Of course."

"Clearly, if his nephew-in-law operates with less than perfect ideals, Hollis should know that. You said yourself, Hollis cares about the type of person he works with." Evan doesn't give me a chance to respond. "I'm telling you, this is the only way to coax Hollis our way."

"This is a bad idea."

"You got a better one? I'm all ears."

"No. I think approaching this professionally, yet with compassion and honesty, is the best tactic."

He leans over my desk. "I don't care how you handle Hollis. Write the listing on a fucking napkin for all I care. Just get it."

twenty

Phoenix averages 211 full-sun days per year. Today is no exception. If not for the condominium complexes and sky-scrapers lining the view beyond my bedroom window, I could see unobstructed for miles. Wes's City Core towers and the dominance they warrant poke into my distant periphery, but I quickly push them and *him* out of my thoughts.

More than a week has passed since our meeting with Hollis. Evan and I have been pleasant to one another, sweeping the latest arguments, like the others, under the rug. It helped that we each had busy weeks, both at the office and with Orchid Lane. I went to a couple more kickboxing classes and Evan was out twice for dinner meetings. We met with Stacee on Thursday, and though Evan and I sat close and he slid his arms around me, planting a kiss on my cheek when I agreed to red velvet groom's cake, I'm certain she sensed we're a bit *off*.

I can't shake Evan's reaction to Hollis's listing. *Soiling a competitor's reputation? Who does that?* We've been together for three years and this is the first I've seen him act this way.

The only way I can make sense of our bickering and his motivations is to chalk it up to stress and anxiety and the weight Hollis's listing carries for his future. Evan doesn't truly mean to play dirty. *Right?*

The sound of SportsCenter on the TV downstairs convinces me to forget about Evan's actions and reactions. Today is not the day for worries.

I reach for my Someday Jar. With a *pop*, the cork falls into my hands and I dump out a slip.

But it's not the slip I expected. My stomach twists into a knot as I stare at my childish handwriting. It's Kit's favorite slip again. *Damn.* I shake my head, drop the fortune into the jar, and thumb through the remaining slips until I find the right one, the one that reads: *Touch an official Cardinals game ball*.

My mood lifts.

Today, not only will I spend the day with Evan, as a committed and supportive other half, but it's Sunday. *The* Sunday. A sweet blessed Cardinals football Sunday. I'm super excited.

After one last brush through my hair, I'm about to head downstairs when my cell phone rings. Mom. It's the nineteenth time she's called. I have nothing to say to her, not sure I ever will. I switch the phone to silent and grab the game tickets. I can't help but wonder what Dad is doing at this very moment. Sipping coffee? Whipping up a batch of blueberry pancakes? Flipping through the sports section of the . . . *Arizona Republic, Boston Globe, Miami Herald*? Which newspaper and whether he reads it with the desert sun at his back or beside a fireplace under a cloudy East Coast sky, I haven't a clue. Tears blur my eyes, but I force them away. Not now. Not today.

I stuff the game ball goal into my pocket and head downstairs.

Evan opens the door for Paige when she knocks at five minutes to ten. "You're prompt." He smiles as if punctuality is equivalent to a cure for cancer.

"Well, I'm excited to be here." She reaches toward Evan for a hug, then turns to me. "Hi, Lanie." She tugs at the sleeve of my oversized and overworn Fitzgerald jersey hanging loose over my favorite pair of jeans. "Aren't you spirited."

I cram the dish towel I'm holding into her mouth.

Okay, I don't.

But I should.

Even though the denim skirt she wears is short enough to spot her ovaries, I refuse to let her spoil my day and I greet her with a smile. "Hi, Paige."

Wes steps from his room in jeans, a brown leather belt, and a silver-blue T-shirt. "Morning, Paige."

Evan, dressed like the team's owner, twists his cuff link and asks, "Everyone set to go?"

We pile into Evan's car and jitters flutter inside me like popping corn kernels as we near the arena. I have Cardinals tickets and a locker room pass in my hand. I clutch them close to my chest.

Evan laughs. "You aren't holding the Hope diamond."

"This is better."

After twenty painfully slow minutes stuck in traffic outside the stadium, we finally pull into our designated parking spot. We cross the asphalt lot toward Westgate, an outdoor shopping center full of restaurants, souvenir vendors, and game-day fun.

Along our path, we pass dozens of tailgaters barbecuing

chicken, burgers, and ribs beside tables full of chips, bowls of dips, and coolers full of beer. Heaven on earth.

"Look at these guys." I point to a group with three operating TVs under a Cardinals EZ-Up. They sit in Cardinals fold-up chairs, dressed in Cardinals jerseys, holding Cardinals coolie cups behind a red Ford truck plastered with yes, Cardinals stickers. I offer a supportive nod. Good people. My people.

A few minutes later, we're seated at a table in the crowded Yard House restaurant and order four beers (light beers for Paige and Evan, Guinness for Wes and me), three burgers, and a spinach salad without dressing (also for Evan).

Our conversation is light and breezy as we talk about the game and how the Cardinals fare for the postseason, Orchid Lane, and Paige's recent trip to Cozumel where her bathing suit top "kept falling off while surfing."

"No tan lines," she joked.

She's adorable. Like a rash.

The moment our waitress clears our plates, I scoot back in my chair and say, "Ready?"

Evan chuckles and taps my hand, which is the teeniest bit sensitive from punching Wes. Thankfully Wes doesn't have a noticeable bruise. "Paige and I still have half a beer."

Kill me. Kill me now. It took every bit of patience I had to sit and enjoy lunch. If I stay here any longer, I will explode. "I don't want to miss a single second of my tour. How about I go on ahead?"

"We should probably stick together; it's crowded out there," Evan says.

Wes swallows the rest of his beer in one gulp, tosses his napkin on the table, and says, "I'll walk her."

"Are you sure?" I ask, knowing I'm smiling.

"Well, I guess that'd be okay. Thanks, Wes." Evan lifts his beer.

"I'll meet you both at our seats." He turns to me. "Let's go."

"Enjoy yourself." Evan stands and kisses me on the cheek. "Have fun."

Wes holds the door and I step outside into the warm air. We pass restaurants and sports shops, dodging between other gamers and beer kiosks. With my swift steps, Wes falls behind.

"You're a freak about football, you know that?" He quickens his pace. "Most girls would rather shop or do just about anything than watch a game. Heck, Julie can't stand football."

My stomach clenches at the mention of her name. "Well, I'm not like most girls."

"No, Lanie. You're not."

We approach a narrow walkway between several restaurants, each with TVs over their outdoor bars. A jumbo screen mounted on a neighboring rooftop airs other football games. A large crowd has gathered, slugging their beers, slapping jersey-clad backs, spouting complaints at referees for botched calls. All at once, the mass cheers and a hundred or more beer bottles lift in unison toward the jumbo screen.

I glance at the TV. With seconds left in the fourth quarter, the Packers score a touchdown, tying the game.

More people hurry close, elbowing for a better view, circling behind us. The crowd packs even tighter. Within seconds, Wes and I are separated. I've lost sight of him, too. All I see is a sea of heads and the nose hairs of the man beside me.

I'm stuck in the middle of the anxious group, which cheers again, presumably for the extra point. In the midst of the celebration, I'm nudged and bumped, pressed into the back of the guy beside me. I nearly lose my footing.

Don't panic. Just worm your way out of the pack. You'll be fine.

"Excuse me," I yell, though no one pays me any mind. Stepped-on toe after stepped-on toe, I inch my way through some people, pushed and bounced like a pinball.

After a few steps I'm stuck, wedged between a man with a 49ers jersey stretched taut over his can't-say-no-to-a-plate-of-potato-skins belly and a Cardinals fan with a faded skull tattoo on his right bicep.

Beer drips off the 49ers fan's hand. "Watch it, fucker!" he says.

"What'd you call me?" The Cardinals fan anchors himself strong like a concrete pillar.

"Hello, boys," I squeak, bracing my palms on each man's chest. "Let me just make my way—"

"You wanna go a round?" The 49ers fan widens his eyes and spits on the ground. He doesn't take his eye off the Cardinals guy, whose chest is now puffed out like a baboon's.

Okay, panic.

This is bad. Very bad. If one of these brutes starts swinging, I'm toast. Somehow I slither out from between them, but bump into people holding themselves steady and eager for the impending fight. I'm inched back toward the men when the fist-pumping crowd shouts, "Fight. Fight. Fight."

"No fight!" I shout, and place a hand on each guy's arm. "He's sorry. You're sorry. Let's calm—"

"Shut your piehole, bitch." The 49ers fan flicks my hand away.

What did he call me?

"Bring it," says the Cardinals guy, who I'm now *totally* rooting for.

"Kick his ass!" I yell.

Beer splashes my ankles as both guys drop their drinks on the ground.

Oh, shit.

"Fight. Fight. Fight." The crowd roars louder.

With hands protecting my face—thank you, Rudy—I lean away from the beasts as they push, punch, shove, and call each other all sorts of names I'm certain they didn't learn in Sunday school.

What is a *cocksack*, anyway?

I duck as the 49er's left hook narrowly misses my cheek and breezes through my bangs. His next swing is a direct hit, and blood spurts from the Cardinals fan's nose. Upon realizing this, he lunges toward the 49ers guy with the speed of a freight train. Rage swells in his eyes.

Oh, God. I need to get out of here. Now. Right now! But how? I'm trapped. My hands tremble and sweat dampens the nape of my neck. It's the first time in my life I've felt *truly* scared. *This is so not good.*

Out of nowhere, Wes pushes through the crowd. "C'mon." He grabs my hand and stiff-arms us through the mass. Beer drips on my clothes, my toes are stomped on too many times to count, and we're nearly pulled apart, but Wes squeezes my hand tighter and drags me along until several minutes later, we break free from the chaos.

"We made it." He laughs, shaking his head at the mess of people.

"Yeah, thank you. That was crazy."

"You all right?"

"I think so. I—" Okay, maybe not. My legs nearly crumple when Wes leans close, his face inches from mine, and reaches

204 · *Allison Morgan*

behind my neck. His fingers brush across my nape, sending prickles along my back. "You had a beer label stuck to your shirt."

"Oh, right. Thanks."

Evan. Evan. Evan. I plant the image of his face in my brain. *Stay, Evan. Stay in my brain.*

"Ready?"

"Yes." I refrain from looking in Wes's eyes. "Absolutely."

We walk silently toward the stadium, the crowd behind us and foot traffic lessened to a handful.

"Your dad got you interested in football, right?" Wes says.

"Yeah. I wasn't always a freak. At first I got bored and complained about watching the games, but one Sunday the Chargers played the Cardinals and Dad bet me that the Chargers were gonna whop the Cardinals. Normally, I didn't care who won as long as I had my coloring books and snacks. But this time, he bet me my bowl of M&Ms."

"Ballsy. What happened?"

"The game got real ugly by the end of the second quarter. Cardinals were down by three touchdowns and a field goal."

"Ouch."

"Yeah. During halftime Dad flipped off the TV, grabbed my bowl of M&Ms and paraded around the room claiming to be the halftime entertainment."

We both laugh.

"They didn't lose that day, you know."

"No?"

"Two interceptions, a recovered fumble, and a blocked punt later, the Cardinals won."

"No shit."

"Yep. I'll never forget the look on Dad's face when I yanked the bowl from his hand and dumped all the M&Ms in my pocket. Bad idea, by the way. M&Ms may not melt in your hand, but they sure as hell melt in the front pocket of your favorite skirt." I tuck a strand of hair behind my ear, aware of the comfort between us. "Ever since that day, the Cardinals have been my favorite team." I look up at the tall silver dome we're shaded under. "Today is a dream come true."

"Let's get you inside, then." Wes knocks on the Guest Services door.

While we wait for an answer, I say, "Thanks for walking with me. And, thanks for saving my ass back there."

"What is that? Twice now?"

"Who's counting?"

The door swings open and, dressed in a red polo with an embroidered cardinal head above the left pocket, a young woman glances at my locker pass, then extends her hands with a football charm bracelet dangling from her thin wrist. She says, "Welcome. I'm Becca, the guest relations coordinator. I'll be showing you around today."

"Thank you. I'm so excited."

"Shall we?" She gestures inside.

"Yes, thanks." I say to Wes, "See you later."

"Have a blast, Lanie. I can't wait to hear all about it."

I smile and step forward. It's then I realize we still hold hands.

"Oh, sorry." He lets go. "I didn't—"

"No, I . . . I didn't even notice myself."

Wes wrings his hands as if they're dirty. "Right, well, you better get going."

"Yeah."

"Aren't you joining us?" Becca asks.

I show her my locker pass. "We only have one."

She ponders this for a second. "You know, the other group for today canceled. I can make room for him."

"Really?"

"Lanie, is that okay with you?" Wes asks.

"Sure. Thanks, Becca."

"My pleasure. Let's go."

We make our way toward the elevator through the forming crowd of gamers funneling early into the stadium. Becca inserts her key and presses the button for a lower level.

My hand is still warm from Wes's grasp, but I try to focus on Becca's words.

"Okay, a little about the facility. It opened August 1, 2006, at a cost of four hundred fifty-five million dollars. The stadium can seat up to eighty-five thousand people and features the first fully retractable natural grass playing surface. Besides seven to eight professional football games each year, we host a number of other events such as concerts, various athletic games, the Fiesta Bowl every January, and most notably two Super Bowls."

As if on cue, the elevator bell chimes and the doors swoosh open. In come smells of damp concrete, steamy showers, sweaty sports gear, and musty locker room air.

I inhale as if it's my last breath.

Wes laughs.

"Follow me." Becca walks through an open set of double doors. "The boys will be in any minute. Feel free to take a quick peek around."

Down two concrete steps and I stand inside the Arizona Cardinals locker room. Painted on the floor, covering nearly the length and width of the room, is a red-and-black Cardinal head with the words *Protect the Nest* in bold underneath the beak. Discarded towels and cleats hanging by their laces adorn lockers that line each side of the room. A banner hanging on the far wall reads NFC Champions.

"I can't believe it. This is so amazing." My hand trails along the glossy wood benches as I study the personalized spread-eagle jerseys displayed above each of the lockers. *#38 Ellington. #21 Peterson. #58 Washington.*

My heart skips a beat when I see it—*#11 Fitzgerald.*

I motion Wes over. "Look at this. It's Fitzgerald's locker." A pressed rich-looking charcoal suit and burgundy-checked silk shirt hangs inside. "He'll probably change into this after the game. I sound like a total creeper, don't I?"

"Yes." He laughs.

On the shelf above Larry's clothes rests an eyeglass case, a silver watch with a gold clasp, and a framed picture presumably of him as a kid, standing knee-deep in snow with what I'm guessing is his brother, mother, and father. Next to that is a bobblehead of himself.

"I don't have that one." I wiggle Fitz's head.

Becca's steps echo as she nears. "Your favorite?"

"Isn't he everybody's?"

"Pretty much."

Becca and Wes move to a whiteboard with X's and O's scribbled in formations. I admire Larry's locker until concrete vibrates beneath my feet and deep voices bounce off the walls. The team stampedes through the double doors. Three-hundred-pound bodies with testosterone spewing from their pores fill the room.

Wes steps beside me and I quickly rattle off, "There's Jaron Brown and Calais Campbell." My eyes dart at each face. "There's

Catanzaro the kicker. I don't know who the blond guy is, but next to him is Andre Ellington." I can't believe Ellington's a stone's throw away from me, close enough to decipher the tattoos on his tree-trunk-sized arms.

"Gentlemen," Coach Arians says, smacking chewing gum. "Quiet down, now. Becca's brought guests." He tucks a clipboard under his arm and says to her, "Just for a second, though. We've got a game to win."

"Thanks, Coach." She gestures toward us. "This is Lanie and Wes."

Sweet Jesus, the Arizona Cardinals team looks at me. The whole friggin' team. I smile and hope there is nothing stuck in my teeth.

They say, "Hey," "Hi," and "What's up?"

"Enjoying your tour?" Coach Arians asks.

"Absolutely. It's the best day ever."

"Nice jersey," says a familiar voice. "You watch much football?"

I look over and see the brilliant, white-toothed smile of Larry Fitzgerald. *Me. He's talking to me.* I clear my throat and hope no one can tell my entire body shakes like a tree in a Category 4 hurricane. I mumble, "Um." *Um? All I can say is* um?

"Yes," Wes answers for me. "Ever since she was a kid."

"Really?" says the blond player. He leans his southern-fed build against the wall, clutching his helmet against his belly. I still don't recognize him and his tone sounds irritated with my presence. "So, tell me, little girl . . ."

Little girl?

"Should we start the game with a two-block-four-over running play or a three-step wide-out pass up the middle?"

Snickers resonate through the room. I scan the players and the several coaches standing by the whiteboard, all waiting for my response. Heat prickles up my neck, but I maintain my cool and return my gaze to Blondie. *Nice try.* "Is that a trick question?"

He laughs. "She don't know football, Larry." He elbows #11. "Just another sucker to buy your jersey. Ask her about shoes or something."

Hearty chuckles reverberate in the room.

"No, wait," I interrupt, my voice loud above the chatter. The guys quiet down and all eyes are again upon me. With confidence, I start to explain. "It's a trick question because you Cardinals are one of the few teams in the NFC West that routinely defers the ball for the first half. You won't have the ball for the initial play because the defense will take the field. And in that case, I suggest you shore up the defensive line with a three-technique-tackle and watch the zone coverage."

One of the coaches crumples a piece of paper and throws it at Blondie. Claps ring through the room while Larry smiles ear to ear and several other players goad Blondie about being outfoxed by a girl.

Wes nudges his shoulder on mine.

"Hey, Coach." Fitz waves his helmet in the air and signals Arians. "How about we let Lanie lead us out the tunnel, maybe do the coin toss with me?"

I stare at Arians, the man who will single-handedly determine if I can die a happy woman.

He hesitates, then says, "Yeah, sure."

My mouth drops open. "Did he just say yes?"

"He did," Wes assures me.

"All right, guys. It's game time." Arians commands the group's attention. "This is our day. No one walks on our field and takes our day."

"Hell, yeah!" a massive voice belts out from somewhere in the crowd.

"Our day," another player shouts.

Some guys smack their hands against their helmets, some jounce their feet against the floor, and all stand like warriors, solid and ironclad. Grunts of battle echo throughout the room. These guys are pumped.

"C'mon." Becca escorts Wes and me up the locker room stairs. The tunnel out to the field is on our left. "Sorry, Wes, but this is where we say good-bye. Security requires a pass for any field presence."

"No problem. Thanks for the tour." He faces me. "Have fun out there."

"I will, thanks."

A few minutes later, the team funnels behind me and the coaches as we walk toward the end of the tunnel. Light from the field shines inside. Stopped by several security guards at the tunnel's exit, we wait until the announcer says over a loudspeaker, "Ladies and gentlemen, welcome your Arizona Cardinals."

Our cue.

Arians nods and we start running. Footsteps pound behind me. This is unreal. God, I wish Dad were here to see this. I'm leading the team onto the field. Thank you, Larson Gates. I will *never* forget this moment.

We exit onto the grass and into the open-roofed stadium among a sea of red seats, jerseys, and #1 fingers waving in the air. The smell of fresh-trimmed grass tickles my nose. The hollers and cheers compete with the Guns N' Roses song—"Paradise City"—that blares through the speakers. The stadium vibrates with energy. The announcer introduces the team's starting lineup.

Becca calls me over and I meet her at the sidelines.

"That was incredible!"

"Glad you enjoyed it."

After an ASU sophomore girl sings the national anthem—
which chokes me up—Fitzgerald steps close and says, "Come
with me."

Explode. I'm about to explode.

We jog onto the grass until we reach two referees and a
49ers player standing midfield.

Larry points at the big screen hanging at the far end of the
stadium. "You're on TV."

Oh, God. I hadn't thought about this part. My hands are
squeezed tight, which makes them look red and blotchy. I
release them, suck in my stomach, quickly fluff my hair, and
smile even broader.

Larry laughs.

One of the referees draws my attention as he tosses a football from one hand to the other while a second referee pulls
out a shiny quarter. He asks Larry, "Heads or tails?"

Larry looks at me for an answer.

"Heads."

"Heads," he confirms with the referee.

We watch as the referee flips the coin into the air.

The 49ers player, who is the width of a Mack truck, steps
back as the quarter bounces near his feet.

Heads.

Yay!

"All right, young lady, you better make your way back."
The referee nods toward the sidelines. "Time for the teams to
get to work."

"Right," I say, disappointed that my moment is over. I shake

Larry's hand. "Thanks again. This was a moment I'll never forget."

"My pleasure," he says.

I turn toward the sidelines, mindful that the TV screens are still on me, so I try to run impressively, like a gazelle or something.

Becca motions me toward her and when I'm nearly there, an image of my dad pops into my head. Is he watching the game? Does he see me? Would he be happy to know that this is a slip from my Someday Jar?

I stop.

I haven't completed a slip. I haven't touched a Cardinals game ball. Time is running out. I'm a few steps from Becca. A few steps from *Tour over, please go find your seat.*

She waves me over.

I quickly scan the sidelines for a random football, but amid the players, cameramen, and tables topped with Gatorade jugs, I don't see any. *Seriously? Not one?*

I remember.

The referee. He spun the game ball in his hands.

All I need is a quick touch.

"Lanie, off the field, please," she says.

"Right, sure." But I spin around and sprint toward Larry, who still talks with the ball-holding referee. Though I don't stop and check, the jumbo screen must display me because the crowd roars. The music switches to a siren. Even above the noise, I hear a man's voice yelling from behind, "Stop! Get off the field."

Okay, maybe this wasn't such a good idea.

But I can't give up now. The ball is within reach. I can read *Spalding* imprinted on the side.

Just a few more feet.

With the force of a sledgehammer, someone shoves me from behind. All the air escapes my lungs as I'm flung forward. My arms flail wildly in the air, desperately searching for something to grab onto. Desperate for something to prevent my body from smacking the ground and my chin from skidding across the grass like a horse-drawn plow.

Larry reaches for me.

In midair, I stretch toward him and grasp his hand. But with the momentum of the shove, my fingers slip through his. In a final effort to save myself I aim for the towel dangling from his waistband, readying for a good grip. My hand skims through the towel and with an urgent clutch I grab onto Larry Fitzgerald's . . . *balls.*

"Aagh," he groans.

Oh, shit. Did I just grab his—?

The crowd goes nuts.

"What are you doing?" Fitz yells with his legs crossed and a slightly higher-pitched voice. He stares at me like I'm some sort of freak who sprinted onto the field and grabbed his balls.

Oh, right.

"You're in big trouble, young lady," says a panting security guard approaching from behind, presumably the one who pushed me. He grabs my arm and shakes me like a rag doll. "What the hell do you think you're doing?" His other hand hovers above the trigger of his Taser.

"Hold up," Larry says to the guard. "What *are* you doing, Lanie?"

"I wanted to touch a ball. It's a dream of mine."

"Huh?"

"No, not yours. His." I point at the referee, who places a hand over his tenders.

214 · *Allison Morgan*

"No, not your balls, either." *God, this is embarrassing.* "That ball." I motion toward the football.

"This ball?" He grabs it from the ref.

"Yeah."

He hands it to me. "Take it."

"Are you serious?"

"Yeah. Stay off the field, okay?"

"Of course, yes. Thank you so much." I clutch the ball to my chest. "Sorry about everything."

Fitz winces as he adjusts his cup.

"Good luck today," I say as the guard hauls me away. "Be careful you aren't sandwiched between defenders up the middle."

"You got it."

The crowd claps and cheers as I'm escorted—with a rather tight grip—toward the sidelines. My face is still plastered on the big TV and, when I wave the ball in the air, the crowd hollers even louder. Okay, I'll admit it. I enjoy the attention. *I did it.* Not exactly as I had in mind—probably not what Fitz had in mind, either—but I still did it. I touched a Cardinals ball. Or should I say, balls?

After an acerbic lecture from the head security guard, who regrettably spits when he says any word ending in *s*, and a cross-armed Becca, I'm released to my seat.

"Hi," I say to my group, and slide beside Evan. Wes and Paige are next to us. "Did you guys see me?"

Evan doesn't look at me. His eyebrows are furrowed together like a long worm resting on his forehead. He's furious. And still in need of that wax.

Paige picks at her nails.

Wes, God bless him, laughs. "Yeah, half of America saw you. What was that about?"

"Yes, Lanie, just what the hell was that about?" Evan snaps.

I'm taken aback by his tone. "I wanted to . . ." I stammer. "Well, I wanted . . ." *Jesus, Lanie, buck up.* Throwing my hand in the air, I say, "It was one of my Someday Jar slips—touch a Cardinals ball. And, I did. Well, technically, I touched a couple." I chuckle.

"What you did was run out on the field like a lunatic, making a complete fool of yourself and me. Are you *trying* to destroy the reputation of my firm?"

"There was no harm done. Who cares?"

"I care! I care about the perception of my firm in this town. What will our clients say, watching you grab an NFL player inappropriately?"

"You mean in the balls?"

"Have you forgotten I'm trying to land the biggest deal of my career?"

"You're worried what Hollis will think?"

"One of us should be."

"Don't. Hollis will be too busy laughing. If he says anything, he'll probably ask if I copped a good feel."

Evan shakes his head. "Embarrassing."

"Evan, I had fun."

"There's more to life than fun."

Whatever. I refuse to give in to his mood. I'm still walking on air, recounting how perfect my day has been. I met the players, stood in their locker room, smelled the sweat, felt the vibrations through the tunnel, made friends with Larry Fitzgerald, and on top of it all, got a game ball. Now, in my seat,

I'm only a few feet away from the field. How much better can it get?

"Anyone want a beer?" I ask.

"I'd love one," Paige says. "Something cool on my lips." She licks them with her wet tongue like she's auditioning for the lead role in a porno.

Give it up, Paige.

"Evan?"

"No." His tone is sharp.

"Wes?"

He springs up. "I'll come with you."

"Great."

We take a couple steps up the stairs. "You met Larry Fitzgerald?"

"I did." A smile spreads across my lips. "A lot of him, actually."

Wes laughs.

Another few steps, and then I climb two at a time. Wes does the same. Soon we're scrambling up as fast as we can, both vying for first place, laughing between breaths. Midway, he presses a stiff arm against my shoulder, slowing me down.

I clutch my football close to my side and yell, "Cheater!"

We poke and pull at one another until Wes reaches the top first. He shoots his arms in the air. "I win!"

"Were we racing?" I say, half a step behind.

"Come along, freak. I'll buy you a beer."

౿

Later, after we drop Paige off at home because the beer "went straight to her head" and Wes at the City Core to meet for dinner with some of his associates, Evan is still mad about the game. His white-knuckled grip on the steering wheel sets the tone for the ride home. Quite honestly I don't know what the big deal is. What's wrong with a little fun?

Kit's text breaks the silence in the car.

> *Rob says he saw you on TV.*
> *Yep. :)*
> *He said you grabbed Fitz in the nuts?*
> *Yep.*
> *Swear?*
> *Swear.*
> *I CAN'T wait to hear the story!*
> *Can't talk now, Evan's pissed. Call you later. XOXO*
> *:(*

We don't say a word to one another until Evan approaches the intersection a block away from our condo and stops, waiting to make a right-hand turn. On the corner, twin girls with matching yellow ribbons in their pigtailed hair sit behind a makeshift lemonade stand. One of the girls reaches up to steady a teetering stack of yellow Solo cups while the other draws squiggly lines around the edges of a handwritten sign taped to the front of the table that reads: YUMMY LEMONADE ~ $.50 A CUP.

It reminds me of the hot chocolate stand I set up when I was nine years old. I still recall the excitement bubbling through me as I organized the cups, sorted the marshmallows in groups of two, lined up the packets of cocoa mix, calculated in my mind how much change a customer would get from a five-, ten-, or twenty-dollar bill. Determined to raise money for a Totally Glitter Me manicure kit, I set up my stand on our street corner on Thanksgiving weekend.

Thing is, Thanksgiving in Phoenix isn't always cold; sometimes it's downright hot. That weekend in particular was a record-breaking eighty-four degrees. No one stopped for my hot chocolate. After three hours of sweating, watching car after car whiz by, with the ice for my milk melted into a pool of water, I started to pack up. Tears stung my sunburned cheeks.

Since that day, regardless of whether I'm thirsty or hungry, in a hurry, or forced to snake through four lines of gridlock, I stop at every lemonade or hot chocolate stand or bake sale. I'd make it a law if I could. Every single citizen must patronize enterprising kids. I'd hate for them to feel defeated like I did.

"Look, Evan." I wave at the twins. "Those are the girls from down the street, the house with the ocotillo in the front yard that's decorated like Santa at Christmas time. They're adorable. Let's stop."

Evan looks briefly in their direction, and then after a quick glance for oncoming traffic, he roars past the girls toward his condo.

"Where are you going?" I spin around and watch the twins fade in the distance. "Why didn't you stop?"

"It's a lemonade stand."

"Exactly."

Evan pulls into the driveway and pushes the remote, opening the garage door.

I stare at him baffled.

"What?"

I hop out of the car and march toward the twins, muttering under my breath, "What type of guy doesn't stop at a lemonade stand? What type of guy makes a big deal out of having a little fun? What type of guy wants to defame a man he doesn't even know?" I cross the street and pull a five-dollar bill from my pocket, then stop dead in my tracks. I peek back toward the condo. Evan disappears inside the house as the garage door closes behind him.

Am I with the wrong guy?

twenty-one

"Broken water line, huh? You're certain?" I ask with hopes that the plumber on the phone will say, *Sorry, I goofed. There's no leak.*

"No doubt," he says.

"It's definitely cracked underneath the kitchen floor?"

"Dead nuts."

Thank you for that lovely description. "There's tile throughout the kitchen. Nice tile."

"If this broken line isn't repaired, water's gonna bubble up through the grout of that *nice* tile."

"What do you do? Jackhammer it all out?"

"We can. Or we can abandon the existing line and run new lines, overhead, in the attic."

That sounds expensive. "I'll need authorization from my seller. E-mail me an estimate."

"You got it." He hangs up.

I rub my temples in an attempt to massage away my headache. Two escrows are on the verge of falling apart, I'm on the sixth counteroffer with a buyer for a duplex in Mesa, Evan and I have hardly spoken since our latest spat—how many fights have we had since Wes arrived?—and now I need to tell the sweet Somerset Lane sellers that their house has a major plumbing leak. What a day. It's only noon.

The phone rings yet again. "Good afternoon, Evan Carter Realty."

"Dentist suffers fatal allergic reaction to toothpaste."

I laugh in spite of the dentist's misfortune because Hollis sounds chipper. "How are you?"

"Fantastic. Bevy and I just finished our swim."

"Good for you." I'm glad to hear he's feeling better. I think about the arrangement I made with Evan. Despite the arguments we've shared lately, I'm still determined to make broker. On my own terms. No dirty play. No cheap shots. No trash-talking. That's why the other day, I assembled a portfolio demonstrating my marketing ideas and messengered it to them. I flip open my copy and scan the first of my two suggestions. An exclusive, champagne, invitation-only property preview party limited to agents who solely represent high-end, prequalified clients. Any agent in their right mind will want a premier showing of the Murphy mansion. Those agents not invited—the poor saps clawing at the door to get a peek—will rush to their office and pull up the listing on the database just to see what they're missing. A win-win.

My other plan is to use technology and incorporate mobile marketing where any agent or potential client can scan a code—listed on every sign, flyer, name rider, social media site, et cetera—linking their smart phones to a full property profile including pictures, data, and video. It's efficient and effective and they're sure to love it. Well, I'm not certain Hollis will understand the benefit, given he doesn't even have a cell phone, but something tells me Bevy will. Hollis mentioned once that Bevy keeps up to date with the latest technology and is obsessed with her iPad. Hollis thought it was a remote for the TV.

"Bevy wanted me to call and thank you for the marketing ideas."

"You're welcome. Now, I know you haven't decided to list your house, and even if you do, I know you don't care much about the extra steps and precautions I'll use to make the sale as painless and noninvasive as possible. Nor the marketing and promotional tools I'll implement to facilitate a speedy sale. You'd rather call me and tell me straight what to do."

He laughs. "You know me well."

"Indeed. But I had a feeling Bevy might be curious."

"Oh, Lanie, you're a good girl. Do you know that?" He sighs. "That's why it pains me to say this."

My heart sinks. "Oh?"

"Hold on a sec, Bevy's handing me my pills." I hear him swallow. "Ugh. Awful stuff." He coughs, then says, "I gotta tell you, Lanie-Lou, getting old is for the birds. But that's not why I called."

I bounce my knee like a hummingbird flaps its wings, hoping he'll rattle off another quirky obituary. Hoping he's teasing. Hoping he doesn't have anything painful to say.

"My nephew-in-law, Timothy Bane, is a real estate developer in Gilbert. Did I ever tell you that?"

My head surges with regained pain. *Shit. Shit. Shit. Just as Evan suspected.* "No, you didn't, but I'm aware of him."

"He's a pompous ass," Hollis says. "So he makes a few bucks, big deal. The boy carries a man-purse. Have you seen those things? It's leather with a silly tassel-tie wraparound thing. It's ridiculous."

A snicker escapes my lips. "I'm sure it's nice."

"If you're a woman." He coughs again. "Anyway, Bevy says I need to call him and discuss the house. Says he's family and if we decide to list, we owe him a chance. I hope you understand."

He *is* going to list his multimillion-dollar mansion with someone else. Can this day get any worse? Evan will be crushed. He's reminded me countless times that this listing carries weight beyond the commission. It carries stature and a level of prowess to secure the Valley's most desired clients. Not to mention, it carries my promotion.

"Sure wish I could talk Bevy out of working with Bane. It's just a hunch, but I don't quite trust him. But my Bevy's adamant. Says a man-purse isn't reason enough not to like someone. Unless I can convince her otherwise, she's hell-bent on him."

Though I didn't agree with the practice, I have done as Evan suggested and investigated Bane. Evan was right. There are more than several questionable dealings on his record. A couple of kickback implications and two fines for misrepresentation. Worse yet, he spent thirty days in jail for a DUI and assault on an officer after a domestic dispute with Hollis's niece eighteen months ago. A fact that Hollis would find unforgivable. Bane must've pulled a few strings, because this information hides under the radar from public knowledge. I only know because I called in a favor from Chett.

Should I reveal this damning evidence and salvage this deal? Switch to broker mode and fight for this listing? Is this what a successful businessperson does? What a good fiancée would do? Is this how the game is played? Hollis would never stand for such immoral conduct; hell, he didn't approve of Evan and me premaritally living together. He'd be aghast at his drunk nephew-in-law beating up an officer. As he should be.

If I don't tell Hollis the truth, I'll lose the listing of a lifetime. I snap the pencil I'm holding in two. Without this deal, I won't earn the half-million-dollar commission. Without this listing, I won't be promoted to broker. Without this deal, I won't complete the slip in my jar. This deal means everything.

But I can't. I can't highlight Bane's behavior. I won't stoop to that level. I toss the pencil in the trash, deciding that Bane may be lower than pond scum, but Hollis is smart enough not to be snowballed. He doesn't need, and likely wouldn't respect, me pointing it out. Nor will I dishonor a man, deserving or not. Bringing up Bane's infractions says more about *me* than it does him.

I realize what this means. Securing the phone between my ear and shoulder, I uncork the Someday Jar and dump out the few remaining slips. There goes my business cards with *Lanie Howard, Broker* printed on them. There goes my chance at truly feeling equal in the business. There goes my promotion. Gone. Like a puff of smoke.

This sucks.

I fiddle with the slips until I find the right one.

Make a sacrifice.

"Did you hang up on me?" Hollis breathes heavily into the phone.

Business is business and my disappointment is no concern of this kind old man. With a professional and respectful voice, I say, "No, I'm here. And, I know that nothing comes before family in your eyes. You should call Bane."

"All right, dear. Thanks for your understanding."

We hang up and I pace around my desk. *Damn. Why did his niece marry a real estate developer? Why couldn't she have fallen in love with a taxidermist?*

I let out a long sigh and wonder how I'll break the news to Evan. This revelation will only add to the tension between us.

Ugh.

Evan's out of the office, so I call his cell phone. He doesn't answer and I don't leave a message. It's not something I want to leave on a voice mail.

A couple of hours later, without any sign of Evan, I nearly scale the walls with the energy and anxiety bubbling inside me. I leave the office at quarter to four and head toward Rudy's for class, knowing I'll feel better if I punch the crap out of something.

As I drive toward the gym, I'm prickly. Though a large part of me says not to feel guilty about the jar, a tiny part wonders if I shouldn't have embarrassed him on the field like that. If I should have been more concerned about his soiled pants. Massaged his shoulders and tried to ease his stress about Orchid Lane, the wedding, and the Murphy deal. We'll be married soon and I should consider his feelings. His sensitivities. Regard the reputation of the firm. Besides, didn't I promise to do that?

⁓

"Hi, Howie." Blue's chipper voice lightens my mood as I set my bag on the bench. She's wearing her customary velour tracksuit. Sea-foam green this time, with a matching necklace and jeweled clip fastened to her bun.

"Hi, Blue. How are you?" I join her on the mat.

"Fantastic." She eyes my gloves, which are on the wrong hands. "You okay, sweetie?"

"Yeah, fine."

"Liar. Spit it out. I'm an old woman, my days are numbered."

"Don't say that." Whether it's her age-spotted hands or lipstick creeping into the wrinkles around her lips, something about her feels unassuming and comforting. I'm completely at ease sharing my private world with this relative stranger and I say, "Lately, I haven't been the best fiancée."

"How so?"

"Well, for starters, he's not a fan of kickboxing."

"Why not?"

"Too dangerous."

"Hogwash."

"I threw up on his pants."

"On purpose?"

"No, I was sick from scuba diving."

"Okay. And?"

"And, the other day, I embarrassed him in front of a lot of people."

"Any harm done?"

"Not really."

"Then who cares?" She waves her hand as if swatting away a fly.

"It's just he's been so stressed about work, our house, and the wedding. Maybe I should be more considerate of that, focus more on him rather than myself."

Blue leans close and whispers, "Bat those gorgeous green eyes and show him a good time in the sack. Trust me; he'll get over it. Hell, it's worked for me for years."

I laugh. "I bet it has."

"Sounds like you're an adventurous girl. Surely he knew

that before he proposed. He shouldn't be too surprised by your behavior."

"Actually, kickboxing and scuba and everything else I've done lately is a reach for me. Normally, I'm pretty reserved."

"Honey, you're far too young for a midlife crisis. What changed?"

"A childhood keepsake from my dad resurfaced, my Someday Jar. It's full of my goals. I'm tackling them one by one."

"Really? Now isn't that a hoot. Hell, I might steal that idea for my grandkids."

"You should. I'm enjoying it."

"Good for you, Howie. What else is in your jar?"

I think about the remaining slips, especially the one that hovers in the back of my mind, the one I can't conceive a way to complete. "Only a couple are left. One is to volunteer as a Big Sister and the other . . . well, I'm terrified to try."

"And if you don't?"

"I'll likely regret it forever."

"Don't be afraid, Howie. Fear reminds us we're still alive. Regret will dig us an early grave. Finish that jar." She pats my thigh.

"Thanks, Blue."

"Ready, Lanie?" Rudy calls me toward the bag.

She points at him. "Go kick his ass."

Inspired by Blue's calm, matter-of-fact confidence in me, I convince myself that not only can I open the jar, but I can knock Rudy's bag over with one punch.

"Today's your day." He smacks the bag.

"Today's my day." *One punch, Lanie. You can do this.* I step into my horse stance, inhale a deep breath, and, with a loud kiai, thrust my fist into the padded bag. It topples over.

"Holy shit! I did it!" I give Rudy a hug.

The women cheer and the girl with the yellow wrist straps offers me a high five.

"You did it." Rudy rights the bag. "I told you. All you had to do was believe in yourself."

⁓

I'm still flying higher than a kite as I reach for my Someday Jar later the next morning at the office. *I did it. I knocked over the bag with one punch.* I even got to write my name on a chart beside Rudy's entrance door. Only four other women have done so.

I still haven't told Evan about Bane, but I decide to wait, until I think of another solution to salvage my broker deal. For now, I pull out the slip I'm looking for, dial the number, and focus on the new task at hand.

"Big Sisters of Central Arizona, may I help you?"

"Yes, hello. My name is Lanie Howard. I'd like to volunteer."

twenty-two

"Elizabeth Baxter, fifteen years old, attends Chapparal High School," I say to Kit, staring at the wallet-sized school photo of the green-eyed girl with a cute blond bob haircut, tiny gold star studs, and innocent smile. "She's an only child and has lived in six different foster homes since the second grade."

"Poor girl." Kit reaches over our coffee cups and shared slice of blueberry loaf and grabs one of the pages from Elizabeth's profile, given to me by the Big Sisters program after I passed the background check and forty hours of instructional classes. "There's no mention of her father, but it says her mom's serving a seventeen-year prison sentence for drug-related charges." She blinks away tears, likely thinking of Dylan. "God, can you imagine? Your mom in prison?"

"Elizabeth's been robbed of her childhood. So unfair."

"This is a good thing you're doing here, Lanie. A really good thing."

"Thanks, I hope you're right."

She pats my hand, then grabs the photo. "Pretty girl, she looks sweet. Think she has a nickname, like Lizzy or Beth?"

"It doesn't say. Lizzy's a cute name."

"Okay, so what are you two going to do?"

"I don't know. Her profile is rather vague. It doesn't list her interests, just says she's an above-average student, which is impressive given her situation. She scores exceptionally high in creativity and comprehension but has limited trust issues."

"Can you blame her? I would, too, bouncing from family to family, house to house. Why'd she move so much?"

"Her profile reads that one family divorced, the other relocated, and the remaining families were designed only as temporary provisions." I look at Kit. "This is going to be tough. Where do I start? How do I connect with her? Should I take her to lunch? A movie?"

"No, not a movie. You guys won't say more than two words to one another."

"Shopping?"

"You could, but it says here you shouldn't spend a lot of money, and shopping is no fun if you can't buy anything."

"Yeah." As I scan the page in front of me, my stomach swells into a knot. "Kit, what if she hates me?"

"Of course she'll hate you. She's fifteen years old. Girls hate everything at that age."

"Awesome." I stab a blueberry with my fork. "I've got to think of something cool to do. Something not too flashy, but not totally lame."

"How about miniature golf? Or bowling?"

"Yeah, I guess we could. What about the zoo?"

"Zoo could be cool."

I imagine Elizabeth and me pointing at the baby elephant

hiding behind its mama or us standing one-legged, mimicking the flamingos. "The animals would give us something to talk about, kinda break the ice. I don't care who you are, monkeys are always good for a laugh."

"I like it. And if she doesn't, you can feed her to the lions."

I stuff Elizabeth's profile into the folder with confidence. "She'll love it. I mean, she may be fifteen, but who hates the zoo?"

⤳

"I hate the zoo," says Elizabeth the moment we step through the turnstile. Except her name isn't Elizabeth, it's E. Just, E. And she's changed dramatically from the girl in the photo. The girl in the photo didn't wear patterned leggings, a white T-shirt with a skull's face cut out of the back to reveal her black mesh bra, and laced-to-the-knee combat boots. The girl from the photo didn't have one side of her cherry-Coke-colored hair shaved above her ear.

"Hate the zoo?" I look up from my map, slightly irritated that she didn't reveal her repulsion to zoos *before* I bought her thirty-seven-dollar ticket.

"Zoos are oppressive, an extension of man's pomposity. They take animals out of their native habitats, transport them great distances, and imprison them in alien environments all for human amusement." She wags her finger at me. "How can you not see that every single animal's liberty is severely restricted?"

Um, what? "Okay . . . well, I . . . I never thought of it that way." I say, trying to keep things light. After all, opinions are good, healthy even. But now what the hell do I do? "Listen, how about I get us some cotton candy?" *And look up the definition of* pomposity.

"Spun white refined sugar? No, thanks. I'd rather be shot by a firing squad." She adjusts the gray beanie threatening to slide off her head and stares at her boots.

"Hot dog?"

She shoots me a look. "I'm a vegan."

Of course you are. "Water?"

I treat her lack of a response as a yes.

"Great. Have a seat." I point at a nearby bench. "I'll be right back." As I head toward the drink kiosk, I give Kit a quick call. "Help!" I scream the moment she answers.

"Not going well?"

"God, no. Elizabeth, I mean E, E is her name by the way, hates zoos and possibly all of humanity. Kit, I bet if a little kid walked by with a lollipop, she'd rip it out of his mouth and throw it on the ground."

"She can't be that bad."

"What am I going to do?" I glance at my watch. "I can't take her back home this early."

"Calm down. Go back and ask E . . . seriously, E?"

"Yep."

"Okay, ask E what she'd rather do. Maybe she'll surprise you with an idea."

"Okay, I will. But if I don't make it home, check the landfill for my body."

"You'll be fine. Love ya."

"Thanks. Love ya, too."

I pay for the drinks and head toward E. Kit's right, I'm worrying too much about this, assuming that all is lost, that today is a failure. But it's not. We're just starting out. E and I will find our groove. We'll find a common ground. We'll . . . Holy shit. Where is she? She's not on the bench. She's not among the crowd. She's not standing near the balloon peddler, peeking into the starfish tank, or wandering through the gift shop. She's nowhere to be found.

E is gone.

Oh, no. Oh, no. Oh, no.

My first day—my first hour—as a Big Sister and I've lost my girl.

"E," I call. "E, where are you?" I hurry toward the exit turnstiles, praying she didn't make a quick getaway. "Excuse me," I ask the zoo attendant. "Did you see a young girl with dark red hair and combat boots come through here?"

"No, ma'am. No one's come through here."

"Okay, thanks." A flicker of relief trickles through me. At least she's still on site. But where? Where the hell has she gone?

Then I see her.

One hundred yards away, leaning against the giraffe exhibit wall, she stands with her back to me, laughing and talking with two teenage boys.

Thank you, sweet Jesus.

As I approach, I tell myself not to freak out, not to act like an overbearing adult because as my orientation instructor said, "You aren't here as their parent, you're here as their friend." *Yes, but friends don't ditch the other the moment their back is turned.*

I'm ten feet away when one of the boys says, "We got smokes. Wanna hang with us?"

"No, she doesn't," I say before E answers. "She's hanging with me." I hand her the water.

E's cheeks flush red and I can't help but feel pleased that she's embarrassed after the panic I experienced.

We turn to leave when of the boys asks me, "Hey, aren't

you that lady from the Cardinals game? The one that ran on the field and grabbed Fitzgerald's—"

"Yes, that's me." I smile at E and ask, "Ready?"

"That was you?" the other boy chimes in. "I saw it on YouTube. The video went viral. It was totally awesome. You ran on the field like the honey badger, all crazy fast and shit."

The other boy laughs. "Yeah, and that security guard pummeled you, but dang, girl, you got right back up. That was so rad." He lifts his hand to high-five mine.

"Um, well . . . thanks." I giggle and smack each boy's hand. "We better go."

Several minutes later E and I reach my car.

"So, I guess I'll take you home then?"

"Whatever."

Right.

We say nothing to each other for twenty painfully awkward minutes as I drive toward her house. This was a complete disaster. What am I going to tell my counselor at the program? Worse yet, what will E say to her?

I pull my car curbside in front of E's house. "Well, it was nice to meet you."

She sits with one hand on the door handle. She doesn't get out.

"Everything okay?"

"That was really you, like on TV and stuff?"

"Yeah. That was me."

"Why'd you do that? Why'd you run back on the field? Not to touch his . . ."

"God, no." I laugh. "That part was an accident."

And for the first time, she laughs, too.

I turn off the ignition. "You see, I have this jar. It's my

Someday Jar. And inside, written on the back side of fortune cookie slips, are my ambitions, things I've always wanted to do. So, I ran on the field because I wanted to touch an official Cardinals game ball." I shrug. "Silly or not, it was a dream of mine. And you know what? I did it."

"That's cool." She kicks her foot onto the seat and plays with her shoelaces. "What else is in your jar?"

I list off the tasks I've completed, telling her about kick-boxing, scuba diving, right down to the speed dating, in which she agrees with Seth: Xboxes are bitchin'.

"If you had a jar, what would you put in it?" I ask.

"I don't know."

"Nope. That's not fair. I'm sure something comes to mind. Tell me."

"You'll probably laugh."

"Me? After I made a fool of myself on national television, you think any idea you have is more embarrassing?"

"Okay. Um . . . well, when I was little, before my mom . . ." She stops and stares out the window. "I've always wanted to draw. Like spread out a blanket and get a sketchpad and some charcoals and just draw, you know?"

"That's beautiful."

She shakes her head. "No, it's silly."

I peek at her house, then the clock on my car radio. "E, do you want to go home now?"

She shrugs. "Not really."

"Great." I peel away from the curb.

"Where are we going?"

"Not to a zoo, I promise you that."

An hour later, E and I carry our armful of supplies to the park. We spread out our red-checkered blanket and carefully arrange the charcoal pencils, erasers, pastel chalks, and bag of Reese's peanut butter cups between us.

I hand her a sketchbook. "Let's do this."

She smiles for the first time.

Truth is, I have no artistic ability. I can't draw to save my life. Even a decent stick figure is difficult for me. But I'm sure as hell not going to make E feel uncomfortable, so I grab a pencil and sketch a few wispy lines across my page, deciding to render Camelback Mountain, my view beyond the grassy park.

A couple of hours and an empty bag of Reese's later, I'm lost in my design when I sneak a peek at E's sketch.

"Holy shit!" I cover my mouth. "Sorry. I mean, wow. I can't believe . . . you drew that? Now? I mean, of course you did . . . but you drew that?"

"Yeah. Do you like it?"

I stare at her drawing: shaded for depth and perspective, defined with charcoal, an oversized remarkably detailed hand scooping up a handful of sand, tiny granules falling between the fingers. In the center of the palm, on top of a mound of sand, rests a tiny butterfly. It's simple. It's profound. It's beautiful.

"That's amazing. Absolutely amazing."

"Really?"

"Really. You have a gift."

She looks into the distance. "I draw all the time, but never in peace. Thanks for doing this."

"You're welcome." I wrap my arm around her shoulder and squeeze. "Can I have it?"

"You want it?"

"Yes, I really do."

"Okay." She tears out the sheet.

"Sign it first."

"Why?"

"Because someday you're going to be famous."

Trying to hide her smile, she signs the print at the lower right corner and hands it to me.

Elizabeth Baxter.

"Thanks."

"Now, let me see your picture," she says.

"You know, why don't we—"

She grabs it from my hand. "Oh . . . um. . . . What is it exactly?"

I point at the mountain.

It's then I notice she holds my drawing sideways. I don't tell her because honestly, right side up looks worse.

"It's good," she says.

"Liar."

We laugh.

Later, after pretzels and ice cream, I take her home.

Before she steps out of the car she asks, "So your Someday Jar, you complete each goal and then what, you're done with it?"

"I guess so, yes."

"So that means, like, you're done with me?"

"Not unless you want me to be."

She says nothing, just presses her lips together.

"There's an art exhibit at ASU next week. Wanna go?"

"Yeah."

We wave good-bye and I scream with delight. I had the best day. The very best day.

I call Kit.

"You survived?"

"More than survived. We had a fantastic time together. You were right, I just needed to scratch the surface with her."

Kit laughs. "I can tell by your voice, you really like this girl."

"She's amazing. And an amazing artist. We went to the park and sketched. You should see what she drew."

"I'd love to."

"Thanks for your help earlier."

"I didn't say anything you wouldn't have thought yourself. So, this is another slip completed, right?"

"Yep. And we're going to meet again. I've made a new friend."

"That's awesome. Hopefully I can meet her, too."

"Absolutely."

"Hey, I gotta run, Rob and I are taking Dylan to Chuck E. Cheese tonight."

"Fun. What time do you leave tomorrow morning?"

"I'm Maui bound at eight-oh-five."

"Tell Rob's mom to call me if she needs anything."

"Already did, thanks."

"Okay, give Dylan a kiss for me."

"Will do."

We hang up and I call Evan, but he doesn't answer.

I pick up tacos and drive home, recalling the afternoon as all my favorite songs play on the radio (REO Speedwagon and the Lumineers), all the lights stay green, and I swear, even the sun shines brighter.

When I step inside the condo, I find Wes on the couch studying a set of plans spread on the coffee table. Evan is nowhere around.

"Hey, Someday Jar girl, need help with those?" He points at the bags of food.

"Sure, thanks." We set the food on the counter, and then I call Evan again. Still no answer. He texts me a few minutes later. *Driving. I'll call in a bit.*

I unload the tacos, salsa, beans, and rice, realizing I got enough for a small army. And, really, it'd be rude not to offer Wes dinner.

"Hungry?"

He looks up from his plans. "Starved." He grabs two beers.

Wes twists off both the caps, then says, "So, you've tackled how many of your slips?"

I think for a moment, then count off with my fingers. "Learn something new, break a record, scuba dive."

He folds his arms across his chest, listening.

I pretend that his interest doesn't affect me and I continue. "Let's see, I touched a Cardinals ball, which will crack me up every time I think about it, made a sacrifice, and last but not least, today I had the most amazing day. I volunteered as a Big Sister and met the most remarkable girl." I explain the zoo and the park, then show him her drawing. "Isn't it good? Like really good?"

"It is." His smile is infectious.

"Anyway, I wouldn't say I've excelled at any of the slips, although I'm getting better at kickboxing. Did you know I knocked over a six-foot bag with one punch? One punch!"

"That's great."

"I'm proud of myself for the tasks I've done. Every single one. Who cares if I haven't accomplished them with grace or expert skills? Hell, I've done them. I've set out toward a goal and I'm meeting it. I'm determined to make broker one way or another."

"Absolutely. There's no fault in that."

I pick at a piece of taco shell while the impossible slip I wrote as a teenager comes to mind. I still have no idea how to handle that one. No idea at all. Sooner or later, I need to find a way.

He grabs a lime from my plate and squeezes it over his tacos before returning it. "Ready for the wedding?"

"What? Oh, yeah. Pretty much, I guess. I still need a dress, but everything else is planned. Are you . . ." I stall. "Are you and Julie coming to the wedding?"

"Julie, no."

"You?"

"I don't think I'll make it, either."

I nod and dip a chip into salsa. There's an awkward silence between us for a minute and before I realize what I'm asking, I say, "Do you think Evan's right for me?"

Wes chokes on his chip and reaches for his beer. "Where did that come from?"

I say nothing.

He looks away, then returns his focus to me. "You want the truth?"

"I do."

"Evan's a hell of a guy, but I see you with someone lighter."

"Like an albino?"

"No," he chuckles. "A lighter personality. Someone who laughs at your jokes and appreciates your quirks."

"Quirks? I have no quirks."

"Really? I've been living at the house, too, you know?"

"Yes, and for the love of God will you please hang up your towel after you shower?"

"About *your* quirks," he says. "You fluff and turn over each couch pillow, three times."

"I like the puff and uniformity."

"You can't walk by a penny on the ground without picking it up."

"I have good financial sense."

"You tense when palm trees blow in the moonlight."

I think of the windy night after dinner at The Hill. "They make a frightening sound."

"You cry during the national anthem and I've watched you painstakingly flick off every walnut from a brownie before you eat it."

"You sound like a stalker."

"Perhaps," he says with a definite voice. "Or maybe someone who pays attention."

"How do I like my coffee?"

"A two-pump mocha."

"What's my favorite color?"

"Brown."

"What color are my eyes?" I close them quickly.

"Green with tiny specks of brown."

How does he know all this about me?

I open my eyes and swirl a chip in the salsa.

"Look, I've nothing against Evan. He's not necessarily someone I'd hang out with, but I appreciate his drive. Hell, I worked with his parents for a long time, they've been a tremendous account for me, but at the end of the day, I see you and Evan wanting different things in life."

"Different things? Like what?"

"He's into appearances, the right restaurant, the right car, the right clients. He likes the spotlight, which is fine. But you're more, I don't know, behind the scenes."

"Haven't you ever heard that opposites attract?" I say, defensively.

"I have."

"Not every relationship is ideal. I'm not falling for someone just because he fulfills some Cinderella fantasy for me. I don't want empty charm. I want security and stability."

"Then marry a concrete pillar."

"I sense your sarcasm."

"You should." He crumples his taco wrapper in his hands and says, "Listen, you asked how I felt and I told you. I just picture Evan with someone more—"

"Classy? Sexy? What?" I cut him off. "Smart? Sophisticated? Say it. Say what you really mean. Someone more—"

"Forgettable."

Oh.

He looks at me and I open my mouth to say something, but close it again. Speechless.

My phone rings and I nearly jump.

It's Evan.

I spin away from Wes and answer. "Hello."

"Sorry, I didn't get back to you sooner. My meeting with the roofer lasted longer than expected."

"No problem. I have a busload full of tacos here and I want to tell you what I did today."

"Picked out a dress?"

Damn. "Actually, not yet, but I did—"

"Listen, we'll need to talk later, I'm late already. Whatever it is, can it wait until tomorrow night?"

"Tomorrow night?"

"Yes, remember, I have that early agency class tomorrow morning. I'm leaving for Flagstaff now."

"Oh, yeah. I totally forgot. Yes, I suppose it can wait."

"Okay, I'm turning onto I-17, probably gonna lose service in a minute. Have a good night."

"Yeah, okay. Wait. Before you hang up." I cup my hand over the mouthpiece and peep at Wes, who thankfully listens to a message on his phone. "How do I like my coffee?"

"What?"

"My coffee. When we go for coffee, how do I order it?" My phone beeps its low battery warning.

"I don't know? With cream? Why are you asking me this? Do you want some?"

"No, no. That's okay. I'll talk to you later."

"Okay. Bye."

We hang up and I'm a bit deflated. But then again, who cares about silly coffee? Who cares that he doesn't know how I order it? That's a silly detail in the scheme of life. *Right?*

"Everything okay?" Wes asks.

"Yes," I lie. "Totally fine."

We finish our tacos in silence. He tosses the trash and wipes the counters, then says, "Thanks, that was really good."

"Sure."

"Lanie, um . . . I'm sorry for what I said about Evan. I probably overstepped."

"No, it's okay. I asked for the truth."

He finishes his beer, then says, "Got time for me to show you something?"

"What?"

"Just something, it's not far from here, twenty minutes or so."

I don't feel like sitting home all evening alone; I'm still revved up from my day. "All right. Mind if I change first?"

"Sure."

After a quick shower, I dress and before heading downstairs, I catch my reflection in the full-length mirror. I wear a gray

Puma hoodie, jeans, and tennis shoes. Kit would hate this outfit. She says white tennis shoes and jeans look like people don't care about their appearance. Like they've given up.

She's right.

I spin on my heel and turn toward the closet, but stop. I don't want to appear like I'm trying to impress Wes. No. The given-up look is best.

"Ready?" he asks as I step into the kitchen.

"Where are we going?"

"You'll see."

Except for a couple of comments about the weather, as the wind has picked up and the threat of a desert storm hovers on the horizon, and recent movies we've each seen, we ride in silence. I'm surprised how comfortable I've become in the stills between us. We can enjoy the ride without feeling the need to talk. And though the console and gearshift separate Wes and me, maybe this comfort, this ease, is why I feel guilty, like we sit too close? I reach for my phone to call Evan, hear his voice, and let him know where I am, but my phone won't turn on; the battery has died.

"Mind if I borrow your phone? I thought I'd call Evan."

"Yeah, sure. It's right . . . damn." He pats both front pockets.

"What?"

"I left my phone on the kitchen counter."

"What? You don't have a phone?"

"Apparently not."

"It's okay. We won't be long. Believe it or not, people roamed the earth for millions of years without cell phones."

"Yes, and they're all dead. Just think how much easier their lives would have been with GPS."

"Is that why the dinosaurs went extinct, too? No smart phones?"

"Nope, lung cancer. They were chain smokers." I bite my lip and quell my smile.

He laughs.

I'm about to ask how much longer this drive will be when he flips on the blinker and makes a right-hand turn onto a long cobblestone road canopied with mature trees.

Although the road was seemingly charming at one time, neglect and Mother Nature have taken their toll. Most of the tree branches either droop or have snapped off completely and fallen on the ground. Wind stirs the dried leaves, which litter the pavement, and several landscaping lights that line either side of the drive are either cracked into pieces or missing altogether.

"I haven't been here for a while," Wes says, squeezing the steering wheel tighter; his knuckles flex, and he slows his speed. "It's changed."

"Where are we?"

Before he answers, a small adobe-style chapel comes into view at the end of the road, with heavy iron doors and vines snaking along the stucco.

This must be where Wes married.

Without any comment, Wes parks the car beside the chapel and we step outside. Swirling dust and the smell of rain tickle my nose as we walk across the gravel toward the three stone stairs, leading to the dark arched front doors encased in matching steel, one of which sags from its hinge. Whoever owns this place must be remodeling, for the two front windows are boarded shut and scaffolding surrounds the four walls. Planks of wood are piled in the corner.

"This place sure needs work." He squints as he gazes up toward the belfry.

"Yeah. It's beautiful, though, so quaint and . . ." My voice trails off, not knowing what to say as Wes seems lost in memories.

He shrugs. "I don't know, I just thought you might like to see it."

"I do. Thank you for bringing me here." I peek at the front doors. "I bet it's lovely inside."

"There's a mural of angels painted on the far wall."

A gust of wind forces me a step back and a tumbleweed skips between us and Wes's car. My hair blows wild and sand granules pelt me in the cheek.

"Let's go in," he says.

With my hand shielding my face, I glance at the small gap between the front doors. "Are you sure we should?"

"C'mon. Just for a second. It's miserable out here and we won't hurt anything."

Large drops of rain ricochet off the ground, and the metal poles that support the planks wobble in the wind, squeaking as they flex. The sky has turned an ominous blue-black. Storms in Arizona are fast and deadly. I shout above the wind, "There's a storm coming. Maybe we should head back."

With that said, a wicked grumble of thunder cracks in the sky and a burst of lightning strikes a tree near Wes's car. Rain pours down in sheets, blows sideways in the wind, and splashes our legs and feet. Water, dirt, and leaves surge snakelike between the cobblestones until they overcome the road, and the path to Wes's car is now a river of mud. An Arizona flash flood.

We dunk under the plank and at the same time, another blast of wind flings open the sagging front door.

He points at it. "Now, that's a sign from God."

We hurry inside.

Only shards of light filter through the stained-glass windows, which span the length of each side wall, near the roof line. Exposed and ornately carved wood beams decorate the ceiling and just as Wes said, an arched mural of three flying angels graces the far wall. Underneath the painting sits a rustic cabinet, reaching the width of the room, with a dusty candelabra and several half-burned candles on top. Pews border both sides of the aisle and an altar has been pushed toward the east wall. The entire chapel couldn't hold more than thirty people. It's old. It smells of damp wood and clay. The tile floor is smooth and slippery from a thin layer of dust, which causes me to slip. I grab onto Wes's forearm. "Oh, sorry."

His hand covers mine. "Easy there."

"I'm fine, thanks." I release my hand.

Wind whistles through the boarded windows and there's a kidney-shaped water stain on the wall nearest me. But, like Hollis, age and wear have made the chapel rich with love and history. It's the most romantic place I've ever been.

"It's beautiful." I wrap my arms around myself, chilled from the dampness.

Wes says nothing and I'm touched by the power the memory has for him.

Rain pours through a hole in the roof at the far end, soaks the floor, and catches his attention.

"Over there." I spot a bucket, probably left behind from the construction workers.

Wes hurries and places it under the leak.

We both gaze at the foot-wide hole in the ceiling and the increasingly gloomy sky. At the same time, another gust of wind howls through the chapel, and the front door slams shut, followed by a scraping sound and thud, leaving us in near darkness.

"What was that?" I ask.

"Don't know." Wes steps toward the front. He pushes on the heavy wood door, but it doesn't budge.

"Put your back into it," I tease, but soon discover he's pushing hard. Really hard. "What's wrong?"

"It won't open. I think the scaffolding fell. It's blocking the door."

"Are you serious?"

Wes grunts as he pushes.

I help, but the door resists.

"Is there another way out?" I squint toward the rear of the chapel, but it's lost in the blackness.

"Nope, this is the only door. And I think we'll go straight to hell if we try to kick out the stained-glass windows."

"What are we going to do?"

"I guess we're gonna stay here until the workers show up in the morning. I noticed a tool bag hidden on the side. I bet they'll be here tomorrow."

"Tomorrow?

What about Evan? I can't call him or anything."

"Yeah, that part's no good."

Thunder cracks again and a flash of lightning briefly lights up the chapel.

"Holy crap! Did you see that?" I blurt, then cover my mouth. "I probably shouldn't say *holy crap* in a church."

"Probably not. Stay right here." A moment later, his voice echoes from across the room. "Let there be light," he jokes. Small flames glow beside his face and the darkness lessens, as he lights each candle. Shadows flicker along the walls and the mural illuminates as if lit by heaven itself. Once all our candles are lit, he blows out the match. "Luckily, I found this matchbook in the cabinet."

I sit in the front pew.

He sits beside me.

"We're stuck," I say.

"We are."

"For the night."

"I think so."

"Got anything to eat?"

"No."

"Anything to drink?"

"No."

"I'm craving margaritas."

"You're screwed."

"Yeah."

I trace my finger along the grain in the pew. "Who sat here?"

Wes thinks for a moment. "My dad. Then my mom and sister. My brother stood beside me at the front."

"You're the oldest?"

"Yep."

"Where's your family?"

"Mom and Dad are in Florida and my sister lives in L.A." He stands and walks to the spot, presumably beside where the altar once stood. He kicks at a splinter of wood on the floor. "She was too good for me. I knew it the moment I saw her." He pauses, stuffs his hands in his pockets, and gazes toward the entrance. "But when she stood at those doors in her wedding dress, with the sun haloed behind her, honest to God, I thought she was an angel." He stares at the floor. "I've tried

hard to focus on that memory, block out her pain, the monitors, the hopeless look on the doctor's faces. Her cold hand
in mine. When I think of her now, I try to remember only the
moment when she stood right there, in the doorway."

No wonder it's hard for him to see a woman in a wedding
dress.

"Anyway." He sits beside me and clasps his hands between
his knees. "I guess hearing the talk about your wedding has
surfaced some memories for me, made me remember things
I've forgotten. Made me remember how important love is."
He pauses. "Listen, I shouldn't have said what I did about you
and Evan, earlier. I shouldn't make judgments. I'm sure you
know exactly what you're doing."

"Thanks," I whisper. And although my thoughts are completely unfair and unfounded, I find myself angry with Julie.
I've never met her, never set eyes on the woman, and yet I
want to stand inches from her face, grab onto her shoulders,
and scream. Does she have any idea how lucky she is? Does
she realize what a beautiful heart Wes has? What a tender
soul? She'd better nurture and cherish him. She'd better give
him the love he deserves. She'd better be his angel.

"Enough of that sad stuff." Wes interrupts my inner rant.
He leans against the backrest and says, "We're stuck here for
a while. What should we do?"

I take a moment, clear my head, and then look at him
square in the eye. "You know what I want to do?"

"Run naked through the church?"

"No." I smack him on the shoulder. "This." Before I come
to my senses, I slip out of my tennis shoes, roll up my jeans
two folds, and run toward the front with my palms and back
pressed against the doors. A smile spreads across my lips.

"What are you doing?" Wes stands and watches me.

Without answering, I inhale, find my kiai, and rather than use my kickboxing skills on the door, I sprint as fast as I can in his direction. Once past the second pew, I stop running and slide in my socks. Momentum glides me as I pass the third pew, then the fourth, squealing and slipping in the dust, my arms flailing in the air. "Aagghh." I nearly reach the fifth pew, fall onto my knees, and laugh.

"What are you doing, Lanie?" Wes's sharp voice echoes off the walls. "Don't you know you're in a church? A house of worship?"

Stupid, Lanie. What was I thinking? This place is sacred to him. This place holds his respect for his first love. I've made light of his pain. I scramble onto my feet and apologize. "Wes, I'm sorry, I didn't—hey!" I shout as he darts past me, rips off his shoes, and tosses them aside. Once at the entrance, he spins around, bolts down the aisle, and slides in his socks. He stops an inch or two after the fifth pew.

"That's the best you got?" I draw a line in the dust with my foot where he stopped. "Give me some competition." With a confident stride, I reach the doors, then skate toward him and pass his mark by at least a half inch.

"Whatever." He pushes me aside and tries once more. His arms pump forward and backward, his chin juts in and out, and his face is lined with determination. He picks up speed, gliding fast. Really fast. Odds are, he would've passed my line, easily, if he hadn't caught his foot on the next-to-last pew, lost his balance, and crashed onto his butt.

I shouldn't poke fun. But I do. Obviously. "You looked—" I start to laugh. "You looked—" I laugh harder, so hard I can't manage a complete sentence. I finally compose myself and say,

"You looked like an ostrich with arms." I mimic his pumping arms and jutting chin.

"Shit," he mutters, dusting off his hands.

"You shouldn't say *shit* in church."

He joins my laugh, climbs to his feet, and steps an inch from my face. "All right. Show me how it's done. Five bucks says you can't reach right here." He points on the floor. "Right where I stand." He's a solid foot past the line.

I tap his chest twice and say, "You're on." I stride past him and head toward the entrance. My cheeks have the slightest ache from smiling.

He stands with his feet shoulder width apart and his arms crossed at his chest. "Bring it." He motions me forward with two fingers.

"All right, but I'm not holding back this time. And, when I win, no quarters, or dimes, or pennies. I want a crisp Abraham Lincoln in my palm."

"Just go."

I paw the ground like a bull preparing to charge and, with a smile wider than the church, take off full blast. Hovering my arms for balance, I zoom down the aisle. My socks glide faster than last time and I pick up even more speed. The mark is easily within reach. I'll blow it away. The money is mine.

Except I'm sliding fast. Really fast. Too fast.

Wes must recognize the panic surely plastered across my face and he opens his arms to catch me.

I crash into him and we tumble backward, landing on the hard floor. My body sprawls across his, our legs entwined, our faces inches apart.

Wes groans and his face wrinkles into a grimace.

"Are you okay? Did you hit your head?" I ask, and scan the floor for drops of blood but thankfully don't see any.

"Lanie." His voice is barely above a murmur. With a curled index finger, he motions me closer.

Oh, God. He's really hurt, something must be broken. A femur? Forearm? Dear God, not his back. What if I've paralyzed this poor man?

His breath tickles my skin as he whispers, "Jesus, woman, how much do you weigh?"

"What?" I shoot him a scowl and dig my knee into his thigh as I climb off.

"Ouch." He groans again.

"You owe me five bucks."

We sit beside each other, leaning against the cabinet. Night has completely darkened the church. The candles are still lit, but the flame's light reaches just beyond our feet. The pews and doors are lost in blackness.

Wes says, "You've been rather quiet during the renovation talks. Tell me, Lanie, what would you like to see done with the house?"

"Me?" I do have several ideas. "I'd cut it in half. Maybe fourths. Okay, eighths. It's much too big and ostentatious. It feels like a hotel."

"I can see that."

"And that breakfast nook off the kitchen, it's all boxed in. I'd window that whole wall, open it up, and bring in the outside."

"Good idea."

I sit tall and crisscross my legs, facing him. "If I ever designed a house, it'd be two-story with a double-door entrance. Tall, knotted-wood doors that I could open at the same time and welcome people into my home. You know what I mean? Double doors just seem so inviting. I want four or five steps leading to the entrance so I can set pumpkins on each step. I love decorating for Halloween."

"Okay, what else?"

"I want a master bedroom at the top of a winding staircase with a sitting area by the window, so I can read by natural light. And tiny fiber-optic lights sprinkled in the ceiling above the staircase. Or maybe in the foyer. When you flip the lights on in the evening, they look like stars. I love it. Have you ever seen those?"

"I have." He folds his arms across his chest. The flame casts a shadow across his face.

"Speaking of stars, I've always wanted a huge tree in the backyard." I'm excited now. My words come quickly. "Wouldn't it be cool to read and take naps under the shade of a ginormous tree?"

"It would. What else? An area for Larry Fitzgerald memorabilia?"

"Only if there's room." I laugh and dust a piece of lint off my jeans. "I'd love a separate little space of my own, an office kind of thing. Nothing big, you know, just a spot that I can retreat to, hang a few pictures, maybe a wall of bookshelves. Oh, and I want a greenhouse. I'd plant strawberries, basil, and cilantro." I catch my breath and stop. "Sorry." I wave my hand. "There I go again, talking your ear off."

"It's not so bad."

We sit in silence, until Wes groans, "I'm sore."

"Me, too. My legs are dead. Whose idea was it to skate in socks? That was too much like exercise."

"Hey, look, the rain stopped." Wes points at the ceiling.

I follow his gaze. "Leave it to Arizona. Storms pass as quickly as they come."

The sky has cleared and only remaining drops of rain slide off the roof and into the bucket. Through the hole, hundreds of tiny stars decorate the night sky. They glow brighter and bigger the longer we stare.

"Stars aren't stars, you know," I say to Wes.

"No?"

"Nope. When I was a kid, my dad told me stars are actually peepholes of light from heaven. He said angels get dressed up and love to dance, and when they do, their high heels poke holes in the sky, and out shines the light."

"That's sweet."

"Yeah." I fall quiet, thinking of my dad.

Wes and I say no more. We just stare silently into the night.

⁓

Outside the chapel, voices stir me awake. I lift my head only to realize where I am. And who I'm with. Wes. I slept on his leg, curled on my side with my head on his thigh. His arm wraps around my waist, warm, safe, and heavy. He still leans against the cabinet, his head fallen to one side.

Wes stirs at the screeching sounds outside the front doors.

As soon as he's aware, without a word, he pulls his arm away.

I sit up, mindful of the intimacy and the cold void from the absence of his arm.

Blinding morning sun invades the room as both doors swing open. A short dark-haired man stands in the doorway, a tool belt hanging from his hand. "*Hola*," he calls.

"Hello. Over here." Wes waves. He stands and reaches for my hand to help me up.

We step toward the doors.

"Thank you for opening the doors. I thought we might be trapped in here forever," I say.

The man, shorter than me, smiles with a missing bicuspid. By the look on his face, he didn't understand a word I said. He rattles off something in Spanish, and the look he sees on *my* face assures him I didn't understand a word he said. A year of Spanish in high school, two more in college, and I can't remember anything except *más cerveza, por favor.* Yep, my hard-earned college tuition dollars were spent on *more beer, please.*

"Guess we can go now," Wes says.

"Yeah, guess we can."

We climb into his car and he switches on the windshield wipers, cleaning off the rain spots.

"Thank you for bringing me here."

"Thanks for coming."

My eyes hold on to the reflection of the chapel through my side mirror as we drive away. I wonder how the place will look once restored, once the water stains darkening the stucco dry, the scaffolding is gone, the doors are adjusted, the trees are trimmed, and the hole is patched in the roof. The stars hidden.

There's a qualm rippling through my body. I don't want to leave. I want to stay in the chapel. I want to stay in Wes's arms.

Oh, God. My body tightens and I twist my engagement ring around my finger, staring through the windshield, praying that Wes can't read my thoughts. Wishing I couldn't, either.

I don't see Wes during the day and Evan isn't home when I return from work later that evening. He left a message on my phone, saying several fellow brokers are meeting for dinner, and then he'll start the two-hour drive home.

As I step out of my shoes and line them up beside the entry rug, I feel the moisture in the air from Wes's bathroom. He must've recently showered and left, for the house is quiet. I pour myself a cup of tea and linger in the solitude.

Aimlessly, I meander through the house, straightening the picture on the wall in the entryway, fluffing the couch pillows, three times just as Wes said, and picking a few stray pieces of lint off the armrest. The plants have enough water, the blinds are twisted closed for the night, and the hall bathroom has plenty of toilet paper. Before I realize it, I find myself in the guest bedroom.

Wes's room.

I shouldn't be here. I shouldn't be in his room, invading his space like some sort of creeper. I ignore that voice of reason and convince myself it's technically not his room. Legally or anything.

Slung over the backrest of an armchair is the light brown T-shirt Wes wore to the chapel. Although I specifically order my legs otherwise, they walk over to the chair. I pick up the shirt, soft in my hands, and before I can stop myself, I lift the shirt to my nose and inhale Wes's scent. It smells like oak. It smells like the church. It smells like him.

What are you doing, Lanie? Put the shirt down.

As if the cotton catches ablaze, I throw the shirt onto the

chair, slinging it over the backrest as it was. Something slips from the breast pocket. I reach behind the chair and pick up a small photo, creased and folded in half. I shouldn't open it. It's none of my business. Nothing that concerns me.

Okay, just a peek.

I unfold it and find a picture of a strikingly beautiful woman with olive skin and long dark hair. Julie? She's at the beach, sitting on a blue-and-white striped towel, smiling in her profile at a small boy, probably Trevor, as he digs with sand buckets and shovels beside her. The boy's bottom tooth is missing, leaving an adorable gap. There is a sweet innocence in this boy's eyes. Eyes that share a resemblance to Wes. Eyes that blind me with reason.

Get out of here, Lanie Howard. Get out of here now.

Carefully, I fold the picture and tuck it into the pocket. I clamp my hand around the body of the shirt, making it look messy like it did initially.

Good. He'll never know I was—

"What are you doing?"

I spin around and see Wes standing at the door. He leans against the jamb with his hands folded across his chest.

"Hi, I was, um . . . just looking for my tiara. Yes, my tiara. I thought it was behind this chair, but now I remember it's in the closet. I mean, why else would I be here? In your room." I laugh as if I told a hilarious joke.

He stands still.

"Right. So, anyway, may I?" I point toward the closet.

"By all means."

"Great, thanks." I dig open the top box and pull my tiara free from the bubble wrap. "Here we are. Got it. Got what I came for. Okay, I'll be going now. Excuse me."

"Nice tiara."

"Thanks."

"I can see why you'd want that now, so many years later." There's a tease in his voice.

"It's special to me."

"Aren't you going to wear it?"

"Sorry?"

"Aren't you going to put the tiara on?"

"Right, right. Of course. That's why I'm here." I rest the crown on my head and smile.

"You look ridiculous."

I meet his gaze.

"Lanie," he whispers, his voice slow and thick. His lips inches from mine.

"Yes?" My heart hammers hard enough that I'm afraid he'll spot it through my shirt.

"I, um, you—" At that very moment, his phone rings. The familiar jingle. Once again. And, as if electrocuted, he quickly steps back, stares at the wall behind me, and says, "Excuse me."

"Yes, of course."

He strides toward the front door. "Hey, there, how's Trevor?"

The picture of Julie and Trevor comes to mind. I recall the smoothness in her face, the gap in Trevor's teeth, and the simple beauty of the moment.

The photo was crinkled and lined, like it's been folded and unfolded a thousand times.

Julie. What would she say if she discovered I'd spent the night in Wes's arms? What would she think of me? What would Evan?

The tiara slips from my head and falls onto the floor.

I want to cry.

 ᴄᴏ

Later, it's after eleven o'clock and I lie in bed, waiting for Evan to come home. I contemplate calling Kit, but she's in Maui. The last thing I want to do is sour her trip with my problems. Wes is downstairs. The TV is on a sports show, I think. He's opened the fridge twice, and from the clanking glass, I assume he's retrieved a beer. Wes and I are still alone.

My mind wanders to the familiarity and comfort and confidence I feel when we're together. The safety of his arm wrapped around me. The fact that I long for his touch, even if just a quick brush of our fingers.

I pull the comforter over my head, trying to hide from my musing, trying to block out my feelings, trying to suffocate my conscience, but it doesn't work. *Why can't I get him off my mind? Why can't Wes be more . . . forgettable?*

I punch at the blanket until it slips onto the floor, then let out a long sigh.

It's more than that.

It's more than my feelings for Wes.

It's more than just wedding jitters.

I can't do this.

I can't pretend any longer.

Evan and I need to talk.

twenty-three

I didn't hear Evan come to bed and it isn't until the following morning, when wafts of coffee drift by my nose, that I see him. I open my eyes and find him dressed in the navy suit and tie I bought for him last month, holding four coffees tucked safely inside the cardboard carryout tray. Two dozen roses decorate the nightstand beside me.

"What's all this?" I sit up.

Evan joins me bedside, and says, "Here." He hands me the coffee tray. "I got four different types." He refers to the black hash marks on the side of each cup and says, "This one is a white mocha, this is a macchiato, and this is a—"

"It's okay, Evan. You can set them on the nightstand."

"Listen, I need to apologize. I've been a beast, lately. All this talk about listings and remodels and promotions and wishes has really got me thinking."

"Me, too." I smooth a bedsheet wrinkle with my palm, sigh, then say, "Maybe we're rushing into this. I'm not sure we should—"

"Marry me." Evan interrupts me and by the focused look in his eyes, I'm not certain he heard what I started to say.

"That's what I want to talk to you about. I don't think we—"

"Today."

"What? Today? Why today?" I scrunch the sheets with fisted hands. "What about all of Stacee's plans and the lily centerpieces, and the cranberries, and . . . and why today?"

"I'll call Stacee and write her a check for her effort. Let's hop over to the courthouse this afternoon."

I stare at him confused. "Evan, I—"

"I got to thinking. Remember when Hollis acted surprised that you and I were moving into Orchid Lane before we're married?"

"Yes."

"Let's honor him."

"What?"

"Call me old-fashioned, but let's get married before we move into the house. Speaking of the house, we're going to remove that dining room wall so you can have more light, just as you asked." He chuckles. "You're speechless."

"Evan, this isn't a good idea."

"Are you kidding? This is an excellent idea. Let's be spontaneous. Isn't that what all this Someday Jar business the past few weeks has been about? A little fun? A little impetuousness?"

"I suppose, but—"

"C'mon, love. You and me, the courthouse, four o'clock. We'll spend the night at some swanky hotel and finish what Wes interrupted." He winks. "Let's have some fun together."

I'm shocked. I don't know what to say, so I spout what comes to mind. "Um, I don't have a dress."

"Come with me."

In my pajamas, I follow him downstairs.

A wedding dress drapes across the couch.

Evan gathers the clear plastic covering, bunches it near the hanger, and reveals the sheath gown. Pearls, beaded along the sweetheart neckline, reflect in the sunlight and the ivory-colored silk looks spun from clouds. It's gorgeous. Exactly as I would pick. "Stacee said you left without selecting a dress, so I took the liberty and chose one for you. It's simple, yet classy. Just like I like. And see, here—" He points at the eggshell-colored sash tied into a small bow at the hip. "—It'll match the napkins you selected." With a smile, Evan says, "I'll meet you at the courthouse. Yes?"

Before I answer, Wes steps from his room in a V-neck charcoal sweater and dark jeans. He glances at the gown. "That's a beautiful dress," he says, looking at me.

"Isn't it, though?" Evan says, pleased with his selection and unaware of the static hovering in the air between Wes and me.

I don't turn away, willing Wes to speak. *Tell me the night in the chapel meant something to you. Tell me not to marry Evan. Tell me how you feel. Say something. Anything. Please.*

He doesn't.

With a half nod, he excuses himself and heads toward the front door.

My stomach drops at the sound of it closing behind him.

Gone.

Just like that.

Fine.

Good.

Walk away.

Honestly, what does he expect me to do? Run after him and scream his name? Flag down a cab and whisk through the city streets like in those stupid romantic comedy movies? Does he expect me to chase after him like a schoolgirl with a silly, lustful crush? Isn't this all it is, anyway? Wild pointless thoughts about a man I barely know.

For Christ's sake, Lanie. Forget it. Forget all of it. For the last time, stop thinking about Wes. Stop thinking about his strong hands, his captivating jawline, his gentle nature with Hollis and Maria. Stop thinking how the tips of your fingers tingle every time he says your name. Stop thinking about all of that and start thinking about Julie and Trevor. He's got a family. A boy that desperately needs him. What do I want to do? Break that up? Of course not. Get him out of your head and focus on your future. Focus on Evan.

"Lanie?"

Evan's voice jars my thoughts. I stare into his hopeful eyes.

What I have in front of me is real. It may not be perfect, and we may have our differences, but it's right now. It's here. My future will be set. Never will I have the financial worries that Mom did. Never will I have a tumultuous, roller-coaster life, wondering what lies ahead. My days will be smooth, calm, and consistent. Each day congruous with the next. I've said my whole life that fireworks don't exist. That stability and security are what's important.

I stand beside Evan and realize I haven't given him enough credit. He's steady. He's constant. He colors inside the lines. And what's so wrong with that? He's a spring day with no wind and a chilled glass of wine compared with Wes, who is a sultry summer day and a shot of tequila. Though that may be fun for a while, I know from experience that too much sun blisters my skin and tequila makes me sick.

Evan directs my attention with a shake of the gown. He waits, expecting my answer.

Most women in America wouldn't hesitate to marry someone like Evan Carter. Not even for a fraction of a second.

"Yes," I say with a smile, and accept the dress. "I'll meet you there."

"Wonderful." Evan throws his fists in the air in victory. "You've made me a happy man. Okay, then, I'm off. See you later." He kisses me hard. "Oh, and don't forget to tell Hollis." With a wink, Evan dashes out the door.

Upstairs, I lay the dress on the bed and stare at it for several minutes.

I pick one of the coffees and take a sip, but as soon as the liquid hits my lips, I hurry toward the bathroom sink, and spit it out. Awful.

∽

After a shower, I head downstairs and pop a blueberry bagel in the toaster.

"Hey." Wes's voice startles me from behind.

I spin around. "I thought you left."

"Just took a walk, wanted to give you and Evan some privacy."

I nod, unsure what to say.

Wes steps forward. "So, congratulations are in order."

"Yes, thanks." Right away, I busy myself, cleaning crumbs off the counter, avoiding his eyes. "You probably think it seems hasty, but we decided, why wait?" *You have Julie. I have Evan. That's the hand we've been dealt.*

"Why should you wait?"

I lift my glance and his eyes bore into mine. *Why should you wait?* His voice echoes in my head, over and over. From the corner of my eye, I notice his bags are gathered by the door.

"You're leaving?"

He stuffs his hands in his pockets—I love when he does that—and says, "Yes, I called Evan and told him the plans are essentially done. I'll finish the rest at my office. The City Core opening isn't for a few weeks. It's time I get back home."

"Right. Of course."

"Well, good luck today, Lanie. I'm sure you'll be a beautiful bride."

I chew on my lip. "Thank you."

"I almost forgot." He turns around and grabs a tube lying on top of his bags. Walking back, he shakes out a rolled set of plans into his hand. "Here. These are for you." He offers me the papers.

"House plans?"

"Something like that. Oh, and this." He pulls a small bubble-wrapped package from his bag. "A wedding present for you."

Accidentally-on-purpose, I let his fingers brush mine. "Thank you."

"My pleasure." We stand in awkward silence before he says, "This is silly." With a chuckle he opens his arms for a hug. "Congratulations, Lanie."

I accept his embrace and though I shouldn't, though it's wrong and weak, I linger. I close my eyes and rest my cheek against his chest. Our arms entwined. Our bodies close. There's no denying the draw between us.

It isn't until the doorbell rings that we let go.

"My taxi," he says.

I wipe a tiny tear from my nose. "Sorry, I'm just extra emotional this morning. A big day."

"A big day for sure." He steps back. "Well, good-bye. It was great meeting you."

"You, too."

Walking toward his bags, he slings the empty tube over his shoulder, opens the door, and disappears outside.

The moment he's gone, my body feels hollow, disconnected from reality, like some sort of bad dream. Before I can stop my legs, I run outside, toward the taxi. "Wes!" I shout.

He turns around and walks toward me.

My palms are sweating and my mouth has forgotten how to move. Wiping my hands on my pants, somehow I manage, "You're really leaving?"

Wes's jawbone flexes beneath his cheeks as he glances at the ground and shifts his feet before looking back at me. "Can you give me a reason to stay?"

There are a million reasons for him to stay, but only one— the most important reason—for him to go. *Julie.*

I reach my arm across my chest and clasp my bicep, pinching it tight. *Damn!* Honestly, what does he want me to say? *Stay. Stay because I might be in love with you.*

"Aren't you getting married today, Lanie?" Wes asks.

It's as if he slapped me across the face. "Yes." I wring my hands together. "I am. Four o'clock. I just thought you might like to stay and see the wedding."

"Nah," Wes says with a short tone. "You know how I feel about a girl in a wedding dress."

Wes climbs into the cab and disappears into traffic.

This time, he's truly gone.

Inside the condo, I toss the plans into the spare bedroom closet and pretend not to notice how much the room smells like Wes. I close the door and shut out Wes and my childish fantasies behind me. For good.

I return to the kitchen and unwrap Wes's present. Tears flow from my eyes as a Larry Fitzgerald bobblehead rests in my palm.

twenty-four

At the office, a few hours later, I think of the Someday Jar and the slips I've pulled out. Kit was right. Stepping out of my comfort zone and tackling these challenges has given me confidence. Yes, the slips have been good for me. All of them. Of course, I haven't technically made broker and there are one or two slips left, one being unquestionably difficult, but overall, I've done pretty well. And, today my focus will be on the wedding.

God, I wish Kit were back from her vacation. She could walk me down the aisle. Never did I think I'd get married without her present. Or my mom. Or Dad.

Before I back out of the parking spot toward home to get ready for the courthouse, my phone rings.

I fumble for it, buried deep in my purse, and on the fourth ring, I answer, "Hello?"

"Lanie-Lou, it's Hollis."

At once, my mood lifts. "How are you?" I switch off the engine.

"Fine as frog's hair," he replies. "You?"

"Fit as a fiddle."

"Hey, I read a good obituary yesterday."

"Oh yeah? What'd it say?"

"Not much on how the guy died, but what caught my eye was the funeral will be held at Hooter's. All-you-can-eat hot wings, but there's a two-drink minimum. Want to be my date?"

"Sure."

Hollis's breathing turns into a raspy cough.

"Have you had that cough checked out?" I ask.

"Rubbish." He pants. "Doctors are rubbish. They'll just pump me full of medicines. I'm dizzy enough without drugs interfering."

"Dizzy?"

"Damn. Don't tell Bevy I said that. She'll cane me with my walking stick if she knows."

"Hollis?"

With a somber voice, Hollis says, "Lanie, it's time."

"Time for what?"

"We need to sell the house. It's more than I can handle. Yesterday, I sat down twice in the hallway because the damn kitchen is clear across the other side of the house. It's too big for my tired body."

"Hollis—"

"Yeah, yeah. So it goes. I hate to leave."

"I thought you listed it with your nephew?" It occurs to me I never saw the listing on our database.

"He's a schmuck. He passed the listing on to some newbie agent whose idea of marketing residential properties is posting the house on Craigslist and a friend's blog. His friend sells air compressors. I unlisted the house with him today."

"Sorry, Hollis."

"No, don't be. I'm the one who's sorry. I want you to list the house, should've done it days ago."

My excitement swells like a balloon. I maintain my composure and reply, "I'm honored. Want to come by tomorrow? I'll have the papers ready."

"Tomorrow? Won't you be on your honeymoon? Evan called this morning."

Oh, right. I thought he told me to call. He must be excited. Well, I'm sure Evan won't mind. In fact, the Murphys' listing will be like a wedding present. "We aren't going out of town or anything. Shall we say ten o'clock? Does that leave enough time for your morning swim?"

"Ten, it is. I'm gonna rest now. See you tomorrow, Lanie."

"Looking forward to it, Hollis. Take care."

"Don't worry." His breathing is labored. "I'll have a candy cane for you. Do you remember why?"

"Because every girl needs a candy cane."

"That's right," he replies with satisfaction. "That's right, indeed."

"Good-bye, Hollis."

"Woo-hoo!" My screams echo in the car. The Murphys want to list their house with me. Me. I can't believe it! I did it. I secured the Valley's most coveted listing. And I did it before we got married. I did it on my own. And now, Evan will grant me a partnership. This is so fantastic. Today has turned out to be a fantastic day.

Oh, but wait . . . the wedding. I'd really like to check the latest pending and expired listing reports before the Murphys come in tomorrow, make sure I'm prepared for any questions Bevy might ask. Given the nature of this deal, I bet Evan won't mind postponing our ceremony for a day or two. Besides, after the Murphys sign the papers, we'll have even more to celebrate.

~

"Evan, guess what?" I blurt as he answers my call. "Hollis called."

"And?" His voice fills with anticipation. "Is he coming to the wedding?"

"Better. He wants to stop by the office tomorrow at ten o'clock and list the house with me. List the house, Evan. Isn't that awesome?"

"You're kidding. Goddammit, Lanie, that's incredible news. I knew the wedding would work."

"What?"

"It's nothing, really. I just knew he'd be impressed with our nuptials."

"Right, well, not only did I secure the most desired listing in the Valley, but remember, you promised me a partnership."

"Let's get the listing signed first. Job well done." He's happy. "Very well done."

"Thanks, Evan." I pause. "Actually, there's one more thing."

"Anything. You name it. Damn, Lanie. Nice work."

"Well, that's the thing. There's quite a bit of paperwork I need to prepare before they come in tomorrow. Would you mind if we postponed—"

"Postponed their signing?" Evan interrupts.

"Not the meeting. The wedding."

"Oh." He hesitates. Finally he says, "I guess that would be best."

"Okay, good. I'm staying here at the office, then. Lots to do."

Stepping from my car, I replay Hollis's voice in my mind. He didn't sound good. I hope Bevy persuades him to see a doctor soon.

Once inside the soon-to-be Evan Carter and Lanie Howard-Carter Realty office, I retrieve the listing documents. My feet bounce around the office as if there are mini-trampolines attached to my shoes. I'm so dang excited. And proud of myself.

I dig for my Someday Jar in search of the Broker slip. The first one I unfold reads *Broker*. Perfect.

The office line rings, and after I answer questions on a triplex in Mesa, I tackle the stack of listing documents and then get started. I want to have most of the paperwork completed ahead of time so the Murphys won't have to stay long.

After three and a half hours, I've completed the exclusive listing agreement, the seller's agency disclosure, the swimming pool addendum, and a dozen other forms equivalent to an entire tree in paper. Here I thought we lived in an environmentally friendly world. I also generated a trifold brochure, accentuating the features of the gorgeous property. I've highlighted the many areas requiring their signatures, and once they've signed, I'll schedule an appointment with our photographer. While he shoots pictures, I'll measure the rooms and compile the list of amenities for the Property Detail Sheet.

I can't wait to see my name as broker on this property. But more than that, I can't wait to get this house sold, alleviating some stress for my sweet old friend.

⌒

Early the next morning, my cell phone vibrates across the dresser and wakens me. Scrambling out of bed, I hurry toward it, but am too late. *Missed Call* highlights my screen. Beside my phone is a note jotted by Evan. *Stopping by the house this morning, before heading to the office. Big day.*

What time is it? My phone blinks 7:00 a.m. Evan got an early start. I glance at my phone again, still not recognizing the number. Must be important to ring this early, so I return the call.

"Hello," a man's voice answers.

"This is Lanie Howard. I believe you tried to call me a minute ago."

"Lanie, yes, hello. My name is Tucker. I'm the Murphys' caretaker."

"Yes, good morning," I reply, wondering why his voice shakes.

"I'm calling about the meeting planned for ten o'clock this morning."

Oh no. Please don't tell me they've changed their mind. Please don't tell me their nephew's friend's blog got a hit and the house sold. "Yes, I'm looking forward to it." Caution laces my words.

"About that," Tucker starts.

"Is there a problem?"

"Mr. Murphy suffered a stroke last night. He didn't recover. He died a few hours ago."

My legs waiver and I grab onto the dresser for support, but still, I fall to my knees. I press the phone close to my ear, hoping I heard him wrong. "What? How did he . . . is he . . . oh, God." Tears soak my cheeks. "He died?"

"Mrs. Murphy wanted me to call you."

"Yes, thank you," I stutter through sobs. I feel dizzy and my breathing is labored like I just ran ten miles. *Hollis.*

"Okay, miss. I'm going to hang up now."

"Wait!" I scream and clutch the phone as if keeping Tucker on the line is somehow holding on to Hollis. "Do you know about services?"

"Not yet. Mrs. Murphy mentioned waiting a few days, allowing time for all the kids to come home. I'll be sure and let you know."

"Thank you, Tucker."

"Yes, ma'am." He hangs up. Just like that, Hollis is gone.

The phone slips from my fingers and onto the floor. I cover my face with both hands and cry. Not because of the stupid listing or the lost commission, but because this sweet old man who smelled like mothballs and granola is gone. No more long hugs. No more stories. No more candy canes.

"Dammit!" I scream, feeling sorry for myself, wishing I had a shoulder to cry on, someone to hold me. Wes's face pops into my mind. I shake my head. *Foolish girl.* Quickly, I gather my purse and head out the door. Evan. I need to find Evan.

Evan's Mercedes is in the driveway of Orchid Lane along with a silver Tahoe that I don't recognize. One of the subcontractors? I pull behind Evan's car. Before I step out, I let a wave of emotions overcome me and cry for several minutes. When my tears run dry, I catch my reflection in the rearview mirror. My face is blotchy and my eyes are swollen. I haven't changed out of my PJs, or brushed my teeth, or combed my hair.

Who cares what I look like? All I want is to be held and cry more about Hollis.

The front door is locked, but the side garage door is open. Once inside, I step over plastic drop cloths, five-gallon paint buckets, and boxes of twenty-inch travertine tiles.

"Evan?" I call, my voice echoing in the vacant house. He's not in two of the guest bedrooms, the living room, or the den. Drywall dust accumulates on my shoes as I near the kitchen. It's not until I turn the corner that I hear gasps of breath and some sort of knocking. *Dear God, Evan, are you okay?*

I hurry through the threshold.

Evan's bare ass is the first thing I see. His pants and paisley silk boxers pool above his loafers, while his hands grasp either side of—*holy shit*—Stacee's hips. Her skirt is gathered above her waist. Bent over, she braces herself with palms pressed into the granite countertop. My wedding coordinator screams, "More, Evan. Give it to me! More."

Wait a minute? She's wearing a veil. My veil.

Evan smacks her on the ass.

It's then, I burst out laughing.

They both turn around.

"Oh, God!" Stacee screams.

Evan pulls away from her. "Lanie, shit." He hikes his pants and secures his belt.

Stacee rips the veil from her head and splits her skirt, pulling it down with such haste.

"Lanie, it's not what—"

I hold up my hand to stop him. Not because I'm hurt or mad or crying, but because I can't stop laughing. With my other hand I clutch my stomach and squeak out, "Give me a second. Let me catch my breath. Oh, God, this is hilarious." Between belly laughs I say, "You guys, are . . . oh, God . . ." I can't stop laughing. I can't. "Is this how you're repaying her, Evan? She's . . ." My words cut short between my laughter. "She's getting cheated. Oh . . . this is so funny . . . you two are such a cliché."

"Lanie, why are you laughing? Please let me explain."

I hardly hear his words. My laughter reverberates through the house, drowning Stacee's embarrassed squeals as she slips into her shoes and gathers her things. This is so funny. So goddamn funny. But then, in a moment of clarity, I stop laughing.

"Are you okay?" Evan asks.

"I just thought of something."

Evan asks with eyes more tender than a week-old puppy, "What is it, love?"

"Paige will be pissed." I try to say this with a straight face, but I can't, and before long, my hysterics become too much and I snort, which makes me laugh even more. "I'm so much better than this. So much better. Oh, God, I've gotta go before I pee my pants."

Evan stares at me, stunned, his face drained of color.

Stacee scrambles like a rabid animal into her underwear, catching her foot on the lace. She falls forward onto the floor.

I belt out another snort. I can't stop. I just can't stop. Tears drip from the corners of my eyes, my cheeks ache, and my hand grasps my belly. It's then I think of my Someday Jar. I throw my hand in the air, then say in between laughs. "Hang on a second."

Digging through my purse, I find my jar and dump out a couple of slips. I find the one I need and keep the other in my palm. I face the slip toward Evan.

"*Laugh until tears run down my face,*" he says.

I catch my breath with a smile stretching the width of my face. "Yes. Thank you, Evan."

"For what?"

"For helping me with my Someday Jar. I know how much

you've supported it along the way. Oh wait, you didn't." I spin on my heel, head toward the front door, and fling the heavy, expensive door wide open. It smacks hard against the wall, chipping off a piece of paint.

Who gives a fuck?

It's not my house.

⤿

Two hours have passed and my frame of mind has settled to sadness. My head pounds from the storm of emotions as I sit at the coffee shop that Hollis and I frequented. The same table where he insisted on keeping the dent I caused in his truck in place. The same table where only a cup of coffee would suffice for payment. I'll miss that man. *Hollis. Sweet, sweet Hollis.*

I catch my reflection in the window. My eyes are swollen and my hair is frizzed. I look like hell. It's more than Hollis. Today Evan cheated on me and regardless of the state of our relationship, that always sucks. Staring at myself, I realize I'm alone. No one but myself to feel sorry for me. Kit's in Maui. Mom and I haven't spoken since dinner at Ivy House. Wes left. Now Hollis is gone, too.

Right then and there, I realize there's only one person for me to turn to.

The last slip from my jar.

After a quick shower and twenty minutes scouring through my boxes in Evan's closet—thankfully, he doesn't come home—I find what I'm looking for. I hop into my car and follow the familiar side streets until I park underneath the Golden Lantern restaurant's sign. It's here I feel the closest to him, the most strength.

My fingers quiver as I dial the number I retrieved and the

phone nearly slips from my palm, but I can do this. I can. I grip the receiver tighter, listening to the line ring while glancing at the childish handwriting on the slip in my lap.

The connection is poor and I'm not sure the number is still good. After a half dozen rings, I'm ready to hang up when a man's voice answers the phone. A familiar voice.

"Hello?"

"Hi, Dad."

twenty-five

We talk and cry for two hours, unearthing and burying the pain we've each felt over the years. Our perspective about the past is different, but our hurt is the same. We've both decided not to waste any more time, wipe the slate clean, start anew.

I tell him about E, kickboxing, scuba, Larry Fitzgerald, and all that I've accomplished with the Someday Jar. I tell him about Hollis and Evan. I tell him about my plans. I tell him I love him.

We hang up and with a newfound vitality, I'm ready to take a stand in my life. I hadn't realized what my future holds until I said it out loud to Dad and, with his words of encouragement, I'm off. I've got a lot to do.

It isn't ten minutes later that my phone chimes with an e-mail. My dad's itinerary shines on my screen. He's flying to Phoenix next month.

Fueled with energy by both love from my dad and anger toward Evan, I head toward the office.

Once inside, I scroll through my Rolodex and find the number.

Chett answers on the second ring. "Arizona Department of Real Estate, licensing."

"Chett. Hey, it's Lanie."

"Hey, Lanie, how are you?"

"Great. Listen, I need a favor."

"Anything."

"Would you mind faxing me a broker change form?"

"Sure, I'll send it right now. But why?"

"You'll find out soon enough." The fax machine rings behind me. "How long does it take to process?"

"Seven days unless you know people."

"Do I know people?"

"You do."

"Thanks, Chett. I owe you one."

"I'll keep you in mind when I need a kidney transplant or something."

"Fair enough."

We hang up and I retrieve my form. After filling out the necessary questions and signing on the dotted line, I fax it back to Chett and leave a copy on Evan's desk.

The computer warms up and while I'm waiting I decide to make a few calls. First to Larson. He answers on the first ring.

"Larson, it's Lanie."

"Lanie, you say? Is this by chance the same Lanie that paraded around the University of Phoenix football field?"

"You saw that?"

"Are you kidding? The entire country saw that. It was an ESPN highlight."

"Oh, God."

"Ah, forget about it. Did you have fun?"

"You know, Larson, I had a blast. That's one reason why I'm calling, to thank you."

"No problem, I'm glad you enjoyed the day. Besides, you've done so much for me the past few months, it's the least I can do."

"It's been my pleasure and I'm not giving up. I'll find you the perfect home."

"I have no doubt."

"That's sort of the other reason why I'm calling. I wanted to tell you personally that I will no longer be at Evan Carter Realty. Effective today."

"Really? Why not?"

"Oh, Larson, it's a long story." I stop and think, no, it's not. It's rather short. "Truth is, Evan was screwing our wedding planner. I caught them this morning."

"No shit?"

"No shit."

"Lanie, I'm sorry."

"Thanks, but it's okay. It was a swift kick in my rear. I needed it."

"What are you going to do? Are you going to get a job at another real estate company?"

"No." I take a deep breath. I haven't revealed my plan to anyone yet, except my dad. Only said it out loud once to myself.

"Lanie? You still here?"

"Yes, sorry. I'm here." After a deep breath, I say, "No, I'm not going to another company because I'm going to start my own. I'm opening Lanie Howard Realty." Wow. That sounds amazing out loud.

"Good for you. You'll be a dynamo in the business. Watch out, Phoenix, here she comes."

"Thanks for the vote of confidence. Listen, when I find the

perfect house, mind if I call you?" I ask, remembering that he never signed a buyer's broker agreement. He's not contractually bound to Evan.

"I'll be waiting by the phone. Take care."

We hang up and I call a few more of my favorite clients—not to lure them away from Evan, well, sort of—but also to make sure they know the situation. Most of our clients talk entirely with me, meeting with Evan only if they pass each other in the office. I've developed a friendship with these people and that's by far the hardest thing to leave. I'll miss the weekly updates of bridge game scores, fudge plates at Christmas, and "my grandson did the funniest thing the other day" kind of stories. So more than anything, I don't want them feeling neglected.

While I'm on the phone, Evan walks in, holding a huge bundle of pink roses. He winks at me and mouths, *I'm sorry*. He sets the bouquet on my desk, wipes his hands on one another, and heads inside his office with an air about him that suggests his escapade was nothing more than a blip on the radar.

I toss the flowers in the trash.

Evan returns a moment later as I hang up the phone. "What's this?" He waves the broker change form in his hand.

"Exactly what it says. I am no longer affiliated with you or this office."

"Lanie?" He steps close and with a patronizing tone, says, "What are you doing?"

"Leaving."

"C'mon, we had a bump in the road, but let's move on. You don't want to do this." He points at the paper.

"A bump?" I scoot back in my chair, distancing myself from him. "You call screwing Stacee a bump in the road? You can't be serious."

He throws his hands in the air in surrender. "You're right. I'm a fool. I'm sorry. Look, I've been busy lately, stressed out about work and the house. The thing with Stacee, it just happened. It's not like I snuck around behind your back."

"Technically you were behind Stacee's back."

"We can work this out. You don't need to leave."

"Maybe I don't need to, but I want to. There's a difference. A huge difference." I gather my things and place them in an empty Xerox paper box.

He crumples up the paper and throws it in the trash, frowning as he notices the flowers. "Well, I don't accept your resignation."

"Too bad. The Department of Real Estate already has a copy. Here is your ring." I drop it on the desk.

His tenderness is quickly replaced with irritation. He folds his hands across his chest. "What are you going to do, Lanie? Get a job at Kinko's?"

"Clearly, you weren't worried about me earlier. Why start now?"

"This is a big mistake. You can't leave."

"Oh, but I can. It just took me a while to figure that out." With a thrust kick, which I learned last week from Rudy—thank you very much—I swing open the front door.

Even though my future is uncertain and the box I'm carrying is heavier than hell, I've never felt lighter on my feet. I've never felt more confident. I've never felt more alive.

I set my box in the backseat, pull out of the parking spot, and leave Evan Carter Realty behind.

twenty-six

With Evan at the office, it's a perfect time to gather my belongings from the condo. There really isn't much, besides clothes, toiletries, and the boxes in the guest bedroom closet. The rest of my life is in storage since it didn't blend with the decor of the condo. Funny, I never saw that as a sign we were doomed from the start. After a few full armloads of stuff, I'm done.

As I scan the condo, with all my items removed, there really is no visible difference of my presence. Almost like I was never here.

Even though it was surprisingly easy to walk away from the condo, I feel dull when I climb into my car, alone. Where am I going to go tonight? Kit's on vacation. I can't bear the thought of a hotel. That seems depressing and somehow gives Evan the upper hand. So, I do what any twenty-seven-year-old dreams of: I go to my mommy's house.

"Oh, Lanie." There's relief in her voice and tears in her eyes as she opens the door and motions me inside. "I've called you a million times."

"I know."

"Come in, sweetie. Please, please, come in."

I smile weakly and step into the family room. I'm still upset, but after reconnecting with Dad, aware of the precious time lost with him, I don't want to do the same with her. Avoiding Mom doesn't solve anything. I plop on the couch and she sits beside me.

"I'm glad you're here. I've been such a mess since we fought. You haven't returned my calls." Tears pour from her eyes. "I feel awful."

I reach for her hand and say, "Mom, I'm really upset about what you did. You took time away from me, time with my dad that I'll never get back."

"I know." She nods and strokes my hand with hers. "I thought I was doing the right thing, protecting you from his reckless behavior and indifference toward stability. I'm aware now how much I hurt you and for that, I'll always . . ." Her voice trails off, her shoulders tremble, and she breaks into sobs.

I pull her close for a hug. Soon, I start to cry. She squeezes me tighter. We comfort each other.

We hold one another for a long time and though I'm still mad—probably always will be to some degree—I can't fault her for doing what she thought was best for me. Even if I disagree. I choose to look on the bright side. My dad is coming to visit. He and I can make up for lost time.

We pull apart and Mom grabs each of my hands in her own.

She notices my empty ring finger. "Heavens. Where's your ring?"

"Evan and I broke up, Mom."

"No!" She gasps as if I were pregnant with a serial killer's child.

"Yep." I nod.

"You aren't getting married?"

"Nope."

"What happened?"

"I caught Evan and Stacee in a compromising position."

"That sweet wedding planner?"

"The very one."

Mom frowns. "Honey, maybe you're jumping to conclusions."

"The sweet wedding planner was bent over the kitchen counter and my bare-assed fiancé was screwing her. What conclusion should I come up with?"

"Must you be so vulgar?" she scolds, then pats my knee. "Call Evan and tell him you've reconsidered. Use the phone in the kitchen."

"No." I let out a little laugh. "God, you're incredible."

"Lanie, Evan slipped. Is that really such a big deal? Men have needs, you know."

"Yes, Evan's needs were to keep me under his thumb and have me do all the work at the company, without the credit, while he had fun on the side. Isn't that like having your cake and eating it, too?"

"I don't know—"

"And the other thing, I quit."

"You didn't?"

"I did."

"Oh, for goodness' sake." She places two fingers inside her wrist, checks her pulse, and counts to herself. After a moment she says, "No worries, I'm fine. Tell me, what are you going to do now?"

"Open my own business," I say decisively.

"Was this one of your slips?"

"Nope. But the Someday Jar taught me I could do it. I'm going to be my own boss."

"This world is tough, Lanie. Things don't always turn out as planned."

"I know that. I know that as well as anyone."

"Honey, there are a lot of challenges and uncertainties with a business. Hands on or not, Evan was instrumental in the company. How do you plan to pull this off by yourself?"

"By myself? That's the least of my worries. I have money saved. I've projected my expenses and I can cover my startup costs, utilities, and at least six month's rent for an office space. In fact, there is a place on Twenty-fourth Street that'd be perfect."

"Evan is a good man. If you don't march down to the office and tell him so, you'll regret it forever. You can't expect perfection."

"I don't expect perfection, Mom. I do expect respect."

"It's a minor indiscretion," she pleads. "I wouldn't throw him out over this tiny issue. Think of your future. Trust me, Lanie, a solid man—"

"Mom, stop! This is my life," I say with fire in my words. "Not yours."

Her shoulders slump in defeat and she purses her lips. "You're right. I haven't made the best decisions. Who am I to tell you what to do?"

"It isn't your fault, or mine, that you fell in love with a man who didn't sign up for happily ever after."

She sighs.

"I know what I'm doing." I rub along her back. "It's funny; since I caught Evan and Stacee, I've felt this relief, like a weight has been lifted off my shoulders. I feel carefree. Alive. I'm excited and I have a new sense of direction. Yes, it scares me to death to take on this adventure, deplete my cash savings, and jump into a new business, but I've never felt more inspired. This is the very feeling Dad wanted me to find. This is what the Someday Jar is all about. I have no idea what tomorrow may bring, but I'll tell you what, I'm not going to fret about it, or let negative thoughts scare me away from my future."

Mom reaches out for me and hugs me close, nearly choking me. "Mom—" I tap her shoulder. "I can't breathe."

"Oh, honey." She swipes away a tear. "You're much smarter than I am. Much, much smarter."

"And another thing, I called Dad."

Her eyes catch mine. "You did?"

"I did."

"He's flying here in a couple of weeks."

"To see you?"

"Yes."

"Oh, Lanie. I'm so glad. Distancing you from your dad was beyond incomprehensible. I've been a mess these few days, realizing what I'd done. Regardless of my feelings toward him, I had no right to take him away from you."

"No, you didn't. But let's not focus on the past. Let's focus on the future." I give her hand a squeeze and say with a wink, "Besides, he asked about you."

"Me?" Her face lights up.

"Yep."

"Oh, my." She laughs and we hug again.

When we part, I ask, "Can I stay here for a little while, just until I get things settled?"

She presses her palm against my cheek. "You stay as long as you like."

"Thanks."

"Oh, and Tuesday is half price at St. Vinny's. We'll go shopping."

Her enthusiasm is hard to resist. "Okay, sounds great."

"You go upstairs and get yourself squared away. I'll take some chicken out of the freezer for dinner. I'm so glad you're here."

Evan doesn't call in the evening and I'm thankful for it. I don't know what we'd say, anyway. Besides, I've been too busy to talk. I've scheduled a preview of the commercial space for the morning, submitted all my fees online for a broker's license, and while Skyping, E and I came up with a fancy slogan for my business cards: *Lanie Howard Realty—Making Your Someday . . . today.*

Early the following morning, I meet the property manager at the office space on Twenty-fourth. Located within a strip mall, between a Whole Foods and a Chase Bank, it's a perfect location with lots of foot traffic.

She invites me inside after unlocking the front door and flipping on the lights. "Go ahead, take a look."

Filled with several desks and chairs, the space is large and bright. Near the front window is a reception area, and hidden under a sheet is a wingback chair, leather couch, and wood coffee table flipped upside down on top of the sofa's cushions. The ceiling fans look new, the walls are painted a soft silver-sage, and the Berber-style carpet is cream-colored. *Is that ecru or eggshell?*

"Something funny?" she asks.

"No, nothing, sorry."

"Well, what do you think of the place?"

It's even better than I hoped. But without revealing my

excitement, I saunter toward the glass-walled corner office in the rear. *Lanie Howard* could be etched on the door. My stomach flitters like a thousand butterflies took flight.

"A galley-style lounge area with a refrigerator and round table are opposite the bathroom," the manager says, pointing in that direction.

"Interesting. Does all the furniture stay?" I ask with a nonchalant tone.

She refers to the listing. "Yes. All furnishings are included."

"Something to consider, then." I wonder how long I need to scan the ceiling for leaks or open several of the desk drawers before I can scream, *I'll take it! I'll take it right now!*

Luckily she puts me out of her misery and says, "It's a steal at twenty-eight hundred dollars a month, and won't be on the market long. In fact, I've got another showing at—"

"I'll take it."

"Wonderful. I brought a lease agreement with me. You'll want possession when?"

"Right away."

"Super. I'll draw up the paperwork."

"Thank you."

As she fills in the blanks of the contract, I study the space. With a little elbow grease, a few plants and bright-colored pillows from Ikea—maybe burnt orange?—this place can be perfect. The desks are a bonus and they'll save me a bundle of money.

"Okay, Ms. Howard. I need your signature here and here." She points at two separate locations. After quickly reading the standard rental agreement, I sign.

"All right, let's see what I need to collect from you today." She punches numbers into her phone's calculator.

My heart palpitates as I write out the check. Not only for the serious ding to my bank account, but because I'm doing this. *I really am.*

"Wonderful," she says, handing me the keys. "I'll e-mail you copies of the lease agreement. Anything else before I go?"

"No, thank you. You've been very helpful."

"All right, then." She heads toward the door. "Good luck to you, Ms. Howard."

"Thank you." My hands clamp over the shiny key.

After she leaves I jump up and down and let out a little shriek.

Holy hell, Lanie. You did it!

twenty-seven

Hollis Murphy regrets to announce the passing of himself. Born November 11, he kicked the bucket after living longer than some probably wanted and probably longer than he deserved, based on his diet of bacon, cream soda, and Three Musketeers candy bars—a surprisingly tasty combination. He hoped to have died from something exciting like a space-borne alien parasite, blown to smithereens after diving over a detonated nuclear device, thus saving the entire world from ruin.

Hollis enjoyed swimming in the nude (you're welcome for the image); chasing his glorious wife, Bevy, around the house with a pair of snapping tongs; and turning wine into urine. His life on earth was splendid and, though he likely used all his luck married to his cream puff, he asks for a bit more. Bury him facedown and ass up so his grandchildren have a place to park their bikes.

A separate sentence followed.

The Murphy family has requested privacy in their grief.

I sit in the coffee shop near Mom's house and read the obituary a dozen times, knowing full well those are Hollis's own words and charm, but hoping I've gotten it wrong. Hoping it doesn't say *Hollis Murphy.* Hoping Tucker's phone call was just a dream.

But it wasn't. Hollis will no longer hug me or tell me a funny story. He'll no longer brighten my day. Hollis is gone.

Tucker left a message a couple days ago, inviting me to attend a celebration of Hollis's life at the Hyatt Regency Club in Scottsdale.

"Lanie." Kit waves from across the room.

"Kit!" I scream like a four-year-old on Christmas morning and rush into my BFF's arms as she nears the table, thankful for her cheery face. "Look at you. You're so tan." She dances around, showing herself off. "Maui looks great on you."

"Doesn't it? We spent tons of time on the beach. Lanie, we had the best vacation." She sits across from me. "You should've seen my husband, all relaxed and spontaneous. Island Rob, I called him, and he was fantastic."

"Sounds like a blast. You guys deserve it."

"Thanks," she says, and I swear I see pineapples flickering in her eyes. I already ordered and the barista calls out our drinks.

I return with our coffees and Kit says, "What's with you?" She tosses her purse onto the nearby chair and studies me. "You look different. Have you changed moisturizers or something? You're glowing. Oh my God, are you pregnant?"

"No, no, no." I laugh at the thought. "Not even close. I did land a spinning back fist at Rudy's the other day, knocked the bag over and everything."

"Wow. I always knew you had a bad-ass in you somewhere. But that's not it?"

"Nope. A lot has happened while you were drinking mai tais on the beach."

"Mudslides." She corrects me. "Go on."

I count on my fingers. "I got in a whopper of a fight with Evan, spent the night in a church with Wes, lost a dear client, lost my broker promotion, caught Stacee wearing my veil while my fiancé was screwing her, broke up with said fiancé, quit my job, called my dad who, by the way, is flying out soon, made up with my mom, and fell in love with Wes." Not sure where the last part came from. It sort of slipped out.

Kit stares at me with her mouth half open.

I take a sip of coffee and let her process.

"Jesus, Lanie. I was only gone a week."

"I've been a busy girl."

"I don't know where you should start." She shakes her head, and then, in a moment of decisiveness, points at me. "Wes. Tell me about him first."

"Aren't you curious about Evan?"

"Nah, he's a schmuck."

"You never told me that."

"Looks like you figured it out on your own, sweetie." She blows on her coffee.

"Well, it doesn't matter how I feel about Wes. He's gone, back to his family in California." I pause for a moment, flick a piece of lint off my sleeve, let out a deep sigh, and blink away the gathering tears in my eyes.

"You know, I've learned that you can't make someone love you. All you can do is stalk them, hope they panic, and give in."

"You always know how to make me feel better."

"It's a gift."

I dig into my purse. "There's more."

"More?"

The key catches the sun as I dangle it between my fingers. "You're sitting across from a business owner. Lanie Howard Realty."

"Swear?"

"Swear."

Kit rushes toward me, practically tackling me with a hug. "Lanie, I'm so proud of you." Her voice mumbles and tickles my neck. "So damn proud of you."

I rattle off all the details, and bless Kit's heart, she sits and listens to every word as if I'm explaining the location of the coveted Holy Grail. She asks about the unit, the color of the walls, and Evan's face when I told him. We leave the coffee shop and Kit insists on driving me over to pick up the box of my business cards from Kinko's.

She takes the first one.

twenty-eight

"Hold it together, Lanie," I whisper while staring at my image in the elevator's mirrored paneling. "Hollis wouldn't want you sad."

"Regency Pool Level," chimes the elevator voice as the doors whoosh open at the top level of Scottsdale's Hyatt Hotel.

"Welcome. Thank you for coming." A suited gentleman in black tie stands outside the elevator. He smiles, then motions beyond the covered walkway, lined with flowers and various pictures, black-and-white framed photos of Hollis in his younger days. I stop and look at them, enjoying the glory of the old man. A couple in particular catch my eye.

One is a side shot of a younger Hollis, probably early twenties. He wears a pair of high-waisted bathing shorts; sand sticks to his shins. He points at a pier stretching into the ocean.

There's another from the same beach. This time, it's taken from behind as Hollis, and presumably Bevy, walk along the shoreline. She wears a floral swimsuit and large straw hat with one hand holding it from taking flight. Hollis's arm is wrapped around his wife's waist.

I think of Wes and his arm draped around me while we slept in the chapel, heavy and warm. *I miss him.*

The elevators chime open and other guests arrive.

Quickly, I trace the curve of Hollis's smile before moving outside toward the gathering, and once through the walkway, I join the large crowd.

Women dressed in heels and men in suits and ties quietly sip white wine and speak in soft tones. Several waiters with black shirts and ties meander about, offering appetizers and square napkins from silver platters. The poolside lounge chairs and tables have been stored and replaced with white wood folding chairs positioned toward the imminent sunset. The stickiness from spilled daiquiris and the smell of sunscreen have been washed from the flagstone ground, the pool towels folded and hidden from view. A few people part and between the bodies, I see the long, rectangular pool glisten in the sun. A beautiful reminder of a beautiful man.

I marvel at the serenity of the afternoon and accept a glass of wine. Without trying to stare, I look for Bevy. I'd love to see the woman who captivated Hollis.

Within moments, a man with a hint of gray hair sprinkled above his temples stands on the far end of the pool and commands our attention. He smiles and his face shapes into a younger version of Hollis. "Ladies and gentlemen." The crowd suddenly quiets. "Thank you all for coming today. I'm sure my dad is looking down at us right now, pleased that so many showed up."

The crowd laughs.

Instinctively, my eyes glance upward as if perhaps I'll see

Hollis peeking through the clouds like a mischievous boy with a candy cane tucked behind one ear.

"My dad loved to swim," Hollis's son continues, focusing on the pool with a thickness in his voice. "It was a ritual to him, an activity he enjoyed nearly every day of his life. He taught my brothers and sisters and our children how to swim. As a family, we spent countless hours in the water. Since Dad wouldn't want us to drone on and on about his life in a dark and dreary church or funeral home, we thought it only fitting to remember him here, outside in the sunshine, beside a pool."

Several other family members and young children encircle the son. None are dressed in black. They wear cheerful-colored dresses, button-down shirts and ties, linking their arms and nodding in agreement with his words. A man with tear-soaked eyes and a similar jawline clutches what I assume is his brother's shoulder.

The brother speaking covers the man's hand with his own and squeezes tight. "He'd want us to celebrate and enjoy the moment. With that said, we won't recite a long speech, but rather, we ask that you join us for a moment of silence in our father's honor."

The crowd is hushed, most with clasped hands and bowed heads.

My eyes shift toward the shorter, older woman standing in the middle of the family. Her children and grandchildren surround her like the peel of an orange protecting its fruit. Dressed in a pale pink pantsuit and cream blouse, she grips the strings of a satin bag. Her face is hidden beneath a lace-canopied hat, but I can see her lips pressed together into a frown.

Bevy.

The son closest places his arm around her.

After a moment, the woman nods slightly, and then with a trembling hand opens the bag by the drawstring. She offers the bag to each of her sons, daughters, and grandchildren who stand so close to one another, barely any light slivers between them. Each person silently takes a handful of something, but I can't tell what it is. The smallest granddaughter, probably two or three years old, bounces up and down, then tosses her filled hand in the air. White rose petals cascade down around her. A couple stick in her hair. She laughs and does it again, quickly scolded by her mother's harsh whispers.

Hollis would've loved it.

"Father, we love you and are thankful to have had you in our lives. We will forever honor your memory," says the eldest son, swallowing his tears.

In unison, the family tosses the rose petals high in the air. The grandchildren point and laugh as the soft breeze catches some of the flowers and dances them through the air before they land softly in the pool. The grandchildren hurry, collecting petals that landed on the concrete and toss them into the air again. Bevy twirls a petal between her thumb and finger, keeping her head low.

Hollis's daughter rests her head on her brother's shoulder. He kisses it. With Hollis's family linked in each other's arms, sharing knowing glances of love and memories, and the mountains and lacy clouds in the background, it's one of the most beautiful moments I've ever witnessed.

The family hugs and cries together and even though they are standing amid a hundred people, I feel intrusive, watching their sacred moment. I'm about to turn around and leave when Beverly Murphy lifts her veil, leans over, and kisses her grandson on the cheek. Her hat threatens to slide off, and in the midst of reaching for it, she glances across the pool.

Our eyes lock.

"Howie?"

⁓

Underneath the veil isn't Beverly Murphy. Well, technically it is, but to me, it's Blue. Beverly Murphy is Blue. My heart skips a beat and a smile spreads across my face. All this time I knew her and didn't even know I knew her.

"Howie, my goodness, how kind of you to come," she says a few minutes later, walking toward me with open arms. We hug and then she asks, "Is Kitty-litter here also?"

"No. Just me. Listen, I'm truly sorry for your loss. Mr. Murphy, he . . ." My voice trails off and tears seep out. She blots my tears with her fingertips and hugs me as if my husband of fifty-four years were the one who just died.

"My apologies, Howie, but I didn't know you knew my husband," she says after we separate.

"I didn't either. You know me as Howie but my real name is Lanie—"

"Lanie Howard." She finishes for me. "Well, hot damn. You're Lanie Howard." A smile the size of Texas spreads across her lips and she shakes her head, "My, my, my. No wonder my husband adored you. No wonder at all."

"Thank you."

"Now wait a minute." She scans the crowd. "Is your fiancé with you? I'd sure like to meet him."

"No," I reply. "Evan and I are no longer together."

"What? You were engaged to Evan Carter? I had no idea."

She grabs my hand and escorts us to a nearby set of chairs. "What happened?"

"You don't have time for this right now. Surely there are more important people here."

She raises her hand to stop me. "Howie, between you and me, I wish all these people would go home. I have cried my eyes out for the past week and I don't need another goddamn hug. Please take my mind off my troubles and tell me about yours."

"When you put it like that—"

"I do," she says, giving my knee a gentle pat.

"Okay, then. Well, apparently our wedding planner offers more than just advice on flowers, cakes, and table settings. She's full-service."

"The slut."

An older couple steps close and offers their condolences to Bevy. She graciously replies, then directs her attention back at me. "You dumped the loser, right?"

"Yes, moved out right away. See, don't you feel better now? Listening to my sad stories."

"Much."

Mrs. Murphy's youngest son calls her over, waving a leather-bound notebook. She exhales a deep sigh. "God bless that child of mine. He's in the arts, you know, a dancer for *Wicked*, off-Broadway. He plays Fiyero. We're really quite proud of him and how sensitive he is, but if he asks me to journal my feelings in that notebook one more time, I'm going to stab him in the neck." My eyes must widen like quarters because she adds, "I'm just kidding. I'd only nick him with the serrated edge."

"Oh, in that case."

We stand for another hug and after our embrace, she starts to turn away but stops and says, "Now wait a minute. Hollis told me you were the brains and the balls of that real estate firm. Don't tell me you're still working with Evan?"

"No, I'm not." I beam with pride. "I'm opening my own company. Lanie Howard Realty."

"Lanie Howard Realty," she repeats. "I like it. Call me when you get settled. We'll go for lunch."

"I'd like that."

"Mom," her son calls again.

An irritated scowl crosses her face. "Lord, give me strength," she whispers.

Bevy hurries away, leaving a smile on my face.

While waiting for the elevator doors to open, I notice an earthen jar of candy canes on the foyer table. I reach for one and clutch it close to my heart.

twenty-nine

The next few days are a flurry of activity. I've had the carpets cleaned and the phones connected, collected necessary listing and sales forms, bought pens, printer paper, tape, and enough paper clips to form a noose should this business fail.

Kit and Mom have been godsends. Dividing and conquering, they've washed the desks, lounge area, and bathroom. They've vacuumed, replaced lightbulbs, and stocked my fridge with water and snacks. They get along well and I think it's because they both appreciate a bargain and like sharing their stories of discounted buys. The only difference is Mom shops at the senior center and Kit at Nordstrom's.

E's helped, too. Aside from keeping Dylan entertained with piggyback rides and paper airplanes, she and I framed and hung her "hand" sketch along with a couple other drawings she made for me. She also designed my logo, a simple and elegant calligraphy-swirled L and H, which I've printed on letterhead, envelopes, et cetera.

While they've all decorated, scoured, and scrubbed, I've

been on the phone with my web designer, diligently arranging a user-friendly site. I placed ads in the *Arizona Republic* and *Scottsdale Press* and e-mailed the nearly seven thousand real estate agents in the Valley, announcing my grand opening.

A young man dressed in a worn T-shirt and jeans with a sparsely grown-in goatee, which makes him look like he's sixteen, walks in and says, "Hi, I'm looking for Lanie." He holds a clipboard with a sticker blazed across the back that reads, *Decal Guys Do It Better.*

"I'm Lanie."

"I'm Eric, from Decal City."

"Oh, yes, Eric." I shake hands with the young man Chett referred to as a "kick-ass decal guy." By the glaze in his eyes, I'm pretty sure he's stoned. "Pleased to meet you."

He nods. "So, want to show me where I can stick it?"

"Excuse me?"

"Yeah, where do you want it?"

Okay, apparently this half-man doesn't know how to talk with a woman respectfully and I'm about to give him a piece of my mind when he shows me the rolled-up decal.

"Here's the decal. Where do you want it?"

"Oh, yes, of course. The decal." I gush, suddenly feeling like an idiot. "I'll show you."

After Eric gets started, I dash inside, grab Mom and Kit. E follows behind, holding Dylan's hand. With joined hands, we watch through the window as Eric unrolls the decal. He smooths it with a roller thingy, sprays some sort of cleaner on the window, and polishes with a cloth before I pay him and he leaves.

We hurry outside and I stand there amazed. Totally amazed. No matter how many times I blink to clear my eyes, I see the same thing and yet it doesn't seem real. It's surreal. Without touching the fresh decal, I trace in the air along the curve of my name, Lanie Howard Realty, scribed in an ivory—not ecru or eggshell—straight-letter font with a big loopy "L." *I really did it.*

"Oh, Lanie," Mom gushes. "I'm so proud of you." She squeezes me hard.

"Really cool, Howie," E says. She calls me this ever since she went to a couple of kickboxing classes with me. Rudy didn't give her a nickname, said "E" was cool enough.

Kit hasn't let go of my hand. She inhales and stares at my name as if it's the code to eternal youth. "It's wonderful, just wonderful."

"It is, isn't it?" I know I shouldn't brag—well, that's just what people say—I should totally brag. Dammit, I worked hard to get here. Though my bank account has dipped to a shockingly low level and I've triggered my low savings account balance fee—thank you, Bank of America, for pointing out my independence—I'm proud of it.

Not to mention, I completed the jar.

Three days later, I sit in the office perusing the day's list of expired listings. My phone has rung exactly six times since I opened the doors. Three times it was Mom, the newspaper called once to see if I wanted to renew the ad, one was a wrong number, and Dylan called after school on Tuesday asking if I wanted an ice cream cone. Which, of course, I did.

Though I'm off to a slow start, I'm not going to lose hope. It's early yet. I'm just getting going. It'll take off. My business will grow. It has to.

With a red pen, I circle the expired listings I'm interested in pursuing and chew on a candy cane. I have a filled jar on my desk. A couple of the vacant land listings look promising, and there's a condo that's slightly overpriced. I know the area well and reach for the phone, while mentally composing a list of comparable properties, aimed at talking them into lowering their price and listing with me.

I start to dial when I remember Bevy. She asked me to call when I was settled. I bite off a chunk of peppermint and wonder if she really meant it. Is it too early to call and see how she's doing? I haven't seen her at Rudy's and I miss that firecracker personality. I'm sure she's grieving, will be for a long time, and I hate to bother her, but I'd love to hear her voice. Well, one thing's for sure, if she doesn't want to talk with me, she'll say so.

"Lanie, I hoped you'd call. I haven't been at class, just can't seem to get my butt there."

"It's understandable, though we've missed you."

"I've been telling that to my thighs, but they don't give a damn." She sighs. "Seriously, the past week I've had plenty of time to think."

"Yes, I can imagine. You doing okay?"

"Not really," she replies with a longing I've never heard in a voice. "I'm miserable as hell. I sure miss that old man."

"Me, too," I whisper.

"But I know he wouldn't want me wallowing in self-pity. Hell, he probably has a girlfriend already."

"No one that holds a candle to you. Can I take you to lunch? Maybe tomorrow or the next day?"

"That would be lovely. First, I'd like you to do something else.

"Name it."

"List my house."

What? Did she say list her house? The house?

"I can't be here without him," she continues. "The nothingness I feel in this big old place is killing me."

"I'm so sorry."

"No, no." She breathes heavily into the phone. "I don't want your pity. I just want you to sell this house. I've decided to move near my son. Both Hollis and I were impressed by your analysis and marketing ideas. I know he wouldn't want it any other way. Draw up the papers. I'll come by tomorrow and sign."

"Are you certain about this? It's a big decision."

"Hollis and I talked about this before he . . ." Her voice trails off. "I'm certain."

"Thank you for your faith in me, Bevy. I won't let you down."

"I have no doubt. I'll come by around nine."

We hang up and I simply can't resist. I climb on top of the table and dance.

⤴

I've arranged bagels, coffee, tea, juice (orange and guava), water, and hot chocolate. On the way into the office, I bought a huge bouquet of lilies and set the vase in the center of the polished coffee table. Even with my limited budget, I have to admit, the place looks good.

Before Bevy arrives, I scan my notes just to be sure I'm on top of all the important parts.

She walks in at the stroke of nine, seemingly in lighter spirits than a couple of days ago, as if a weight has been lifted. She tells me she knows listing the house is the right decision. After a bagel and a bit of negotiating the details, Mrs. Murphy signs the six-month listing agreement with a reasonable asking price. We hug and talk for a moment about the man we both adored.

As soon as she leaves, I input the listing into the MLS. It feels incredibly gratifying to add my name beside the listing. *Hello, real estate world, my name is Lanie Howard. And I'm a broker.*

For the next hour, I finish the necessary paperwork and fiddle with a trifold brochure. Working on the presentation, I receive a flash of genius. "Why didn't I think of this before?" I shake my head at my own ignorance and scroll through my phone to find the number. I press Call just as my door swings open.

"What the hell is this?" Evan stomps toward me. His eyes are dark and his face is blotchy with anger. He holds a printout of the Murphy listing.

That didn't take long.

Calmly, I press End and set my phone on the desk. "It's a listing, Evan. I'm sure you're familiar with them. Oh wait, maybe you aren't. I did most of the work around there."

"Don't get cute with me. How dare you undermine my efforts. I've been working this listing for years."

"No, Evan." I rise from my seat. "*I've* been working the listing. And you don't get it. It's not *working* the listing," I say with air quotes. "It's assisting some really great people."

"You don't want to mess with me. Hollis is mine."

"Apparently you haven't removed your dick from Stacee"— cheap shot, I know—"long enough to discover that that sweet old man has passed away and his wife listed the property with me."

He curls his lip into a cruel smile. "What do you know about real estate?"

"Plenty."

"You're a fool to think you can get away with this." His smile shifts into a scowl—still hasn't gotten that wax—and he waves the listing in the air. "I'll take this up with the Department of Real Estate. I'm the procuring cause."

"Good luck. We both know you have no agreement with the Murphys establishing a binding relationship. You have nothing. 'Procuring cause'? Please. The only reason you know Hollis is because of me."

My mind lingers on the last word. *Me.*

Oh my God. The only reason Hollis knows Evan is because of me. He stepped foot in Evan's office because of me. *Me.* I was Evan's connection to this man. I was Evan's connection to a multimillion-dollar real estate collection. *Me.*

Clarity slams into my head like a freight train. Evan approached me in the coffee shop three years ago and later proposed because of my friendship with Hollis. Evan's and my relationship was a business deal, a sham, nothing more. How did I not see this? To think, I almost married this asshole.

But I no longer give a damn about him or what he did. I have a house to sell. "Evan, I'm busy, so—"

"I screwed up."

"What?"

Evan braces his hands on my desk and drops his head like a flower too heavy to hold its weight. With a whisper he says, "I screwed up." Slowly, and with his check-me-out-I'm-trying-to-be-adorable look, he lifts his gaze toward mine and repeats, "Lanie, I can't believe I let you get away from me." Tears glisten his eyes.

Please.

"I don't know what I was thinking. I had perfection right

in my grasp, this beautiful little bird, and I let it slip away." He demonstrates my flight by fluttering his fingers in the air.

It's all I can do not to throw up.

He shakes his head. "God, I'm such an idiot. I didn't appreciate what I had until I lost it. You, Lanie Howard. I lost you and everything that's ever mattered in my life."

I'm afraid to move for fear of the shit I might step in. There's a lot of it spewing from his lips.

"Please come back to me. Say you'll forgive me. I'll make you partner right away." His eyes widen. "We'll go to the Department of Real Estate, right now. C'mon, Lanie. What do you say?"

"Hmm." I lean back in my chair, fold my hands across my chest, and tap my foot on the floor. "What do I say? It's a good offer. Enticing. Really enticing."

His face lights up. "I love you. Please. Let's go."

"You know what I say?" I reply, sweetly.

"What?" He steps toward my side of the desk and grasps my hands. "Tell me, love."

I rip my hands from his and snap, "I say no. You don't love *me*. You love my connection to Hollis and I can't believe it took me so long to realize it. I say, get the hell out of my office!"

He steps back and looks stunned, stupefied as if he just woke up from a ten-year coma and his VHS tape won't work. "What?"

"You heard me."

"You'll be nothing without me," he snarls. "Do you hear me? Nothing."

I hear him all right, but I'm not listening. And at the same time, my cell phone rings. I hold up my finger and silence Evan. "Hi, Larson," I say into the phone.

"I'm talking to you!" Evan shouts.

"Can you hold on just a moment, please? Thanks." I cup my hand over my phone and whisper to Evan, "I need to take this call, so take your temper tantrum somewhere else. Besides, you're getting my carpet dirty with all the crap spewing from your mouth."

"After all I've done for you? Signing your paycheck all these years. The fancy dinners. The goddamn house on Orchid Lane."

"Orchid Lane? That's just lumber and tile."

"Oh, really? You're so high and mighty now that a little indiscretion on my part justifies your disloyalty? Always thinking about yourself, aren't you?"

Wes's face comes to mind. *Not always.*

"You ungrateful bitch."

Now he's gone too far.

"One tiny second more, Larson. Okay? Thanks." I set the phone down, recoil my right arm and with the strength of my kiai, punch my ex-fiancé square in the jaw. "Get out of my office."

He clutches his chin with his hand and whimpers, "Ouch! What the—"

"Want some more?"

Shock is frozen on his face.

Evan turns on his heel and yells before he slams the door. "You'll regret this. You will definitely regret this."

I doubt it.

Returning to my phone, I cradle it beside my ear and say, "Larson, I'm so sorry to keep you waiting."

"It sounded like you just punched someone."

"Really?"

"Ha." He laughs. "Please tell me it was Evan."

"The very same."

"Good for you. He deserves it."

"Thanks, Larson."

"Hey, I think you just tried to call me."

"Yes, I have something even more amazing than my fighting skills for you."

"What's that?"

"The perfect house."

◌

Six days later, I stare at a signed contract for the Murphy mansion. Larson made a solid offer and Bevy accepted. It's a quick close, three weeks, no contingencies. Bevy has already flown to California to look for a new place and, by the sound of her voice, she enjoys giving her son a hard time. Hollis's parents are buried outside La Jolla, as will Hollis be, so it's fitting she's near them.

I'm exhausted and plop into my office chair. It's been a whirlwind. Once word spread that I listed and sold the Murphy mansion in a matter of days, my phone has rung nonstop. Mom signed on to work four days a week answering phones. She agreed once I promised good health insurance.

When Dylan is at school, Kit hangs out from time to time and helps me with odd jobs and difficult decisions, like where to order lunch. Even E stops after school a couple of days a week to do her homework or teach Mom computer tips.

Though the commission I'm about to receive will set me up financially for a very, very, very long time, and I should be elated with all that I've accomplished, I can't bury this melancholy feeling still plaguing me. It drapes over me like a wet blanket and often, I meander around the office, lost.

I know what it is. It's Wes. And as many times as I've told myself to stop thinking of him, I just can't. It's more than a crush. Much more. With a long sigh, I flick my Larry Fitzgerald bobblehead and watch it wiggle, recalling that walk toward the stadium, Wes's hand in mine.

One Friday afternoon, Kit nudges open my office door with her butt and places a box on my desk. "I found this in the back room. What should I do with it?"

I peer into the box. "This is my stuff from Evan's." I poke through the picture frames, last year's calendar I bought from the Girl Scouts, and a remote control that completely eludes me. "Trash it."

"What's this?" Kit grabs a rolled tube of paper.

"These are blueprints for Orchid Lane." *Wes drew them.*

"Let's take a look. I never saw the house."

"Go for it." I pull a listing from my file cabinet. "I don't need to see Orchid Lane ever again."

Kit slips off the rubber band and unrolls the prints, holding it wide with outstretched arms. "You know, maybe I should become an architect. I love to look at plans. Oh, that reminds me, I got you a subscription to *Architectural Digest*. I thought it'd be good to have on the coffee table. They do such cool covers."

"Thanks."

"Lanie?" she says a few minutes later. "This doesn't look like what you described Orchid Lane to be. What's all this?"

"All what?" I don't lift my focus from my file.

"This. Take a look." She lays the oversized papers across my desk and points.

With a quick study, I determine these aren't Orchid Lane's

finished plans. They're mine. *My house plans.* They're exactly as I described my ideal house when Wes and I spent the night at the chapel.

Drawn at the end of a cul-de-sac named Lanie Lane, the house boasts three bedrooms, a family room with a double-sided fireplace off the kitchen, a kidney-shaped pool, a garden, a winding staircase, a large master bedroom with a sitting area by the windows, twinkly lights in the foyer, and double front doors. It's perfect.

"Kit." I stare at her. "Wes drew these for me. I told him and he drew them." I'm nearly speechless, barely able to make a coherent sentence. I trace the lines with my fingers, hoping Wes's scent lingers, woven between the threads of paper.

"I knew he liked you."

"What? You never met him."

"Sure I did. At Lucinda's speed dating."

"It was pitch-black in there. He and I argued that day."

"Yes, but if he didn't care, he wouldn't have shown up."

"Well, it doesn't matter." I step away from the plans. "He left. I haven't heard from him since."

"What's he supposed to do? Draw a sword and fight Evan for you?"

"If he wanted me, yes. Is that so much to ask?" Tears pool in my eyes. "Look at me. I'm a mess. This is ridiculous. I'm ridiculous."

"No, you aren't." She rolls up the plans.

"I have enough to worry about around here without clouding my head with thoughts of him. Look at my desk. It's a disaster." I spread my arms across my desk and shake my head. "This should be more organized." Quickly, I grab a few files and stack them straight. "This pencil cup is a wreck. Some of the pencils are upside down. Can you believe that? Where are my pens? I swear—"

"Lanie," Kit interrupts. "Sit down for a second. You've gone nonstop for weeks."

"No. I'm fine. I'm busy. Busy. Busy." I wipe a tear with the back of my hand. "I need to stay busy, keep my mind focused. This would look better over here." I grab my dad's picture and the Someday Jar by its cork, moving it to a side table on the opposite side of my office. In my haste, the cork slips free and the jar falls onto the floor. It cracks in half.

"Damn," I mutter, then plop onto my knees and bury my face in my hands. "I broke the jar." More tears pour down my cheeks.

"You *are* a mess." Kit wraps her arms around me and holds me for a moment. "Um, Lanie?"

"What?"

"I thought you emptied the jar."

"I did."

"There's still a few slips in the jar."

"Can't be. I finished them all."

"Look."

I lift my head. Kit's right. As I pick up the broken crock, three slips falls out.

"Kit?"

"Read them."

I wipe my eyes, then unfold the fortunes. I recognize the handwriting, in capital letters, and for the moment I forget how to breathe. I stare at Kit. "They're from Wes."

She peers over my shoulder and reads out loud. "Ride a motorcycle from Alaska to Arizona. Throw the first pitch at a San Francisco Giants game. Kiss Lanie Howard." She smiles at me. "Honey, that's beautiful."

"It's about time you found those," Mom says from the door's threshold. "I was about to break the jar over your head."

"You knew?"

"Of course. Wes mailed them and asked me to stuff them in the jar."

I swallow hard and stare at his words. *Kiss Lanie Howard.*

"He's here, you know," Mom says.

"What?"

She slides the *Arizona Republic*'s business section toward me and points at a picture of the City Core. "Read it. He's here."

City Core Ribbon-Cutting Ceremony—Today 1:00 p.m.
Phoenix mayor Judith Glaskey, along with Heuer Con-
struction Group, is pleased to announce that it will hold
a ribbon-cutting ceremony for its newly constructed mul-
tiuse complex, the City Core, onsite, at 1:00 p.m. today.

"We're happy to introduce our latest accomplishment
to both the city of Phoenix and those who helped bring
this project to fruition," said Derek Heuer, CEO of Heuer
Construction Group. "We're delighted that several of our
investors, city officials, and Wes Campbell, our esteemed
architect, will join us for today's activities.

I glance at my watch. "One-oh-five."

Kit's focus meets mine.

"Swear?"

"Swear."

"Let's go." I squeal, grabbing Kit's hand, and lead us toward the door. "Mom, watch the office for a bit."

"Go get him!"

Kit and I dash outside and climb into her car.

"I can't believe I'm doing this. Aagh!"

"Move!" Kit shouts at the bicyclist slowly passing her parked car. She pulls away from the curb, honks her horn, and quickly switches lanes. Her Audi roars under her heavy foot. "I love that you're doing this. Now if we can get these damn cars out of the way."

I hang on to the dash and the door handle for support as she zigzags from lane to lane. "Don't kill me on the way there."

"Go, go, go!" she yells at a slow cabdriver in front of us.

Ten excruciatingly long minutes later, we pull into the parking lot of the City Core. Kit and I jump out of the car and run toward the shiny steel and glossy windows, gleaming bright in the sun. Hand in hand, we dodge through the side-street traffic and pedestrians until we're swallowed in a sea of people and stand beside one of the several angled-steel spouting-water features on the north end of the project. The fences have been removed, the concrete swept, and the glass polished clean. The complex is stunning as it slants high into the Arizona sky. Tall, strong, and dominant. *Like Wes*.

"Wow," Kit says, looking above the crowd at the towers.

A woman's voice echoes through the speaker system. A stage is assembled on the south end, near the tower's entrance doors, quite far from Kit and me. "We appreciate the community's support and look forward to a mutually beneficial relationship in the future. Thank you for coming." Cheers and claps spread through the crowd as the lady steps away from the podium.

"Oh, no, it's over." People swarm around us, heading

toward their cars. "There are so many people, Kit. I'll never find him."

"Yes, you will. We'll think of something."

How? How will I find him in this mass of business-suited heads?

I get an idea.

Quickly, I climb on top of the concrete wall surrounding the water feature.

"Be careful. Don't hurt yourself."

"Help me look for him," I shout, standing above the crowd, scanning.

"How?"

"He's gorgeous. Find the cutest guy here."

Within minutes, a large-muscled man with *Core Patrol* emblazoned across his uniform shirt points up at me from the driver's seat of his golf cart with a red siren affixed to the roof, and says to me, "Ma'am, you'll need to get down from there."

"No, it's okay." Kit stands between the guard and me. "She's trying to find someone. She'll just be a second."

The guard steps from his cart and says again with a stern voice, "Ma'am, get down."

I don't see Wes anywhere. Several others in the crowd, some way across the plaza, also point at me.

"My purse. It's been stolen. Help!" Kit screams.

The guard ignores her. "Ma'am, I'll ask you one more time. Get down."

"Just another second, please," I beg, focused on the crowd. *Where is he?*

"I've been stabbed and I'm bleeding to death," Kit says.

"Are you trying to cause a disturbance?" he asks with a less-than-friendly tone.

"If it'll buy her some time, then yes."

"Ma'am—"

"Can't she have a minute?" Kit pleads. "She's trying to find someone."

"Who?"

"Wes Campbell."

"The architect?"

"You know him?" I crouch down toward the security guard.

"Say, you look familiar." He eyes me with curiosity.

"Wes? Where is Wes?"

"He's over by the stage." The guard shakes his finger at me. "Hey, aren't you the chick who grabbed Larry Fitzgerald's—"

"Yes." I glance at his cart. "Think you can give me a ride?"

The guard laughs and reaches his arms out toward me, helping me down. "Get in."

"Kit, c'mon." We jump into the cart and the guard steers his way through the slow-moving crowd.

Without asking, I flip the switch and the siren flashes. The crowd parts and lets us through.

He shoots me a look.

"Punch it," I scream.

"I am. This is a golf cart, not a Maserati."

We reach the other side of the plaza and before the cart comes to a complete stop, I thank the guard, jump off, and run toward the stage. Kit follows close behind.

There are many groups in twos and threes of suited men and women, congratulating one another with pats on the back, posing for photos, shaking hands, and clinking glasses of champagne.

No Wes.

I rush toward the stage, prepared to climb on and shout his

name into the microphone, when out of the corner of my eye, I see him.

He stands beside two older men, talking and pointing at the roofline of the towers, in a charcoal suit and white tie.

He's here. In front of me. Ten feet away. And he's gorgeous.

Every strand of hair on my scalp tingles. My toes curl inside my pumps when Wes lifts his gaze from the gentlemen and finds me. His lips bend into a full smile.

The sounds around me silence. Heat rushes through my entire body as he excuses himself and steps away from the men, toward me. The huge smile across my lips is meaningless, for I know my eyes reveal everything I feel as I walk toward him, narrowing our gap.

Only a couple of feet apart.

He's delicious.

He's strong.

He's married.

Guilt clamps around my heart. *What in the world am I thinking? God, Lanie, you're an idiot.* I spin away from Wes.

"What are you doing? Turn around," Kit says.

I walk past her.

"Lanie?" She hurries after me, grasps my wrist, and stops me. "Where are you going? He wants you. Go get him."

"Julie. He has Julie. I can't do this, Kit. I can't." I drop my head into my hands. "What was I thinking?"

"Lanie?" Wes says.

I look up. Damn him. Why can't he be more *forgettable*?

"Where are you going?"

"Why did you write this?" I show him the slip.

"You asked me what I'd write in my Someday Jar. It's what I want." He reaches for my hand.

I stumble half a step back from his touch, his hand wrapped around mine. I can't tell where his fingers end and mine begin. A perfect fit.

No. No. No. "Julie." Like a Band-Aid ripped off skin, I tear my hand away and dash toward Kit's car.

"What's going on?" She slides into the driver's seat.

"Drive."

"Where am I going?"

"Just drive."

For twenty minutes we circle through the streets of downtown Phoenix before she says, "Should I stop for gas?"

I exhale. "No, just head back to the office."

"Okay, sweetie. Want to tell me why you ran?"

"Julie." I drop my head into my hands.

Kit rubs my back. "Oh."

I avoid Mom's inquisitive eyes as I step inside my office. I don't feel like explaining.

"Lanie, there's someone here to see you."

Shit. I don't feel like meeting with a client now. "Mom, can you please make an excuse for me? I'm going home."

"Hi." Wes stands from the couch.

"What are you doing here?"

He steps toward me and it's then I notice that he holds my fractured Someday Jar in his hands. But it's no longer broken into pieces, it's together. Cracked with a sliver missing from one side, but together.

I step toward him and reach for the jar.

He holds up his hand. "No, not yet. It's still drying. Thank you for the glue." He peeks at my mom.

"No problem."

"I'm Lanie's best friend." Kit jumps in, her voice a bit higher than normal. She thinks he's cute. I can tell by her pitch.

"Nice to meet you, Lanie's best friend. I'm Wes."

"She likes you," Kit says, nodding toward me with a rise in her eyebrows.

"That's good," Wes says, not taking his eyes off me. "I like her, too."

Kit giggles and says, "Um . . . Jane and I are going to get a coffee."

"You go on ahead. I'm fine," Mom says.

Kit grabs my mom's hand and pulls the resisting woman out the door.

"You can't be here. You have Julie. I saw the picture."

"The picture? Oh, right. You mean when you stalked my room?"

"You have a beautiful family."

"I do."

"Julie wouldn't appreciate me chasing after you. You need to go, I need—"

"Are you chasing after me, Lanie?"

There's a sexiness in his tone and it rattles every nerve in my body.

"It's not her concern," he says.

"What? How can you be so heartless? You think your wife would want you standing here, smiling at me like this?"

He laughs.

"This isn't funny."

"I'm not married."

"Fine. Your girlfriend wouldn't—"

"She's not my girlfriend, either."

"Jesus." I'm frustrated, feeling more and more like a fool with every passing second, and he stands there, mocking me. "Fine. The mother of your child—"

"Nope."

He's enjoying this. He *does* like to watch me squirm.

But I'm confused. "The picture?"

"Will you?"

I pretend shivers don't trail up my arm as he slips the jar into my cupped hand.

He digs into his wallet and retrieves the photo. "This picture is of my nephew, Trevor. And this"—he points at the woman—"is Julie. My sister."

"Sister?"

He nods and stares at the photo for a moment before returning it into his wallet. He shifts his feet and says, "She married a wreck of a guy, took off a year ago once Trevor was diagnosed with autism. I like to keep an eye on them because Trevor has trouble sometimes."

"I had no idea."

Fixing on the tiny scar above his lip, wanting to outline the curve of his face with my fingers, I process what he says. He's not married. *Not married.*

"Evan told me about the breakup and that you opened your own business. I told him he was a self-righteous jackass and pissed away the best thing he'll ever know. I'll probably never work for Evan's parents again. Or him, for that matter." He steps closer. "But I don't care. And I don't want to talk about him."

"No?"

"No. I don't want to talk at all." He traces his finger from my shoulder, along my arm, down to my fingertip, sparking more goose bumps along the way. He grabs my empty hand and kisses inside my palm.

"What do you want to do?"

Wes draws me close with his hand at the nape of my neck. His thumb strokes my cheek. "This." He opens my lips with his, pressing his mouth on mine.

My body curves into his as Wes's other hand finds the small of my back and pulls me closer, the Someday Jar snuggled between us. My head spins, mindless from the heat shared between our bodies, dizzy from the desire Wes stirs within me. Our kiss is sexy, solid, seamless.

Never have I felt so certain and confident in a moment and yet so completely powerless. Wes is like a drug. At once, I'm addicted. I want more.

Minutes—hours—days?—pass before we part. After I exhale a long satisfied breath, I smile at him.

"Just so you know." He carefully sets the jar on the desk beside us, squeezes me closer, our bodies pressed tight together, his lips a fraction of an inch away from mine, and says, "I prefer you to a hundred milk cows."

Read on for a special excerpt from the
next novel by Allison Morgan

Can I See You Again?

Coming Summer 2016 from Berkley Trade!

"What's wrong with this one?" I aim my cellphone toward my approaching client, Nixon Voss, and show him the lengthy text from another of his disappointed dates.

He settles into the chair across my desk in smooth dark jeans, nearly swallowing the leather slingback with his long California-tanned frame. Nixon tugs at the cuffs of his pale pink button-down shirt, a color not many men can pull off. "It's nice to see you, too, Bree. You look good. Beautiful morning. Don't you think?"

"Forgive me." I match the tease in his voice. "I figured we skipped the pleasantries once you started breaking hearts in the double-digit range. How many does this make now? Eleven?"

"She's hollow."

I glance at her text and count three rows of crying face emojis. Okay, so she's not a nano-physicist. She is, however, a blue-eyed San Diego Chargers cheerleader whose toned thighs make me regret the wedge of Oreo-crusted cheesecake I

330 · *Allison Morgan*

ate for breakfast today. And yesterday. "You know, there's no bonus for the most dates. No, buy eleven get the twelfth free."

"Now you tell me. All this time I've been holding out for a Bree Caxton and Associates keychain."

"Where'd you take her? And don't say for coffee."

"Then I won't say it."

"My God, Nixon. You're impossible." I flick a stray paper-clip in his direction. He reaches for it, but the wire fumbles through his grasp. "You do realize you're trying to impress these women?"

"Why suffer through dinner if we can't muster a decent conversation during a cup of coffee?"

"Because women like dinner. Women shave their legs for dinner. Dinner shouts to the world that you chose her, above all others, even if just for the evening. And trust me, a valued woman is ten thousand times more likely to open up. In all ways." I arch an eyebrow in his direction. "Dinner is the slow seduction."

"'Slow seduction,' huh? I'll try and remember that." He laughs and pulls his chiming phone from his pocket. "Excuse me, one sec?"

"Sure, go ahead."

I flip my phone end over end and think about how revealing ringtones are. When waiting for a dentist appointment or pedicure, I try and peg other people's chosen signals based on their magazine selection, shoe style, tattoo, or haircut. It's judgmental. Based on conjecture. But given that my livelihood depends upon my ability to read energy and body language, I'm happy to report that nine times out of ten, I nail it.

Hard to say if my sixth sense stems from my psychology degree, books I've devoured on human behavior, college parties where I bet my friends twenty bucks I could hook up total strangers, or because I was born on Halloween.

Whatever the reason, I'm grateful for the intuition and over the last six years, I've capitalized off of people's unique characteristics.

Nixon remains focused on his screen and I consider my own ringtone, realizing I don't differ much from the predictable. My hair is draped around my shoulders in loose curls and my makeup is minimal: peach lip gloss, mascara, and a dusting of bronzing powder. I'd rather suffer a kick to the liver then eat a McRib—real pork, my ass—all my cleaning products are paraben and phthalate free, and, I'm a pointed toe away from conquering an eight-angle yoga pose.

So, it's no surprise that my ringtone is a Fratelli's song, an organic indie rock band I fell in love with after my boyfriend, Sean, took me to their concert last spring. We drank too many Amber Bachs, danced until a blister formed on my pinkie toe, then wired and giddy—likely from marijuana smoke blanketing the air—fooled around like teenagers in the back of his Audi A4. For two weeks, I had a cup-holder-shaped bruise on my left hip.

"Sorry," Nixon says, pointing at his phone, "small fire at the office. Give me a minute?"

"No problem."

Nixon types his reply and I spin around to face my computer. I delete a few junk e-mails for last-minute Ensenada cruise deals and detox vitamins, suppressing my giggle when I come across an offer from Size Matters that reads: SMALL PRICE, BIG PENIS.

I then order three rolls of Christmas-themed wrapping paper from my landscaper's daughter who's fund-raising for a field trip to the San Diego Zoo. They're $18.95—per roll—but who can say no to a pigtailed second grader with a gap between her front teeth?

Allowing Nixon a few more moments, I open the *New York Times* webpage, clicking on the bestsellers list. The familiar black-and-white page fills the screen.

It's surreal to think that in two months' time my very own book—which is without a doubt my hardest fought and proudest accomplishment—will hit the shelves. My self-help debut *Can I See You Again?* chronicles a handful of my most memorable matchmaking love stories, funny anecdotes about first meetings that didn't go well—one guy arrived in a U-Haul, tossed his date a pair of gloves, and asked her to help him unload—along with tips and suggestions to find the one-and-only.

Not only will a successful book explode my business, but the bags under my eyes from late nights fixed at the computer, tears of uncertainty pooled on my keyboard, and calloused fingertips from typing, deleting, and typing again will culminate into something tangible. Something I created.

As I scroll down to this week's current number one bestseller, *Fallen*, a twinge of wistfulness prickles my heart.

Jo.

My grandmother's smiling face and apple-wallpapered kitchen flash through my mind as I recall the countless Sundays we spent together during my early teenage years, lingering in bookstores or lounging on her sofa, soaking up every number one novel on the list, even those with saucy parts. We shared a yellow highlighter and marked our favorite lines, writing comments in the margins.

Then, anteing with raisins, Ritz crackers, pretzel sticks, or her favorite—liqueur-filled chocolates—we'd wager on the upcoming week *Times* bestseller rankings. We'd bet which novel jumped to the top spot, which fell below twenty, how many authors were female, the number of times *Love, Forever,* or *Dead* was used in titles, how cute we thought the male authors might be.

It never mattered who won. We combined our snack piles and munched on the winnings, laughing at nothing special, enjoying the afternoon with just us two before my parents came to pick me up. I can still smell the hint of black cherry on Jo's breath when she kissed me good-bye.

It's hard to believe that fifteen years of Sundays have passed. Its even more disheartening to admit that since the day I moved out for college, my visits became less frequent, less welcome, more guarded. Worst of all, Jo's smile has faded into a thin line of disappointment and it doesn't take a body language expert to recognize the layer of regret clouding her eyes.

So along with sidebars and strategies, curse-filled rants, doubt and resurgence, I've invested my heart and soul into *Can I See You Again?*—not to mention a sizable chunk of my savings account for a publicist—and there's nothing I want more than to earn the coveted ranking.

Ease the sting of all that I've ripped away.

With a cleansing breath, I clear my thoughts and return my attention to work. My book means nothing without a successful business to base it upon.

Nixon remains concentrated on his screen and it occurs to me that he's a capable guy. The woman he marries will never need to call a plumber to fix a leaky toilet or a handyman to repair a screen door. On top of his handiness, Nixon's a sharp, diligent businessman with an iron-will dedication to his company. So, it seems fitting, as he *tap-tap-tap*s at his keys, that his phone's alert is a series of three rigid bumps. *Thump-thump-thump.* Like the knocking on a door.

Given that I appreciate his work ethic and value his account—especially his on-time monthly payments—I don't mind waiting another minute or two for him to finish his conversation.

He's still typing.

Okay, that's long enough. "Medical emergency?"

He says nothing.

"Beached whale?"

"Mmm?"

"Have you been called to deliver a baby on the freeway? Should I take cover because we've launched into WWIII?"

Nixon lifts his focus to offer a what-the-hell-are-you-talking-about scowl.

"We're discussing your life, remember?" I point at his phone. "What's more important than love?"

"Look." Nixon tucks his phone into his pocket. "I appreciate your help. I really do. But you know this whole arranged dating thing isn't me. I'm here because my mom forgets I have a business to run and insists . . . actually, commands . . . that I have a date on my arm for my cousin's wedding. If I don't, she'll have to explain to friends and neighbors and the caterer that the Voss family name is in jeopardy because I haven't married and spawned a grandchild, which in her eyes, is equivalent to the earth slipping off its axis. So, according to my mom, if I don't have a girlfriend at the party, I'll be responsible for the end of humanity. And, I'm man enough to say, my mom scares the shit out of me."

I fiddle with a file, trying not to laugh at Mrs. Voss's expense even though Nixon's not off base. I recall her unannounced visit several weeks ago. She fixed herself in the very chair where

Nixon sits now, wagging her plump middle finger at me, explaining that each passing day is one less she'll be alive to spend with her grandchildren. And the Holy Lord can strike her dead before she'll allow children without marriage. She's giving Nixon until his cousin's wedding before Mama-bear steps in and finds a daughter-in-law herself. She all but threatened to cut Nixon out of her will if he doesn't produce a grandchild in the next couple of years. Truth be told, she scared the shit out of me, too.

No, that's not true. Yes, her approach is abrasive, but I admire her conviction, her certainty. Who can fault a woman for pinpointing exactly what she wants from life? A woman who isn't afraid to stand up and declare it. And though Nixon may disagree, he's a lot like his mom, confident and steadfast. But the two differ in the sense that work is his baby. And, I imagine it's hard to spoon-feed mashed sweet potatoes to a Fortune 500 Company.

"Let's be honest." I tuck my hair behind my ears and prop my elbows on my thick glass desk. "You're not here because your mom said so. You're here because you're a thirty-six-year-old man with no one to share your life. Your house is cold and sterile. There's probably expired milk in your fridge. And more than likely, grey hairs are sprouting up in inappropriate places. Your comfort zone is shrinking and, at the end of the day, you're alone."

"Shit, Bree. Don't sugarcoat it. Give it to me straight."

"I know it sounds harsh."

"It sounds like you're stalking me."

"Only when your shutters are open."

He laughs.

"Seriously, though, love isn't easy. Don't get discouraged

because we had a few misfires. I'm good at this. I know what I'm doing." I thumb toward the wall behind me blanketed with framed pictures of some of my happy couples I've introduced over the last six years. "Seven of my clients have named their firstborns after me, three their dogs, and another his pet squirrel."

"A squirrel?"

"Yeah, that guy was kinda creepy. So are squirrels. Anyway, my point is," I scoot toward the edge of my seat and say, "I've facilitated relationships between aging lounge singers and triathletes. I've married pilots to prison guards, CEOs to sanitation workers, vegans to Paleo dieters. Bree Caxton and Associates is one of San Diego's most prolific matchmaking companies. I've devoted my life to finding love and have a ninety-eight percent success rate." I lean closer toward him. "Do you realize, Nixon Voss, you're my two percent?"

"Are you really afraid of squirrels?"

"I wish you'd take this seriously."

"Is it the soft, bushy tails or the doe-like eyes that terrify you?"

"Very funny. You know, if I had a nickel for every time you said a girl's too dull, too fake, or too—"

"You'd have fifty-five cents." He folds one leg over his knee and ties the laces of his charcoal suede oxford-style shoes, noticing my sneer. "Hey, now . . . my mom makes that face at my dad. You and I aren't married. You're not allowed to give me that look."

I flip open his last date's file, reaching for her headshot. "Here is a perky blond with a smile worthy of a Colgate commercial. She's gorgeous. You chose her. But you don't care to see this darling girl again, because . . . ?"

"She seemed too obvious, a little young."

"Young? That's what I've said for months. And for months, you've continued to override my choices and select girls, eleven to be exact, that aren't your right match. And for some crazy reason, I've allowed it! But no more." I wave her picture in the air. "You think you want a twentysomething model/actress with big boobs and a tight ass, but you're wrong."

"How are big boobs and a tight ass ever wrong?"

Fair enough.

"Fine. Think of it this way, you're a venture capitalist who negotiates with financiers across the world, right?"

"Right."

"You speak three languages and have a master's degree in business."

"I do."

"How can you expect to find a connection with some barely legal play toy? It isn't probable. You don't share the same energy. Girls that age don't care about exchange rates or investment returns. They don't care about variances in sea levels or the shipping economy. They care about hair extensions, polishing their nails with the color of the season, and mango-flavored vodka. That's who they are. That's who they should be." I point at Nixon. "But that's not you."

"It's not?"

"It's not. You need a thirtysomething, strong, independent, less obvious woman who is filled with a driving passion. Someone who challenges you."

Nixon leans against the chair's backrest and scans me from head to toe through my desk. My neck muscles tighten. Not because I regret my clothing choice. After all I'm dressed in Tony Burch buckle flats, dark-rinsed jeans, an ivory blazer, and a grey v-neck cotton top with an oval stone pendant dangling from a long gold chain. I tense with hopes Nixon doesn't recognize the outfit from the Banana Republic window mannequin across the street.

Yes, sure, I may be unoriginal, but at least I look cute.

A mischievous corner-smile curves his lips. The same smile that I'm certain has garnered its way into countless women's panties. Not that it matters, but the smile does have its charm.

"So . . ." he says, "I need someone like you?"

"What? No, not like me." I reach for a pencil, though I've nothing to jot down. "Well, yes, technically, I suppose . . . exactly like me." Bree, what have you done? You've given Nixon the wrong impression with your flirty and sassy 'you're my two percent' garbage. Some expert you are, leading the poor guy on. I pull the lapels of my blazer closer together, then with the eraser, tap the framed picture of Sean and me paddle boarding in Cabo. "Sorry, Nixon, not me. I'm here for you professionally."

"Whoa. I was kidding. Did you think . . . me and you?" He laughs loud enough to grab a glance from my secretary, Stacia, seated in the next room.

It isn't that funny. No funnier than that spotted patch of jaw fuzz you call a beard.

"You're too old anyway," he says.

"I'm thirty-one!"

"Yep."

I shoot him a look, but, truth be told, his comment stings, more so since I filled out a health insurance questionnaire two weeks ago and, thanks to my last birthday, had to check a lower box. A lower box.

But my eggs won't shrivel up until I'm forty-something, right?

"I'm just giving you a hard time," Nixon says. "You've

made yourself clear." He nods as if about to say something more, but stops. For the briefest moment, his jaw bone clenches and he stares at his feet.

I've struck a nerve.

Two seconds ago I was prepared to kick Nixon in the shins—hard—but now, a wave of loneliness washes over me. Not for me. For him. Nixon's a good man. Yes, a tad smug, making a mockery of my livelihood, but all the same, he deserves a loving relationship, someone to hold hands with when shopping for air filters on Saturday afternoons or snuggle close to on lazy Sunday mornings. The type of effortless connection I have with Sean.

As I think about my boyfriend of four years, a sense of calm replaces my unease. I think about how his beach-colored hair reflects the season, dark like wet sand in the winter and light as dry sand in the summer, a result of surfing and impromptu weekend volleyball games. His skin bronzes the color of a mocha latte and we mark the calendar noting how long his swim trunks tan line lasts. January 9th is the record. My sunscreened body never makes it past October 1.

We hardly argue—aside from him getting upset when I fall asleep during Bruce Willis movies (try as I might, his acting is like a horse tranquilizer to me)—or the few times I didn't laugh at one of his lame lawyer jokes. But, at the end of the day, there's a treasured comfort level that we share, a priceless familiarity.

My eyes dart to my purse where I tucked the Post-It note Sean stuck on my bathroom mirror this morning while I showered.

You, me. Antonio's. 8:00 p.m.

Today is our anniversary. Leave it to Sean, scrawling a note about our special evening. That's so him. Such an adorable little quirk he has, writing everything down on stickies. I swear there isn't a day that goes by where I don't find something scribbled and stuck somewhere; on his apartment's medicine cabinet, dash of his Audi, upper right corner of his latest deposition. I bite my lip, quelling my smile as I remember the other night when I found Sean, naked in my bed, with a smiley face drawn on a Post-it, and stuck on the tip of his—

"Bree?" Nixon redirects my attention. "Wasn't it you that chewed me out for not being present?"

"Sorry." I pat my cheeks, hoping they haven't flushed as pink as they feel. "Yes, let's continue with your situation. You're paying me to find you love, so its time to let me call the shots and—"

"You win." Nixon raises his hands in surrender. "My cousin's wedding is a couple weeks away and my mom will see right through me if I show up with a piece of arm candy. Get my mom off my back so I can focus on work. You pick the woman this time."

"Finally!" I raise my fists in victory.

"Settle down, crazy lady." He laughs. "Just find me my lovely."

I sit upright, pulled like a puppet on a string, caught by the tenderness of his words. My lovely. "Why, Nixon Voss! Underneath this smooth-talking, systematic, number-crunching, all-business-all-the-time exterior is a mushy center."

"There's nothing mushy about me."

"A soft underbelly."

"I don't think so."

"Beneath your thick crust, you're as gooey as a marshmallow."

"Okay, then, time for me to go." He stands, but before

turning away, points at the *New York Times* bestseller webpage. "People buy their way onto that list, you know."

"What?" I spin around for a quick peek. "No, they don't." Do they?

"Sure they do. It's not about quality. It's about how many aunts in Wisconsin got their garden club friends to buy her niece's book in a particular week. It's manipulation and marketing."

It's all Jo reads.

Nixon braces his fingers on my desk's edge. For the first time, I notice tiny specs of brown sprinkled in his blue eyes and catch a whiff of his Giorgio Armani cologne. I recognize the woody scent because I bought a bottle for Sean last Christmas.

He exchanged it.

"So, how many weeks?" Nixon asks.

"Until the release? Eight."

"All I'm saying is, don't put too much weight on the *New York Times*, Amazon, or *USA Today* lists because they have as much merit as what's etched on the bathroom stall of a gas station. It's not the only threshold of success."

My tattoo tingles. It does this at random times: writing a check, reading an e-mail, pouring detergent into the wash.

I glance at my parents' initials, L and S, scripted around an inch-long scar, snaking the inside of my wrist. The toughened pink flesh tingles and as I trace the letters, I see the hint of my mom's narrow hands and slender fingers in my own. I'd never noticed the similarities until the night I sat rigid in the backseat of Dad's Jeep Cherokee with arms folded across my chest in an adolescent act of defiance. Illuminated by the dashboard lights, Mom's thumb massaged Dad's vein, bulging above his temple, soothing his anger as he drove us toward home.

I think about the deafening screams and shattered glass, the hissing fluids, the smell of fuel, the twisted steel. I think about the suffering in Jo's eyes and the arms-length distance she's kept me ever since my dad and mom, Jo's only daughter, died. I think about the reverence Jo gives bestselling authors and the purpose and compulsion I've invested into *Can I See You Again?* I think about how it'd feel for her to be proud of me. To like me again. To share something besides loss.

I glance again at the bestseller list. Not the only threshold of success? It is for me.

Nixon taps my desk, redirecting my attention a second time.

Honestly, Bree, hold it together.

"Find me the right woman."

"Will do." I step around my desk and slide my hands on my hips. "You know what they say, twelfth time's the charm."

"Sounds good."

"Leaving so soon?" Stacia purrs, sauntering toward us in a borderline-too-short-for work shift dress and wedge heels, twisting the end of her long blond ponytail, this week's hairstyle. She colors, straightens or curls her hair, adds or removes extensions, more frequently than I empty my dishwasher.

I chuckle at Stacia, my closest friend since our freshman year at UCSD. Assigned as roommates, we shared a two-hundred square foot dorm room and a wicked fight three weeks into our first semester—who knew that turning my hair dryer on and off, on and off, on and off, as I readied for my 7:00 a.m. class rather than leaving it on until my hair was completely dry, hovered her on the edge of sanity? The following day she bought me a sleek, quieter hair dryer and we hugged it out. We've been tight ever since.

"Gotta get to the office," he says.

"Be prepared, Nixon," I say, "the woman I choose will count past six."

"I'll bring my abacus."

Once he's a few feet away, Stacia whispers, "He's smokin' hot. One of those silent but deadly guys."

"What are you talking about?"

"He's the kinda guy that's aloof and guarded just enough to be sexy, but not conceited." She watches Nixon leave. "You don't see it?"

I follow her gaze.

The paperclip is stuck to Nixon's butt.

That's what he gets for calling me old.